PRAISE FOR [

"Daniel Judson is so much more than a crime-fiction novelist. He's a tattooed poet, a mad philosopher of the Apocalypse fascinated with exploring the darkest places in people's souls."
—*Chicago Tribune* on *The Water's Edge*

"Shamus winner Judson once again successfully mines Long Island's South Fork for glittering noir nuggets."
—*Publishers Weekly* on *The Violet Hour*

"A suspense masterpiece."
—Bookreporter.com on *The Violet Hour*

"Judson hits you with a twenty-five-thousand-volt stun gun in chapter one and doesn't let up until the satisfying end."
—Alafair Burke, author of *The Wife*, on *Voyeur*

"Judson is a thoroughly accomplished writer."
—*Kirkus Reviews* on *Voyeur*

"A searing, brooding look at the bleak side of the Hamptons . . . an intense novel."
—*South Florida Sun-Sentinel* on *The Darkest Place*

"Action packed. Loss and redemption rule in Shamus Award–winning Daniel Judson's third novel, set in Southampton nights so cold that they could cool off a reader sizzling in this summer's heat. It's noir on ice."
—*USA Today* on *The Darkest Place*

"This taut thriller is far from predictable, and its dark and mysterious plot suits Judson's understated writing style."
—*Publishers Weekly* on *The Poisoned Rose*

THE
COTTAGE

OTHER TITLES BY DANIEL JUDSON

THE AGENT SERIES

The Temporary Agent
The Rogue Agent
The Shadow Agent

THE GIN PALACE TRILOGY

The Poisoned Rose
The Bone Orchard
The Gin Palace

THE SOUTHAMPTON TRILOGY

The Darkest Place
The Water's Edge
Voyeur

STAND-ALONE TITLES

The Betrayer
Avenged
The Violet Hour

THE
COTTAGE

DANIEL
JUDSON

THOMAS & MERCER

Text copyright © 2021 by Daniel Judson
All rights reserved.

Published by Thomas & Mercer, Seattle

www.apub.com

Amazon, the Amazon logo, and Thomas & Mercer are trademarks of Amazon.com, Inc., or its affiliates.

ISBN-13: 9781542010016
ISBN-10: 1542010012

Cover design by Shasti O'Leary Soudant

Printed in the United States of America

for Liz Pearsons

PROLOGUE

Taking a boy into the cottage was a clear violation of the rules the two sisters had agreed to, rules that were in place—they were assured often by their stern but beloved grandfather—for their own good.

Now that they lived here year-round, all that was asked of them was that they do their assigned chores, excel at school, and respectfully obey.

Kate did all that, as did Rebecca, up to a point.

Taking in that boy—that odd boy, as their grandmother used to say— was expressly forbidden. He had followed them around since they were younger, picking on them occasionally until Rebecca punched him in the nose for taunting her kid sister, after which they'd all become friends, or at least friendly.

Rebecca was fourteen, and Kate, a year and a half younger, was scared of her, though she hadn't always been. The sisters had held hands during their parents' wake, and again while standing at their gravesides. During the car ride from the cemetery, sitting together in the back seat, they had all but clung to each other, a seven-year-old and an eight-year-old whose world, while not perfect, had been turned upside down.

Rebecca played the role of older sister well, even when Kate didn't need her to. But Kate was always grateful. In her darkest moments, usually at night when she couldn't sleep, she would imagine what it would be like to have no sister at all, no confidante or protector. She saw herself alone in her grandparents' home and felt her heart go cold.

But lately all that had changed. Rebecca had changed. Rebellious, impetuous, compulsive.

And, at times, cruel. She smoked, to Kate's dismay. She swore, though never in the presence of their grandparents. She disappeared for hours, refusing to tell Kate where she had gone. She flew into rages when challenged or questioned by those in authority.

Kate covered for her sister, or tried to. She became the peacemaker, finding herself caught between their outraged grandparents and the granddaughter they no longer recognized.

Nothing was broken, though; Kate told herself that often. If her sister could change, seemingly overnight, couldn't she just change back? And then the chaos Rebecca caused would end and be forgotten. Kate and she would once again be what they had always been, ever since Kate could remember: sisters and best friends.

Those hopes were dashed that Sunday afternoon Rebecca sneaked him into the cottage for the purpose of having sex for the first time.

They'd fought before that, Rebecca and Kate, when the boy was on his way over. Rebecca had asked Kate to be on the lookout. Kate had pleaded for her sister not to do this. Not like this, and not with him.

If Kate told, Rebecca would never forgive her. Those were the words Rebecca had spoken as he appeared at the top of the driveway—a twelve-year-old, like Kate—here for what had been promised to him.

TWENTY-FIVE YEARS LATER

ONE

Waking, Kate hears through her half-open bedroom window the sound of something moving in her backyard.

Sitting up, she listens to dead leaves crumbling beneath dragging feet, and though the movement ceases completely after several steps and is followed by a moment of silence, it resumes soon enough. This continues—starting, stopping, silence, starting again—and with each cluster of steps she hears, their source grows closer.

It doesn't take much for Kate to be sent back to the moment when her life was shattered to pieces, or for the rush of gut-wrenching fear that accompanies that memory to be triggered.

But nothing does that job better than the sound of footsteps in the dark of night.

She is feeling it now, that primal and overwhelming terror, as strong tonight as it was the night her husband was murdered just steps beyond their front door.

Motionless except for her darting eyes and the rapid rising and falling of her chest, Kate can only listen to the sound that causes her blood to run cold.

But the concern for the safety of her children, asleep upstairs, kicks in, becoming more powerful than the numbing fear, and Kate throws off her blanket and moves to the edge of her king-size bed. She is barefoot, clothed only in boxer shorts and a tank top, which serves to compound the deep sense of vulnerability she feels as her feet hit the floor.

With no weapon of any kind to reach for, she snatches the cordless phone from its charging cradle with shaking hands, thinking of the long minutes she'd be required to endure, should she, in fact, call for help, before the police would actually arrive.

Phone in hand, Kate moves toward the window that overlooks the backyard, open with the blinds partially raised, to let in the cool spring air. The knowledge that she is, for the moment, all that stands between her children and some unspeakable harm gives her the steel she needs to peer out.

The backyard has always been a safe haven—for her own children now, but also for Kate and her older sister back when their grandparents lived in this home and she and Rebecca would spend their summers with them before finally moving in year-round following the death of their parents.

Just large enough for a swing set, sandbox, and aluminum tool-shed, the yard is surrounded on three sides by dense woods, and the motion-activated light mounted in the second-floor eave illuminates every corner of that space.

The light also confirms for Kate that something has, in fact, entered her property.

She stands at the window for a moment but sees and hears nothing, then concludes that whatever was there has perhaps by now moved around to the front of the house. Turning, her heart thudding, Kate scrambles to maneuver the small room, negotiating the narrow pathway between the bed and dresser. She reaches the bedroom door in a matter of seconds, hurries through it and down the short hallway, passing the steep stairs that lead to the two upper bedrooms where her twins are asleep. Pausing there, she listens for any sign that her children are awake, but hearing none, she enters the living room.

It is the largest room in a house of small rooms, but the picture window at its opposite end is still just seven or eight strides away. Crossing quickly and standing before the plate glass, her body surging with adrenaline, Kate can see the front lawn, roughly double the size of the backyard, and the driveway that winds at an incline alongside it toward Old Town Road. Not far from the house are two towering oaks, and just beyond them, standing in the dark, is the empty cottage.

Kate again sees nothing, but despite her all-out panic she has presence of mind enough to note that the motion light at the front of the house has yet to be activated.

Watching the scene frantically, she desperately holds on to the hope that she will soon view a meandering deer or some other animal cross into the front yard. Much of Westport is still heavily wooded, and all manner of animals traverse her property in search of food day and night.

And yet as often as that occurs, it is always the fear of another kind of animal—a two-legged animal—that strikes Kate hard when strange noises are heard.

Within seconds of her surveillance, Kate's attention is quickly drawn back to the cottage, and there she sees the very thing she fears most.

A figure is moving near the small building. Maybe two seconds tops—that's the time between Kate spotting the trespasser and them slipping behind the cottage and out of her sight. Her gut tightens hard, as if against a punch sensed at the last second, and a violent shiver spirals down her spine. She can barely breathe as she looks at the phone in her hand and begins to punch in the seven-digit number she memorized long ago, which would connect her directly with the police station dispatcher rather than the 911 operator.

But Kate has only managed to complete the prefix when the figure draws her attention again. Reappearing, it bolts up the sloping lawn toward the road, another following close behind.

Her legs are suddenly heavy, as if filled with water, and only her head is capable of movement as she tracks two runners. Being a high school teacher, Kate is familiar with the way young people move, and she realizes soon enough that these are teenage boys, likely neighborhood kids.

Kate presses "End" on her cordless phone but keeps her eyes on the boys until they have reached the pavement, where they turn right and race away. The fact that they stayed by the cottage and didn't venture any closer to the main house is the reason the front light didn't activate. But their location doesn't explain what caused the backyard light to come on.

Could something back there—or someone—be what sent the boys running?

Making the walk back to the bedroom on weak legs, Kate returns to the window overlooking the rear of her property. The explosion of courage and physical strength she experienced moments ago are waning now, but she forces herself to once more look through the glass. This time she spots the culprit.

It is exactly what she should have expected to see in the first place.

A deer—a fully pregnant doe—stands not far from the swing set. Aware of the commotion up on the road, it has paused, frozen, to listen with cocked ears.

The creature holds perfectly still for several seconds before suddenly turning and darting across the yard. Leaping through the barrier of shrubs, it quickly disappears within the dark woods.

A full minute passes before Kate steps away from the window. The adrenaline in her blood is like alcohol, in that it will take time for it to dissipate, and her hands are still shaking violently and her heart is still pounding like a trapped animal against her breastbone.

Every cell in her body is reacting as though she'd just fought for her life.

She has been through these bouts of blinding terror enough times in the past two years to know exactly what the fight-or-flight reflex is capable of doing to her, and what to expect once she is at last free of it.

A few more moments go by before her heart, beating at a dangerously high rate, finally starts to slow, first to a dull throb and then to the high range of her resting heartbeat.

And it is at this point in the long unwinding that the anger always comes.

As the last of the lingering effects of terror fade, Kate is consumed by a frustration that ultimately transforms itself into a slow-burning rage, one that takes everything she has to contain—during those times when she is able to contain it, at least.

There have been too many instances when her fury grows too big to hold back and she explodes into fits of violence that are both frightening and impotent—for all her thrashing and screaming and stomping about, no change comes and nothing is made better.

Following the surges of raw emotion—those contained and those let loose—are crying jags that make her body shudder, as if she were being battered by an outward storm as well. These can last minutes, sometimes longer, but no matter how long they endure, these outbursts leave her face smeared with tears.

Tonight, everything comes to her on schedule, and though the crying lasts less than a minute, it is enough to force her to sit down on the edge of her bed and lean forward with her arms folded across her stomach, as if bracing herself against some terrible pain.

The only pleasing thing about this latest incident for Kate is that she manages, yet again, to keep it and its ugly aftermath from her children. They are twelve years old now and sharp, and more and more, there is less and less that she can hide from them.

———

Lingering on the edge of the bed, Kate attempts to reclaim her focus and composure by remembering Leif.

She does her best to recall her husband's smell, which is, luckily, still a vivid-enough memory to comfort her. Then she homes in on the confidence he had exuded and the safety his physical size and choice of profession had promised.

A town cop, and the son of a cop, Leif was a former state wrestling champ, undefeated in his senior year of high school, as fit the night he was killed as he was when he and Kate first started dating. Six foot plus with shoulders as wide as a doorway—like his father—there was for Kate no feeling safer than when Leif was beside her.

As it turned out, of course, that promise of security was one that he could not keep, despite all his strength and skill.

Kate is back in the past now, lost in the memory of the man that had been taken from her by a single act of meaningless violence.

She is on the verge of reliving that experience—feeling the depths of its shock and horror all over again—when the phone in her hand rings, piercing the late-night silence of her dark bedroom and sending yet another jolt of cold fear through her tired body.

TWO

To prevent the ringing of the phone from waking her children asleep upstairs, Kate presses "Talk" with her thumb without first looking at the Caller ID display, then quickly brings the receiver up to her ear and says softly, "Hello."

She hears, though, only dead silence, and her eyes go to the alarm clock on her nightstand. It is eleven fifteen.

After a few seconds, Kate says again, more firmly, "Hello."

A familiar voice finally comes through the earpiece. "It's me," Rebecca says. "I'm sorry; I know it's late there."

While Kate is grateful that this isn't turning out to be a prank call—the initial silence had her concerned—the sound of her sister's voice brings no sense of relief.

It takes a moment for Kate to respond. "Where are you?" Her voice is flat, her tone a well-rehearsed mix of hostility and disinterest.

"I'm in Colorado still."

The last time Kate and Rebecca spoke was a year ago when Rebecca had just arrived in Colorado. A year in the same place is a radical change in Rebecca's behavior; she rarely stays put longer than a few months. But Kate has no desire to get into that.

"What do you want?" she says.

"Did I wake you? This is really my only chance to call. Things are hectic."

Kate repeats, "What do you want?"

"I didn't call to fight, Kate. And it wasn't easy for me to call you like this in the first place."

"So why did you?"

"I was wondering whether you were going to be renting out the cottage this summer."

"I haven't thought about it. Why?"

"I wanted to talk to you about me staying in it for a while."

"You only have access to it November through April. Grandpa's will is very clear. I can do what I want with it in the summers."

"Yeah, well, since I haven't done anything with it in two years, and you didn't rent it out the past two summers, I thought maybe you'd make an exception."

"Like I said, I haven't thought about what I'm going to do with it yet."

"It's the third week of April, Kate. Time is running out to line up a summer rental."

"That's my problem."

"Look, I know you don't need the money."

"My finances aren't any of your business, Becca." Kate takes a breath, lets it out. "Listen, I don't want to do this. I'm tired and in a bad mood. You can have the cottage in November, like it says in the will. November through April. I can't stop you from using it then."

"So generous of you."

"It's not about me. You're the one who pushed everyone away. Grandma and Grandpa. Me."

"And that's unforgivable? Forever?"

"It has nothing to do with forgiveness," Kate says. "All I can do is to follow Grandpa's instructions. The house went to me, and use of the cottage during the off-season went to you. That's what he wanted."

"And what do you want?"

"What I *don't* want is chaos."

"I get it. I was chaos. But I'm not anymore."

12

Kate shakes her head dismissively, despite the fact that Rebecca cannot see her. The gesture has become automatic when talking to her sister. "It's too late, Becca. Too many things have been said. The damage is done."

"It can be undone, don't you think? Wounds heal. Anyway, there are some things going on with me. Things you should probably know about. Can we talk sometime?"

"I don't know. I can't think about it right now. I really need to get back to sleep."

"When would be a better time?"

"Let me get back to you."

"You promise you'll call."

"Yeah, yeah."

"How are Max and Callie? I miss them."

"They're good. But I really should get going."

The line goes silent. Kate wonders if the call was disconnected, would be grateful if it were, but then Rebecca speaks.

"I miss you, Kate. I miss the way things used to be. When we were kids, I mean."

Kate nods at that, though absently. Finally, she says, "We're not kids anymore, though, are we? Look, I need to go."

"Call me—"

Kate ends the call and returns the receiver to its charging cradle, but she is moving hastily and fails to properly seat it into its slot, so when she takes her hand away from the device, it falls from the nightstand and clatters to the floor.

———

Kate pours a glass of Malbec, leans against the kitchen counter, and takes a mouthful, swallowing it without bothering to savor it.

There are rituals she follows when she is too riled up to sleep, and she sees nothing to gain by not indulging in those tonight.

After climbing the steep stairs to the second floor, she first looks in on her sleeping son, then steps across the hall and checks on her daughter. In their own ways they are each versions of their mother and aunt. Like Kate, Max has dark hair, is the quieter of the two children, the bookworm who tends to want to please and not ask questions. Callie, on the other hand, has blonde hair and is naturally skeptical, though lately it is a skepticism that strikes Kate as an all-too-familiar desire to rebel.

The older Callie gets, the more Kate sees shades of Rebecca in her, not only in behavior but in appearance as well.

Kate watches Callie the longest, is concerned the most about her—not just how the next few years will play out as Callie enters her early teens, but also what kind of future, given what she sees in her daughter, the two of them will have.

Will the same clash of personalities that first drove Kate and her sister apart repeat and drive Kate and her daughter apart as well?

Returning downstairs to the kitchen, Kate takes her glass of wine into the living room, grabbing her photo album from the bookcase with her free hand and sitting on the couch. Placing the album on the coffee table, she opens it and begins to randomly flip through its pages.

She glimpses photos of herself and Leif, spanning from as far back as high school to as recently as a few months before his death, when the last one of him was taken.

Though they'd first dated in high school, they went their separate ways the following summer—Kate off to college in Boston, and Leif to Ohio, where he continued his wrestling career and studied criminology, followed by grad school for Kate and the police academy for Leif. By then Kate had inherited her grandparents' house and moved back to Westport. A chance meeting in a grocery store brought them back together.

The photos remind her of a life that once made sense: college, careers, marriage, and children. On good days it is a life that seems, if only vaguely, recoverable. Somehow, one day. It has been over two years since Kate was widowed, and according to her colleagues and select few friends, she should be dating again by now.

On bad days, however, the life that Kate lost feels forever gone. Seeking it again would be a hollow gesture—going through the motions for the sake of going through the motions. At least what she is left with—career and children—makes half sense.

The photos are a mix of Kodak Instamatics, Polaroids, and print-outs of digital pics on photo paper. Moving through the album, Kate sees the children grow and her and Leif age from their teen years through their twenties and into their midthirties. She always assumed there would be photos of them in their forties and fifties—graying but still as vibrant as they'd always been, still loving and in love. She also expected to add photos of them in their sixties and seventies and beyond—images depicting them delighting in their grandchildren, possibly even great-grandchildren, as they faced together and side by side the twilight of their lives.

The final photo in the album is the last photo of Leif, taken on his birthday, smiling not for the camera, but at the woman holding it.

The remaining pages are empty. All pictures now—school photos of the kids, ones taken by friends of Kate and her children—go instead onto the refrigerator, held in place by magnets on which are printed inspirational sayings by Thoreau, Emerson, Gandhi, Eleanor Roosevelt, and so on.

Sayings that, at the time of their purchase, *were* inspiring, only to have whatever hope for change the daily reading of them promised fade shortly after being displayed, if not before that.

Normally, Kate closes the album once she has reached the end, but tonight she flips the collection of heavy pages back to the very first, where a handful of photos from her childhood are preserved.

All were taken on this property—Kate and Rebecca as toddlers on the swings, as young children in leaf piles under the oaks, and as teenagers standing outside the cottage, where Rebecca had first begun to paint and Kate would spend hours reading.

These photos track not only their growth from children to young women but also their growing apart. Smiling and hugging in early photos, their closeness unmistakable, they are by the later ones standing apart and barely interacting.

More than that, Kate can see on her own face and in the way she stands the strain that her older sister's wildness took on her. What was once a haven from neglectful and self-absorbed parents had become a battleground of four wills—Kate's, Rebecca's, and their grandmother's and grandfather's.

Kate remembers now the distress Rebecca had caused them as well. The heart attack that took their grandmother shortly before Kate left for college was, according to the doctors, the result of congenital heart disease, but Kate knew better. She'd witnessed their grandmother weaken and shrink as Rebecca grew more brazenly defiant.

The passing of their grandfather six years later was due to natural causes, but it was evident to Kate, those times when she visited, that the man had died of a broken heart, having lost the woman who had been at his side every day for sixty-five years.

Closing the album, Kate leaves it on the table as she carries her glass of wine into the kitchen, stands over the sink, and takes one last sip, then pours what remains down the drain.

Tomorrow is Monday, and though that will be the first official day of spring vacation, Kate really doesn't want to be dealing with any degree of hangover.

Back in her bedroom, she closes the window and returns to bed. The sheets, warm when she'd left them, are cold against her bare legs and arms. Drawing the blanket to her shoulders, she sees the empty charging cradle on the nightstand, then reaches down to pick up the receiver off the floor.

She decides to check the number Rebecca called from, so she can recognize it, should her sister try to call again, and decide then whether or not to pick up. In all likelihood, however, she will opt to ignore the call, telling herself that she is simply putting it off till a better time, knowing in her heart there will never be such a time as far as dealing with Rebecca is concerned.

After placing the receiver on its charger, Kate rolls onto her right side, facing the nightstand and the door beyond it, which is left open in case one or both of her children need her in the night. It is a habit that began the day she brought them home from the hospital, but since Leif's death, it is one that she has struggled with.

She feels her best in small, closed-off spaces. And to the point of obsession, she finds herself closing and locking every door that she can.

Despite her exhaustion—from the usual long day to the upheaval of the past half hour—Kate is unable to fall asleep. Lying with her eyes open, she looks down the narrow hallway and into the dark living room, waiting for another random sound to trigger the madness all over again.

The last thing she remembers is the bedside clock reading three forty-five.

THREE

Even though today is the first day of her vacation, and despite the late night, Kate is up at five thirty.

She lingers in bed, however, hoping to fall back asleep, but all she really does is lie there and play back in her mind the events of last night—waking to the footsteps outside, the teenagers by the cottage, the phone ringing just as she was calming down, the conversation with her sister and all the unpleasant memories that it brought up.

She has learned not to stay in bed and dwell, so by five forty-five Kate is up and making what she is certain will be the first of many cups of coffee. Since it is likely that Callie and Max will sleep in this morning, Kate decides that the best thing for her is to get and stay busy. She is exhausted—it's only after the second cup that her grogginess begins to wane—but after two years as a working single mother, she is used to performing on very little sleep.

In her bedroom, Kate removes from her closet several pieces of heavier winter clothing she will no longer need and lays them in neatly folded piles on her bed. She brings up from the basement an empty Rubbermaid container labeled WINTER CLOTHES, and after placing each pile into the container and sealing its lid, she returns to the basement and places the container on a metal shelf next to the washer and dryer. She then takes a container marked SUMMER CLOTHES from the same shelf and carries it upstairs, laying its items—lightweight cardigans and slacks, several silk blouses and knee-length skirts—in piles on her bed.

Retrieving the ironing board and iron from her closet, she sets the board up and plugs the iron in, then irons each piece meticulously before placing it on a hanger and, after close inspection, hanging it up in the closet.

Back in the basement, she organizes months' worth of newspapers—the free local weekly as well as the daily *New York Times*—into two-foot-tall bundles that she secures with twine, making them ready for Wednesday's trash and recycling pickup. Her next project is to take inventory of the paint cans leftover from when Leif last painted the house five years ago. The paint on the garage door is peeling badly, and it is her intention to scrape and repaint it once it is warm enough. One and a half cans remain, and though she isn't certain, she believes that should be more than enough.

The sun is visible through the still-bare trees by the time Kate returns upstairs to mop the kitchen floor and, as it dries, sit in the living room and sort through her pile of mail. After that, she strips her bed and puts the sheets and pillowcases into the washing machine.

She continues moving from project to chore to project until a little before eight o'clock, when Callie comes downstairs and passes through the kitchen. She finds her mother kneeling on the counter in the pantry and wiping down the empty shelves, several stacks of canned goods on either side of her.

Callie asks, "What are you doing?" She is not yet fully awake, and her tone is even more skeptical than usual. She is at the age now when she questions much of what her mother says and does, often doing so as if annoyed.

Kate responds to her daughter's question with a question of her own. "What does it look like I'm doing?"

Callie looks at the dozens of cans. "Making a mess." Then she looks into the kitchen. "Did you mop the floor?"

"Yes."

"I can smell the bleach."

"That means it's clean."

"Why are you doing all this? It's your vacation."

"It's the only time I have. I've got a lot of things for us to do this week."

"Is this because Auntie Becca called last night?"

Kate stops scrubbing and looks at her daughter. "What makes you think she called?"

"I heard the phone ring late. I heard you talking. And you always do this after you talk to her. You always go on a cleaning spree like some obsessed person."

"That's nice," Kate says. She resumes her scrubbing. "And I'm not a crazy person. I'm just trying to get things done while I can."

"Which is what a crazy person would say."

"Instead of standing there criticizing, how about helping me?"

"The bleach is making me nauseous."

"Nauseated."

"What?"

"The bleach is making you nauseated. Saying you're nauseous means you cause nausea."

Callie moans, "Oh my God." Turning, she starts to walk away.

"Go wake up your brother," Kate says. "Maria's kids are coming over at nine. They're spending the day here, remember?"

Callie mutters, "Stop being so nauseous." Then she quickly adds, "Yes, I remember. We're going to do something fun this week, though, right?"

"You like D. J. and Alice."

"They're kids."

"Alice is only two years younger than you."

Callie moves into the living room. "You're not making the argument you think you're making."

Kate hears her daughter on the stairs, her footsteps a tad louder than they need to be. She knows this is Callie's way of informing her that she has moved out of earshot and the conversation is over.

Since she was a child, Callie has always preferred to be the one who gets in the last word, and in this regard Kate recognizes she and her daughter are alike—or, more accurately, too much alike.

———

Callie and Max are in the kitchen, bickering over who gets to use the toaster oven first, when Kate finishes wiping down the final shelf and begins the process of extricating herself from her precarious position on the pantry countertop.

After sliding her left knee off, she lowers her foot to the floor, then does the same with her right knee, only to lose her balance at the last second and knock over a stack of canned soups, one of which falls to the floor.

The loud slap of the single can landing is enough to cause Kate to react with a gasp. Flinching, she clutches the edge of the counter with one hand and covers her mouth with the other. Suddenly unable to breathe, she freezes.

From the kitchen, Callie asks, "You okay in there?"

Kate exhales and lowers her hand from her mouth. "Yes," she says. "I'm fine."

Max appears in the doorway before Kate is able to fully compose herself. "You all right, Mom?" He is chewing, his mouth overfull, and in his hand is a half-eaten pastry.

Kate forces a smile and nods. "It's just your mother being a klutz, is all." Her eyes immediately go to his hand. "What's that?"

"A Pop-Tart."

"Where did you even get that?"

"School."

21

"Your school is handing out Pop-Tarts."

"Jimmy gave it to me. His mom can't do gluten anymore, so he keeps a box in his locker."

"That's not going to be your breakfast; you know that, right?"

"Why not?"

"It's junk."

"I was hungry. Callie is hogging the toaster."

"What is she making?"

"Frozen waffles."

Raising her voice so she'll be heard in the other room, Kate says, "I'll be there in a minute to make you guys some egg whites."

Callie calls from the kitchen, "I'm bored of egg whites."

"You need a protein," Kate responds. She can hear the stress in her own voice, so she exhales, then looks at Max. "Go on," she says, her voice softer. "I'll be right there."

"You're sure you don't need help?"

"I'm sure. I'll finish this later."

Max pauses to look at her, but Kate maintains her fixed, assuring smile.

Max finally turns and leaves the doorway. Kate waits until she knows he is in the kitchen before dropping the forced expression of happiness and ease. She looks down at her hands. They are trembling. Watching them, she gives the rush of adrenaline still moving through her the time it needs to pass.

Her hands are nearly steady when she picks up the errant can and places it on the countertop.

FOUR

Maria arrives, D. J. and Alice with her. As Kate offers her neighbor a cup of coffee, the four kids pair off—the boys heading into the living room to watch a Blu-ray DVD that D. J. has brought, and the girls up to Callie's bedroom to listen to music.

"No coffee for me," Maria says. "I've already had two cups."

Kate refills her own mug from the stained Mr. Coffee carafe. "This will be my third so far today."

"Derek said you were up early."

"How'd he know that?"

"He saw that your lights were on."

"Ah," Kate says. She returns the carafe to the outdated coffee maker.

"Thanks again for watching the kids," Maria says.

"No problem. They'll keep Max and Callie busy, so I should be able to get a lot more done."

"I'm not sure how long all my errands will take, but Derek is going to pick them up around three. If you want, the twins can go back to our house with them. That'll give you more time, and they can eat dinner with us, and I'll send them over after."

"No, that's okay."

"Take the extra free time while you can, Kate."

"We'll see what's going on when Derek gets here."

"Oh, before I forget, apparently last night someone let the air out of the tires of Derek's work truck. At first he thought someone had slashed them, but he checked them out and they were just flat, so he was able to fill them back up with his compressor."

"Shit," Kate says. There is a hint of alarm in her voice.

Maria asks quickly, "What?"

"Last night I saw two teenagers by the cottage."

"What time?"

"After eleven, I think."

"What were they doing?"

"All I saw was them behind it for a second, and then they were running away."

"Did they do any damage?"

"Nothing that I've noticed. And I would have heard it if they broke any of the windows or anything like that. My bedroom window was open. Anyway, there's nothing inside worth stealing. Just furniture and some of Rebecca's old artwork."

Maria's expression transitions from curiosity to concern. "That must have scared the shit out of you."

"No, it was fine."

"You don't have to lie to me, Kate."

Kate pauses. "Yeah, all right, it scared me a little."

"Do you want me to go with you to check out the cottage? Or I could check it out for you?"

"I'm sure it was just kids being kids. I mean, they got you guys, too, right?"

"Still, something like that is the last thing you need."

"It was nothing, Maria. If I were worried, I'd say something." She pauses. "We ask for help. That's what we're supposed to do, right?"

"Right," Maria answers. "You can call me, you know. If something scares you. No matter how late."

"I know."

"To be honest, I don't know how you've stayed here. If I lost Derek the way you lost Leif . . ." Maria doesn't complete her thought, and it

24

is obvious to Kate by her friend's abrupt shift in body language that she regrets having even touched upon that subject.

Before Maria can apologize, Kate says, "Don't worry about it. It's fine. Life goes on, one way or another."

Maria nods for a moment, watching her friend in what is likely an attempt to gauge whether or not she, in fact, is fine. As is more often than not the case, however, she finds getting an entirely accurate read on Kate a less-than-easy thing to do.

Finally, Maria says, "Why don't we take the kids and go walk Compo Beach right now, get you out of here. We can grab lunch at Chef's Table."

"No, you have your day planned."

"Are you sure?"

"Very."

Maria nods again. "Do you need anything while I'm out?"

"No, thanks."

"Text me if you think of something."

"I will."

Maria heads toward the back door. "And if my kids give you any shit today, feel free to beat them," she jokes.

Following her friend to the door, Kate jokes back, "Always do."

She watches as Maria walks down the back steps, then crosses the driveway and gets into her car.

Kate is still at the door after Maria has driven off, though now, instead of looking through the window, she is staring at the heavy-duty dead bolt lock that she'd had installed two years ago.

After a moment of indecision, Kate reaches out for the brass knob and turns it to the right, seating the inch-thick steel bolt in place.

Kate returns the canned goods to the pantry shelves as the boys watch D. J.'s movie, *Mission: Impossible—Fallout*. Kate watched it once before, with Max, but since then she has listened to it a half dozen times at least, as she worked around the house while it played in the background. The fact that the boys have rewatched it so often tells her that it is Max's current favorite as well, and though she enjoyed it well enough the one time she viewed it, the exciting score and frequent action sequences, many of which feature prolonged shoot-outs, are difficult for her to bear this morning.

Even before Taylor Swift started blasting upstairs—Callie's room is directly above the pantry—Kate was feeling a stress-induced headache beginning to form.

She hurries to finish restacking the cans, then grabs the handheld vacuum from the utility closet and carries it down to the basement, where she drags the dryer away from the wall and disconnects the vent pipe from the exhaust duct. Hoping that the sound of the vacuum motor will drown out the combined racket from upstairs, Kate proceeds to clean the dryer's exhaust, after which she inserts the vacuum's nozzle as far into the flex pipe as it will go, clearing out cloudlike strands of trapped lint.

But the vacuum's motor sounds shrill to her, like an emergency alarm running continuously, and by the time she has finished her task, her headache is verging on a full-blown migraine.

Leaving the dryer vent disconnected, Kate walks to the darkest corner of the basement, where Leif's workbench is located. On its surface are cleaning kits for his duty pistol and carbine, various gunsmith tools, two pairs of yellow-tinted safety glasses, as well as two pairs of ear protectors, one of which Kate puts on.

Relieved by the complete silence, Kate takes a seat on the metal stool and looks across the workbench at the half dozen framed photos that hang at eye level on the concrete wall.

Two photos are of Leif and Kate at an indoor shooting range, both wearing the same safety glasses and ear protectors that lie before her. In one photo, Leif is standing beside Kate, adjusting her grip on his duty pistol as her arms are outstretched and pointed forward. He is behind her in the other photo, peering over her shoulder as she fires the weapon at a silhouette target hanging seven yards downrange.

Though Kate was never a fan of firearms, she recognized the importance of the wife of a cop knowing how to handle one safely and effectively.

The remaining photos are of Leif and his father posed together, each photo taken at various occasions—Leif's graduation from the police academy fifteen years ago; the day Leif joined the Westport PD, where his father was chief of police; Leif being awarded an Officer of the Year citation by his father; and Leif at his father's retirement party, the two men embracing.

Despite the fact that she is in the darkest corner of the basement, there is still enough light present to require that Kate close her eyes. She begins the breathing techniques she'd been taught by the therapist she worked with in the months following Leif's death. She prefers not to take the Imitrex that was prescribed to her if she can avoid it, and so far she doesn't feel the wave of nausea that always presents itself whenever a migraine is about to reach its full potential.

If she holds still in a quiet, dark place long enough, she can keep the worst at bay, providing that she catches the early-warning signs in time.

Taking out her cell phone, she navigates to an ongoing group chat between herself and her children, composes a text instructing them that she is in the basement and to come get her if they need her, then sends it off.

She waits for a reply from both of them before she places her phone on the workbench. Sitting as still as she can, her back straight and shoulders relaxed, she begins counting her breaths.

In, out, one; in, out, two; in, out, three . . .

The migraine does not arrive, and though the initial headache remains, it has lessened just enough to be an annoyance that allows Kate to continue with her chores but keeps her on edge.

After lunch, she has had enough of the noise to veto the boys' second viewing of the movie and sends them out to the backyard. And minutes later, when loud music resumes upstairs, Kate does the same with the girls—over Callie's objections, of course.

"There's nothing for me to do out there, Mom."

"Swing on the swings," Kate says.

"God! How old am I?"

"Just sit on them, then. Or hang from the bar like your brother does. I don't care what you do. It's a nice day out, and the fresh air will do you good."

"I can open my bedroom window if I want fresh air."

It is all Kate can do not to explode. "Just go," she says. "Please."

Alice, the peacemaker in her family, just as Kate was in hers when she was a girl, discreetly grabs her jacket from the coat hooks by the back door and slips outside.

"Mom," Callie pleads. "It's boring out there."

Kate faces her daughter. "Don't push it, Cal. Not today. Just please, get outside."

By the look on her daughter's face—a mix of confusion, contempt, and concern—Kate understands that she has spoken louder than she'd intended to.

Taking a few steps back, Callie looks at her mother for a moment, her complex emotions swiftly melding into simple shock. After a brief standoff, she grabs her jacket as well and storms through the back door.

Alone in the house, with the sounds of the playing boys muted by the closed windows, Kate tries to pull herself back from the breaking point.

She whispers, "Keep it together, Kate. Keep it together."

By two forty-five, Kate has showered and is outside with the children, waiting for Derek to arrive. She is dressed in khakis, a dark sweater with a white Oxford shirt beneath, and mud boots.

Maria's children are aware of the tension between Kate and Callie. Sitting motionless on the swings, they keep quiet as Max kicks a soccer ball back and forth across the yard.

Whenever one of his mother's dark moods descends, his coping mechanism is to occupy himself with an activity that requires focus. Callie's reaction is to shut her mother out, and seated on the back steps, she takes it a step further by ignoring everyone. House rules forbid her from using her cell phone when there is company, and Kate knows that the moment Alice and D. J. are picked up by their father, Callie will retreat to her bedroom, and into her phone and the direct connection with her chosen friends that it provides.

It is 3:04 p.m. when Derek's work truck turns into the driveway and rolls down the incline, passing the cottage. At the bottom of the driveway, where the property levels out, he slows to a stop and leans across the seat, opening the passenger door and folding the seat forward, providing access to the bench seat in the rear of the truck's extended cab.

D. J. and Alice hurry to the truck and climb inside while Kate approaches the driver's-side door.

Derek lowers the window. "Hey, Kate."

"Hi, Derek."

"Maria texted me, said you saw teenagers last night."

"Yeah."

"You didn't by any chance see who they were?"

"No, sorry. And sorry to hear about your tires."

Derek shrugs. "Deflated is better than slashed."

"That's true."

"Maria also said that Max and Callie might be coming back with me."

"They're going to stay here instead. We've got things to do."

"Sounds good." Derek leans across the seat and pulls the passenger door closed, then checks to make sure D. J. and Alice are buckled in. "Say thank you to Kate for having you over."

In unison, and sounding a bit forced, they say, "Thank you, Kate."

"You're very welcome."

"See you, Kate."

"Bye, Derek."

Kate steps back onto the lawn. Derek turns his truck around, then heads up the driveway. Turning toward the backyard, Kate sees Max standing with the soccer ball held under one arm.

Then Kate looks at the back steps, but Callie has already gone inside.

Turning back to her son, she shrugs, as if to say, "Oh, well." Max returns the gesture.

They head toward the house together, but Kate stops when her cell phone rings. Max stops as well, waiting as Kate fishes the phone out of her pocket and looks down at the display.

She announces that it is Derek calling as she presses the "Talk" button and brings the phone to her ear. "Hi, Derek."

"Hey, Kate." There is something about his tone that strikes Kate as odd.

She asks, "What's up?"

"Driving past the cottage just now, I glanced at the front door, and it looked ajar to me. Did you go in it today and forget to close it?"

"No. I haven't gone in it yet."

"I can come back after I drop the kids off and check it out for you, if you want."

"No, don't bother."

"It'll only take me a minute."

"Thanks for the offer, but I can do it."

Derek hesitates. "Are you sure, Kate?"

"Yes."

"Call if you change your mind."

"I will. Thanks. Bye."

She ends the call and looks toward the cottage, but since its front faces the driveway and not the main house, she cannot see the door.

Yet the idea of it being ajar—when she is certain that the last time she was in it she locked up after exiting—triggers in her a sense of dread.

Max asks, "What's going on, Mom?"

Her instinct is to keep the news Derek shared with her, as well as her reaction to it, from her son, even though he is twelve now and sees himself as the man of the house, which, in fact, he is.

Max was ten when he lost his father, and in the two years since he has grown by several inches, bringing him close to his mother's height of five foot ten. Kate has no doubt that he will surpass that soon enough.

Still, she struggles to see anything other than her child—her baby boy—whenever she looks at him, despite all evidence to the contrary. And now is no different.

She answers, "Nothing's going on, sweetie. Derek forgot to tell me something, that's all. C'mon, let's get inside. We'll need to start thinking about what we're going to do for dinner soon."

FIVE

It's another hour before Kate leaves the house and heads for the cottage.

Attacking a few more chores helped her put off this task, but it will be getting dark soon, so continued stalling is no longer an option. Walking along the edge of the driveway, Kate reminds herself that whatever she finds at the cottage now, it was the work of teenagers, nothing more.

As she walks closer and the front door enters her line of sight, she at first doesn't think it is ajar at all, but after a few more steps she sees that, in fact, it is open, though by barely an inch.

Pushing through the sudden urge to slow down, she maintains her steady pace for a short distance but then actually widens her stride and quickens her steps until she is close enough to see the damaged wood surrounding the lock. Once at the door, she recognizes marks in the frame indicating that it likely was forced open with some kind of lever—a crowbar or tire iron.

Here she pauses, suddenly uncertain whether or not to continue, but her hesitation lasts only seconds. Pushing the door open, she scans the room beyond, finding what she was expecting to see—an open art studio with a couch against the left-hand wall and a kitchen counter against the right. Straight ahead at the far end of the room are two doors, one leading to the bathroom, the other to the bedroom.

Both doors are open, and Kate can see the fixtures in the bathroom and the foot of the unmade bed in the bedroom.

The cottage has that dormant feel places that have been closed up for a period of time have, but Kate knows that doesn't mean anything. If someone entered and walked around last night, that wouldn't really erase the stuffiness that comes with months of inactivity and closed windows.

Stepping through the door, Kate pauses again, this time to listen, but hears nothing. And there are no indications that anything has been disturbed—the few pieces of furniture are in place, and the dozens of paintings that Rebecca left behind remain leaning in stacks against the walls.

Since there are no closets or any other rooms, Kate need only cross the open space to the two rooms at the far end to determine once and for all that the cottage is truly as empty as it feels.

As she walks, she continues to look for indications that something is out of place, but everything is exactly as Rebecca left it two years ago. Kate also searches for anything that might tell her why teenagers would break in—cigarette butts, remnants of joints, empty beer cans, or liquor bottles. She also scans for condom wrappers or, worse, a condom that was discarded after use.

But she sees no such items anywhere.

Reaching the bathroom, she stands in the doorway and peers inside. The room is small and has only a shower, sink, and toilet, so it doesn't take long for her to confirm that no one is there and no damage has been done.

She steps then to her right and looks into the bedroom, which is little more than double the size of the bathroom. The four corners of the room are clear, and the unmade platform bed appears undisturbed.

Kate decides to look closely for the same items she kept an eye out for as she crossed the cottage. After all, if she were to find any discarded condoms or wrappers, they likely would be somewhere on or around the bed.

Entering the room, she looks down at the floor, scanning the narrow space between the right side of the bed and the wall. Seeing nothing, she takes a few steps farther into the room, passing the foot of the bed, and looks down at the floor running along the left side of the bed. Still nothing. And since the bed is really just a mattress set upon an enclosed wooden platform, she need not get down on her hands and knees to check the floor underneath.

She is relieved to find no damage or trash, but the strangeness of the situation is confusing to her. Did the teenagers make so much noise prying open the lock that they got spooked and ran? Did they break in to steal, only to find nothing worth taking?

Or did they just break in to see if they could? Out of boredom? For the fun of it?

Kate tells herself that the "why" doesn't matter, and that most importantly, this is just the work of boys being stupid, which boys are known to be, and nothing more.

All this careful rationale, however, is rendered moot when Kate turns to head back toward the door.

On the wall, roughly dead center, is the last thing in the world she expected to see, and it takes a few seconds of her staring at it, dumbfounded, before she fully understands what it is she is looking at.

Protruding from the wall, the tip of its blade sunk a good three or four inches into the drywall, is a large kitchen knife.

Instantly, her body shudders violently and the hairs on the back of her neck are standing. She stands too frozen to even gasp, her shock total and overwhelming.

All she can do for far too long is stand in place and stare and hold her breath.

Then she breaks free of the utter fear and hurries out of the bedroom. Every step she takes as she recrosses the room is faster than the one before, so that by the time she is approaching the front door, she is close to an all-out run.

Once she is outside, instead of experiencing relief, Kate feels deeply vulnerable, as though she is certain that whoever stuck the knife in the bedroom wall is still watching from somewhere. She forces herself to walk to the house, though, not run like she wants to, because Max or Callie may be watching her, and the last thing she wants is for them to see her frightened. Nonetheless, she is out of breath when she enters the empty kitchen, mere seconds from hyperventilating.

From the living room come the familiar sounds of *Mission: Impossible—Fallout*, and Taylor Swift is again playing loudly upstairs. This time, however, Kate is grateful for the noise since it gives her cover. No one can hear her now, and no one is likely to walk in on her as she speaks on the phone.

Using the landline, Kate keys in her father-in-law's number, then waits for him to answer. Her hand is shaking, and she taps her right toe impatiently. Finally, the call is answered at the tail end of the third ring.

"Hello," Leo Burke says.

Kate speaks quickly. "I'm sorry to bother you, Dad, but could you come over right now?"

"What's wrong?"

"Everyone's okay, nothing like that. But the cottage was broken into, and whoever did it left something."

"Left what?"

"Can you just please come over? And don't make a big deal out of it. I'd rather keep Max and Callie out of this if possible."

"I'll be right there."

As Kate hangs up, the movie playing in the living room enters one of its action sequences, the orchestral music swelling and the gunshots ringing out.

———

Standing at the foot of the driveway, Kate watches as her father-in-law exits the cottage and starts walking toward her.

He's been inside for only a few minutes, and during that time Kate frequently turned her attention to the house to confirm that neither Max nor Callie was watching from a window. And when she wasn't looking at the house or the cottage, Kate was surveying the yard, front and back, and the rows of trees and saplings that border them.

All the places from which someone could be watching, unseen.

Leo Burke is as tall as Kate—five ten—and sturdily built. At sixty-six, he is still as vital and tireless as he was when Kate first started dating Leif in high school. Up until his retirement five years ago, the man was almost always in uniform, and it is still strange for Kate to see him in civilian clothes.

The fact that he is dressed more or less in the same dark pants, dress shirt, and black shoes every time Kate sees him tells her that he has merely traded in one uniform for another.

Burke is still a few steps from Kate when he says, "Chief O'Neil should see this. Why don't you take the children out to dinner while he and I have a closer look around?"

Kate shakes her head. "No. I want to hear what O'Neil has to say. I'll send them next door."

Burke considers that, then nods. "Okay. But it'll be getting dark soon. Is the power to the cottage on?"

"I'll switch it on before I walk the kids over."

"You'd better drive them, Kate," he says.

She looks at him squarely.

He shrugs and says, "It's safer."

Back at the house, Kate tells Max to turn off the movie and get his sister, and before he can ask why, she explains that the two of them are going to Maria's for dinner after all and that they need to leave right now.

Max asks, "What's Grandpa doing here?"

The boy is reclining on the couch and has no view of any part of the driveway through any of the windows.

"How did you know he was here?" Kate says.

"I heard his car."

"He's helping me with something in the cottage." Kate heads toward the door to the basement. "Please just turn off the TV and go get your sister."

In the basement, Kate hurries to the circuit breaker box and opens it, exposing the panel. Finding the six switches marked COTTAGE, she flips them to the right, then swings the door closed and returns upstairs.

Callie voices her complaints about the change in plan, but Kate doesn't engage. Instead, she composes and sends a text to Maria, then tells the twins to get their shoes and jackets on.

The reply comes through in less than a minute, after which Kate leads the kids through the back door and down the steps to the driveway. Burke's Ford Explorer is parked next to Kate's Subaru Outback.

Callie asks, "When did Grandpa get here?"

Max answers, "He's helping Mom with something in the cottage."

"With what?"

Kate gets behind the wheel as the twins occupy the back seats.

"Wait," Callie says. "Why are we driving?"

Kate starts the engine and then pauses to fasten her seat belt. Looking back, she watches as Max and Callie fasten theirs. "It's quicker," she lies.

"If we took the path through the woods, we'd already be in her yard by now."

Kate replies, "We don't want to get our shoes dirty."

Callie says under her breath, "Crazy."

37

Kate ignores that, too. Shifting into gear, she heads up the driveway, traveling faster than she usually does.

"What the hell?" Callie says.

Kate gives her daughter a scolding look via the rearview mirror. Then she glances down at the speedometer. The Subaru is doing thirty, but Kate doesn't want there to be enough time for Max, sitting behind the passenger seat, to see the broken lock, so she makes no attempt to reduce speed.

Callie asks, "Why are you being a maniac, Mom?"

Kate tries to keep things light. "I've had too much coffee today; that's why."

"You know, we'd be inside their house by now if we had walked."

"Shut up," Max says softly.

Callie looks across the seat at him. "What's your problem?"

Max doesn't answer. Kate glances over her shoulder at him. He is watching her with his all-too-familiar expression of worry.

"Everything's okay," Kate says. It takes all she has to sound convincing. "Your crazy mom just has a lot on her mind."

Max looks away, but his face is unchanged.

———

The late-afternoon sun is well below the tops of the bare border trees when Kate turns back into the driveway. Parked on the grass by the cottage are a Westport PD sedan and SUV. The sedan belongs to the current chief of police, James O'Neil, and the SUV is one of the department's dozen-plus patrol vehicles.

Kate rolls past the cottage, its many windows lit, and parks and exits the Subaru. As she approaches the open front door, the first man she sees is Officer Eddie Sabrowsky, bent at the waist and examining the broken lock.

As Kate steps onto the stone pathway leading to the cottage, Sabrowsky straightens his back and faces her. "Hey, Katie."

"Hi, Eddie."

Having attended high school together, they still address each other by the nicknames assigned to them as youths. Very few people call Kate "Katie" anymore, and she hasn't heard anyone refer to Ed as "Eddie" in years.

Kate asks, "Did you just get here?"

"I pulled in right after you pulled out. O'Neil was right behind me."

"Did Leo call you, or did O'Neil?"

"Leo. The minute I answered the phone I knew something was up. And then when he told me what it was . . ." Sabrowsky doesn't complete his thought. "The last thing you need is this shit again."

Sabrowsky has been like a member of Leo Burke's family since junior high school, when he and Leif became friends. As time went on, there wasn't a family get-together—from Sunday dinner to holidays— that Sabrowsky didn't attend, or at least make an appearance.

Leif, Kate, and Sabrowsky had been members of the same class in high school, and Leif and Sabrowsky had graduated the police academy together, with Leif being hired by his father right away and Sabrowsky a year later.

It wasn't until after Leif's death that Leo Burke, in his grieving, began to see Sabrowsky as a second son, and the two men had grown only closer.

It is no surprise to Kate, then, that her father-in-law would take it upon himself to call his surrogate son immediately after alerting Chief O'Neil, even though doing so was something of a breach of protocol.

She wonders if, when Leo was police chief, he would have taken kindly to such a jump in the chain of command.

Still, regardless of whatever trouble it may have caused, she is pleased that Sabrowsky is here.

At Leif's funeral, Sabrowsky had promised to do whatever it took to take care of her and the twins.

Sabrowsky gestures to the broken lock. "Sorry about this, Kate. They did a number on it. The whole thing will need to be replaced."

"I figured."

"But it's a chance to upgrade, which you were due for anyway, since this one was definitely out-of-date."

"Always looking on the bright side, Eddie."

Sabrowsky smiles. "I try."

Visible through the doorway are Leo Burke and Chief O'Neil. Standing face-to-face in the center of the studio, the two men speak over each other in low but intense voices. Because Kate can't hear their words, she can only guess at the cause of the tension between them.

While Leo's call to Sabrowsky could be the reason, there are a number of other issues between the two men that would lead them so quickly to a confrontation.

Sabrowsky glances into the cottage, then looks back at Kate and shrugs, as if to say he has no idea what the problem is between Leo and his chief. "O'Neil said to send you in."

As Kate steps into the doorway, the former and current police chiefs immediately cease their hushed discussion.

O'Neil is quick to shift his demeanor. "Hello, Kate," he says. His tone is serious to the point of being grave. "Come in, please." In one hand is a gallon-size baggie containing the kitchen knife she found stuck into the bedroom wall. With his other hand he waves her forward.

Despite the invitation, Kate stands in the doorway. The intensity of the private conversation she interrupted has left her feeling like an intruder.

Leo nods once and says, "It's okay, Kate. Come in."

Kate briefly studies both men before stepping into the cottage.

SIX

Chief O'Neil says, "I'm going to ask you a few questions."

"Of course."

Burke steps away from O'Neil, moving to the table along the left-hand wall, which he leans against. Kate recognizes this action as her father-in-law casting himself as merely an observer—and making a point of it.

Sabrowsky has followed Kate in, but he remains behind her, stepping to her left as well so he can view both Chief O'Neil and Burke.

O'Neil says, "I understand you saw what looked to you like two teenagers running from the cottage last night."

"Yes."

"What time was that?"

"After eleven."

"You were awake?"

"No, something woke me up."

"What?"

"A deer walking through the backyard." She anticipates the chief's likely next question and adds, "My window was open a little. I only have one, and it can get stuffy if I keep it closed overnight."

O'Neil nods, then holds up the baggie and says, "This is your knife, correct?"

"I don't understand."

O'Neil gestures toward the kitchen area. "There's a knife holder with an empty slot. I'm assuming this is the one that's missing."

Kate looks at the kitchen counter running along the wall to her right. Indeed, there is a knife missing from the wooden cutlery holder located between the sink and the toaster oven.

"Yeah, it looks like part of that set."

"Do your children ever use the cottage?"

"No. But if they did come out here for some reason, they know where the key is, so they wouldn't need to destroy the lock."

"Is it possible they use this without your knowing it?"

"I drop them off at Maria's every weekday morning; she drives them and her kids to school, and then I pick them up at her house at five o'clock. I'm with them the rest of the time. So no." She pauses. "Obviously, I'm not keen on letting them out of my sight."

"Understandable," O'Neil says.

"I'm curious," Kate says. "Why are they your first thought?"

"They're not. I'm just ruling things out. It's possible they were in here doing something they shouldn't have been doing and decided to break the lock to cover their tracks."

"Possible, maybe, but not likely," Kate says.

"Is there any chance that the two teenagers you saw were Maria's children?"

"No, the ones I saw were both male, and they looked older to me. High school age."

"How long did you see them?"

"For however long it takes two teenage boys to cover the distance between the cottage and the street. Ten seconds, maybe."

O'Neil nods, then says, "To me, *teenagers* can also mean *young adults*. Someone who has been out of high school for a year or two, maybe even more."

"I suppose, yeah. You're thinking students of mine, or former students, aren't you?"

"Is there anyone who might have a reason to hold a grudge against you? Maybe someone who is failing or that you failed in the past few years?"

"I teach AP English. The students that make it into my class aren't the kind to fail. And if one of them were struggling, I'd help them out."

"Maybe it's a student who is attracted to you and feels, I don't know, rebuffed?"

"I doubt that's the case."

"The mind of a teenage boy isn't exactly a mystery, Kate. Haven't you ever noticed one of your students looking at you a certain way?"

Embarrassed, Kate laughs, then says, "Boys who 'like' their teachers tend to be the ones who excel. That has been my experience, anyway."

"So there isn't anything in particular that stands out in your mind. No recent difficulties with a student? No unusual interactions, nothing like that?"

"Nothing."

"I guess, for that matter, it wouldn't have to be a student in one of your AP classes. There are other students at the school, ones that don't make the cut for Advanced Placement classes but still know who you are and see you every day."

"Yes, of course."

"But you don't decide who makes your class and who doesn't, right? It's not like you passed over someone."

"I don't make that decision, no."

O'Neil looks down at the baggie in his hand. After a moment, he says, "When you were experiencing that wave of vandalism the year prior to Leif's death, did you discuss it with the people in your life—colleagues, friends?"

"You wanted us to keep it quiet."

"So you told no one."

Kate says, "I confided in Maria and her husband."

"Anyone else?"

"My principal needed to know. I had exceeded my personal days. It was a rough time."

"Well, if Harwood knew, then so did everyone in the PTA. What I'm asking, Kate, is how much detail did you go into? Did you give examples of the vandalism?"

"Not to Harwood."

"But to Maria?"

Kate nods. "She needed to know."

"Because she was your neighbor. Because it was happening right next door to her."

Kate nods again. She is experiencing once more the feelings of desperation that had overwhelmed her at the time. Finally, she shrugs and says, "I had to tell someone."

From behind Kate, Sabrowsky speaks. "Can I ask what difference that makes, Chief?"

O'Neil glances at his officer briefly, his displeasure evident. Then he looks back at Kate.

"What I'm getting at is all that prior vandalism, while disturbing at the time, was pretty mundane stuff compared with this. And honestly, when it was occurring, I'd always believed it was directed at Leif, because of what a hard-nosed cop he was, especially with the high school crowd. And, of course, it stopped after his death, so case closed." O'Neil looks at the baggie again. "But this, this is different. This is . . . disturbing on a whole new level. And with Leif gone, I can only assume that this time it's directed at you."

SEVEN

The room is silent until Burke speaks.

"Jesus, man, scare the shit out of her, why don't you."

O'Neil addresses his former chief. "I would think that of all people, Leo, you'd want this taken seriously."

"I'm taking this very seriously. But I think maybe you're jumping the gun here. This cottage has been unoccupied for two years. Vacant structures invite vandalism, and you know that."

"No other damage was done."

Burke shrugs. "They could have gotten scared off. Breaking the lock would have made noise."

"Yet they made it all the way to the back room, after grabbing a knife from the kitchen counter. And why do that? Why stick a knife into the wall? A bedroom wall, at that."

"They could have seen it in some horror movie. And, yes, if they were determined enough—or drunk enough—I could see them rushing to accomplish what they came to do before beating it out of here. For that matter, this could have been a crime of opportunity. They broke in without any plan, saw the block of knives, and decided then what to do."

Sabrowsky chimes in again. "Teenagers do crazy things, Chief. For all we know, some neighborhood kids have decided that this place is haunted. This could have been a dare, or something along those lines."

O'Neil says, "These are all interesting theories, gentlemen, but last I knew *I* was the chief of police." He addresses Kate. "I can't ignore what happened before, but even with my suspicions, this isn't something I can devote a lot of man-hours to. I can send the knife to the state police forensics lab, but that's about it. I'm not trying to scare anyone, and to be frank, I think I know you well enough to know that you're scared already. How could you not be? But Leo has a point. This place has been empty for a long time, and that *is* the kind of thing that catches the attention of bored teenagers. What happened last night could have absolutely nothing at all to do with what happened before, but whatever the case—whether this is an escalation or a dumb prank—there is a relatively simple solution."

O'Neil pauses, then says, "As I recall, you and Leif used to rent this out in the summertime. A bike ride to the beach and to the town, a short Uber ride to and from the train station—it's a perfect getaway for New Yorkers. That's who you used to rent to, right? Artist types from the city."

"Yes. We learned quickly enough that when we described this as a cottage, most people who came to check it out were expecting something out of *The Great Gatsby*. Calling it what it is—an art cottage with bare-bones essentials—caused less confusion. And it always seemed to draw the same kind of tenants."

"There's still plenty of time to run an ad and get someone in here. I'll be more than happy to run a background check on any candidate for you, and with the right person living here, maybe you'll feel a little more secure. You might even be able to find someone looking for a short-term lease. That way they'd be on the premises for more than just weekends. Like I said, it's a relatively simple solution. The only other actions you could take are to invest in a security system or ask people you know and trust to take turns spending the night. But that would mean putting people out, which I know you don't like, and why spend the money on a system—a real system, not some unreliable cloud camera setup—for what has basically become a place to store your sister's paintings?"

In the weeks following Leif's death, Kate had been encouraged by her father-in-law to consider installing surveillance cameras in key positions on the property. But she had no interest in turning her home into a fortress, mainly because she thought doing so would mean that she was giving in to her fears. Also, the idea of being watched as she came and went, even by a closed-circuit system over which she had total control, unnerved her.

Of course, at that time she was out of her mind with grief and anger, and all her energies went into keeping herself together for the sake of her children, who were coping with the loss of their father. In that moment-to-moment, hour-to-hour way of living, Kate was often incapable of making even the most basic of decisions—what clothes to put on in the morning, how to get through the day, what to prepare for dinner, how to deal with the horrific nightmares that plagued her during those few hours when she managed to find sleep.

There was a part of her then that wished her father-in-law would take it upon himself and make the decision for her. In fact, she was surprised that he didn't. But he was bereft as well, stunned at the loss of his flesh-and-blood son to what Chief O'Neil concluded after a weeks-long investigation was an attempted robbery gone wrong—nothing more and nothing less.

The rift this determination caused drove the two once-close men apart. More than that, it sent Leo Burke into a rage that resulted in him launching his own investigation, one in which Sabrowsky secretly played a key role. But that investigation offered no other explanation for Leif Burke's death, a result that Leo Burke blamed on the time that had been lost as he'd waited out O'Neil's official investigation.

And now, two years later, it is clear to Kate that her father-in-law is no more healed than she is. He is watching his former protégé—the man he had handpicked to succeed him—with a hostile scorn.

Kate says to O'Neil, "Thanks for the advice. I'll think about it."

"I'm sorry I can't offer more than that, Kate. The board of selectmen I have to deal with aren't the same Leo dealt with. In a lot of ways, they've tied my hands. I'm more of a politician most days than I am an officer of the law."

Though Kate understands that this last comment is meant more for Burke than for herself, she feels compelled to reply.

"I get it," she says. "The last thing they want is for people to think Westport is a dangerous place."

"I appreciate your understanding that, Kate. With that in mind, let's keep this between the four of us for now, okay? No one else need know at this stage."

Leo Burke scoffs then, and shaking his head, stomps to the door and exits the cottage, leaving Kate with O'Neil and Sabrowsky.

In the silence that follows her father-in-law's noisy departure, Kate is uncertain what to say. Finally, she shrugs once and leaves it at that.

"We'll get through this, Kate," O'Neil says. "Keep your alarm set and maintain your situational awareness at all times. You have my cell number, correct?"

"Yes."

"If you need anything, anytime, call me directly."

"Thanks."

"In the meantime, I'll ask around and see if there's anyone looking for a place to live for a few months—the right 'anyone,' of course."

Kate thanks him again. O'Neil heads for the exit, pausing briefly at the open door to look at Sabrowsky. The officer meets his chief's stare, but neither man speaks. Eventually, O'Neil turns to glance back at Kate before stepping through the door.

Another quiet moment passes; then Sabrowsky asks, "You okay, Katie?"

Glancing around the cottage, Kate says, "Maybe I should just have this torn down."

"Now, why would you want to do that? It's a moneymaker."

"I don't care about that."

"But what about Rebecca? If your grandfather's will gives her access to it November through April, is it really yours to tear down?"

"You're not making the argument you think you're making," Kate says. "No cottage, no reason for her to come back here."

"Things are still bad between you two?"

A shrug is Kate's only response.

"I've known the two of you for a long time," Sabrowsky says. "Longer than anyone else in my life. If you ask me, it's time to forget and start over."

This time Kate offers no response at all.

Sabrowsky nods. "I know; it's none of my business."

Kate says, "No, that's not what I'm saying."

"You're not saying anything, Katie. Something's on your mind."

She takes a breath in, lets it out, then says, "Chief O'Neil is right about my options. What do you think I should do?"

"Would a stranger living here really make you feel any better?"

"I honestly don't know."

"Obviously, offering it to Rebecca is out of the question. But something you have to keep in mind, Katie, is that O'Neil has an agenda. He wasn't kidding about the board of selectmen climbing up his ass every day over shit that should be left to law enforcement. Because of that, all he wants is for there to be the appearance of Westport being crime-free. It doesn't actually have to be crime-free, just the appearance. That's his job now, and everything he just said is clouded by that."

Sabrowsky pauses. "I'm not just saying this because it's what we all want, but this bullshit here, what happened last night, it's just kids. It was kids before—kids pranking the town cop they hated—and it's kids again. But I'm on this, okay? I'll make sure a patrol car drives by here every hour. There isn't a cop in the department who wouldn't do whatever you needed them to do. You know that. You're one of us, you and your kids. You always will be."

49

Kate sighs and says, "Thanks, Eddie."

"After Leif died and O'Neil closed his investigation, I helped Leo out of loyalty to him. I know he complained that too much time had gone by and too many leads had gone cold, but O'Neil was right: there was no connection between the vandalism you guys endured and the armed robbers that came to your house. They both had criminal records, and we'll probably never know why they decided to attempt to rob a cop's home. My guess is that they chose your house as a target because of the layout of the yard—the trees surrounding it, the fact that the house is set so far back from the road and at the bottom of a knoll. Their arrest histories indicated that they weren't particularly bright, and I don't think they had any idea who lived here. I think they just saw what they saw and went for it."

"You've already told me all that, Eddie. Why are you telling me again?"

"Because I don't want you to be so afraid that you rush into something you're not ready for. To be honest, I don't like the idea of a stranger living here, no matter how much vetting the chief does. I know you're still struggling with your post-traumatic stress. I know you didn't sell the house and move because you don't want to be driven out of your home—a mortgage-free home at that. I give you all the credit in the world for staying and facing all the reminders of Leif and how he was taken from you, but tenants are a roll of the dice. And yeah, while it would be good to have another presence on your property, do you really want to surrender your privacy? Are you really ready for that? I mean, there's a reason why you haven't rented the place out the past two summers, right? Someone here would be just another person you have to wear a mask in front of."

Kate half smiles—the very mask Sabrowsky is referring to.

"When did you become sensitive?" she teases.

He smiles in return. "We all have our masks, Katie. I'm not really the dick I pretend to be, believe it or not."

Kate laughs at the joke. "Good to know." She takes another breath in, holding it briefly before letting it out. "I have a lot to think about, I guess, huh?"

"Yeah," Sabrowsky answers. "But like I said, someone will swing by every hour, me or one of the other officers on patrol. Who knows, maybe I'll see your two teenagers. If I do, I'll put a scare into them." He smiles. "Like Leif used to."

Sabrowsky steps outside. Kate hears him speaking briefly with Leo Burke before getting into his SUV and starting up the driveway. Reaching the top, he turns onto the street, the sound of his engine gradually receding.

Kate remains in place and has another look around. Then finally she takes her hands out of her pockets and glances down at them—at the trembling she cannot control.

After switching off the lights, she exits the cottage as well, pulling the door closed behind her. But when she releases the knob, the door doesn't stay closed, drifting back about an inch before stopping on its own.

Burke is standing beside his Ford Explorer. "We should probably leave some lights on," he says. "I'll run out now and get a latch and padlock. I'll turn the lights on when I come back to secure the place."

Kate looks at him and nods her thanks. "You can come up for dinner after," she says. "The kids have already eaten, so it'll just be me."

"I wouldn't be very good company."

She half smiles again. "And when has that ever stopped you?"

Despite himself, Burke laughs. "Yeah, all right. But I want to swing by my place and grab some things. I'm going to stay the night."

"You don't have to do that, Dad. I'll set the alarm, and Maria and Derek are right next door. Plus, Eddie is going to drive by every hour. We'll be fine."

"Let's just say it's for my sake, then."

"Okay," Kate says. "I'll see you in, what? An hour?"

"Give or take, yeah."

After her father-in-law drives off, Kate lingers in the driveway. Full darkness has come, but as much as she wants to, she doesn't make a move toward the relative safety and privacy of her vehicle. Remaining in the open, she looks down at the pavement, unwilling to engage her peripheral vision for fear of seeing something lurking along the edges of her property.

Standing there, she tells herself that she is a mother, for God's sake, and that she had been married to a cop whose father was a cop, one as tough as the other. Fear was never something that controlled her as much as it does now. In fact, her life had been decidedly fear-free, at least free of the life-or-death fear that assaults her and violates her until she can barely stand, never mind move.

She feels both its grip upon her and the inner powerlessness it renders that all but stakes her feet to the ground.

It takes a moment, but finally Kate pulls herself together enough to break free and head toward her Subaru.

She finds her pace quickening, though, the closer to the vehicle she gets.

It is when she is behind the wheel with the door closed that Kate realizes she neglected to mention that her neighbor's tires had been flattened last night.

She considers calling Chief O'Neil to pass on this important detail, but instead she sends the information by text to Sabrowsky.

She decides, too, not to share this with Leo—at least not tonight.

Revisiting the subject is the last thing either of them needs.

By the time Kate reaches the bottom of the driveway, Sabrowsky's reply comes through. It is a simple two-word missive that brings Kate a degree of comfort.

ON IT.

EIGHT

After dinner, the twins and their grandfather gather in the living room. Max wants them to watch the new *Mission: Impossible* movie but Kate steers them away from that, tuning the TV instead to reruns of *The Office*. Callie ignores the program in favor of her cell phone, but during commercials, when Leo Burke asks them questions about school and their friends, she does place the device faceup on her lap and interact with her grandfather.

Long ago, he began to influence their personalities, mainly by demanding that they act with discipline and courtesy at all times, just as he had done with their father when he was young. And even though the traits he has pressed upon his grandchildren are most evident in his presence—in the presence of any authority figure, really, with the exception of their mother—Kate is grateful that her children have a positive male role model, one who expects them, just as their father had, to always be their best selves.

She is particularly grateful that Callie, who is proving more and more unruly as she approaches young adulthood, has someone she wishes to never disappoint.

Kate and Rebecca were close to the age Callie is now when the differences in their personalities began to emerge. After that, it wasn't long before Kate barely recognized her older sister.

Kate joins her children and father-in-law for part of one episode, then excuses herself and grabs her laptop from its carrying case. After setting it up on the kitchen table, she goes online and signs in to the account she has with the local paper. Navigating to the "For Rent" page, she begins to compose an ad.

It is difficult for her not to recall the last time she'd done this. The house was different then, had a singular energy—the energy of a family of four, one that was as yet untouched by sudden violence and irreparable loss.

The best Kate can hope for now is the chaos of daily life, though that is, of course, not the same thing at all.

She completes her standard ad—the same ad she will, after this, post in the online classifieds of the *Village Voice* and *New York Times*. But she is hesitant to take the final step of this process and make the ad active in the local online classifieds. Sabrowsky's words play in her mind, and she asks herself if she really wants this. Does she really need to seek out more activity—a single tenant or couple coming and going as they will—as if it were some kind of balm? As if it could fill the Leif-shaped gap that still remains? As if the old adage that there is safety in numbers applies to her situation?

In the end she clicks on the "X," closing the window without posting the ad. Then she shuts down her notebook computer and returns it to its carrying case.

Better to sleep on it, she thinks.

She realizes that what she needs to do—and can do with no problem—is to arrange for a locksmith to repair the broken lock on the cottage door. In her phone is the contact information of the man she used to switch out all the locks when a summer tenant failed to return his keys. Four texts total—two from her and two from him—are all it takes to make an appointment for eleven o'clock tomorrow morning.

———

Kate is making up the foldout bed in the living room as Leo Burke sees the twins off to bed.

She has laid out the bottom sheet and is unfolding the comforter when her cell phone buzzes in her pocket. Looking at the display and recognizing Chief O'Neil's home number, she quickly answers.

"Hello, Chief."

"Sorry to call so late."

"No problem. What's up?"

"So, listen, I may have found someone for you."

"Who?"

"His name is Jack Guarnere. Actually, I think you may have gone to high school with him."

Kate shakes her head. "I don't recognize the name."

"Maybe you'd graduated before he got there, then. Anyway, he's moving back to Westport and is looking for a short-term rental."

"How did you find him?"

"I didn't; my wife did. There's a connection to his family somewhere in hers. His mother was her cousin or something like that."

Though that sounds oddly vague to Kate, she doesn't dwell on it. She has kicked in to landlord mode, which means she is on the lookout for any indication that she should pass. "Why does he want a short-term rental?"

"From what I understand, he's had a run of bad luck and is coming back home to regroup."

"Does he have a job here?"

"I'm not sure. Angela and I only discussed it briefly, when I mentioned that you were looking for someone. I doubt he's a bum, though, but I'll ask her later anything you want me to."

"I'd need a few days to clean the place up, get Rebecca's paintings out of there and into the attic. No one has really been in there for two years. And I'll need to have a new lock installed. Right now all we have is a padlock."

"You can at least meet with him, right? See if he's a good fit. If it turns out he isn't, that'll save you the trouble of cleaning up for nothing."

"When is he free?"

"Tomorrow."

Kate pauses. "Okay, yeah."

"What time should I tell him to be there?"

"Eleven?"

"That sounds like a question."

"Eleven," she says.

"He'll be there. And no pressure, Kate. It just seemed like . . . I don't know . . . kismet that you need a tenant and he needs a place."

"We'll see, I guess."

"I won't bother running a background check, because I know Leo will want to run his own. I'll email him Jack's info."

"Thanks."

O'Neil asks, "He's there now, right? Leo?"

"Yes. How did you know?"

"Sabrowsky drove by and saw his Explorer."

"Oh, yeah," Kate says.

"With him there you should at least be able to sleep through the night."

"Hope so."

"Try not to worry so much, Kate. You have a lot of people looking out for you."

"Thanks, Chief."

"Have a good night."

"You too."

Kate ends the call and lays her phone on an end table. She is finishing up with the couch when her father-in-law appears at the bottom of the stairs with his own cell in his hand.

His eyes on the screen, Burke asks, "What's this email from O'Neil?"

"It's the info on someone who's looking for a place. He says his wife is related to him."

"That was quick."

Kate shrugs. She guides a spare pillow into a pillowcase, then holds the case by its end and bounces it until the pillow has slipped all the way in.

Burke reads the name aloud. "Jack Guarnere." He repeats it several times before asking, "Why is that name familiar?"

Kate tosses the pillow onto the couch. "O'Neil says he might have been at the high school the same time Leif and I were."

Burke nods, then asks, "Are you considering renting to him?"

Kate shrugs again. "Having someone here might make things feel safer. Anyway, I won't know until I meet him."

"When's that?"

"Tomorrow at eleven."

"That gives me time to run a check on him. If he's bad news, I don't even want him on the property."

"If O'Neil suggested him, I doubt he's bad news."

Burke pauses. "It doesn't seem strange to you that hours after telling you to rent the cottage he finds someone?"

"I'm not really the best judge anymore of what's strange and what's not, Dad. I know things aren't good between you and O'Neil these days, but maybe he's just trying to help. Anyway, there's no harm in meeting the guy, right?"

"I can be here. I'd rather you weren't alone."

"The locksmith will be here."

"Which one?"

"Your guy," Kate answers. "Tony. The one you recommended to me."

Burke considers that, then says, "And what about the kids?"

"What about them?"

"What did you tell them about the cottage?"

"I haven't told them anything yet."

"What will you tell them?"

"Not the truth; that's for certain."

"Tell them there's a plumbing problem."

"Okay."

"And maybe you should send them to Maria's house, so they don't see Tony's truck. Or this Jack guy."

"Maria's taking her kids to visit their grandmother in Litchfield. They'll be gone all day."

"I'll take them to lunch, then."

"They won't even know anyone's here, Dad. They'll likely be in their rooms on their devices. Anyway, I'm taking them to Tutti's at one. It's Max's favorite."

Burke takes another moment. Finally, he shrugs and says, "Okay. It's your call."

Kate realizes that her failure to include her father-in-law in the family's lunch plans might have left him feeling slighted.

"Do you want to come with us? I'm sorry; I didn't think to ask."

"It's not a problem, Kate," Burke says. "I'll run a check first thing in the morning and let you know what I find out."

"I'll be here."

"Your vacation isn't off to a very good start, is it?"

"It can only get better, right?"

"Let's hope so." Burke looks at the email once more, reads it aloud, then says, "Why do I know that name?"

It's obvious to Kate that the question isn't directed at her, so she doesn't answer.

A moment later Burke repeats himself. "Why do I know that name?"

NINE

Kate dreams of Leif.

It is a warm summer night, the windows throughout the house open, and Kate is sitting on the edge of the bed, applying hand lotion while Leif brushes his teeth in the bathroom. Earlier that afternoon, Kate had brought Max and Callie next door for a sleepover, and shortly after a quiet dinner together, she and Leif had engaged in rowdy and intense sex.

Leif had just finished two weeks of night shifts, and they were long overdue. Satisfied and exhausted, Kate looks forward to a full night's sleep with her husband beside her, as well as sharing another quiet meal in the morning.

She is getting into bed, Leif still in the bathroom, when the first sound comes—a *thunk* from an unknown direction. Though initially unidentifiable, the noise is more than enough to get Kate's attention, and Leif's, too. He steps out of the bathroom and asks, "What was that?"

"I don't know."

"Could you tell where it came from?"

"No."

A pause, then Leif says, "Wait here."

Kate is aware now that she is dreaming, and she desperately wants to wake but cannot. All she can do is watch as Leif walks to the nightstand on his side of the bed, pulls open the drawer, and removes his unloaded duty pistol. From the drawer below he grabs two magazines, inserts one into the weapon and tucks the other into the waistband of his boxers. Racking the slide to chamber a round, he steps into the bedroom doorway, where he pauses to listen before stepping through and entering the dark living room.

Kate already has the phone in her hand and is ready to dial 911, should Leif call to her and tell her to do so, or should something—anything—give her reason to believe that they are in danger.

But she remains seated on the edge of the bed, waiting for this to turn out to be nothing. There have been late-night noises for the past two years, coming on an average of once a month, but those always turned out to be acts of petty vandalism—someone throwing eggs at the picture window or pelting the front door with tomatoes.

So she has every reason to hope this is just more of the same as she watches Leif step from her line of sight, after which she tracks him by the creaking sound that comes with nearly every step he takes as he moves across the one-hundred-plus-year-old floorboards.

His footsteps cease as he reaches the front door. Then he unlocks and opens it, and Kate can hear the hinges of the door as it is pulled back.

A few seconds of silence follow, and Kate is left to wonder what Leif has seen now that he has opened the front door.

Her answer comes when he barks an angry command, ordering someone to freeze. His single word is spoken outside, meaning that he has left the doorway and moved into the yard. He calls out several more times, each command sounding fainter as he moves farther away.

Kate stands and hurries through the bedroom doorway, stopping at the foot of the stairs. This could still be what it has always been—vandals. Only this time Leif saw them and is running them down. But that hope is ended almost immediately by the sharp crack of a gunshot.

Kate flinches, but before she can make any voluntary movements—before she has even fully processed the sound—a barrage of gunshots follows.

A cluster of overlapping pops that sound like fireworks but hit her ears like thunder.

The gunshots last only five seconds, which gives Kate time to overcome the shock that has rendered her motionless. Finally, she scrambles through the living room, rushing toward the door.

The dream skips forward then, and she finds herself outside the house, moving toward where Leif has fallen.

Where he will die as she kneels over him, struggling with bare hands to contain the blood gushing from his chest . . .

———

Kate finally opens her eyes.

First she rolls onto her side to prevent herself from falling back to sleep and reentering the dream, which has happened too many times before. But lying on her side isn't enough; she is drowsy and feels herself being pulled back toward unconsciousness, so she sits up and focuses on her surroundings in an effort to will her mind clear.

She reminds herself that she is in her bedroom, safe, and that her children are upstairs, safe, and that her father-in-law is asleep on the couch just outside her open door. She can hear in the silence the sound of his breathing, slow and steady.

Walking through the living room, she passes the couch as quietly as she can, avoiding the wide planks that creak the loudest. Then she reaches the large window overlooking the front yard—there to check on the cottage, though her eyes cannot avoid the spot where Leif had died, feet from the two would-be home invaders he'd killed.

Maria and Derek had joined Kate by then—Maria, a former nurse, had grabbed her trauma kit as she left her house and was attempting to stanch the bleeding while Derek, who had put the call in to 911 the moment the first shots were fired, had remained in the house to attend to the children.

Their arms and hands and clothing soaked with blood, Kate and Maria worked together until the first police officer arrived—Sabrowsky. But by then it was too late. Leif was gone.

Maria saw the shock set in. She took charge, guiding her friend back to the house and sitting her down at the kitchen table.

Kate's mind wanders, and she remembers a conversation that she and Maria had weeks later about Kate having run outside instead of remaining in the house. Leif had long ago established a protocol that Kate was to follow, should something like this happen, and she had broken that protocol.

The kids were safe and Leif wasn't, Maria said. *And it probably was more of a reaction than a choice—the reaction of a fighter, which you are.*

Kate pushes the memory from her mind, though not without first recalling her response.

Was, maybe, she'd scoffed.

It was Maria who encouraged Kate to pursue counseling—each family member individually at first, and then, months later, together as a family. And it was Maria who ran both families during Kate's grief, handling the things that Kate suddenly couldn't. She did so, happily, until Kate and her children were finally ready to return to their home and resume their lives.

But the Kate who emerged from those weeks of grief relieved occasionally by numbness—that Kate was a different Kate, a broken Kate that in no way resembled the one she'd always been.

The Kate who could always be counted on.

The Kate who had rushed toward gunshots.

The Kate who had never really known fear.

Standing alone in her darkened living room, she does not trust the silence that surrounds her now. Something will shatter it, if not in this very moment, then in the next. Or an hour from now. Or tomorrow. Or the day after that . . .

TEN

Kate is unloading the dishwasher when Callie enters the kitchen and says, "Some of my friends from school are meeting in town. Can I go?"

Examining a dinner plate as she towel-dries it, Kate shakes her head. "It's vacation week. This is when we get to do family things."

"So we're actually going to do something today."

Kate first glances at her daughter, then places the plate onto the stack in the cupboard. "Yes. We're getting pizza this afternoon at Tutti's. Remember? Today is Max's choice."

"What time?"

"One."

"I'll be back before then. They're only going to walk around for an hour and a half."

"Who's taking them?"

"Tracy's mother. She's picking everyone up along the way."

Kate glances at the clock. It is ten fifteen. Though the idea of having only Max around during her appointments appeals to her, she cannot let Callie change plans—at least not easily.

"What time would she pick you up?"

"Ten thirty."

"Why so last-minute?"

"No one plans things, Mom. Not everyone is like you."

Kate again pauses to look at her daughter. Placing another hand-dried plate in the cupboard, she asks, "Could you be ready in time?"

Suddenly cooperative, Callie nods eagerly and answers, "Yes."

"Okay. But you have to be back before one. No texting me to ask if you can stay longer."

"I promise."

"Are you sure?"

"Yes! God!"

"All right; go get ready."

As Callie darts from the room, the landline rings. Kate picks up the kitchen extension and glances at the Caller ID. Answering, she says, "Hi, Dad."

"Sorry it took me this long to call," he says. "I had to run to the high school and take a look at the yearbooks."

"Why'd you have to do that?"

"I ran a background check on O'Neil's friend, and everything looks good except for his credit rating, which recently took a dive. Did O'Neil happen to say if it was just him looking for a place, or was it him and someone else?"

"I was under the impression it was just him. Why?"

"Ten years ago he married a woman named Helen Veitzer. I didn't find any record of divorce."

"Maybe they're separated. Anyway, it doesn't really matter, does it? If his credit is bad, I'm not going to rent to him."

"Normally, I would agree with that, but here's the thing: we know him."

"What do you mean?"

"That's why I went to take a look at the yearbooks."

"I'm not following."

"I knew I'd heard the name before, but I couldn't figure out where until I found out that he spent the last twelve years teaching at a prep school in New Hampshire—where he also coached wrestling."

"I'm still not—"

"Jack Guarnere was a freshman when you and Leif were seniors. He was on the wrestling team with Leif."

Burke pauses, and Kate gets the sense that he is waiting for her to make some kind of connection. Though it takes a moment, she suddenly understands.

It is a vague memory of an event that occurred so many years ago that it may as well have been from a previous life. She remembers being at the Burke home, where she was to meet Leif. The exact night she cannot recall, though it was likely in the week between Christmas and New Year's Day—a week of parties, several of which took place in the homes of friends whose parents were away. She can see Leif now in her mind's eye, walking in more than an hour late, his face bruised and bloodied. He'd gone to a package store in Norwalk where he'd successfully bought liquor several times before, intending to pick up some bottles of cheap vodka for that night's house party. He explained that three men in their twenties had cornered him in the far corner of the lot, where he had parked so that he would be out of sight of the main road. Leif was cocky then, all too willing to fight—*a wrestler's arrogance*, his father called it. So of course the confrontation escalated from insults to violence, and being outnumbered, Leif very quickly found himself in trouble.

Kate remembers exactly what Leif said next, and how he shook his head and almost laughed as he spoke.

And then this skinny kid comes out of nowhere and saves my butt.

"Jesus," Kate says into the phone. "That was him. That was Jack."

"Yes," Burke answers. "He actually didn't live in Westport. He lived in Norwalk. But his grandmother lived here, so they used her address so he could go to a better school."

Deep in thought, Kate nods, then says, "I remember Leif pointing him out to me at a match, and how neither of them made a big deal out of it. For the life of me, though, I can't remember what he looks like."

"I never told you this, but two of the three guys who attacked him that night were later convicted of beating a homeless man to death. They were pieces of shit. But that could have easily been Leif. I've always thought that. We could have lost him, then, if not for his teammate showing up."

Kate won't let herself imagine what her life would have been like had that been the case. It is simply too much to process at this moment. "I've noticed that you've been uncharacteristically quiet on the whole should-I-or-shouldn't-I-rent debate."

"You didn't need me to add my opinion. We both know all the pros and cons. I'd be more than happy to sleep on your couch every night, if that's what is needed to keep you and my grandchildren safe. Frankly, yeah, I would rather that than having some stranger on the property, all things considered. But this changes things, Kate. He isn't a stranger. And if he's in some kind of trouble, which I'm thinking he might be, then the least we can do is to help him out."

"What do you mean by 'trouble'?"

"If it is just him looking for a rental, then I'm guessing his marriage is either over or ending. That can certainly ruin someone financially. And for whatever reason, he gave up a job he held for twelve years. The fact that he held a job for that long is in itself a good reference, but to walk away from that—from what sounds to me like a pretty cushy setup—that tells me that his wanting to come back to the area is more than nostalgia. It sounds to me like he's someone looking to regroup."

Kate cocks her head slightly. O'Neil used the exact same word. She is considering whether or not to point that out when Burke speaks.

"Who among us hasn't been forced to do that at some point?"

Though her father-in-law cannot see her, Kate nods.

Leo Burke is a principled man—too principled, at times. Kate knows this better than anyone. And he believes in such things as loyalty and good character. But Kate suspects this isn't the only reason for his eagerness to help Jack Guarnere. Having someone around who once was connected to Leif would be for her father-in-law like having a little bit of his son back. Even if it were someone who hadn't saved Leif from harm, and possibly death—if it were, say, any one of Leif's former teammates or school friends—then Leo Burke would still be on board.

Sabrowsky, Callie and Max, and Kate—each one of them is a way of keeping Leo Burke's beloved only child alive.

Kate says, "Thanks for the information, Dad. I'll let you know how the meeting goes."

"If the rent you're asking is too high, find out how much he can pay, and I'll subsidize the rest."

"You don't have to do that. I'm not doing this for the money. If he seems like a good fit, I'll take whatever he can pay."

———

Rushing down the stairs, Callie calls, "My ride's here."

As her daughter hurries through the living room, Kate glances at her bedside clock. It is 10:50 a.m.

Half-dressed after her quick shower—and with a twelve-year-old boy in the house—Kate can't leave the room, so she calls back, "Just because they're late doesn't mean you can come home late. Understand?"

"Yes."

"Before one, no later."

"*Okay!*"

Kate listens as her daughter opens the front door and then carelessly lets it slam closed behind her after she has exited. Once Kate has finished dressing, she walks to the picture window at the other side of the house to watch as Callie hurries up the long driveway toward the waiting minivan at the top.

The vehicle belongs to Tracy Higgins's mother, Karen, and as Callie approaches it, the side door slides back, revealing a half dozen of Callie's school friends seated inside.

Kate waits until her daughter takes her seat and the minivan is driving off before she turns away. In her bathroom, she blow-dries her hair, though only partially, then brushes it out and grabs an elastic from the doorknob as she exits. Walking through her bedroom, she pulls her hair back into a ponytail, securing it with the elastic.

At the bottom of the stairs she calls up to Max. "I'm going to the cottage to meet with a plumber."

Through his closed bedroom door, Max replies, "Okay."

"I need you to take a shower and get dressed while I'm gone."

Max doesn't respond, prompting Kate to ask whether or not he heard her.

"Yeah, I did."

"I won't be long, but if you need anything, it's probably better if you text me."

Kate winces at how that statement sounded odder than she thought it would.

"Yeah, okay," Max says. His tone, however, is void of suspicion.

Kate's mud boots are by the back door. In the kitchen, she puts them on, then heads for the front door, where she catches herself glancing at her reflection in the mirror mounted on the wall below the ornamental and seldom-used coatrack.

She is wearing jeans and a zip-up, hooded sweatshirt with an old T-shirt beneath.

Unpolished, she thinks. *Maybe even a little run-down looking.* But that kind of thing hasn't mattered to her in a while. If it weren't for her job, for which she wore tailored blouses tucked neatly into dark slacks or the occasional skirt, Kate would dress every morning as if she were anticipating a day of hard chores ahead.

It is 10:55 a.m. when she reaches the cottage. Four minutes later, Tony arrives. Kate directs him to park on the street side of the cottage so his van can't be seen from the house.

As the locksmith works on the front door, Kate stands on the pathway and watches the street, waiting for her prospective tenant to arrive—a man she only vaguely recalls, and whose face, as much as she tries, she cannot visualize.

Minutes pass, but finally at 11:03 an early-model, four-door Jeep Wrangler appears on the road. Many vehicles passed while Kate waited, but most she recognized, and all maintained a steady speed. It isn't until the Jeep begins to slow to make the turn into the driveway that she allows herself to believe that her wait is over.

ELEVEN

A skinny freshman, Leif had called him, and so that is what Kate has to go on in terms of expectations. But the man who emerges from the Jeep isn't that at all, of course.

He is fit, probably 190 pounds, she guesses, and an inch shorter than she is, so five nine. Since he was a freshman when she was a senior, he must be thirty-four or thirty-five.

Seeing him now—seeing his face—does not awaken any long-forgotten memory of him. Had she passed him on the street, he would be no more than a stranger to her.

He meets Kate on the pathway and offers his hand. "I'm Jack," he says.

Kate shakes it. "I'm Kate."

He nods. "I know."

"You remember me?"

"Of course. I wrestled with Leif. You came to every match. I'm sorry, by the way. I only learned last night what happened to him. He was a big influence on me."

Kate thanks him, then gestures toward the cottage and says, "I don't mean to rush you, but I don't have a lot of time."

"No problem. Let's take a look."

At the door to the cottage, Kate introduces Jack to Tony, who assures her that he'll be done in a few minutes. Stepping inside, Kate leads Jack to the center of the open room.

"It's not much," she explains. "It was originally built in the fifties as an art studio for my grandmother. The bathroom and bedroom were added at some point in the sixties, I think."

Jack's eyes go to the row of narrow skylights running along the top of all four walls. Then he looks at the stacks of paintings leaning against one wall.

"We'll get those out of here," Kate says.

"You won't have to do that. I kind of like them."

"Really? I've never been much of a fan."

"I don't have a lot of stuff anyway. Taking them out might make the place feel empty." He looks again at the upper windows. "This reminds me of the dorms where I went to college."

"Where was that?"

"Goddard."

"Vermont."

"Yeah."

"Leo says you taught at a prep school in New Hampshire. You must have started right after graduation, then."

"I did."

"How'd you get certified so fast?"

"You don't need to be certified to teach at a private school. Of course, the downside of that is they pay you accordingly."

Kate nods. "Ah."

Jack crosses the room to the bedroom and looks inside. "So how much are you asking?"

"We usually get fifteen hundred a month, which is cheap for around here. But that includes utilities, and the place is, as you can see, pretty unpolished, so we think it's fair."

Nodding, Jack says, "Yeah, I can do fifteen."

"Okay. Cool. How long a term are you looking for?"

Jack moves to the bathroom door, making a quick scan of the small room. "Would three months be okay with you?"

"Sure."

"I can pay all of it up front."

"You wouldn't have to do that. Month by month is fine."

"I'd rather we handled it that way, if you don't mind. This way it's taken care of and off my mind."

Kate wonders if he is doing this in hopes that she won't bother checking his credit rating.

She is also wondering how someone who is supposedly struggling financially got his hands on that much cash.

She asks, "Do you have a job lined up?"

"Not yet."

"Are you hoping to find another prep-school gig?"

"If one fell into my lap like that one did, then maybe, yeah. But otherwise, no. To be honest, I wouldn't mind something that got me outside. I did some work for a contractor during the summers. Simple home construction, that kind of thing. I liked it. What do you do?"

"I teach high school, AP English mostly. What did you teach?"

"History, civics, philosophy, psychology, the whole kit and caboodle. But that's life, teaching at a prep school." Jack completes his self-tour. Facing Kate, he says, "I like the open layout and all the light."

"I should tell you that someone broke in here Sunday night."

"Thus the new lock," Jack says.

"Yes. The consensus is it was vandals."

Jack makes another quick scan of the main room. "I don't see any damage."

Kate decides that the knife in the bedroom wall is just too much to explain. "Would-be vandals," she says. She pauses, and then adds, "Teenagers."

"I don't see that being a problem," Jack says. "It looks like a sturdy-enough lock that's being installed. And I'll be here pretty much every night—and every day, for that matter, until I find work."

For Kate, only one question remains. "So, is it just you?" she says. "Not that it matters. I'd just like to know how many people will be coming and going. We like things quiet."

"Just me," Jack answers. "And I like quiet, too."

"When would you be looking to move in?"

"I need to make a quick run back up to New Hampshire for a four o'clock appointment. It shouldn't take more than an hour. If I'm on the road by five, I should be back here between nine and ten."

"Tonight?"

"Yeah. If that works for you, I mean."

Though Kate prefers not to make rush decisions—or snap judgments—she is more concerned with the well-being of the occupants of her home than she is with adhering to a lifelong habit.

She has, in fact, no interests other than that.

"That works for me," she says. "The only problem is, I won't have time to clean up the place."

"I don't think you have to bother with that."

"Are you sure?"

"Yeah."

"No one has been in here for two years. It's kinda dusty."

"I can take care of that myself."

Kate shrugs. "Okay. I guess the only thing left for me to say is welcome home."

Jack thanks her and removes a crumpled envelope from his front pocket. He opens it, and Kate sees that it contains a number of bills.

Jack pulls the entire stack out—it's all fifties—and counts out $4,500, then hands those bills to Kate for her to double-check. She notices that what he puts back into the envelope is, at the most, ten fifty-dollar bills.

Kate finishes counting. "All here." She folds the bills and stuffs them into the back pocket of her jeans.

"If something comes up and you can't make it back tonight, would you do me a favor and let me know?"

"Yeah, of course. Would it be okay if I texted you?"

"That'd be perfect."

Kate recites her number, and Jack enters it into his phone. When he is done keying it in, he says, "I'm sending you a text now so you have my number."

The instant he presses the "Send" key, Kate feels her cell phone buzz in her pocket.

The quickness of it startles her, and though she reacts with a minor flinch, she is able to conceal it from Jack.

TWELVE

Tony is finishing up as Jack and Kate exit the cottage. She follows Jack to the midpoint of the pathway, and then stops as he continues toward his Jeep. He is a few steps from his vehicle when she realizes that he'll need a copy of the new key.

"Oh, wait," she says.

Jack stops and faces Kate. She hurries back to the cottage. Tony has the pair of keys ready and hands them to her.

Jack returns to the pathway's midpoint. Joining him there, Kate hands him a key. "Almost forgot," she says.

He thanks her again, and then retraces his steps back to his vehicle. Climbing in behind the wheel, he says, "I'll be back soon."

Kate replies, "I'll be here."

The Jeep reverses up the driveway and pulls out onto Old Town Road. Kate waits till the vehicle is gone from her sight, then turns back toward the cottage. But she stops when something at the far end of the property catches her eye.

Seated on one of the swings, motionless, is Max. His feet are flat on the ground, his hands deep in his pockets. His eyes are locked on his mother.

Despite the distance between them, Kate can see that he appears concerned, as he often does.

After Kate pays Tony, she begins to walk down the driveway toward the backyard. Max has a clear line of sight of the locksmith's work van as it leaves.

Kate sits on the swing next to her son. She recognizes by his sullen demeanor that he is upset with her, so she decides to let him speak first. Even before the death of his father caused him to withdraw into himself, Max was an introvert who responded best when he was given space. This is among the many ways he is different from his sister, who, if given an inch, would happily take a mile.

Still looking down at his feet, Max finally asks, "Who was that?"

"A locksmith."

"I meant the other guy."

"Oh. His name is Jack. He's going to take the cottage for a few months." Kate pauses. "Your dad knew him. They were on the same team in high school."

"He wrestled with Dad?"

"Yeah. And he was the wrestling coach at the school where he used to teach. Maybe he'll show you some things; that way when you get to high school and join the team, you'll be ahead of everyone."

Though Kate was certain that this information would ease her son's mood to some degree—pursuing his father's sport is something Max has expressed an eagerness to do—it does not. His eyes remain fixed downward, and his worried scowl, if anything, has only deepened.

Another moment passes, and then he asks, "Is he a boyfriend or something?"

"No. Nothing like that. Is that why you're upset?"

Max shakes his head.

"Then what's going on? Why won't you look at me?"

Max lifts his head, but instead of turning to look at his mother, he stares straight ahead. "Why did you lie? Why did you tell me that you were meeting with a plumber?"

Kate nods and looks ahead as well. "Oh. Yeah. That. I thought it'd be best not to worry you."

"Worry me about what?"

"Someone broke into the cottage two nights ago. It was kids; I saw them running away. I talked it over with your grandfather, and we decided the reason why those kids did what they did is because the cottage has been empty for too long. Luckily, though, a friend of ours knew someone who was looking for a place. And since that person was someone we already knew, it seemed like the perfect solution."

"How long will he be staying?"

"Three months." Kate pauses. "You know that your grandfather and I wouldn't ever put you and your sister in danger. Is that why you're upset? I mean, besides the fact that I lied? Are you upset because you saw me with a stranger?"

After a moment, Max nods. It is obvious to Kate that he did so reluctantly.

She says, "I know Grandpa likes to say that you're the man of the house now, and that's true; you are. But I'm your mother, and it's my job to protect you, not the other way around. Okay?"

Max nods once more.

"And we have a lot of people on our side. Maria and Derek. Eddie. Not to mention every police officer in town. Nothing like what happened before will ever happen again. I promise you that. Yeah, I may lie now and then, but don't I always keep my promises?"

"You're sure it was just kids."

"Yes. Positive."

"Maybe it was the Dolans."

"Who are they?"

"Brian and his older brother, Greg. They live on Greens Farms Road. They're bullies."

"Do they bother you?"

Max shrugs. "They just say things sometimes."

"What do they say?"

"They ask me how my father's doing. Or if we played catch together the night before." Max pauses. "They say things about you, too."

"What things?"

"Just stupid things."

"Like what?"

Embarrassed, Max doesn't answer.

A sense of urgency overtakes Kate, causing her to press her son in a way she normally would not. "Max, honey," she says. "Please tell me what they say."

Though it clearly makes him uncomfortable to do so, Max answers. "They ask if you have a boyfriend yet. Sometimes they say things like, 'Sorry if your mom and I made too much noise last night.' That kind of stuff."

Closing her eyes briefly, Kate shakes her head in utter disbelief. She needs a moment to contain the quick rush of rage.

Once she is calm enough, she says, "You should have told me about this, Max."

"They're jerks, Mom. It doesn't matter."

"They're assholes," Kate says. "And it does matter."

Despite himself, Max smiles at his mother's use of a swear word. Her informality—her treating him, for a moment, like an adult—eases his tension.

"It doesn't bother me," he says. "Greg is a dropout, and Brian is failing everything, including gym."

As Kate continues to process her anger, she suddenly realizes that the reason Max got so upset was due to the optics of his mother with a strange man, and the potential for further cruelty that it might create.

She takes a breath, holds it, and then slowly lets it out. "You said their last name is Dolan."

Max nods. "But please don't say anything to Grandpa, okay? He'll want to do something about it, but he'll only make it worse."

"I won't say anything."

"Promise."

"I promise. But you need to promise not to keep things like that from me anymore. Okay?"

"Yeah, okay."

"And I need you to do one more thing for me," Kate says.

"What?"

"I need you to start thinking about what you're going to have on your pizza this afternoon."

"I already know."

"What?"

"The same thing I got last time. Pineapple and bacon."

Kate responds with an exaggerated groan of disgust, then says, "That's just gross, Max. How can you eat that?"

"It's delicious. You should try it."

"No way."

Kate watches her son for a moment. Then she rocks her swing to the left, lightly bumping into his.

"My God," she teases. "Who raised you?"

THIRTEEN

Dinner is a salad with grilled chicken—an effort by Kate to balance out the family's lunchtime calorie overload.

Leo Burke arrives at six, just as Kate and the twins are sitting down at the kitchen table. He makes small talk with his grandchildren as they eat—how their day was, what is planned for tomorrow, is there maybe a movie they want to see that they think he might enjoy as well.

It is clear to Kate that Max is uncomfortable with the questions—answering any one of them could result in him accidentally revealing the secret that he and his mother now share—so whenever possible she speaks for him. Max's natural reticence is well known, so Kate helping to carry his side of a conversation isn't unusual. Still, it isn't long before his grandfather realizes what is going on.

After dinner, Leo Burke remains in the kitchen with Kate on the pretense of helping her clean up. "What's the story with Max?" he says.

"He saw me with Jack at the cottage this morning. I think it caught him off guard to see his mother with a stranger. And it doesn't help that he caught me in a lie."

"What lie?"

"I told him I was meeting a plumber, like you told me to."

"Ah," Burke says.

"He just needs time to process it, Dad."

"Maybe I should talk to him."

"I took care of it," Kate says. She makes certain that her tone is assuring and cheerful. "He just needs time."

Burke considers that before nodding and moving on. "Are you sure you don't want me to stay until Jack gets here?"

"I'm sure. I asked him to text me if his timetable changed, but I haven't heard anything yet, and he should be on his way back by now. We'll be fine, Dad. I'll set the alarm. And Eddie's on duty tonight."

Burke studies his daughter-in-law. "You seem to be doing better than you were last night," he says finally.

Kate's promise to Max that she wouldn't tell his grandfather about the neighborhood boys prevents her from revealing the reason for her appearance of calm. The belief that the event was nothing more than simple mischief is what Kate has chosen to embrace. Still, she knows that her father-in-law is waiting for a satisfactory explanation for her shift in attitude.

She says first, "What other choice do I have, Dad?" Then she adds, "The more I think about it, though, the more I realize it probably was just kids acting stupidly."

Burke nods. "As much as I hate to admit that O'Neil was right about something, that's what I think, too."

Kate takes a breath, then lets it out. "It did freak me out, though."

"You had every reason to be concerned, Kate. Going through hell once is bad enough. Thinking a second tour might be ahead, that would trigger anyone."

"Thanks, Dad. For everything."

He offers his best smile. "Yeah, well, what other choice do I have, right?"

———

It is fully dark by seven.

Kate chooses to keep busy by tackling another project on her list—cleaning out and organizing the kitchen drawers. Despite the fact that her new tenant's ETA is still several hours away, she finds herself listening as she works for the sound of his Jeep. With the windows open to the mild April night, she can hear each car that passes on Old Town Road, none of which slows to make the turn into her driveway.

Still, each vehicle on her road catches and holds her attention, even if only for a few seconds.

By eight she has completed her task and moves on to another—cleaning the glass panels in the upper cupboard doors. Removing the stacks of plates, glasses, and cups so she can wipe down the shelves and change the paper, she will save for another day.

A half hour later she is done, and with the house suddenly chilly, she moves from window to window, closing and locking each one, which requires her to reset the alarm system.

By nine the twins are in their bedrooms upstairs with the doors closed. Since it is vacation week, Kate has allowed them to stay up with their devices for as long as they want, just as long as they remain in their rooms. Keeping them on their schedule as much as possible is crucial, not so much for Max as for Callie, who has a habit of viewing any deviation from their normal routine as a way of setting new and expanded boundaries.

It is nine thirty by the time Kate changes into her typical night-time wear—a pair of pajama bottoms, tank top, and oversize pullover sweater—and takes a seat on the living room couch with a glass of Malbec. Turning on the TV with the volume low—mainly to avoid having to sit in silence—she sips her wine and runs through her mind the projects she has accomplished so far.

Even as she relaxes physically at the end of a busy day, Kate prefers to remain active mentally. It is her way of refusing to acknowledge the absence that still lingers throughout her home—the absence of the man who'd been the one constant presence for so many years.

To allow that awareness at times such as these—the twins in their beds, the house finally still—is to risk experiencing the loss all over again.

Some aspect of that night, or the days that immediately followed, will overtake her thoughts, and from there it isn't long before she is mourning not only the man that was taken from her but also the life-long abilities that were lost.

Specifically, the ability to receive love and the capacity for courage.

Ten minutes pass before Kate's wineglass is empty. She is debating whether to get another when her cell phone buzzes. Looking at the display, she reads the text from Jack.

Stuck in traffic outside New London. Total standstill. Must be an accident.

Kate composes and sends a reply—Thanks for letting me know. Hope it clears soon.

She calculates that his having made it as far as New London means that he had departed soon after his appointment, which makes him a man who can hold to a schedule, not to mention keep a promise to act with courtesy, and she likes that.

More and more, she feels good about the setup that has been thrust upon her, even if it really isn't necessary any longer. Having another presence on the property—another being living his life—will be a welcome change from the routine she has allowed to settle around her.

She decides not to pour that second glass; she is tired enough to go to sleep, and there is no point in even risking a slight hangover in the morning. Moving through the house, she double-checks the doors and windows, all of which are, of course, locked. Back in the living room, she turns off the TV and picks up her empty glass from the coffee table, carrying the glass into the kitchen, where she rinses it out quickly before placing it in the dishwasher. Shutting off the lights and leaving the kitchen, Kate moves into the living room again and turns off the lamp by the couch, but instead of continuing on to her bedroom, she steps to the front picture window and pauses there to look out at the cottage.

Its windows are dark, and the front yard and driveway are empty. After a moment, she turns away and heads toward the bedroom, but just before reaching it, a light behind her comes on, casting her shadow onto the wall directly ahead.

The fact that the light is muted tells her that its source is outside, and that can only mean that the motion-activated floodlight at the front of the house has been tripped.

The instant she turns to face the light, something hard strikes the top-right corner of the picture window, sending a loud thump mixed with a sharp cracking sound echoing through the house. Startled, Kate brings both hands to her mouth to stifle her gasp, after which she, frozen, stares at a fissure in the thick glass running from the top of the pane down to the bottom.

At the center of the impact point is a jagged star pattern no bigger than a fist—the result of a projectile that had been thrown with force at the window where, seconds ago, she had been standing.

Kate remains motionless for a few seconds—far too long—as she waits for a second impact. None comes, and finally she makes herself move to the stairs and take a position on the second step so that she is both out of sight from anyone who may be looking in through the window and standing between her children and whatever danger might soon come.

Her cell phone is clutched tightly in her hand, and at first she is uncertain whom to call, but her head clears just enough for her to remember that Sabrowsky is on duty.

Frantically scrolling through her contact list, she finds his number and presses "Talk" with a trembling thumb.

Her legs are suddenly water, and she sinks down until she is seated on the third step. She listens for any indication that her children have been awakened as the line starts to ring.

Any hope of them having slept through it is dashed when Max's door opens and he appears at the top of the stairs.

The ringing in her ears stops. Kate has only enough time to raise her index finger to her lips, telling her son to be quiet, before Sabrowsky answers.

"Kate, everything okay?"

With Max listening, Kate says, "I think someone threw a rock or something at my front window."

"I'm on the way," Sabrowsky says.

Callie joins her brother at the top of the stairs, her eyes squinting and her mood more annoyed than frightened.

"What's going on?"

Sabrowsky is speaking, so Kate repeats the shushing gesture.

"Get the twins and get somewhere you feel safe," he says.

Kate stands and, with an urgent wave, beckons her children to come to her. Max moves immediately, but Callie hesitates, causing Kate to wave with even more urgency.

Allowing her children to pass, she ushers them into her bedroom, and once inside, she closes and locks the door.

"We're in my bedroom," she says.

"Okay, good. I'm three minutes away."

The idea of being all that stands between her children and some terrible harm for three minutes is something Kate does not care to think about, and yet it's all that is on her mind now.

Sabrowsky asks, "Kate, you okay? Did you hear me?"

"Yes. I'm okay. But please hurry."

"Everything's going to be okay, I promise. Just hang in there. Did you call Leo?"

"No. I figured you were closest."

"Do me a favor and hang up and call him right now, okay? He can stay on the line with you until I get there."

"Okay," Kate says.

She ends the call, navigates to her father-in-law's number, is about to press "Talk" with her thumb, but suddenly she hesitates. Her instinct is to keep this between her and Sabrowsky if she can—at least for now. To engage Leo Burke at this point would likely result in her having to tell him about the Dolan brothers, which she had promised her son she would not do.

She had said nothing about not telling Sabrowsky, however.

Everyone is silent as Kate stares at her phone, but after several seconds pass, Callie's impatience gets the better of her.

"What's going on?" she demands.

His eyes fixed on his mother, Max tells Callie to be quiet.

Kate realizes that he has intentionally maneuvered and is standing now between her and the door. Reaching out, she grabs him by the arm and quickly pulls him closer to her—and out of his protective position.

She now has a clear view of the door as she pockets her phone, which frees up her right hand. With it she grabs her daughter, pulling her close as well.

Kate estimates that thirty seconds have passed since she first alerted Sabrowsky, leaving about two and a half minutes before his arrival.

An unbearably long time, she thinks, to be helpless.

FOURTEEN

"Here's the culprit," Sabrowsky says.

In his right hand is a rock roughly the size of a softball.

Kate met him in the front yard after he texted the all-clear. He obviously knew that she wouldn't want to discuss this in front of the kids.

"I'm surprised it didn't go straight through the glass," he says. "My guess is it was thrown from a distance and lost its velocity."

"Whoever threw it was close enough to activate the motion light."

This piques Sabrowsky's interest. "Do you know how far out the trigger point is?"

"Seventy-five feet. That was the farthest range available when we bought it."

Sabrowsky scans the area between the house and the cottage, then looks back at Kate. "So somewhere between your two oaks and the cottage."

"Yes."

He scans the area once more, though Kate isn't certain what he is hoping to see.

She asks, "Have you ever heard of the Dolan brothers?"

Facing her again, Sabrowsky shakes his head. "No. Why?"

"Apparently, they've been bothering Max. Taunting him."

"Taunting him how?"

"They say shit about him not having a father." She pauses. "And about me."

"What is it they say about you?"

"You were a teenager once, Eddie. Use your imagination."

He nods. "Oh. Yeah, got it. When did he tell you this?"

"Today."

"Did you tell Leo?"

"No. Considering his mindset lately, I think we should keep that from him. But I planned on telling you the next time I saw you."

"I see," Sabrowsky says. "So, Leo's not on his way, I take it."

"He's not."

"Did Max give you a description of the Dolans?"

"All I know is one is in his grade and the other is older. Max says the older one dropped out, so he'd have to be at least sixteen."

"So, teenagers. Which is what you saw running from the cottage Sunday night."

"Exactly."

"Any idea where they live?"

"A few streets over, apparently."

Sabrowsky thinks about that for a moment, then nods and asks, "Is Max okay?"

"He says it doesn't bother him, but how could it not?"

"He is a brave one," Sabrowsky says. "All right; I've got a rough idea what to keep an eye out for now. I'll find out where they live and add their house to my patrol. And I'll run the yearbooks tomorrow and see what the older one looks like. Maybe there's a photo of the younger one in Max's class picture?"

"I'll look for it in the morning."

Sabrowsky pauses again. "I hate to say it, but it looks like maybe Chief O'Neil was right."

Kate smiles knowingly.

Sabrowsky asks, "What?"

"You sound like Leo."

Sabrowsky shrugs. "No surprise there, right?" He drops the rock. It hits the ground with a solid thud. Then he takes another look at the picture window and says, "I'll get what's left of my shift covered; that way I can park up on the street for the rest of the night."

"You don't have to do that, Eddie."

"It's not a problem."

"No, what I mean is I've rented the cottage to someone. He's moving in tonight."

Sabrowsky furrows his brows. "When did this happen?"

Kate can hear in his tone both curiosity and disappointment.

"This morning," she answers. "I know you said not to, but it kind of fell into my lap."

"Oh. I see."

Though it's obvious to Kate that her longtime friend is feeling slighted, she decides not to get into too much detail about how she found her tenant.

"He's actually someone we know," she says.

"Who?"

"He was on the wrestling team with you and Leif back in high school. He was a freshman. His name is Jack Guarnere." She pauses before adding, "He saved Leif from getting his ass kicked one night in Norwalk."

"Oh, yeah, I remember that."

"I had to be reminded of it. I couldn't even remember what he looked like."

"Who remembers freshmen," Sabrowsky jokes.

Kate recognizes that his statement is an attempt at hiding his true feelings.

"Like I said, Eddie, it kind of just fell into my lap."

"You said he's moving in tonight."

"Yes."

"When is he getting here?"

"He was supposed to be here by ten at the latest, but he texted me a little while ago to tell me that he's stuck in traffic near New London."

"Traffic on I-95, this time of night?"

"He thinks there's an accident up ahead."

Sabrowsky considers that for a moment, then nods and says, "I'll check on that."

"What do you mean?"

"I think we should be certain whether he's lying or not."

"Why would he lie about something like that?"

"Some men are liars, Katie. Here's a chance to find out if he's one of them before he moves in."

"Seriously, Eddie, you don't have to bother with that."

"It's what Leif would want me to do."

"I appreciate that, but I don't think it's necessary—"

"Please, Katie," Sabrowsky says. "People change. And doing one good thing a long time ago doesn't necessarily make someone a good person."

To keep the peace, Kate decides to back off. "Okay, Eddie."

"I'm going to take my dinner break now. New London is less than an hour away, so with any luck he'll clear traffic and be here before my hour is up. This way, in the meantime, we won't have to worry about another incident."

Kate decides it would be best not to fight that as well. "Okay," she says. "Thanks."

"Anything more to tell me?"

"Yeah. I was getting ready for bed and looked out the window for a moment, then turned and walked toward my bedroom. Maybe five seconds later the outside light came on, and a few seconds after that is when the rock hit."

"You think someone was watching you."

"I didn't see anyone."

"They could have been somewhere out of sight, beyond the seventy-five-foot line. Which could mean they staked your place out and knew how far to stay away to keep from tripping the light."

"Great," Kate says.

"Sorry. I'm just thinking out loud."

"No, it's fine. I shouldn't ask you to keep things from me, Eddie. I need to hear whatever it is you have to say, whether I'm going to like it or not."

"Then I guess there's no point in denying that, for whatever reason, someone is out to harass you. The good news is, so far the damage is restricted to the kind of things punk kids would do and not anything worse." He pauses. "Max must be upset about this, thinking that it's his fault. Do you want me to talk to him?"

"I will when I get him back to bed. But thanks, though."

"If he's got any of his grandfather in him, he might be thinking about taking matters into his own hands."

"No, I think he has more sense than that."

"Yeah, you're probably right," Sabrowsky says. He looks at the cracked picture window. "Are you going to have your neighbor replace this?"

"Yeah, I'll ask Derek tomorrow. If he can't do it, I'm sure he can recommend someone."

Sabrowsky nods approvingly. "We'll need to keep that from getting worse until it's replaced. Do you have any duct tape or marine tape?"

"I have duct tape inside. I'll get it for you."

"I'll need a stepladder or something."

"I'll get that, too."

———

Later, Kate is in bed but awake when she hears the sound of a car door closing.

Avoiding the picture window, she steps to the front door and peers through one of the narrow panes that frame it.

Parked on the side of the road is Sabrowsky's ten-year-old Ford F-150, and beside the cottage is Jack's four-door Wrangler.

As Jack emerges from his vehicle and steps around to the passenger-side rear door, he spots the pickup. Opening the door and leaning in, he removes a duffel bag, carrying it as he heads toward the cottage, his eye on the vehicle as he moves.

It's then that Sabrowsky steps out of his truck and, still in his uniform, approaches Jack, whose pace slows slightly.

The two men meet at the edge of the pathway and stand face-to-face. Jack's back is to Kate, but it is clear to her that Sabrowsky is doing most of the talking.

After a moment, the two men shake hands. Sabrowsky walks back up the driveway to his F-150 as Jack continues to the cottage, unlocks the door, and enters, switching on the lights.

Kate expects that the truck will drive off right away, but the vehicle remains. Lingering at the window, she watches until she realizes that Sabrowsky is talking on his cell phone.

Another moment passes before he lays his phone down, starts the engine, and finally drives off.

Looking back at the cottage, she catches a glimpse of Jack as he passes a window. A few seconds later he passes another.

Returning to bed, Kate lies still and listens to the silence, praying that it will not be broken, at least for a while.

Would that be too much to ask?

FIFTEEN

For three days—Wednesday, Thursday, and Friday—Kate barely sees any sign of Jack, but that's mostly because of the planned vacation-week day trips that she and the twins take.

Wednesday is one hour first thing at the aquarium in Norwalk, followed by a train ride into Manhattan, where they first walk from Grand Central down to Callie's favorite clothing store in the West Village, and from there up Eighth Avenue to an army-navy surplus store next to the Port Authority Terminal so Max can browse for the perfect backpack in which to carry his books to and from school. After he picks out and pays for a green canvas rucksack, the three take a walk through Times Square, stopping at various chain stores before picking a place at random for lunch.

Thursday is a long drive to Cornwall for lunch at the White Horse—Callie's choice—and then ice cream at Arethusa in Bantam, after which they take a walk through the nature center in Litchfield, as well as strolling around the historic town itself, checking out the small boutique shops and one of the last remaining independent bookstores.

Friday is an even longer car trip to Stockbridge, Massachusetts, to visit the Norman Rockwell Museum in the morning and then have lunch at Red Lion Inn—Kate's choice. She and Leif had spent their honeymoon there, as well as anniversaries until the kids came along.

It is also the place, Kate believes, where her children were conceived, in a small room furnished only with a canopy bed, bureau, and one easy chair. Kate remembers her and Leif being unable to keep their hands off each other that entire weekend, spending more time in bed—or in the easy chair or on the single windowsill or bent over the bureau—than out of it.

———

Evenings are when she catches glimpses of Jack, mainly as he cooks his dinner on a small hibachi grill that he sets up every night on the stone pathway. Sitting in the open doorway of the cottage, he divides his time between staring off reflectively and glancing down at his cell phone. Every few moments he stands to flip what looks to Kate to be a chicken breast, then sits back down until it is time to stand and flip the chicken yet again.

Kate does not know why he uses that grill as opposed to the kitchen stove, but her guess is that he prefers charcoal-cooked meat over panfried.

A minor detail, at best, but it tells her just a little more about the man living a few dozen steps from her and her children.

The only other time she sees Jack is when she glances out a window and he just happens to be passing one of his, which occurs only a handful of times each night. But the fact that the windows are lit and his Jeep is parked outside the cottage tells her—and anyone else—that *someone* is there, and she reminds herself over and over again that this is all that matters.

Never in all the years that she and Leif had rented the cottage did either of them interact in anything more than a passing way with their tenants. And it is her intention to maintain that tradition, if only because her life is complicated enough right now and there really isn't any room for even one more acquaintance.

This, too, she tells herself over and over again.

It is by the weekend—the last two days of vacation—that Kate finds herself looking out at the cottage less. Its occupant's routine has become, for now, predictable, and so she no longer needs to seek out, consciously or unconsciously, the comforting reminder of his presence.

Still, every time she returns to her property, Kate scans it for any indication of vandalism, doing so as subtly as possible, of course, for the sake of her children in the back seat.

She did it when she came home from their various day trips during the week, and she does it still every time she returns from errands over the weekend.

———

Vacation week is capped off with a Sunday-evening dinner at Maria's house—Kate and the twins, and Maria and Derek and their two children, all seated around the long, handcrafted dinner table like an extended family.

Afterward, the children head to the large screened-in porch at the other side of the house to prepare for a game of Pictionary as Kate and Maria begin to clean up—with Derek's usual minimal assistance.

He carries two plates from the dining room to the kitchen and places them side by side on the counter. Kate is also clearing the table, though she stacks the remaining plates together and collects the tableware, which she lays on the top plate before carrying the stack into the kitchen. Maria is already at the sink washing the pots and pans she had used to prepare the meal.

Kate sets the stack on the counter to Maria's left, then steps around to Maria's right and begins to remove the washed pots and pans from the dish drainer, towel-drying each one and setting them on the unlit burners of the large industrial oven to her right.

Her tone hushed for the sake of the children in the other room, Maria says, "I've been wanting to ask: Anything since the other night?"

Kate shakes her head. "No, nothing."

"It looks like your new guard dog is working," Derek jokes. He turns and leans against the counter, his arms folded across his chest.

Kate smiles out of politeness and says, "It seems so, yeah. Though I'd rather not think of him that way."

Maria glances over her shoulder at the still-cluttered table, then says to Derek, "Do you want to start collecting the glasses and putting them into the dishwasher?"

Derek looks at the table and sighs, then nods, but before he can take more than a few steps toward the table his cell phone chimes. Taking it from his pocket, he looks at the display and says, "Oh, I need to take this." Kate hears urgency in his voice. As he heads out of the room, Derek answers the phone. "Yeah, what's the word?" His voice trails off as he walks down the hallway to his office.

"That was well timed," Kate says.

Maria laughs. "Yeah, he usually finds some way of getting out of cleaning up. But we'll probably finish quicker without him, so that's fine with me."

She and Kate work in a comfortable silence for a moment, Maria washing and Kate drying. Then, her voice still hushed, Maria says, "So, you're doing okay, right?"

Kate smiles and nods. "I'm fine, yeah. Surprisingly."

"And how is Max doing?"

"I kept a close eye on him all week. He seems good."

"It's great that he opened up to you like that and told you about his bullies. That's progress."

"I hope so."

"And Callie?"

"You know her. If something doesn't directly affect her, she doesn't pay attention."

"It's the age," Maria says.

"Or she's too much like her aunt." Kate pauses. "I know that has a lot to do with why I'm so hard on her. We get in these battles over everything now. Big, small, it doesn't matter. She reacts in her way, and that makes me react in my way, and the war is on. And she's just so willful, you know? Of course, I'm no different, so in that way she's too much like *me*. Can't exactly have two A-types trying to run the show, right?"

Maria nods knowingly. "No, you can't."

Instead of placing the final pot into the dish drainer, she hands it directly to Kate. Then she takes a handful of the tableware off the top of the stacked plates and begins rinsing them under the faucet.

"Have you two talked recently?"

"You mean Rebecca and me."

"Yeah."

"She called last week, actually."

"Really? How'd that go?"

Kate shrugs. "She wanted to know if she could live in the cottage for the summer. I told her no."

Maria falls silent. After transferring the tableware into the dishwasher, she shifts to the task of rinsing off each plate one by one.

Kate puts away the last pot, then returns to the dining room table to collect the first handful of water glasses. A moment passes before she speaks. "I can't help it; I'm sorry," she says. "I just bristle at the idea of her being around."

"I didn't say a word."

Kate returns to the kitchen and places four glasses on the counter. "You were thinking it, though, right?"

"You shut her out pretty hard," Maria says. "After Leif's funeral."

"I didn't need her help. I had you."

"We're *like* family, Kate. I love you—you know that—but Rebecca *is* family. I mean, true, she's not exactly my favorite person, either, but it had to hurt her to be sent away like that. It was obvious that she wanted to stay. And she hasn't been back since, so what does that tell you? I mean, have you ever considered that she wanted to make amends back then? To be there for you."

Kate walks back into the dining room to retrieve the remaining three glasses. Being careful to keep her tone friendly, she says, "How about we talk about something else?"

"I'm just saying that if you see a chance to start over, you should take it. There was a time not too long ago when being around Derek made me bristle."

"Oh, I remember."

"We were on the fast-track to divorce, and that scared him straight. It scared me straight, too. We saw a chance to start over and took it. Every day I'm glad we did." She pauses. "Well, almost every day."

Kate laughs, then shrugs and says, "It's too late anyway. The cottage is rented."

"I guess that settles it, then," Maria says.

Neither speaks as Maria finishes loading the plates. Kate carries the remaining glasses into the kitchen and sets them on the counter. She takes a breath, and then turns to Maria.

"Go ahead," Kate says.

"'Go ahead' what?"

"Say what you want to say."

"You already know the story. My sister and I hated each other, and our last conversation before she died was pretty shitty. Like the song says, accidents will happen. What if something were to happen to Rebecca? I had just assumed Jen would always be around, and then suddenly she was gone. And again, like the song says, sometimes it's what we don't say that we're stuck having to live with."

"I appreciate what you're saying, Maria. But I have enough going on right now."

"All the more reason to have family around, don't you think? Especially when it's all the family you have left."

Kate pauses so that Maria knows that her advice is valued, and then says, "Everyone's waiting for us. We should finish up so we can get the game started."

She returns to the table and resumes clearing it. Maria is emptying the glasses into the sink.

"I've upset you," Maria says.

"No, not at all. You know my story, too. She can stay in the cottage in the off-season, that's the agreement. But that's as far into my life as she can go. She showed me who she was a long time ago. I haven't seen any reason to think she has changed."

"What if you missed your chance to see that? For that matter, would you even let yourself see it?"

Kate stops at the far end of the long table and looks at her friend. "What's going on, Maria?"

"What do you mean?"

"Something's up. There has to be a reason for you all of a sudden pushing Rebecca on me like this. What's going on?"

Maria waits until she has loaded the last glass into the dishwasher, then crosses the kitchen and enters the dining room. Standing at the other end of the table, she faces Kate.

"Derek doesn't want anyone to know," Maria says, "but his business is cash-strapped, so it looks like I might be going back to work soon. If I do, I won't be able to help you with Callie and Max like I do. I know you don't want a stranger watching them, for obvious reasons, and the last thing I'd want to do is leave you high and dry, so when you mentioned that Rebecca wanted to come back, I started to think that could be a solution to both our problems."

"What about your kids?"

"Derek will have to step up and get them to school and be here when they get home when he can." She pauses. "I guess I'm thinking that on the days that he can't, they could go to your place and Rebecca could watch all four of them. Obviously, I'd rather not spend money on a sitter or an after-school program if I don't have to. And since Rebecca doesn't work while she's here, well, like I said, it seemed like a very real solution."

Kate says, "If your situation is that bad, maybe I could help out. I've got Leif's life insurance money, and my tenant gave me almost five grand in cash that's just sitting in the house."

"I appreciate the offer, Kate, but I couldn't do that. And I've kept my nursing license up to date for this very reason. Derek's business has always been hit or miss."

"I should at least pay him for the hours it took to replace my picture window."

"He wouldn't accept."

"What if I insisted?"

Maria shakes her head. "No. He will always help you out like that, no matter how bad it gets for us."

"How soon would you be going back to work?"

"Unless that call just now was news about a big contract, I'd need to do it as soon as possible. I put out feelers last week."

"Jesus, Maria. I am so sorry."

"No, I'm sorry. I was being selfish. I've been stressing about this since he told me two weeks ago."

"You should have told me what was happening."

Maria shrugs. "I didn't want to bother you."

"Well, that's just stupid," Kate jokes. "We'll figure something out, I promise. You've done so much for me, and for so long, and half the time without me having to ask, so of course I'm going to be there for you. Maybe one of my students can help out after school, someone I trust."

"And asking Leo is a nonstarter."

"He'd be happy to help, of course, but it's a lot, as you know. I couldn't ask him to take that on until the end of the school year, especially if there'll be days when Alice and D. J. need to be watched, too.

I could ask him to do it temporarily, but you know me; I'm not a fan of temporary."

"Plus, he tends to take over, which drives you crazy."

Kate laughs. "Yeah, there's that, too."

"So Leo's out and a stranger is out. Who else is left?"

"To be honest, I'm not sure I wouldn't prefer a stranger over Rebecca."

Maria watches Kate for a moment, nodding thoughtfully. Finally, she says, "You tend to talk about Rebecca as if she has no redeeming qualities. But no one can be all bad. There has got to be something about her to admire. Are there really no fond memories of her, something you two shared before it all came apart?"

It takes Kate a moment to speak. When she does, her eyes are cast downward. "It's hard to remember."

"I'm your friend, Kate, so if I don't say this, who will? And I'm not pushing for a babysitter here. But is what she did so unforgivable? Is there even such a thing when it comes to family?"

Kate looks at Maria and responds in a flat voice, "Yes, there is."

Even Kate is shocked at how automatic—and coldly so—her answer sounded.

Maria waits a moment before replying. "Okay." Her tone is calm, and she musters a reassuring smile.

Kate recognizes this reaction is that of a professional health-care worker seeking to defuse a situation suddenly turned bad.

Maria had adopted the same demeanor as she struggled to save Leif's life, applying pressure to his gunshot wound in an effort to stem the rate at which he was losing blood.

"Listen, how about I finish cleaning up later and we just go and get the game started," Maria says. "Maybe even open a bottle of wine, try our best not to finish it."

"It's a school night," Kate says. "But what the hell, right?"

SIXTEEN

That night, with the twins in bed, Kate sits at the kitchen table and goes over tomorrow's lesson plans, after which she begins her usual nighttime routine—changing out of her clothes and into her sleepwear in the bedroom, then washing her face and brushing her teeth in the downstairs bathroom. The next ritual is to move through the house, examining every window latch, as well as the locks on both the front and back doors, and then pausing at the keypad in the kitchen to confirm that the alarm system is set.

Tonight she only briefly glances out the picture window at the cottage, and seeing that its windows are lit and Jack's Jeep is in its parking space, she heads for bed, switching off the lights as she goes.

The last light to turn off is her bedside lamp, which she does once she is under the blankets. Laying her head on the pillow, she settles in, hoping to doze off quickly.

As she often does while waiting for sleep, Kate runs through her mind tomorrow morning's activities—rising, getting her clothes picked out, starting breakfast, then waking the twins and showering as they eat, and after that drying her hair and getting dressed while at the same time making sure Callie and Max are keeping to the school-day morning schedule.

Out the door by 6:25 a.m., she will drop the twins off at Maria's, and then make the drive to Fairfield and be in her classroom by six forty-five.

The hectic start to a nonstop day.

This mental rehearsal is a comfort, generally, one that allows Kate's mind to wind down while at the same time keeping thoughts or memories—anything that she might dwell on—from emerging.

But tonight this process is an exercise in futility, since all Kate can do is replay what Maria said about Rebecca.

It had to hurt her to be sent away like that.

Kate can barely recall the actual conversation in question, or much of anything else from that time. It took place in Maria's kitchen—she knows that much—on a clear and already warm summer morning. Rebecca was leaning against the counter, sipping from her first cup of coffee, and Kate was seated at the kitchen table.

She'd had little to eat in days, was still vacillating, moment by moment, between states of numbed shock and overwhelming grief.

The more Kate tries to recall the conversation, the more details start to fill in.

Rebecca was dressed in white shorts and a dark tank top, her skin tanned and her sun-bleached blonde hair up in a loose bun.

Where her sister had flown in from Kate cannot recall. Nor can she recall where it was Maria had taken the children that morning so that Kate could talk to Rebecca alone.

What she can recall now, vividly, is the sense that her sister was little more than an intruder. In the way. Not needed, thanks to Maria's stepping up and taking charge.

Rebecca was also an imposition on the neighbor who had taken Kate and her children in, or so Kate believed. The cottage had been rented for the season to a New York City couple who used it only on the weekends, but the news of Kate's loss—and the unspeakable violence that had taken place on the property—kept them away. But despite the place being currently unoccupied, Kate felt that it would be inappropriate for Rebecca to stay there, at least until the money the renters paid upon signing the lease was returned to them.

Thinking back, Kate wonders if, in fact, there had been signs that Rebecca wanted to stay and help. She can only trust that Maria had seen what she claims to have seen.

A caring Rebecca. An empathic Rebecca. A Rebecca wanting to play a part.

But would Kate even know what that looked like? And would she have allowed herself to see it?

As Kate lies still, a few more scraps of that morning's conversation emerge.

I don't want to hold you up, Becca, she said.

She remembers putting it that way, as if it were her sister's well-being that concerned her. And she remembers repeating that same phrase a number of times, and Rebecca gently resisting the idea.

You're not holding me up, Katie.

It didn't take long, though, before Kate decided to simply come out and say what she really meant.

I don't really need you here. I have Maria. You should go.

Rebecca was packed, and the cab she had called parked in the driveway, by the time Maria returned with the children. Kate watched from a window as Rebecca said goodbye to Callie and Max—Callie in tears and Max unable to look his aunt in the eye.

Then Rebecca got into the waiting cab and was gone.

There were phone calls from Rebecca after that—on Callie and Max's birthday, Christmas morning, a day or two before the school year was to start so she could wish them good luck, other such occasions. Rebecca and Kate's interactions were strictly matter-of-fact. No tension or anger, just a mutual disinterest—acquaintances, not sisters, talking only as much as was required to maintain a degree of politeness.

Basic questions, brief or one-word answers, then quick goodbyes.

Rebecca had never stated outright to either the twins or Kate during any phone call that she wouldn't be using the cottage come autumn. She simply never showed up that following November, and the one after that.

It would be days into those months before Kate even realized that her sister had not arrived, and upon each realization she'd feel only relief, as if an inconvenient and dreaded chore had been struck from her list.

Kate tells herself that she had done what she needed to do that summer morning. There were just too many people in Maria's house—that was, for her, the only issue at hand.

Of course, she only need remind herself now of what Rebecca had done, the toll that the years of her stubborn defiance had taken on the couple who'd welcomed them into their home, sacrificing their golden years so that their orphaned grandchildren would have a good and stable life.

Even if sending Rebecca away had been an act motivated by hate, surely she deserved it, no?

Rebecca's actions had had a direct impact on the health of their once-formidable grandmother, leading to her rapid decline and death. The years of loneliness that their grandfather had endured following were not the end of life that he deserved.

Nor was it the proper reward for taking in their granddaughters.

How could Kate not hate—or at least want to—such wanton selfishness?

How could any hint of that in others—especially her own daughter—not cause her dismay?

Several more moments of sleeplessness pass before Kate recalls what else Maria said earlier.

You tend to talk about Rebecca as if she has no redeeming qualities.

Are there really no fond memories of her, something you two shared before it all came apart?

At this point Kate knows that her racing mind is unlikely to slow itself anytime soon, so she casts off the blankets and sits on the edge of the bed, her bare feet on the wood floor and her hands in her lap.

Of course, what has set her mind running is Maria's second question—or rather, the answer to it.

Kate can remember many cherished moments from the childhood that she and Rebecca had shared, memories from when they spent only their summers here, as well as after they had come to live year-round when Kate was seven and Rebecca eight.

Those were the years when they were inseparable, relying on each other for everything, confiding every thought and wish and fear.

It is an intimacy that Kate has never fully replicated, not even with Leif or her own children.

Those years of closeness—a means to their mutual survival—existed prior to the emergence of Rebecca's sexuality, which came on early and with a vengeance, igniting in her previously unknown needs, one of which was the need to push any and all boundaries, and at any and all costs.

This Rebecca was unrecognizable to Kate. And frightening, too. Even when her own maturation began, Kate did not experience that same compulsion for wildness. A year behind Rebecca in high school, she had observed her older sister's behavior and strove to be the opposite.

Of the two sisters, Rebecca was the promiscuous one, which caused Kate to be more conservative with boys. Rebecca was the unmotivated student, which made Kate want to excel. And Rebecca, of course, was the one to challenge authority, no matter how trivial, at every opportunity, leaving Kate to pursue the path of conformity.

The reckless Rebecca embarrassed and annoyed Kate, and had even caused Kate to feel a deep shame, one that offered her no other choice but to remain as unseen as possible.

It wasn't until Kate's senior year, when Rebecca was off for her first and only year of college, that Kate felt free of her older sister's shadow and allowed herself to show who and what she was.

These are the memories that Kate carries with her, and that serve to obscure the memories of better times, when each was the other's only constant in life.

But as surely as Leif is forever lost to Kate, so is Rebecca, no? Surely she is as dead and buried as Leif—buried beneath decades of selfishness and narcissism and a seething contempt for anything resembling normalcy.

And even if there is a chance that Rebecca has somehow changed, is finding that out worth the risk?

Could Kate even bring herself to give Rebecca that chance?

———

It is already past midnight when Kate steps into the bathroom, opens the medicine cabinet, and reaches for the bottle of melatonin on the top shelf.

There are for her side effects to this supplement that she finds unpleasant—vivid dreams that tend toward the bizarre, and a sluggishness that is worse than the kind of tiredness that comes with a lack of sleep.

But there are times when lying awake is worse than what might be dreamed or how she will feel the next day, and tonight is one of those times.

Kate downs two pills, and then returns to bed to wait for sleep.

It comes finally after she has taken several glances at the alarm clock, the last of which is at half past one.

SEVENTEEN

Kate hits the snooze button three times before finally getting out of bed.

As predicted, she is overcome by a melatonin-induced lethargy that slows both her thoughts and movements, but her routine is so set that she need only go through the motions at a slightly accelerated pace to make up for the half hour she lost to oversleep.

By the time she wakes the twins, she has had enough coffee to boost her pace even more, which enables her to get everyone out the door on schedule.

Callie takes the passenger-side back seat as Kate starts the engine, but Max is still outside the vehicle, lingering by the open driver's-side back door and looking toward the backyard.

"Get in," Kate says.

Max, though, doesn't respond.

Kate repeats herself, her tone more impatient sounding than she intended, and Callie, too, looks up from her cell phone and chimes in.

"Max, c'mon, let's go," she says.

Kate lowers her window and leans her head out, looking back at her son. "Max, honey, please, we need to go."

Max's attention is still directed toward the backyard, his brow deeply furrowed and his mouth set in a frown.

Kate asks, "What's wrong?"

"What happened to our swings?"

"What do you mean?"

Pointing toward the swing set, Max says, "Look."

To follow Max's line of sight, Kate has to lean her head out the window even farther. At first she doesn't know what it is she's supposed to be looking for, but then she sees what has her son so puzzled.

The seats of all four swings are missing, leaving the eight chains to dangle motionlessly from the upper bar.

Kate gets out from behind the wheel and stands beside Max. She, too, is perplexed, staring at the apparatus in disbelief. Then she quickly scans the backyard, though for what, exactly, she isn't sure—more signs that someone has trespassed, or maybe the four swing seats themselves, left scattered on the grass.

But to her eye everything else looks as it should, and, of course, the seats are nowhere to be seen.

Max asks, "Did someone take them?"

Kate says softly, "I don't know."

From inside the car, Callie says, "What's going on?"

"It's nothing," Kate answers. Then she puts her hands on Max's shoulders and guides him toward the back door. "Get in, okay?"

"Why would someone do that, Mom?"

"I don't know, Max."

Callie demands, "Do what?"

"Let's just go," Kate says.

She sits behind the wheel and looks at her children in the rearview mirror. Callie is turned around in her seat and looking through the back window. Max, however, is buckling his seat belt, his eyes unfocused and his expression blank.

"What the hell?" Callie says.

Kate ignores that and addresses Max. "It's okay," she says. "I'll call Eddie and tell him what's going on."

"He's going to talk to them, isn't he?"

"Maybe," Kate says. "I'll tell him not to if that's what you want."

Max shakes his head but says nothing.

"We need this to stop, Max."

"I know."

Callie faces forward. "Who is 'they'?"

"Nobody," Kate says.

Max lowers his head. Callie looks at him. Her tone softens. She asks, "What's-his-name?"

Max nods.

"You know about him?"

"Yeah. Brian Dolan. He's a jerk. Everybody hates him. I can get Jimmy Martz to beat him up."

"Who is Jimmy Martz?"

"This boy who likes me. He's huge. He'd do it if I asked him to."

"Okay, one problem at a time," Kate says. "First, you're not asking anyone to do anything, got it? Second, have you been texting with him?"

"Why?"

"Have you been texting with this boy?"

"A little."

"I need you to give me your phone, right now."

"Mom."

"Give me your phone, or I'm calling today and getting it shut off. That was the deal you agreed to when you got it."

Angry, Callie passes the phone to Kate.

"You don't use people who like you, Callie. Do you understand me?"

"Okay. When can I have my phone back?"

"I'll look at your text exchange at Maria's. Am I going to find something I don't like?"

"No."

"If that turns out to be the case, you can have it back then."

"God, you're such a psycho."

Kate ignores that and turns to Max. "Don't worry about this, okay? We'll get it figured out."

"It's my fault."

"No, it isn't."

Callie says to Max, "Tell me next time he bothers you. I'm not afraid of him. I'll get all up in his face."

Getting her daughter's attention, Kate briefly closes her eyes and shakes her head. Callie recognizes that as an indication that her comments aren't helpful.

"I don't want to talk about it," Max says. "Can we just go?"

Kate and Callie look at each other once more; then Kate says, "Yes, of course."

She faces forward, fastens her seat belt, and shifts into reverse. Executing a Y-turn so the vehicle is facing the road, she shifts into first, then eases down on the accelerator and proceeds slowly up the driveway.

Only when they have passed the cottage does Kate glance at the digital clock mounted in the dashboard.

Four minutes behind schedule, and she still needs to check through Callie's text messages.

Kate's carefully planned day is quickly spinning out of control.

———

In her classroom at seven—fifteen minutes later than usual—Kate calls Sabrowsky. Getting his voice mail, she leaves a message, informing him of the latest incident and asking if he'd call her back when he gets the chance to discuss what can be done.

Between third and fourth periods she checks her phone, finding a voice mail from him, which she listens to as her students file in and take their seats. The message offers no information, though Sabrowsky tells Kate to call him back as soon as she can.

It isn't until Kate takes her lunch after fifth period that she and Sabrowsky finally connect.

"I did a little digging around this morning and found out a few things," Sabrowsky says.

"What?"

"The Dolans went out of town the day after spring break started. That was a week ago last Saturday. The day before you saw two kids lingering around the cottage."

"So it wasn't them."

"I'm afraid not."

"How did you find out?"

"I went to their house and talked to their mother."

"You didn't mention Max, though, right?"

"I only told her that some boys fitting their description were seen trespassing during vacation."

"Could she be lying?"

"I confirmed it with a neighbor two houses down. He brought in the mail while they were gone."

"Where did they go? I mean, if they didn't go far away, the boys could have come back."

"They went to stay with the mother's sister in New Jersey. It's not likely that they drove back here just to stick a knife into your cottage wall or throw a rock at your picture window."

"What about the swings? When did they get back?"

"Yesterday around six. But if they weren't responsible for the other acts of vandalism, we have to assume they weren't the ones who fucked with your swings last night."

"So I saw two different teenagers."

"It happens all the time, Katie."

"What does?"

"A suspect can seem perfect for a crime, even well into an investigation, and then suddenly it turns out the real criminal is someone else entirely."

"Then who's doing this?"

"That's the question, isn't it? I went by just now and checked the swings. It looks like the links were cut with bolt cutters. If they were hacksawed, the cut marks would have been cleaner."

"Why is that important?"

"Your swing-set chains are heavy-duty, schoolyard-grade chains. Cutting through them with bolt cutters would require a degree of strength. I don't imagine someone Max's age would have that kind of strength, so that means an older teenager, possibly, or, more likely, an adult."

"I definitely saw teenagers, Eddie."

"I don't doubt you think that, but we can't ignore the fact that it was night and the cottage is over a hundred feet away. That's something else that happens all the time. People see something they don't understand and their mind is suddenly under pressure to create a story that makes the most sense to them. I mean, you said it yourself, Katie. You work with teenagers all day. You could have seen what's most familiar to you. And we all just assumed that the wave of vandalism you went through when Leif was still alive was the work of teenagers, too, so that story was already in your head."

"Great," Kate says. "I'm delusional."

"Not delusional. But the two trespassers you saw being teenagers, well, that's a lot less frightening than the alternative. I mean, the home invaders Leif confronted were adults. Grown men with criminal records. It's possible your brain would refuse to let you see anything that even came close to resembling that."

"Eddie, c'mon, you know me better than that."

The line is silent for a moment. Kate is about to ask if Sabrowsky is still there when he finally speaks.

"You experienced a major trauma, Katie. That changes a person. Trust me, I know. And two years is not a long time, as far as recovering from trauma goes. There's no shame in admitting that you're not one hundred percent. The shame, actually, would be to go on ignoring the signs."

"I'm not ignoring anything, Eddie."

"You jump at sounds, still, right? Any noise even remotely like a gunshot terrifies you. And you wake up in the middle of the night, thinking you've heard something, right? Something—someone—moving around. Because that's what you and Leif heard that night, and if you two hadn't already been alerted, he might not have gotten to the door as quickly as he did, and those three assholes might have made it inside and gotten the jump on him. And God knows what would have happened then—"

Kate snaps, "Okay, Eddie, you've made your point. I got it."

Another moment of silence, and then Sabrowsky speaks, his voice heavy with concern. "And there's that, too. That sudden rage. I've known you pretty much my whole life, and I've never once seen you out of control."

It takes a moment for Kate to calm herself enough to respond. "Sorry," she says. "So what do we do? About the vandalism, I mean."

"All I can do is make the same suggestions as last time. Security cameras, better outdoor lighting, maybe a guard dog."

"Max is allergic."

"It can be an outside dog."

"I don't want that."

"Then cameras," Sabrowsky says. "And upgraded lights."

"You're telling me to basically turn my yard into a border crossing. Checkpoint Charlie, or whatever."

"It'll be a little more subtle than that. But yeah, I think that's where we are. Obviously, having someone in the cottage didn't keep whoever this is away. It just sent them to another part of the property."

"Can you recommend someone to install all that?"

"I'll do it myself on my day off. That way we know it's done right."

"I want to pay you for your time."

Sabrowsky dismisses the offer. "Please, Katie."

"I insist."

"No. Anyway, I should have pushed you to do this a long time ago."

"What are we looking at cost-wise?"

"For a state-of-the-art system, maybe two grand. I'll have to order the equipment."

"Okay, do that," Kate says. "If you swing by tonight, I can give you a check."

"We'll deal with that when I have the gear. Maybe I can get everything for less than two."

"Money's not a problem; you know that."

"I know that's the reason why you're in the situation you're in."

"What do you mean?"

"What I said the other day. Your home is mortgage-free, and you have a rental property that, when you rent it out, probably covers your property taxes. Who'd walk away from that, right?"

"You think I should have moved." Kate pauses. "Afterward."

"Living there, where it happened, that can't be doing you any good. And you could have gotten a million five for the property, easy."

"And if a developer got his hands on it, the house would be torn down and two McMansions would go up. I promised my grandfather I wouldn't ever sell for that very reason."

"But you couldn't have imagined then that something like this would happen."

"It's my home, Eddie. And it's Max and Callie's home. I don't want to move them around. I know what that's like."

"It can't be easy for them, either. To be there still."

Kate cuts him off abruptly. "Listen, Eddie, I need to get going."

"I'm sorry, Katie. I shouldn't have said that. I just care about you, that's all. All of you."

"I know."

"I'll order the gear. It'll take a few days. Will you be okay in the meantime?"

"Yeah."

"Have you told Leo about any of this?"

"Not the recent stuff, no. But I will."

"Tell you what, I'll fill him in on what's been happening, if that's easier. He needs to know. And maybe I can stop him from overreacting."

"That's probably a good idea."

"This is an all-hands-on-deck situation, Katie. I mean, it's obvious that someone is fucking with you, and it's starting to look to me like it's not teenagers after all. If you have been targeted by someone, we need to find out who and why. Your father-in-law can be a pain in the ass, yes, but I think that's what you need right now. Someone who can make this his number one priority. And who won't have a problem getting in Chief O'Neil's face, if that's what it takes."

Kate closes her eyes. The last thing she wants is exactly, according to Sabrowsky, what she needs—her father-in-law's involvement, as well as the full force of the Westport PD, not to mention transforming her property into some kind of secure compound, complete with a CCTV system and floodlights.

The very loss of privacy she has sought to avoid.

Sabrowsky asks, "You still there, Katie?"

"Yeah. Sorry. I was just processing everything."

"We'll get through this, I promise. You've got a lot of people on your side; remember that."

Kate feels the need to offer him some kind of reward, so she says, "What would we do without you, Eddie?"

The words are just a little automatic sounding to her, but that is the best she can give right now.

There is no indication in Sabrowsky's response, though, to indicate that her statement came across as anything other than sincere.

"It's the least I can do," he says.

"I'll talk to you later."

"Hang in there."

Kate ends the call and places her phone down on the desk. It is eleven forty-five, so there are fewer than three hours until her last class is over.

Sitting alone in the silent classroom, she is suddenly aware of tightness at the back of her skull—the unmistakable precursor to a migraine. Eating something would help keep it at bay—going too long between meals can be a trigger—but her appetite is gone.

And anyway, this oncoming storm has nothing to do with low blood sugar.

By the time Kate's classroom is once again filling up with students, the right side of her head is pulsating, and the light from the April noontime sun beyond the windows is a harsh, white glare that stings her eyes.

Midway through that class she is overcome by a nausea that extends from the depths of her gut up through her esophagus and into her throat.

Kate is just moments from it now—moments from the kind of violent migraine that has the potential to stop her dead in her tracks.

But somehow she lingers on the edge of it, pushing through as she keeps an eye on the time and telling herself that all she needs to do is hang on until the end of final period.

After that last bell of the day has rung, Kate abandons her habit of remaining behind for two hours to grade tests and papers and prepare for the next day.

It takes all she has to make it to her Subaru in the teachers' lot, and once behind the wheel she sits perfectly still with her eyes closed for fifteen minutes before she is well enough to drive home.

On the way she nearly veers into oncoming traffic twice, and she closes her eyes at every red light, only opening them when the driver of the vehicle directly behind her honks the horn.

Turning in to her driveway, she anticipates making her bedroom as dark as she can, and then lying down until five o'clock, which is when she typically picks up Callie and Max at Maria's.

If she is lucky, she can continue to hold off the worst, maybe even begin to reverse the near-crippling effects that have laid siege upon her.

Facedown on her bed, her head beneath a pillow and a wet hand towel on the back of her neck, Kate keeps as still as she can, taking long, slow breaths in, and then letting them out.

With each cycle of inhalation and exhalation completed, she imagines herself sinking deeper and deeper into the soft bed.

EIGHTEEN

Kate hears a car door close.

The bedroom is as dark as she could get it—blinds closed, curtain drawn, door shut, making a kind of soft twilight gloom in which to hide herself.

But opening her eyes to even this limited light sends a wave of pain from the right half of her head to the left.

Rolling onto her side and then sitting up just sends the same pain sloshing back to the right side.

Squinting, Kate stands and moves around the bed to her back window, shielding her eyes with one hand while parting two slats of the blinds with the index finger and thumb of the other hand. To the far right of the window is the end of the driveway, and she sees Leo Burke's Ford Explorer parked beside her Subaru.

In the bathroom Kate splashes cold water onto her face, and then quickly dries off with the towel, hoping to make herself as fresh looking as possible. Glancing in the mirror, however, she sees exactly the opposite, but the only thing she can do about that is practice for a few seconds the easy and contented smile that she can switch on and off like a light.

Kate exits the bathroom, surprised that her father-in-law hasn't knocked on the back door yet. Walking through the kitchen, she unlocks and opens the door, but no one is there. She pushes the screen back and leans out, looking down the stairs—again, no sign of the man.

Crossing through the living room, she unlocks and opens the front door, and then she sees him, walking up the driveway toward the cottage.

Reaching it, Leo Burke knocks on the front door, and then takes a few steps back. A moment later Jack, dressed in jeans and a hooded sweatshirt but barefoot, opens the door and steps out onto the pathway. Leo Burke extends his hand and Jack takes it.

Leo Burke does most of the talking. At one point he gestures toward the backyard, and Jack looks in that direction briefly. Kate wonders when in this conversation her father-in-law will bring up Leif. But the fact that the man doesn't once smile gives her the impression that he hasn't yet mentioned the son whose memory he is desperate to keep alive in any and every way possible.

Finally, though, Kate decides that she doesn't need to observe these two any longer and closes the door.

In the kitchen she fills the teakettle and sets it on the burner. Searching through the dozen boxes of tea kept in an upper cupboard, she finally locates the half-filled box of organic golden green tea.

She places a tea bag into a mug and then waits with her eyes closed for the water to boil.

The kettle is roiling when Kate finally hears her father-in-law's trademark authoritative knock on the front door.

Once a cop, always a cop, she thinks.

———

Standing in the backyard with her mug of hot tea in her hand, Kate watches as Leo Burke examines one of the cut chains.

"Cutting through these would have taken time," he says. "Even for a strong man. So he wasn't in and out of here in a minute. More like five, maybe even ten." He looks at Kate. "And you didn't hear anything last night?"

"Nothing."

"Do you think you would have?"

"A deer walking through the yard usually wakes me up, so yeah."

"Did you go out at all yesterday?"

"We had dinner at Maria's."

"It could have happened then, and you didn't see it when you got home."

"I didn't see it at all, actually. Max did."

Leo Burke takes a step back and looks at all eight hanging chains. "It's such an oddly specific thing to do. If no one was home when they came, they could have broken windows or something like that, but instead they go through the trouble of cutting off all four seats and taking off with them. Ruling out for now that this is something a kid could, in fact, do, what we're left with is the possibility that someone wants us to think that this is kids fucking around. They went for the swings because that's something kids might do to other kids. Breaking into the cottage and leaving that knife stuck in the wall, yeah, that's something kids might do. Throwing a rock at your picture window, yeah, kids do that shit all the time. But this, this looks to me like someone is starting to bend over backward to make us think that all we're looking at here is bullies being bullies. Which makes me think there's another explanation that we can't ignore: someone is trying to get to you and has decided for some reason that the best way to do that is to target your kids."

Leo Burke's habit of speaking bluntly is something Kate has long since become accustomed to, and yet this statement still manages to catch her off guard.

"Jesus, Dad," she says.

Leo Burke faces her again. "You should have told me about what happened the other night, Kate. And you should have called me right away about this."

"I didn't want to upset Max any more than he already was."

"Why would telling me about these incidents upset him?"

Kate chooses to be just as blunt as her father-in-law. "If I'd told you what was going on, you would have confronted the Dolan family. Max said he didn't want that. After he confided in me, he made me promise not to tell you or anyone. I wasn't about to betray that trust."

Kate could say more—that she didn't want to bother him and she wanted to handle this problem herself—but she decides to stop there.

Leo Burke appears to be considering what she said about his grandson's desire. The man's reaction strikes Kate as an uncharacteristic moment of self-reflection.

But that moment doesn't last, and Leo Burke says, "It's my job to protect my family."

"Mine, too," Kate replies.

"But if I had gone to talk to the mother, we would have known sooner that they were out of town and something else was going on here. That's all I'm saying."

Kate nods, though like her father-in-law, she offers no apology. "I understand that."

Burke studies her for a moment, and then asks, "Is there anything else I don't know about?"

"No, Dad. You're up to date now."

He nods. "Good. I went ahead and spoke with Chief O'Neil this afternoon. He's posting a patrol car on your road every night until Sabrowsky and I can get the cameras and new lights set up."

Kate realizes that she should have anticipated these actions—that her father-in-law would have immediately contacted his successor, but also that he would be quick to assign himself a role in the installation of the security system.

And though she feels the urge to resist his controlling nature, as a matter of principle more than anything, she opts to ignore that habitual response.

Just as she, earlier, let go of her previous objections to having her every move outside her home recorded, she decides not to resist any part of this plan.

This is an all-hands-on-deck situation, Sabrowsky had said.

"Thanks for doing that, Dad."

"It was that or the three of you sleeping at my house for the next few nights, which a part of me still thinks we should do."

"A police car up on the street is enough. And anyway, I think leaving our home like that would scare the kids even more than they are now. Plus, we rented the cottage so it wouldn't be empty, so why would we want the house to sit vacant?"

"That was before. It's obvious to me that what we're looking at now is some kind of campaign of terrorism being waged against you. That changes things."

"Not for me," Kate says. "I'll turn my property into whatever I have to in order to keep us safe, but I'm not leaving, not even for a few nights. I can't. And it has nothing to do with my grandfather's wishes. Leif was killed trying to protect our home. How could I just abandon it? I would think that's something you'd understand, Dad. I think in that regard you and I are alike."

Leo Burke nods, then smiles and says, "Unfortunately for you, Kate, we're probably a lot more alike than you think."

Kate smiles in return—as genuinely as she can. "What a terrible thing to say," she jokes.

"Listen, I want you to do me a favor."

"What?"

"Reconsider your decision regarding Leif's personal sidearm. I can return it to you; legally it belongs to you, so you keeping it in the house won't be a problem. I could take you to my range this weekend and go over everything with you again."

"I don't want it, Dad."

"If you're worried about safety, I have a lockbox I can give you that requires a three-digit code to unlock. You and I will be the only ones who know it."

"It's not that."

"Then what is it?"

"It would be pointless for me to have a gun."

"Why?"

"Because I don't think I could pull the trigger."

Leo Burke pauses. "Because of the noise."

Kate nods.

Leo Burke takes a breath, lets it out. "Look, Kate, I understand your concern, but when push comes to shove, you'll do whatever it takes to save your family. I know you would."

Kate glances at her father-in-law's SUV. After a moment, she says, "I'm assuming you brought it with you."

"I did."

It takes a moment, but she shakes her head. "I appreciate you doing that, Dad, but no."

"I think that's a mistake, Kate."

"Maybe."

"At least think about it."

Kate nods. "If I change my mind, I know where to find you." She faces the cottage. "I saw you talking to my tenant before."

"I wanted to meet him face-to-face."

"You asked him if he saw anything."

"Yes."

"Did he?"

"No. But he said he'll keep an eye out from now on."

Kate watches the cottage for a moment more. "I didn't tell him before he moved in exactly what was going on. I probably should have."

"He didn't seem to me to be upset."

Kate shrugs and says, "Still, I kept the whole truth from him. I didn't realize it at the time, but I guess I kind of used him."

"You wanted to protect your family, Kate. And anyway, what does it matter if you did use him? It's not like he didn't get anything out of the deal."

Kate ignores the question and turns back to face her father-in-law. "It'll be a while until dinner, but you're welcome to come back."

"Another night."

"You're sure."

"Honestly, Kate, you don't look like you're in the mood for company tonight."

"I'm just fighting a migraine, that's all."

"That's why you're home so early."

Kate nods. "It's starting to ease up a little, though."

Leo Burke glances down at the mug in Kate's hand. "Drink your tea; it should help."

"I will, Dad. Thanks."

"You and I will need to have a talk at some point. Not now, of course. But what's happening is happening for one reason: someone wants you scared. I'm going to need a list of anyone who might think that you've wronged them—a friend, former student, current or former colleague, maybe someone you dated in the past two years."

"There's been no one since Leif, Dad. You know that."

"Still, a list would be helpful."

"It's difficult to imagine anyone hating me enough to go to these lengths. And anyway, I tend to go out of my way not to wrong anyone."

"We all make enemies, whether we know it or not. You should focus on males first. At the risk of sounding sexist, I can't imagine a woman being strong enough to cut through chains. I suppose a female could recruit a male to help her, or this could be a couple, but for now let's start simple and just keep it to men."

"Okay," Kate says.

"I doubt it would be something minor, like a fellow teacher asking you out and you saying no, that kind of thing. I don't think you need to drive yourself crazy or start getting paranoid about every interaction with a man. But like I said, we can deal with this another time."

"Okay," Kate says again. "I really should get back inside and lie down now."

"Yes, of course. If you need any help with Callie and Max later, just give me a call. I can take them out to eat, and we can bring you back something; that way you won't have to cook."

Kate glances once more at the cottage. "Actually, Dad, could you do that?"

"No problem, Kate. Anywhere in particular?"

"Wherever you guys want. Pizza, fast food, whatever."

"I'll pick them up from Maria's at five and have them back here by seven. Would that work?"

"Yeah, that'd be great. Thanks."

"I'll see you around seven, then. In the meantime, get some rest."

"I will, Dad."

———

Once Leo Burke's Ford Explorer has made the turn from the end of her driveway onto Old Town Road, Kate returns inside.

Standing in the kitchen, she downs the tea in one long sip, and then places the mug into the sink. Back in her darkened bedroom, she chooses a pair of jeans, T-shirt, and cardigan, laying them out at the foot of her bed. Each movement she makes sends waves of pain through her head—bigger waves for bigger movements, smaller ones for smaller gestures. But even the lesser pain is enough to cause her to wince.

After undressing, she takes a shower, more to feel the hard spray from the showerhead on the back of her head and neck than to get clean. She stays under the hot stream for twenty minutes, only ending it when she has drained the water heater.

The hair dryer would be too loud, so once she has dressed, Kate towel-dries her hair before combing it straight. Though the shower helped some of the tension—the muscles at the back of her skull and neck, once as hard as concrete, have softened slightly—Kate knows that she dare not apply any makeup to her still-aching eyes.

And anyway, her reason for taking this chance now to visit the cottage isn't one that requires her to appear attractive.

It is not yet five o'clock when Kate is ready, so she stands at the living room window and waits for her father-in-law to arrive at Maria's house, which he does, of course, right on time. Five minutes later, his SUV drives off with the twins inside.

Leaving the house, Kate walks toward the cottage, and though she is taking the same route she'd taken the night that she rushed to her fallen husband's side, she doesn't this time dwell on that memory.

NINETEEN

Jack is placing the hibachi grill on the stone pathway several feet from the cottage as Kate approaches. Yet unaware of her, he returns inside, but by the time he exits again, a lighter in hand, Kate has closed much of the distance and is just a few yards away. Spotting her, he pauses to show his surprise, and then smiles as he continues toward the grill.

Kate reaches the other end of the pathway and, respectful that the cottage is Jack's domain, stops.

He faces her and says, "I hope it's okay that I've been grilling out here. I probably should have asked back when we first spoke."

"It's not a problem," Kate says. "I've been meaning to ask you if something's wrong with the stove."

Jack crouches down and ignites the lighter, placing its tip inside the small pile of fresh charcoals. "The stove works fine. This is just a habit I got into at college. We had a shitty food plan, so a lot of us started to grill our own food outside our dorms."

"I'd think Vermont winters would get too cold for that," Kate says.

"Oh, they did. Snowstorms weren't really a problem. We'd just bundle up and huddle around for warmth. Blizzards or freezing rain were pretty much all that stopped us."

Kate can see that the body of the hibachi is heavily rusted. "Is that the same grill you used back then?"

"Yep, it is."

"You've hung on to it all these years."

Jack shrugs, looks at Kate, and smiles. "It still works. And it reminds me of simpler times, I guess. Before life became too . . . adult."

Her tone sardonic, Kate says, "Yeah, adult life sucks sometimes, doesn't it?"

The charcoals lit, Jack stands. "I'm going to cook a chicken breast. I can throw one on for you, if you'd like."

"No, but thanks."

Jack looks at Kate for a moment. It's as if he is studying or even assessing her.

"I'll be honest," he says finally. "You look like you could use something to eat. Is anything wrong?"

"Tough day is all."

"You're sure that's all?"

"Do I look that bad?"

"The sun's behind you, but you're squinting like it's bothering you. Plus, your eyes are glassy and your face is pale."

"Bad headache."

Jack nods. "Ah. I know them well." He looks at her for another moment. "C'mon, let me make you something."

"No, really, it's okay."

"I think I just saw your father-in-law load your kids into his SUV a few minutes ago, so you're obviously free—unless you have other plans for dinner."

"No other plans," Kate says. "So you saw that."

"Not a hell of a lot else for me to do these days. I heard the car doors close next door and went to take a look. Anyway, I've got some power greens for a salad. And beer, if you don't mind dark. Plus, my guess is you walked over here to tell me something, so why don't you tell me while we eat?"

Kate is too spent to resist. Though she already knows the time, she glances at her watch. "Yeah, okay," she says. "I'll stay for a little while."

"Good. Why don't you go inside and sit down. It'll take me five minutes, tops, to get everything ready."

———

Kate sits at the head of the table positioned along the left-hand wall as Jack finishes preparing dinner.

He exits and reenters the cottage several times, and though he is outside the majority of the time, tending to the grill, when he is in the kitchen, he works busily and doesn't address his guest.

These few moments of solitude allow Kate to look around and recall being here with her sister. Looking at the couch, she sees herself and Rebecca seated there, two young children quietly reading. Then Kate looks down at the other end of the long table and remembers Rebecca there, drawing with a pencil in a sketchbook she had gotten one Christmas.

Kate relives briefly a number of other occasions—the two of them seeking solace here after their parents' death in a car accident, Rebecca teaching Kate to dance, the two of them practicing cartwheels, Rebecca tending to Kate's skinned knee after she fell in the driveway while running from a neighborhood boy who played just a bit too roughly.

Each remembrance is before everything changed—before Rebecca became Rebecca, the wild and troubled one, and Kate became Kate, the judgmental and fearful one.

Next to the table is one of the many stacks of Rebecca's paintings, and with Jack outside, Kate looks at the first painting, then tilts it forward and looks at the next, and on and on until she has perused all eight canvases.

Each painting is signed and dated by the artist, indicating that this batch is from ten years ago. All are self-portraits, one of which is a nude, and every one of them is to some degree unflattering, and jarringly so. Rebecca's face is stretched and distorted, her expression uneasy or mournful or angry.

The nude is perhaps the least kind of them all, showing full but uneven breasts and a slightly sunken sternum and expanded rib cage. Rebecca's body is distorted as well, taller and thinner than it is in reality, but in a way that gives her a frail, almost elderly appearance.

Coming from a family of art lovers, Kate is accustomed to nudity in artworks, but this specific portrait of her sister is difficult to look at because of the brutal way in which Rebecca chose to present herself.

Kate can't help but recall the reflection that she saw in her bathroom mirror earlier today—a woman pained by her own mind.

She also remembers the years she spent comparing her body and face with her better endowed and more beautiful older sister's, and the terrible envy that comparison wrought.

Rebecca was the beautiful sister, the blonde who tanned easily, unlike Kate, the plain and brown-haired sister who, as their grandfather would say, could freckle on a cloudy day.

Did Rebecca, at least for a period of time ten years ago, look at herself and not see what others saw? Could she have been blind—maybe was always that way or grew to be that way—to what Kate saw and compared herself negatively with?

Kate lays the stack back against the wall as Jack carries two plates to the table, placing one in front of his guest and the other in his intended seat just around the corner from her.

She looks down at her plate, on one half of which is a chicken breast, golden with perfectly lined grill marks. The other half is taken up by a salad of spinach and kale with cherub tomatoes and shredded carrots.

"Looks good," Kate says.

"Let's hope it tastes good."

As Jack hurries back into the kitchen area, Kate cuts off a piece of the chicken. She tries it, and to her surprise it is both tender and juicy. Chewing, she says to Jack, "Wow."

He is taking out of the refrigerator a bottle of Newman's Own balsamic dressing. "Oh, good. Honestly, I got lucky. Usually I'm not paying attention and cook it for too long."

Before Jack closes the door, Kate notes that the refrigerator is practically empty—two bottles of Guinness, a bread bag containing what can only be the last few remaining slices, and various condiments are all she sees.

Kate swallows, then takes a sip from her glass of water. Jack returns to the table and takes his seat.

"Thanks for this," she says.

"Didn't want you falling over on the walkway."

Kate smiles. "Yeah, that wouldn't have been good."

Jack begins eating. "Yeah, the chicken's not bad," he says.

"Told you." Kate pauses. "So you're right, I did come over to talk to you. Obviously my father-in-law told you about what's going on. The vandalism, the knife in the bedroom wall here. I just wanted to say that I'm sorry for not telling you the extent of what was really going on when you came to look at the place. Not to make excuses, but we were thinking that if someone was living here, then it would put an end to the whole thing, which unfortunately it clearly hasn't."

"A kitchen knife in the wall is a little freaky, yeah, but Chief O'Neil had already told me all about it."

"He did?"

"Yeah."

"You must have thought it was pretty shitty of me not to at least mention it."

"Not at all."

"Still, it wasn't . . ." Kate searches for the end to that sentence, finally finding after a few seconds what she means to say. "That's not like me, at all. I just wanted you to know that."

"I appreciate that," Jack says. "So your father-in-law mentioned that you've been through this kind of thing before. Back when Leif was . . ."

Now it's Jack who is seeking for the proper ending to his thought.

"It's okay," Kate says. "Yes, back when Leif was alive, we had a run of vandalism. Nothing like this, though. It was sporadic, maybe once a month, and the usual kind of stuff that kids would do."

"Because Leif was a cop."

"Yeah, he was a hard-ass. He wasn't at home, of course—well, not usually. But he didn't make himself popular with the high school set."

Kate realizes that Jack might not know how—and where, specifi-cally—Leif had died. She is about to take on the burden of explaining that as well when, as if reading her mind, Jack speaks.

"Chief O'Neil told me about that, too. Again, I'm sorry."

"Me too," Kate says. She has eaten most of her chicken, and yet Jack is barely halfway through his. Slightly embarrassed, she says, "I guess I must have been hungry after all."

"I'd offer to toss another on the grill for you, but these were my last two pieces."

"This is plenty, thanks. What else did my father-in-law say?"

"He asked if I'd keep a closer watch on the place. And he said some cameras and better lighting would be going up in the next few days."

"That was another thing I wanted to tell you. I hope that's not going to be a problem for you."

"Why would it be?"

"Maybe it's just me, but the idea of all my comings and goings being recorded makes me uneasy. And a bunch of security cameras and lights will change this place from, I don't know, a peaceful haven to a fortress."

"It sounds like the right thing to do, though. And you can take everything down once this is over, if you want."

"That's true."

"Whatever you need to do, don't worry about me," Jack says. "I mean, it's not like I have a lot of comings and goings to record."

"Which brings me to the last thing I need to tell you—unless, that is, you already know."

"That there will be a cop car parked on the street for the next few nights?"

"Okay, he told you everything."

"Do you have any idea who is doing this? Or why?"

Kate shakes her head. "There are theories, of course, but so far they all involve me having wronged someone."

"That doesn't seem likely."

"That's kind of you, considering I was less than forthcoming."

"You seem to be taking it in stride. I mean, you're still living your life and not going into hiding."

Kate shrugs. "I guess I'm still holding out hope that this will turn out to be nothing. And I have a lot of people on my side, most of them cops or ex-cops, so that helps." She pauses, then says, "And when you have kids, you learn to hide a lot of what you're feeling, for their sake."

"I imagine that must get lonely, though. I hope you have someone you can be real with."

Kate takes a breath, nods. "I do. My neighbor Maria." She almost adds "for now" but stops herself.

"That's good. And for what it's worth, I'm on your side, too."

"That helps, actually. Thanks. I know this isn't what you bargained for."

"Like I said, it's not like I went into this blind."

Kate has finished the chicken and moves on to the salad. "Hey, so any luck with the job search?"

"Not yet. To be honest, I was giving myself two weeks to do pretty much nothing." He seems uncertain whether to continue with his thought, then says, "My wife and I split up. Everything kind of came crashing down at once."

"I'm sorry to hear that."

"I'm pretty much to blame."

"What do you mean?"

"Her father was the president of the school where I taught. We lived in a house on the edge of campus that the school owned. I more or less built my world around her, you know. So losing her meant I lost everything else, too. The job, the home, our friends."

"Yeah, I think I'd need a few weeks to regroup after that, too," Kate says. "What was she like?"

Jack shakes his head, and it seems to Kate for a moment that he isn't going to answer. Finally, though, he says, "A handful. But I guess that's what I thought I wanted. We married right out of college."

"I'm sorry if I'm prying."

"No, not at all. I'm living a hundred feet from you and your kids. You should want to know more about me. Ask me anything you want."

"Like what?"

Jack smiles. "I don't know. That was just my clever way of changing the subject."

"Smooth."

"Thanks."

"Actually, I do have a question."

"Go for it."

"You said that you taught a lot of subjects. History, philosophy, psychology. How does one do that, exactly? I mean, how do you know enough about a variety of things to be able to teach each one effectively?"

"A lot of last-minute, late-night cram sessions," Jack jokes. "But my college was an experimental school, so I got to create my own major. Those three were my focus of study."

"You're a renaissance man, then."

"God, no. I'm just an idiot who went out of his way to study the subjects with the lowest possible earning potential. I was lucky to have a steady job for so long, not that it paid great. It was its own little world, though, you know? Classes during the day, practice and matches after school during the wrestling season. Off season, it was faculty wine-and-cheese parties, or dinner and drinks at so-and-so's house. We barely left the campus, which is good because half the time we were lit."

"Sounds idyllic."

"It was, but now I'm back out in the real world and need to make some money."

Kate remembers Jack paying his rent from an envelope of fifties, and that he returned to that envelope what looked to her to be about $500. She can't help but wonder if that $500 was all the money he had left.

"You know, I was thinking, if you are going to play lookout, then you should probably get a break on rent. Maybe a thousand a month instead of fifteen hundred."

"That's not necessary."

"Well, I ate the last of your chicken, so the least I can do is have you over for dinner tomorrow night. That way I can introduce you to the twins. They should meet you if you're going to be around—you know, in case you ever actually do step outside."

"I don't want to intrude."

"I'm inviting you, so how could you be intruding?"

"Oh, I'd manage somehow."

"Stop it. It's settled. You're coming over tomorrow night. Any food issues I should know about? Allergies, preferences."

"Generally, I'll eat whatever's in front of me."

"That's helpful."

Jack studies her face for a quick moment. "Your eyes are looking better," he says. "How's your headache?"

"Easing, thanks."

"Elle used to get crazy-bad headaches if she went too long between meals. That combined with stress were her triggers."

"Elle is your ex-wife?"

Jack nods. "Yeah. It was a nightmare; she'd freak out, bad, but I would make her something to eat and sit her down, and it would begin to go away." He smiles. "There were other tricks I learned, too, for when they got so bad that eating didn't help."

Kate is beginning to get a better idea of what he meant when he referred to his ex as a "handful."

"You'll have to teach me those tricks one day."

"Sure. I'd be happy to." Jack takes a sip of his beer, then places the pint glass on the table and glances at his guest's empty plate. "I'm sorry if you're still hungry. I don't have any dessert to offer you."

"No, this was great. I should get back soon anyway. There are some things I'd like to get done before Dad brings Max and Callie back." Kate pauses. "And it was nice for me to have someone else do the cooking for a change."

"It was nice not to eat alone," Jack says. He turns in his seat, getting ready to stand. "Here, I'll walk you out."

"No, I'll sit with you until you're finished. I'm not in a rush. They won't be back until seven, at least."

Jack returns his knees under the table and picks up his fork. Kate looks around the room.

"I really should have cleared out these paintings."

"I like having them here. As you can see, I don't have a lot of stuff, and the place would feel too empty without them."

"Really? To me it feels like clutter."

"I actually spent my first few days looking at them all. You said they were your sister's, right?"

"Yes."

"She's very good. Is that how she makes her living?"

"No."

"What does she do?"

"Honestly, I don't know."

"How can you not know what your own sister does for a living?"

137

"We're . . . estranged."

"I'm sorry to hear that."

Kate shrugs. "It happened a long time ago." She pauses, and then adds, "She's a handful."

Jack nods. "Ah. Gotcha. I don't remember her. I'm assuming she went to high school here, too."

"She was a year ahead of me, so she had graduated and was long gone before you were a freshman."

Jack nods again, then asks, "Any idea where she is now?"

"Colorado, last I knew. Why?"

"I don't have any brothers or sisters, so I don't know what it's like to be estranged from one. It has to suck, though, right?"

Kate continues to look around the room.

Finally, she says, "I guess it does, yeah."

"Now I feel like I'm the one asking too many questions."

"It's okay," Kate says. "We're getting to know each other. And like you said, we're neighbors, and who wants to live next door to a stranger?"

TWENTY

At seven fifteen Max and Callie return, bringing Kate a tuna club sandwich and side of coleslaw in a Styrofoam take-out container. Despite having eaten with Jack less than two hours ago, Kate finishes the entire sandwich standing at the kitchen counter, hoping that a full stomach will further diminish what is now just a steadily throbbing headache.

The twins are seated at the table with their grandfather, who relays to Kate as she eats every detail of where they went—the diner on the Post Road, and what they ate—burgers all around, followed by ice-cream sundaes.

It takes a few moments, but Kate finally realizes that her father-in-law is stalling, not wanting to leave until Chief O'Neil's man arrives, which he does at seven thirty.

Shortly after that, Leo Burke says good night and departs. Once on the street, he parks his SUV facing in the opposite direction of the Westport PD SUV, so their driver's-side windows align. They talk briefly, and then Leo Burke drives off, leaving just the cop at the top of Kate's driveway.

It isn't until she is getting ready for bed that Kate gets to think about her interaction with Jack. What may have been a significant age gap back in high school is hardly consequential now. Maybe outwardly Jack looks a little younger, and maybe the fact that Kate is an inch or so taller somehow casts her as the older of the two, but there is no doubt in her mind that he is an adult man now, one who has experienced his share of triumphs and setbacks.

She can't help but replay how he sensed that something was bothering her and immediately offered help, taking charge and not allowing Kate to refuse.

There is a confidence to him that seems equal to his courtesy, and Kate finds that appealing.

She is surrounded by too many cops and chiefs, former and current, and she, of course, carries with her always the memory of the cop she loved and married and with whom she had children.

So many alpha males, but here now, suddenly, is something very different from that.

A teacher, like she is. And, like her, coping with loss that has him looking to start a new life, which is a task Kate knows that she will need to face at some point.

Despite her initial favorable impressions of Jack, however, there is a part of her now that regrets having invited him to dinner. Yes, it seemed the thing to do at the time, but in her mind it is at this moment *one more thing* to do in a day that is already blocked out down to the minute with all that must be done in the seventeen-plus hours between her predawn rising and often-too-late bedtime.

Washing her face in the bathroom sink, Kate recognizes that she is finally, totally pain-free, though the action of brushing her teeth moments later causes the muscles at the back of her skull to tighten slightly. But that sensation ends once she is done, after which she moves through the house, making her usual pre-bedtime check of the locks and alarm system. Tonight, though, that routine includes taking a moment to confirm that the Westport PD SUV is still parked at the top of the driveway.

Sitting on the edge of her bed, Kate is applying hand cream when her cell phone vibrates. The display screen shows an incoming text from Maria. Once Kate's hands are dry enough, she picks up the device from her nightstand and navigates to the message.

Are you awake?

Kate replies: Yes. What's up?

It takes close to a minute for Maria to answer. First interview tomorrow afternoon. Derek will be here when the kids get off the bus. Wish me luck!

Kate is caught off guard by this news. Last she knew, seeking a job was something Maria thought she might need to do.

Kate sends a reply text. Did something happen?

Within seconds Maria responds. Business not just low on cash. Majorly in debt. He admitted it tonight. So pissed. Need to act now.

This is immediately followed by another text. Sorry!

Kate ignores her initial reaction—alarm verging on panic—and shifts into friend mode, quickly keying in and sending off her reply. Don't be. Sorry your life has been turned upside down. You don't deserve that. How badly in debt?

A half minute passes before Maria replies. Will tell you next time we talk.

Kate needs a moment before she can compose and send her response. K. Good luck. Let me know how it goes.

Maria's text contains a thumbs-up emoji and nothing more, and though Kate senses that the conversation has ended, she nonetheless hangs on to her cell phone, just in case she is mistaken and more is to come. She remains seated on the edge of her bed, but the phone doesn't vibrate again and eventually she returns the device to the nightstand.

She lingers for a moment in silence, and then mutters to herself, "Shit."

Kate runs through the limited options that she and Maria discussed the night before, but none seem any more possible now than they had then.

The knowledge that Max and Callie were being watched by someone who was akin to family has been one of Kate's few comforts these past two years, and the idea of that disappearing from her life feels like one more thing being taken from her.

Too keyed up to sleep, Kate roams her dark house, pausing for several moments in every room—living room, kitchen, even the narrow pantry—as if in one of those places she may come across something that might reveal to her a yet-to-be-seen solution to this problem.

But instead, everywhere she goes she hears what Maria said the night before.

You tend to talk about Rebecca as if she has no redeeming qualities.

Standing in the kitchen now, Kate remembers mornings when Rebecca would walk from the cottage early to make breakfast for her niece and nephew, and how Rebecca had a way with Max that, to a degree, Kate herself didn't have—an ability to draw the boy out of his shell without calling attention to the fact that she was doing so.

Of course, Callie adored her aunt, though for Kate the idea of Rebecca being Callie's caretaker, even on a part-time basis, would be to solve one problem while inviting another.

Callie is already too much like her beloved Aunt Becca, and continued exposure would only add more fuel to that fire.

The trade-off there is that Callie and Max would be safe—physically safe, watched over by someone who would fight and die to keep harm from befalling them.

At the basic-needs level, Kate would be able to spend her workday free of fear and worry. And she would make the drive home every afternoon secure in the knowledge that upon turning in to her driveway, she would not be confronted with some devastating tragedy from which she will never recover.

As flawed as this option is, Kate knows that there is no other.

———

In her bedroom, Kate picks up the cordless phone from its cradle on her nightstand and scrolls through the list of incoming calls until she arrives at Rebecca's current number.

Pressing "Redial," Kate takes a breath and lets it out before bringing the phone to her ear. With each ringing sound she hears, she feels the urge to hang up. But she fights it, and finally, midway through the fourth ring, the phone is answered.

Rebecca's voice is quiet, but her surprise is evident. Kate knows by this that Rebecca has seen the landline number displayed on the Caller ID.

"Hey," Rebecca says.

Kate replies, "Hey."

"Everything okay?"

"Yeah—I mean, no one's hurt or anything."

"What's going on?"

"Is this a bad time?"

"No. You don't sound good, Katie. What's wrong?"

"I'm calling because you said last week that you were interested in coming back here for a while, and I was wondering if that was still the case."

"I thought that wasn't a good idea. You seemed pretty adamant about that."

"I know."

"What has changed?"

"It turns out I'm going to need someone to look after Callie and Max."

"Ah. What happened with Maria?"

"She's going back to work. Derek's company is in debt."

The line is silent for a moment.

Kate asks, "You still there?"

"Yes. So now that it suits you, my coming back is not such a terrible idea after all."

Kate chooses to ignore the jab, if only for the sake of propriety. "You know I wouldn't ask if it weren't an emergency."

"That's what I'm saying, Katie. You only want me there because Maria is bailing on you. You don't want me there because I'm your sister and I wanted to come home."

Again, Kate sees it as her role to keep the conversation from turning less than civil. "I realize now that I hurt you, Becca. And I'm sorry for that. I wasn't thinking straight. I should have probably let you stay."

"'Probably'?"

"I really don't want to do this. You offered to help out, and now I want to take you up on that offer. Are you interested?"

"What are we talking about, exactly?"

"Getting Max and Callie to school in the morning and picking them up in the afternoon."

"So, I'd be your nanny."

"You'd be their aunt playing a part in their lives. I thought that's what you wanted."

"It is. And what happens when school ends for the year? You won't need help then, right?"

"If you want to stay, maybe I can help you get an apartment or something."

"Wait, won't I be in the cottage?"

"That's the thing. I've rented it, so you'd be staying in the house with us."

"But how would that work with only three bedrooms? I don't really want to sleep on your foldout couch for two months."

"I really haven't thought about that yet, but I'd probably get the spare cot out of the attic and set it up for Max in Callie's room. Or vice versa. Obviously, I know you'd want your own room."

Again, the line falls silent.

This time Kate waits for her sister to speak.

"You must be desperate—I mean, if you want me to live in your house."

Kate knows that the possessive pronoun is the main point of that sentence—*your* house instead of simply *the* house. And if that's bait, she doesn't care to take it, leaving Kate with nothing to say in response.

Once a peacemaker, always a peacemaker.

Again, it's Rebecca who ends the silence. "I don't know, Katie. When you shot me down last week, I went ahead and made other arrangements."

"Are they set in stone?"

"No. I'm curious, though. Why did you rent the cottage all of a sudden?"

"It's a long story," Kate says.

"Is something else going on?"

"What do you mean?"

"You sound scared."

It takes a moment for Kate to answer. "It's happening again."

"What is?"

"It's nothing, I'm sure. Actually, I take that back. We don't know what it is."

"Katie, what are you talking about?"

"Someone's . . . fucking with me. Like before. Random acts of vandalism. But it's different this time."

"Different how?"

"They're happening more frequently. And what they're doing, there's something . . . creepy about it."

"Creepy how?"

"The first incident was inside the cottage. Someone broke in and stuck a kitchen knife in the bedroom wall."

"Jesus," Rebecca says.

"That's why we rented it. We thought it was just kids screwing around."

"But you don't think that anymore?"

"We don't."

"'We'?"

"Everyone's involved in this. Leo, Eddie, Chief O'Neil. I'm sure they'll figure it out. It would just help me out if I knew someone who cares about Max and Callie is looking after them."

"I'd need a couple of days. What's today? Monday?"

"Yes."

"I should be able to get there by Thursday. Can you guys hang on till then?"

"Of course, yeah."

"The number you called is my new cell. I'll text you from it when I know exactly what time I'll be arriving."

"Do you need to be picked up at the airport? I'll be teaching if you're coming in during the day, but maybe Derek could get you."

"No, I'll make my own way."

"Are you sure?"

"Yes."

"I appreciate this."

"Yeah?"

"Yes."

Rebecca pauses. "It's nice to be appreciated," she says. "I'll see you Thursday."

She ends the call. Kate returns the handset to its charger, staring at it briefly before finally turning away and looking down at the floor.

Her mind isn't any calmer now than it had been prior to making these arrangements.

And though she is relieved to have taken care of that problem, there is a part of her that feels as if she has done wrong, like she rushed into a deal with the devil.

This thought brings her back to something else Maria said last night.

No one can be all bad. There has got to be something about her to admire.

TWENTY-ONE

Callie asks, "Why is he having dinner with us?"

Kate has been nonstop since leaving school at four—dropping by the supermarket for a few things, hurrying to get the twins from Maria's, and then home to change and get dinner prep started.

As she answers her daughter, she continues chopping two stalks of celery set side by side on a cutting board. "Because you and Max should get to know him."

"Why do we need to do that?" Callie's tone conveys confusion with a touch of annoyance.

"He's our neighbor. It's the polite thing to do."

"He's just a renter, Mom. What's the big deal?"

"It's only a big deal because you're making it one."

"What's he like?"

"He's a nice man."

"So, we'll have to, like, sit there and talk to him?"

"That's usually how we get to know someone."

"I have homework I wanted to get done."

"There'll be plenty of time to do that after."

"But I was going to group-chat with my friends."

Kate looks at her daughter and says, "I don't know what to tell you." Lifting the cutting board, she transfers the celery into a wooden salad bowl, then returns the board to the counter and proceeds to cut a large English cucumber into thin slices.

"You don't, like, like him, do you?" Callie says. "I mean, you're kind of stressing out right now."

Kate looks up again and stops her work briefly. Though she does not answer the question, she realizes that her daughter is right, she has been moving frantically from the minute she walked through the door, so when she resumes her careful slicing, she does so at a slower, more deliberate pace.

Callie says, "You don't, do you?" It is more a demand than a question.

"Grown men and women can get together and just be friends."

"Then why do you freak out whenever I talk to a boy?"

"I said 'grown men and women.' Teenagers are another story."

"I'm not a teenager yet. Way to know your own daughter's age."

"Twelve is close enough. Hey, here's an idea: Why don't you start your homework now? That way you won't have so much to do after dinner."

Callie rolls her eyes and says, "*Fine.* What are we having, anyway?"

"I'm making salmon."

"Ugh."

"I don't want to hear it. You like salmon. Go get started on your homework. I'll let you know when it's time to set the table."

"What time is he supposed to get here?"

"Six."

Callie is turning to leave the room, but then stops and asks, "By the way, where was Maria this afternoon?"

"She had a job interview."

"Where?"

"At a hospital. I don't know which one."

"Does that mean Derek is going to meet us after school from now on?"

"We'll talk about it later."

"You know, we don't need a babysitter. We're old enough to look after ourselves."

"I know you think that, but you're not."

"It wouldn't be any different from having Derek watch us. He was on the phone the entire time. All he did was open the back door and point at the cupboard where they keep their junk food."

"Like I said, we'll talk about it later."

"Why can't you tell me now?"

"Callie, you're working my last nerve here. If you don't want to do your homework, then you can help me cut up vegetables for the salad."

Turning again, Callie this time exits the kitchen. Moving through the living room, she says, "I'll do my homework. Just stop stressing out already."

She climbs the stairs, her feet landing on each plank with a little more force than necessary. Once her bedroom door closes, the only sound in the house is the *tut-tut-tut* of the cleaver on the cutting board. After a moment, Kate realizes that she is once again working at a hurried pace. She pauses to take a full breath in through her nose, and after first holding it deep in her lungs as she silently counts to four, she slowly lets it out.

But it doesn't eliminate the nervousness she is feeling, so she opens a bottle of Malbec and pours a glass, opting for a half serving but then adding a little more to it. Taking sips as she continues making the salad, Kate forces herself to move at a more mindful pace, and perhaps it's the combination of the two, but her edginess begins to diminish.

After she has emptied the glass, which takes less than ten minutes, Kate is tempted to pour herself another half portion, but she decides against it.

Having not eaten anything since noon, she is already a little buzzed.

But more than that, a man is about to sit at her table and meet her children, so she will need to remain in full control if she is to ensure that the evening goes smoothly for all involved.

At five forty-five, while Callie and Max are setting the table, Kate slips into her bedroom to change into a clean blouse. After that, she stands before the bathroom mirror and quickly applies enough eyeliner to make her appear less tired.

Back in the kitchen she removes the salmon from the oven and sets it on the stovetop as Callie and Max orbit the table, Callie setting down the dinner plates and Max following her with the tableware. Walking to the refrigerator to take out the salad, Kate notices from the corner of her eye that Callie has stopped mid-chore. Kate, too, stops and faces her daughter, who is obviously fixated on Kate's eyes.

Kate asks, "What?"

Callie shrugs and continues to the next place setting. "Nothing," she says. Kate remains where she is, and Callie looks at her mother again, smiling to herself. "You look nice, that's all."

———

Jack arrives promptly at six, dressed in khaki pants, a gingham shirt, and tie, and carrying a half-gallon container of Turkey Hill vanilla ice cream.

"I brought dessert," he says.

He offers the container to Kate, who takes it and steps back, waving for her guest to come in.

"You didn't have to do that, Jack," she says.

He enters and Kate closes the door, and when she gestures toward the kitchen to show him the way, she sees Callie standing in the doorway, smiling again, though this time knowingly.

Stepping forward with her right hand extended, Callie is suddenly a model of good manners and warmth. She introduces herself, and as she and Jack shake hands, she looks him in the eye with a confidence that strikes Kate as an act, but one that is disturbingly believable.

The fact that her daughter can switch on the charm in this manner—and for a man more than twice her age—is yet another reminder for Kate that this twelve-year-old is becoming more and more like her aunt.

TWENTY-TWO

Callie is an active participant in the dinnertime conversation, which is surprising to Kate since her daughter is often a sullen half presence at the table. The girl asks Jack questions that cover the same ground that Kate covered the night before, but so their guest can actually eat his meal, Kate frequently answers a number of those questions for him.

On the other hand, Max must be drawn in to the conversation, though when, after they've all finished eating, Kate mentions again that Jack coached wrestling at his old job, Max perks up slightly. Though intrigued, he nonetheless maintains his reserve, his attention for the most part focused on his dinner plate as he absently moves around his half-eaten salmon with his fork.

But when Kate reminds Max that Jack had been on the same wrestling team as Max's father, the boy's reluctance gives way and he, too, joins the conversation.

"You knew my dad?"

"A little bit, yeah."

"Your grandfather remembers Jack very well," Kate says, adding a piece of information that she thinks might serve to put the boy at ease even further.

Max, however, doesn't acknowledge the statement, instead asking Jack, "Were you good?"

"I was pretty good. I made it to the state finals my senior year."

Max looks at his mother. "Dad made it to state, right?"

"He did."

"How did he do?"

Unable to recall, Kate defers to Jack, who answers, "He took first place."

Max asks, "And when you went?"

"Fifth. Like I said, I was pretty good, but your dad was great."

Suddenly cut out of the conversation, Callie pushes her way back in, asking her mother, "Did you and Jack know each other in high school?"

"Sure," Kate answers.

"Did you hang out?"

Kate is caught off guard a bit by the question, though she immediately realizes that she shouldn't be since it goes directly to the ongoing argument that she and her daughter have regarding girls and boys being friends.

Kate dodges the question. "We were in different circles."

"I was kind of invisible, especially my freshman year," Jack adds.

Callie looks at him. "What does that mean?"

"I lived in Norwalk, not Westport. But my mother wanted me to go to school here because the schools are better, so we used the address of someone who lived here so I could enroll. Since it had to be a secret, I couldn't really make a lot of friends."

Kate is caught by surprise by this as well. Looking at him, she says, "I didn't know that. About keeping it such a secret, I mean."

Jack shrugs. "Like I said, it was a secret."

"So you commuted back and forth from Norwalk," Callie says.

"Yeah. After school I'd make it look like I was walking home, but my mom would be waiting a half mile away to pick me up. It was a whole operation."

Callie can't hide her delight at the idea that their guest, at one point at least, was what her mother would call a "bad influence."

Though she is looking at her mother, Callie addresses Jack. "Isn't that against the law or something?"

He nods. "It was, yeah."

Even more delighted, Callie is on the verge of laughing. "You're a criminal, then."

"Callie," Kate scolds. "That's rude."

Jack smiles. "I was underage, so technically my mother was the criminal. But she wanted what was best for me, which is what mothers do."

"See?" Kate says to her daughter.

Callie rolls her eyes, annoyed. "Whatever."

Calmly, Kate says, "Okay, I think that's enough from you for one night. Why don't you go upstairs and finish your homework."

"I was kidding."

Careful to maintain an even tone, Kate responds, "No, you were showing off."

"C'mon, Mom."

"Just please go upstairs."

"What about ice cream?"

"I'll have Max bring you a bowl after we clean up."

Her cheeks reddening, Callie tilts her head to one side and whispers, *"Mom."*

"I don't think we need to make a scene, do you?"

The girl's embarrassment shifts quickly to anger. *"Fine."*

Standing, Callie storms out of the kitchen. Seconds later, she is stomping up the stairs.

Kate waits patiently for the sound of her daughter's bedroom door closing before saying to Jack, "Sorry about that."

"Don't be. I get it. It's the age."

"If only that's all it was. I'm afraid we're getting too good at pushing each other's buttons. I try not to overreact, but . . ."

"I don't think you did," Jack says. "Anyway, that happens, right? Parents and children argue. It comes with the territory."

"I guess I was hoping that wouldn't happen to us."

"What wouldn't?"

"That we'd turn on each other."

"Is that what you think is happening?"

Kate shrugs. "I don't know. That's what it feels like sometimes." Wanting to change the subject for Max's sake, she shifts her attention to the boy and says, "You didn't finish your salmon, sweetie."

The row, though brief and relatively undramatic, has caused the boy's shyness to return. His eyes cast down, he says, "I'm not hungry."

Softening her tone still more, she teases, "Then you won't want dessert, either, right?"

Max says nothing, though by his expression it is obvious that he realizes his mistake and is trying to think of what he could say to get him out of it.

Before the boy can say anything, though, Kate says, "You know, I bet Jack would be happy to show you some wrestling techniques sometime."

Jack looks at Max. "Absolutely, yeah."

Max shrugs and says, "Okay."

"The thing is," Jack says, "if you want to be a great wrestler like your dad was, you'll need to eat up and get strong."

Max mumbles, "I know."

Kate says, "If you're done eating, then, would you like to be excused?"

"Yes, please."

"Go ahead."

"Can I watch a movie?"

"Is your homework done?"

"Yes."

"Okay. Not too loud, though, please."

Max rests his fork on the plate and stands, then hurries into the living room.

After a moment, Jack says, "Sorry; I thought that might get him to eat."

"I appreciate the effort," Kate says. She pauses, then stands. "I'll clear the table a little, and then we can have dessert."

Jack stands as well. "Let me help you."

"No, you're the guest."

"We'll get done quicker with two pairs of hands," Jack says. He begins collecting the dinner plates, picking up the tableware as he does.

Minutes later, the two are standing side by side at the sink, Kate washing the plates and Jack drying them.

Kate says, "As you can see, between Max being too shy and Callie being too outgoing, I've got my hands full."

"Looks to me like you're doing a great job."

"Thanks. I can't remember if I asked; did you and your wife have kids?"

"No, we never took that leap."

"Any particular reason why?"

"I think we were too attached to our lifestyle to even consider it."

"Yeah, everything changes when you have kids," Kate says.

She washes a plate and hands it to Jack. As he towel-dries it, he asks, "How's the headache, by the way?"

"Long gone."

"That's good to hear."

"It wasn't the worst I've had, but it was bad enough. How was dinner?"

"It was great. I almost forgot that there was something other than chicken."

Kate smiles and hands him the last washed dinner plate. "I'm glad you enjoyed it."

Later, Kate and Jack walk up the driveway toward the cottage. The sun is already below the tree line, and dusk is just moments away.

"I noticed your lawn could use a spring cleanup," Jack says. "I'd be happy to take care of that for you. And the grass is starting to grow, so if you have a mower, I could do the lawn while I'm at it."

"Seriously?"

"Sure. I think I've sat around long enough. I need to do something."

"I'll pay you for your time. I usually hire a crew to take care of all that anyway."

"You don't need to pay me."

Kate briefly considers bringing up her concerns about his cash situation, but instead she says, "How about this: you get a dinner—one that doesn't include chicken—for every job you do around here."

"That sounds fair."

Kate is reminded by this that in two nights there would be another adult joining them at the kitchen table.

"Oh, yeah, I should tell you that my sister is arriving Thursday. She'll be staying here at least until the end of the school year."

"I thought you two were estranged? Unless it's a different sister."

"No, I only have the one. My neighbor Maria usually looks after Max and Callie for me, but she's going back to work. Rebecca offered to help out." Kate pauses. "Also, it has come to my attention recently that maybe I've been less than fair to her over the years."

"That's a big thing to admit. Good for you."

Smiling, Kate shrugs and says, "Well, I did say 'maybe I've been less than fair.'"

They reach the pathway to the cottage. Kate stops, and Jack turns to face her.

"Thanks again for dinner."

"I guess we'll be doing it again soon."

"I figured I'd get started tomorrow."

"The lawn mower is in there." Kate points to an aluminum toolshed in the southwestern corner of the backyard.

"Is it locked?"

"No. And there should be enough gasoline in the red plastic container-thing."

"I'm actually looking forward to it."

Kate studies him for a moment, and then says, "You're a genuinely helpful person, aren't you?"

Now it's Jack who shrugs. "What's the point in being otherwise, right?"

"Right," Kate says. "Anyway, I should probably get back. Have a good night."

Jack replies, "You too."

As Kate starts down the driveway, she hears the cottage door open and close. After taking a dozen or so steps, she suddenly realizes that either or both of her children might have been watching her. Looking toward the house, she sees that the large living room window is empty, but then she looks up at the bedroom window directly above—Callie's window.

The girl is there, and she and Kate make eye contact.

Kate then has a second realization: her exchange with Jack has left her with a lingering smile.

Lowering her line of sight, Kate continues toward the house.

She reaches the front door as a vehicle rolls to a stop on her street. Turning, she sees that a Westport PD SUV is parked at the top of her driveway, its driver masked by tinted windows.

Though she has no idea if the unknown officer is looking at her, Kate waves before stepping inside.

———

Callie is still texting with her friends at bedtime.

Standing in the doorway of her daughter's bedroom, Kate says, "Time to put the phone away for the night."

Seated cross-legged on her bed with her eyes on the screen, Callie continues to work the keypad with two thumbs. "Okay. Let me just send this and say good night."

As Callie continues thumbing the keypad, Kate crosses the hall to Max's room. His door is closed, so she knocks and waits for his permission before opening it.

The boy is lying down on his bed with his head propped up on a pillow, reading.

Kate says, "It's bedtime."

Max closes the book and places it on his nightstand, then turns onto his left side. He flattens his pillow, adjusts his position, and pulls the covers to his shoulder.

Kate steps into the room, stopping midway between the door and the bed.

Though they are facing each other, Max avoids eye contact.

Kate moves closer to the bed by a few more steps and asks, "You okay, Max?"

His head on his pillow, the boy nods.

Kate closes the remaining distance, putting herself squarely within her son's line of sight and leaving him no choice but to look at her.

"You know if there's something you want to say or ask me, you can," Kate says.

Max glances down at his mother's feet and, without lifting his head, whispers, "When do you think he'll show me stuff?"

Kate whispers back, "You mean Jack?"

The boy nods. "Yeah."

"We can ask him. Maybe this weekend, if he isn't busy."

Max thinks about that for a moment, then asks, "Is he going to be your boyfriend?"

"No, Max. He's just our neighbor."

After another thoughtful silence, Max says, "It'd be okay, you know."

"What would be okay?"

"If he became your boyfriend. He's nice."

"Hey," Kate says. She steps to the bed and sits on the edge of the mattress. Max rolls onto his back, and Kate brushes his hair from his eyes with two fingers. "You don't have to worry about that," she says. "There are a lot of things more important than that right now."

"I'm not worried. I'm just saying I'd be okay with it. I wouldn't care what anyone said."

Kate had almost forgotten about the teasing Max has had to endure, and she suddenly realizes how something as innocent as her walking to the cottage with her tenant might appear to anyone watching—particularly anyone with a cruel streak. This error in judgment causes her to cringe slightly.

"Maybe if I know how to wrestle I can beat them up," Max says.

"Is that why you want to join the wrestling team?"

Max doesn't answer.

"First of all, I don't want you fighting, okay? Not anyone. Promise me that you won't."

The boy looks at his mother, nods once.

"And we keep our promises to each other, right?" Kate says.

Max nods again.

"Second of all, I protect you, not the other way around. Got it?"

Yet another nod, though Kate gets the sense that this one is hesitant, which indicates to her that her son's concession might be less than sincere.

"Listen, I know things are weird right now, but we have a lot of people looking out for us. And between you and me, yes, that's why Jack is here. Between him and your grandfather and Eddie and all your father's friends, I don't think we're going to have any more trouble. Okay?"

159

"Okay."

Kate leans down, putting her face closer to his, and, whispering even more quietly, says, "You know, there's a surprise coming on Thursday, for you and your sister."

"What?"

"If I tell you, it wouldn't be a surprise anymore, would it?" Kate pauses, then says, "Auntie Becca is coming to stay with us for a while."

This makes the boy smile. "She can meet us after school," he says. "Right?"

"That's right. And send you off in the morning. And have dinner with us every night. That sounds good, right?"

"Yes."

"And you two are her favorite people in the world, so you know she'd never let anything happen to you."

"Will she be here when we get home from school on Thursday?"

"I'm not sure about that yet. It depends on what time her flight is. But she'll definitely be here waiting for you on Friday."

"That'll be cool," Max says.

"Good. Now get some sleep, okay?"

"Okay."

Since Kate is already so close to her son, she leans forward the rest of the way and quickly kisses him on the forehead, making a point of doing so playfully because the only way she can get kisses now that he is twelve is by stealing them.

To Kate's surprise, Max doesn't make a big deal out of it. As she stands, he rolls onto his left side again. Though tempted to push her luck by adjusting his blanket, which no doubt would count as tucking him in, Kate leaves the boy be and quietly exits, softly closing the door behind her.

Crossing to Callie's room, Kate is not surprised to see that her daughter is still texting.

Before her mother can speak, however, Callie says, "I'm just saying good night."

"Please don't make me play phone cop tonight, okay?"

Callie says impatiently, "Okay."

As Kate waits, Callie types frantically.

Finally, she places her phone on the nightstand. "Okay, I'm done."

"You finished your homework?"

"Yes."

Kate's eyes go to the half-eaten bowl of melted ice cream on her daughter's desk.

Kate holds out her hand. "Can you hand that to me, please?"

Callie gets out of bed, marches to her desk and picks up the bowl, then carries it to the doorway. Even when she complies, the girl can still convey defiance, simply by acting as though what she is being told to do is her pleasure.

Callie smiles and asks, "Anything else, Mother?"

Kate recognizes that her daughter is still under the impression that she knows her mother's secret and therefore has the upper hand.

"Maybe you could drop the attitude."

"What attitude?" Turning, Callie crosses the room and resumes sitting cross-legged on her bed.

Looking to make peace, Kate says, "So, I've got some good news and some bad news. The good news is your aunt is coming to stay with us. She's going to be taking you and Max to school every morning and watching you in the afternoon until I get home from work."

"For how long?"

"The rest of the school year, at least."

"When is she getting here?"

"The day after tomorrow."

"Cool."

"Don't forget there's bad news."

"What?"

"You and Max are going to have to share his room."

"*What?*"

"I'm moving the cot in there."

"I don't want to sleep in his room. Why can't Auntie Becca sleep in here with me?"

"She needs her own room."

"So do I! Why can't she sleep on the foldout couch downstairs, like Grandpa does?"

"You know that's not comfortable."

"Then why can't Max sleep downstairs?"

"I don't want someone camping out in our living room for two months. He's your twin brother, Callie. You can deal with it."

"That's not fair."

"It seems to me a small price to pay to have your aunt here."

"But why do I have to be the one to sleep on a cot?"

"Maybe if you ask your brother nicely he'll trade with you."

"Ew. I don't want to sleep in his bed."

"I don't know what to tell you, then."

"Why don't you tell your boyfriend to move out so Auntie Becca can stay in the cottage, like she normally does?"

The "boyfriend" comment is obvious bait, so Kate ignores it. "Jack and I have an agreement. You can't go back on an agreement, Callie, just because it's no longer convenient."

"Says who?"

"I'm not going to fight with you about this," Kate says. She turns to leave, grabbing the door handle. "Go to sleep. I'll see you in the morning."

As Kate closes the door, Callie says again, *"This isn't fair!"*

The last thing Kate sees is the girl slapping her mattress with both palms. And the last thing she hears from her daughter is a sustained grunt of frustration.

At the kitchen sink, Kate washes the bowl and spoon, sets them in the dish drainer to dry overnight, and then makes her nightly check of the doors and windows and security system.

A quick glance out the living room window shows Kate a cottage with its windows lit, and a marked police SUV parked up on her road.

———

Kate is undressing for bed when her landline rings.

Wearing only her underwear, Kate hurries from her bathroom and crosses to the bedside nightstand, snatching the receiver from its charging cradle. Though she is anxious to silence the ringing, she first checks the incoming number on the display screen. The lateness of this call has her expecting to see Rebecca's number, but instead of a series of digits, the display shows two words.

"Unknown Caller."

Suddenly uncertain whether or not to answer, Kate is still staring at the display as the second ring begins, then ends. Her thumb remains hovering over the "Talk" button as, a second later, the third ring starts—only to cease abruptly midway through.

The display goes dark.

Kate hangs on to the receiver, waiting for a possible second call, but a half minute passes and the device remains silent. Still, another half minute goes by before Kate is able to slip the receiver back into its cradle.

Turning finally to head back to the bathroom, Kate is stopped when her cell phone suddenly buzzes. The device is on the nightstand as well, and displayed on its brightly lit screen are the same two words—"Unknown Caller."

Since that phone's ringer is shut off, Kate need not hurry to silence it, though each vibration, amplified by the thick wood of the tabletop in the otherwise quiet room, is as unnerving as an alarm.

Kate waits as the first buzzing sound ends, and then does the same for the second. The third begins, though unlike what had occurred a moment ago, the call isn't abruptly ended. The buzzing continues for a fourth and finally fifth time, at which point the call rolls over to her voice mail.

Picking up the device, Kate waits for a notification of a new voice message, but she receives none.

Eventually, she places her cell on the table and returns to her bathroom. As she washes her face, she anticipates another call to her landline or cell phone, and while brushing her teeth she stands in the bathroom doorway, eyeing both devices.

After rinsing with an astringent, Kate removes her bra and puts on a tank top, then exchanges her boy shorts for a pair of loose-fitting boxers.

In bed, she takes one last look at her devices before switching off the light and getting under the covers.

It takes a while, however, for her to relax enough to even begin the process of falling asleep.

TWENTY-THREE

At seven, Kate is dropping Max and Callie off next door when Maria exits through her back door and approaches Kate's Subaru.

Maria offers a quick wave, and Kate lowers her driver's-door window.

"Hey," Maria says. "I haven't heard from you since my text the other night about the job. Is everything okay?"

Max and Callie exit the vehicle and pass Maria on their way toward the back door. Callie has been ignoring her mother all morning, so only Max says goodbye, though Kate makes a point of wishing both her children a good day, and to do so by name.

Then she says to Maria, "Yes, sorry. I've been scrambling. Everything is fine. When do you start?"

"Monday. So you're not upset with me? Because it kind of felt like you were maybe ignoring me."

"No, not at all."

"Any idea yet what you're going to do—kids-wise, I mean?"

"It's all sorted out, actually. Rebecca's coming for the rest of the school year."

"Really? That's great."

"I hope so."

"Well, I'm glad you and I are good. You had me worried."

"Sorry. It wasn't intentional."

Maria takes a step closer and speaks in a conspiratorial half whisper. "Oh, and Derek has this notion that he and I should host a potluck family dinner this Saturday night. He wants to invite as many people as possible—neighbors, former clients. I think he thinks he can drum up some pity jobs if people know he's in a bad way. Anyway, he told me to invite you and to tell you to invite anyone you want—your father-in-law, Eddie, anyone else from the department you can think of."

"Okay," Kate says. "Is your house going to hold that many people?"

"No, but he seems to think it's going to be an indoor-outdoor kind of thing. I mean, I guess it's not the worst idea, right? You know, unless it rains."

"Sounds like it might be fun, but also a lot of work for you."

"Yeah, exactly."

"I'll help out if you need."

Maria smiles. "Oh God, that would be great. When is Rebecca getting here?"

"Tomorrow at some point. I'm taking a personal day, so I can get everything ready. Maybe I'll take one Friday, too. If I do, I could help you get ready then."

"That would be amazing."

"We'll talk more about it later, though, okay? I'm running a little late."

Maria takes several steps back. "Yes, yes, go."

Kate checks her rearview mirror as she shifts into reverse. "Thanks." Easing out the clutch, she backs down the driveway and pulls out into the street, and after a quick wave to her friend, she drives off.

———

The first text comes through during third period, but Kate doesn't see it until she checks her phone in the five minutes she has between that period and fourth.

The number isn't recognizable as one belonging to someone she knows, and the area code isn't one that Kate is familiar with.

Since she is waiting on a text from Rebecca regarding tomorrow's arrival time, Kate at first assumes this is that message, only sent from a different phone. After all, Rebecca changes cell phones often, generally every time she leaves one place for another, so it would be in keeping with that habit for her to make the switch now.

This text, however, is not what Kate was expecting.

Missed you last night.

For a moment Kate is uncertain what to do. Should she inform the sender that he has the wrong number? Or maybe first ask who the sender is? The words strike her as possibly being in reference to some kind of intimate gathering, though on second thought she supposes it could be otherwise—a friend telling another friend that his or her absence from some event was noticed.

Of course, there is no one in Kate's life with whom she has any intimacy—the closest would be Maria—and no one, not even her neighbor, was expecting Kate's presence anywhere last night.

Still, the timing isn't something Kate can ignore—a strange text sent to her cell the morning after two late-night hang-ups, and just days after an unnerving act of vandalism.

With only a few minutes between classes, and needing to use the restroom, Kate decides to hold out hope that the simplest explanation is the most likely one, that this is nothing more than an innocent missive sent to a wrong number.

And anyway, there really isn't anything that she could do about it right now.

Following fifth period is Kate's lunch break, and sitting at her desk with a salad she brought from home, she retrieves her phone from her top desk drawer with the intention of texting Maria to ask whether there was anything specific she wants Kate to bring on Saturday. Also, there is still the matter of finding out from Rebecca when she intends to arrive, which Kate realizes will require a prompting text from her.

Placing the phone faceup on her desk, Kate sees on the unlocked display the same unrecognizable phone number, and below it, a preview of a second message.

Maybe I'll see you soon?

Kate unlocks the phone and opens the actual message, but it contains no more than the five words visible in the preview.

Again, Kate is unsure how to proceed. Does the fact that a follow-up message has been sent increase the likelihood of this being an innocent mistake or decrease it?

But she is skilled at compartmentalizing things while teaching—commanding a classroom filled with high school juniors and seniors requires a level of focus equal to that of a lion tamer—so she tells herself that she can't be bothered with this now.

And anyway, the thought of engaging a sender who might have bad intentions triggers a rush of fear.

Instead, she first texts her question to Maria, and then sends a request for an ETA to Rebecca, after which she resumes eating her salad as she awaits replies.

To Kate's surprise, Rebecca is the first to respond, doing so within a minute of Kate having sent her request.

Landing at JFK tomorrow morning. Planning on taking an early-afternoon train. Not sure yet which one. Can I let you know?

Kate responds, Of course. Will you need to be picked up at the station?

Rebecca replies, I'll call a Lyft.

Kate keys in and sends, Are you sure?

Rebecca's response is a thumbs-up emoji. In keeping with Kate's belief that the appearance of an emoji in a text exchange is a sign-off, she sends the "okay" emoji and puts the phone down.

As she continues to eat, though, Kate is aware of a steady feeling of unease—a tightness in her chest—but she attributes it to the fact that communicating with her sister in such a casual manner is not something she is accustomed to. More than that, it is antithetical to all the steps she has taken over the past two-plus decades designed to establish ever clearer and harder boundaries.

To suddenly put herself in the position of trusting her sister—never mind making arrangements for a prolonged visit while maintaining a civil tone—is a transition she finds less than easy to make, or even natural, for that matter.

But she knows that this is learned behavior and therefore can be unlearned, given enough time and consistent effort.

After finishing lunch and using the restroom again, Kate decides to make use of the last few minutes of her break to take a screenshot of the two texts and forward them to Sabrowsky, along with a request that he look up the number for her if he could. She also mentions the two late-night phone calls, just as an FYI.

Sabrowsky responds immediately.

Will check out and get back to you. Everything okay otherwise?

Kate texts and sends, Yes. All quiet.

She then informs Sabrowsky of Maria and Derek's party on Saturday, telling him that he has been invited. His reply to that doesn't come as quickly.

Cool.

TWENTY-FOUR

Kate is driving home at four thirty when Sabrowsky calls her cell.

"Hey, Eddie."

"I figured I'd wait till you were out of work before I got back to you."

"No problem."

"The number you sent me is a prepaid cell phone that was sold in Trenton, New Jersey, two years ago. The fact that it's a prepaid phone, as opposed to one that would be easily traceable to a specific individual through a contract with a carrier, is a pretty good indication that whoever sent the two texts is intent on maintaining anonymity. That puts the odds that those texts are an innocent mistake at close to zero."

Kate says, "Shit."

"I tried to call the number from the station, figured it wouldn't hurt for Westport PD to show up on the Caller ID, but the call went straight to voice mail, which means the phone is likely shut off now. An easy solution to this would be for you to block the number, but I'm thinking maybe you should let it ride another day or two, see if anything more comes through—something more definitive."

"What do you mean by 'definitive'?"

"Something less vague and more explicit, like a threat or a comment of a sexual nature, that kind of thing. While we can get some cell-related information without a warrant, it wouldn't really help us pinpoint the exact location of the phone when the texts were sent. To get that kind of detailed data, we'd need a warrant, and no judge is going to issue one based on the texts you received."

"I'm not really sure I'd want to see anything threatening or sexual show up on my cell phone, Eddie."

"No, you're right," Sabrowsky says. "I get it. Just block the number, then."

"There's nothing else you can do?"

"I'm afraid not. One of the problems we're facing is that the phone was sold two years ago, so it's not like we can go to the point of purchase and take a look at the store surveillance tape. Nobody holds on to surveillance videos that long. And for all we know, since the phone was originally sold back then, it's possible its current user bought it secondhand. Anyway, I seriously doubt that whoever is fucking with you actually texted you from his home."

"What about the calls last night from the unknown number?"

"Those are traceable, but we'd need a court order for that, and again, a pair of late-night hang-ups isn't going to cut it with a judge. And chances are we'd probably come up with the same number anyway, or the number of another prepaid cell phone that was purchased anonymously years ago in another state and is now shut off. One thing we could do is I could come over now and we could star-sixty-seven from your landline, but only if last night's call was the last one your landline received. The way telemarketers are these days, though, you've probably gotten ten calls while you were at work. That's how many my home phone gets every day. And of course, we can't star-sixty-seven them from your cell because I just called it."

"But if the phone he called from is shut off, what would calling them back get us anyway?"

"Exactly."

After a pause, Kate says, "What the fuck is going on, Eddie? Why is this happening?"

"I'm sorry, Katie; I wish I knew. But this is another reason to eliminate some neighborhood kid as our guy. And to me this is a long way for a student or coworker with a grudge to go. I hate to say this, but it's starting to look to me like a . . ." He trails off.

"Like a what, Eddie?"

"Like a professional operation."

"What the hell does that mean?"

"Maybe 'professional' was the wrong word. I'm just saying that whoever is behind this knows what he's doing—so far, at least. Contacting you from phones that can't be traced to an individual, which is saying a lot in this day and age. Texts that wouldn't be perceived as threatening or harassing by a judge, but are weird enough to unnerve you. No one is perfect, though, Katie, so he's going to make a mistake at some point, and we just need to wait for that. In the meantime, I've ordered the camera equipment, and I should get it by Monday. I've already taken the day off so I'll be able to install it. All you need to do is hang on till then. Obviously since there has been an escalation, Chief O'Neil will continue posting one of us on your street between now and when I've gotten the equipment up and running."

Kate is silent, driving with one hand on the wheel and the other bridged across her forehead.

Sabrowsky asks, "You there?"

"Yeah," Kate answers. She shakes her head. "I guess since there hadn't been anything since Sunday, I convinced myself that this had blown over."

"And that to me is another indication that we're dealing with someone who knows what he's doing."

"How do you mean?"

"He strikes, and then he backs off long enough for you to think 'maybe it's over and done, maybe I can relax.' That way when he strikes again, you shoot right back up from a state of calm to terror. It's basic psyops."

"Psyops?"

"Psychological warfare."

"Jesus, Eddie."

"I'm sorry, Katie. I think it's important that we don't turn a blind eye to any possibility right now, no matter how uncomfortable it may be."

Speechless, all Kate can do is shake her head.

After a moment, Sabrowsky says, "Listen, maybe Leo should stay with you for a while. Or maybe you and the twins should go live with him."

"I'm not giving up my home," Kate says. "And anyway, Rebecca is coming to stay."

"Really? When is she getting there?"

"Tomorrow."

"Well, at least that'll be one more adult on the property," Sabrowsky says. "I'm assuming she's staying in the house, since the cottage is rented."

"She is. It's going to be a tight fit, but all of us at Leo's house would be even tighter."

"Is she going to be at Maria and Derek's party?"

"Probably, yeah. I mean, with everything that's going on, I wouldn't want her hanging out in the house all alone. But you're still coming, right?"

"I think so."

"I know it might be weird for you to see her again, but please come. I haven't told him yet, but Leo is invited, too. I'm sure he'd like the chance to spend some time with you."

"Yeah, I would like that, too," Sabrowsky says. "I forgot who's watching your place tonight, but if you want me to I can find out and switch with them."

"You don't have to do that."

"I don't mind."

"If I were scared, I'd maybe want you to do that."

"You're not scared?"

"I'm more pissed off than anything. I really don't need this shit. But we're safe, right? The twins and me? There's someone living in the cottage, there's a cop parked on my street at night. And like you said, all I have to do is make it till Monday."

"Listen, if any of us thought you were in actual physical danger, we'd drag the three of you out of that house and hide you somewhere very safe. I'm serious. And it's good that you're pissed, because that means your wannabe tormentor is failing. Just keep living your life; that's the best thing you can do. I'll try the number a couple of more times tonight. If it doesn't go straight to voice mail, that means it's on, in which case we can find the general location. At least we'll know if the fucker is local or out of state. It's not much, but it's a start."

Kate takes in a breath, then lets it out and says, "Thanks, Eddie."

"Have you blocked that number?"

"Not yet, but I will the minute I get home. And maybe I'll unplug my landline for tonight."

"I think that's a good idea." Sabrowsky pauses. "Hey, I'm sorry I said that stuff about psychological warfare. You know me; I say things without thinking first. This is just someone being a nuisance. And maybe this isn't a long way for some former student or colleague to go after all. You can find out how to do pretty much anything on the internet now, this shit included. We'll just keep putting up obstacles, and if our guy doesn't give up, then he'll eventually trip over one. And when he does, I'll be there to nail his ass."

Even though Kate knows that Sabrowsky is backtracking to put her at ease, she is grateful for the note of optimism. His change in perspective allows her to feel less overwhelmed by these disturbing events.

"I appreciate that, Eddie. I really do."

"We're family, Katie. We've known each other forever, right? In fact, I realized the other day that it was thirty years ago this summer that I first met you and Rebecca."

"First of all, that's not possible," Kate teases. "I'm only twenty-seven."

Sabrowsky laughs. "Yeah, you and me both."

Kate makes the turn onto Old Town Road. "I'm almost at Maria's," she says.

"I'll let you go. If I find anything out, I'll give you a call."

"Okay. And I'll see you Saturday."

"Yeah, if not sooner. Hang in there."

"I will."

———

Minutes later, with Max and Callie in the back seat, Kate is steering her Subaru past a freshly mowed lawn that is clear of a winter's worth of fallen twigs and branches.

She feels a rush of excitement at the sight of her suddenly clutter-free yard, only realizing at this moment that its state of disarray has been weighing on her since spring began.

Jack's Wrangler is parked in its space beside the cottage, and once Kate is inside her house, she calls Jack's cell to thank him and invite him over for dinner, as promised.

"Can I take a rain check?" he says.

"Yes, of course. Everything okay?"

"Yeah. I have to make another run up to New Hampshire. I just got the call a few minutes ago."

Kate does quick math in her head—it is almost five o'clock now, so Jack wouldn't arrive in New Hampshire until at least nine, and if he stayed an hour like he had last time, he wouldn't be getting back here until around two in the morning.

The excitement she'd felt moments ago is replaced by disappointment. "That sucks," she says. "I mean, that you have to do all that driving." It is on the tip of her tongue to ask why he has to return to New Hampshire, but instead she says, "If you haven't eaten already, I

175

can make you a sandwich. You must be hungry after working out in the yard all day."

"I'll grab something on the way. But thanks."

"Of course. And thank you for doing such a great job."

"Happy to do it. It felt good to do something for a change. I needed that."

To Kate's surprise, she is reluctant to end the call. But as she is scrambling for something to say to keep it going, Jack speaks.

"I should really get going now. I'll probably hit rush-hour traffic on I-95."

"Of course. Drive safe."

"I will. Have a good night."

"You too."

Ending the call, Kate heads into her bedroom to change out of her work clothes. Dressed in jeans, a loose-fitting T-shirt, and sneakers, she returns to the kitchen and begins making dinner, but then remembers that she needs to block the number that the two odd texts were sent from.

Once that is done, she resumes putting together tonight's dinner salad.

Five minutes after she ended the call with Jack, she hears his Jeep start up and then drive off.

———

Kate adds disconnecting the landline extension in the kitchen to her bedtime routine. In her bedroom, she disconnects the extension on her nightstand as well, and then decides to do something she has never done before: set her cell phone to "Do Not Disturb."

Between now and tomorrow morning she will be cut off from everyone, which, of course, includes anyone who may want to upset her.

Any discomfort caused by the thought of such a prolonged isolation, however, is allayed by the promise of six hours of undisturbed sleep.

And anyway, what are the chances of any of the few people in her life needing to get hold of her tonight?

———

Kate is dreaming of Leif when her alarm goes off.

Pressing the snooze button, she rolls onto her back and lies still, hoping that she will fall right back to sleep and return to that unfinished dream.

But she is still awake, and barely hanging on to the memory of that dream, when her alarm goes off again nine minutes later.

The first thing she does after sitting up is check her cell phone for any messages or missed calls. To her relief, there are none. Reconnecting her landline, she then rises and walks to the bathroom, taking her cell off "Do Not Disturb" as she goes.

A few minutes after that, she is in the kitchen, starting the coffee maker. The thoughts of Leif, as well as the feelings the dream of him stirred, are gone by the time Kate has her mug filled. Taking her first few sips, she crosses through the living room to check that the police SUV is still parked on her street.

It is, but the parking space alongside the cottage is empty. A rush of concern moves through her, but she tells herself to remain calm, that there are a number of reasons that would explain why Jack isn't back yet, the most likely being that he decided to wait until morning to make the four-hour-long return trip.

Her first instinct is to text him, but then she realizes that 5:20 a.m. is probably too early for that. Her second thought is to check the landline's Caller ID, though she quickly dismisses that as well since it wouldn't show any incoming numbers that arrived while she slept because she unplugged both phones from their wall jacks.

And anyway, she only gave her cell phone number to her tenant. Of course, Jack could have looked up the number to her house phone, but why would he go to the trouble of doing that?

It takes a few moments, but Kate is able to set her worries aside. Jack is a grown man and can take care of himself. And if his reason for spending the night in New Hampshire had nothing to do with sleep, well, that is none of her business.

Since she has taken a personal day, she won't have to rush through the next hour, getting ready for work, before Max and Callie wake up.

She can do whatever she wants with this time, but her list of projects and chores does not interest her. She considers doing absolutely nothing, but that isn't really in her nature, and never has been.

What does interest her is the unfinished dream of her husband—or more specifically, the lingering arousal that has only increased as she has become more awake.

Once Rebecca arrives this afternoon, there won't be a lot of privacy—this Kate knows, so it's now or never.

Leaving her coffee mug beside the microwave so she can reheat it later, Kate returns to her bedroom, closing and locking the door behind her before stepping to the half-open window, shutting it and then the blinds.

She can't remember the last time she's taken care of herself. Certainly it had to be before the recent turmoil started—well before it, more than likely. And no doubt it was a similar dream that put the need in her.

A dream of Leif pleasuring her, dominating her with his strength, his powerful body pressing down on hers, his mouth covering hers, muffling her gasps . . .

Removing her boxers and dropping them to the floor, Kate gets back under the still-warm covers. Sitting up, she pulls off her tank top and tosses it aside, then lies down, her head propped up by two pillows, the blankets over her.

It isn't long before she gets overheated and kicks down the blankets, exposing herself to the cool morning air. The climax she chases is elusive, however, and though thoughts of Leif were what got her started, she will need something else—something *more*—to get her the rest of the way.

In dire situations such as these, Kate has occasional thoughts of Maria, though that act has less to do with attraction and more to do with the fact that her neighbor is the only person with whom she has shared any kind of intimacy recently, which for Kate is critical.

So there were times that she would imagine an experienced Maria, skillfully and lovingly tending to her, their eyes locked, and though doing so now brings her closer, it's not what she needs to put her over the top.

Growing more desperate, Kate adds Derek to the mix, but only briefly, as he is as selfish in her fantasy as he is in reality.

She then replaces him with Jack—there is no other male in her life with whom she feels any kind of closeness—and focuses on a scenario in which she and Jack and Maria are three entangled bodies on a bed, but not this bed, a hotel bed, a Manhattan hotel bed, the city lights beyond the row of floor-to-ceiling windows the room's only illumination, and the reflection of Kate being touched by two pairs of hands, watched by two sets of eyes, doted on by two expert mouths clearly visible on the glass.

Her climax finally arrives, causing her body to shudder and a light sweat to break out on her skin, but once the overwhelming pleasure passes into relief, Kate feels a rush of embarrassment at her choice of fantasy and laughs to herself.

She isn't surprised that tears come once the embarrassment has faded—the sudden tightness in her throat was all the forewarning she needed. But this second reaction, an all-too-common occurrence, is also to be expected.

Nor is she surprised by the speed with which an acute sorrow overtakes her.

What does surprise her, though, is the sense of peacefulness she feels once her crying jag eventually ends. Lying still, naked and spent and utterly exhausted, she lingers in this strange calm for as long as she can hang on to it.

———

It isn't until after nine that Kate hears the sound of a vehicle rolling down her driveway.

She is upstairs in Callie's room, putting a fresh set of sheets on the bed, and can see the cottage from her daughter's window.

The vehicle is Jack's Wrangler, and Kate watches as he walks to the cottage, unlocks the door, and enters.

As she continues making the bed, Kate glances out the window several times, only stopping when she sees that all the curtains have been drawn, no doubt so Jack can get some sleep.

She wonders about his night—why he is called away like this, and what kept him from coming back during the night, as he said he would.

By ten Kate has gotten the frame of the folding cot down from the attic and set up in Max's room. Then she returns for the mattress, which is encased in a plastic protector. Kate unzips the cover and removes the mattress and, using her only spare set of sheets and extra pillow, makes up the cot.

After that she clears Callie's closet of winter clothes, storing them neatly in several plastic bags before transferring them to a shelf in the basement. The idea of Rebecca and Callie sharing a closet doesn't concern Kate—the two will, no doubt, spend plenty of time together behind closed doors, as they often do, talking about whatever it is they talk about.

At eleven Kate begins to wonder why she hasn't heard from Rebecca yet. It wouldn't be uncharacteristic of her sister to completely blow her off—as in not show up at all. Nor would it be unlike Rebecca to forget about the text she'd promised to send, and simply arrive, unannounced, when it suited her.

Kate is growing agitated, but she is aware that her reaction is probably more of a conditioned response than a proportionate one.

She wonders if she will ever be able to break that habit and offer her sister the same benefit of the doubt that she offers others.

Despite her being conscious of the true nature of her state of mind, Kate's aggravation is nonetheless bordering on anger by noontime.

She is about to give up on the whole thing—an all-too-familiar act of self-preservation—when her cell phone chimes.

The incoming text, from Rebecca's current number, reads: Sorry for the delay! Catching the 2:34 train. Should be there by four.

Kate takes a breath, lets it out. It is official—Rebecca is actually on her way—and there are, suddenly, only three and a half hours of quiet left.

Three and a half hours before a chaos she has never been able to control invades her home.

She waits a moment before sending her reply. We will be here.

A follow-up text comes through a moment later, its words catching Kate off guard.

Looking forward to seeing you.

Unable to think of a reply that doesn't feel forced, Kate decides not to send one.

Pocketing her phone, she then checks her list of projects for something that will keep her occupied—and free from any and all thought—for these remaining hours.

TWENTY-FIVE

A few minutes before four, Max and Callie are seated on the front steps, waiting.

Kate is inside, squeezing in one final chore—shifting around the contents of the refrigerator to free up space, should Rebecca require some kind of specialty food.

As she works, Kate composes in her mind a list of several other boundary lines she will need to draw and point out to her sister. While in residency in the cottage, Rebecca was free to live her own life her way, which usually meant, sooner or later, entertaining men. And though Rebecca was for the most part monogamous—she tended to get involved with one man during her six-month stay—there was the occasional year when she would, over the course of her stay, burn through several relationships, many of them tumultuous.

Arguments that took place inside the cottage, even in the winter months when windows were closed, often could be heard in certain parts of the main house.

So, too, at times, could the sound of a sexual encounter.

Whatever Rebecca did in the cottage was her own business, but obviously such behavior would not be acceptable while she occupied Callie's bedroom. Knowing too well that Rebecca has no fondness at all for rules, Kate isn't looking forward to having that discussion. And perhaps with any other person Kate wouldn't have to point out such basic courtesies. But everyone who knows Rebecca understands that she is driven by impulse, and always has been.

It was, after all, Rebecca's lack of discipline that first drove the once-close sisters apart.

And it was that same character-defining flaw that gave rise to Kate's own often-rigid code of conduct.

———

Kate is washing her hands in the kitchen sink when she hears Max and Callie leave their post outside the front door and hurry down the pathway to the driveway.

It is the sound of a car door closing a moment later, followed by the excited voices of her children, that causes Kate to shut her eyes and brace herself.

Then she dries her hands with a towel, which she returns to the rack mounted on a cabinet door. After first making sure the towel is folded evenly and hanging neatly, she steps toward the back door, opens it, and exits.

From the back steps she sees a dark Chevy sedan parked at the rear of the driveway. Its driver, a neatly dressed man in his midtwenties, is lifting two suitcases from the trunk. Standing a few feet from the rear bumper, Rebecca is embracing both Max and Callie. She kisses first the boy on the top of the forehead and then the girl.

Right away, Kate takes note of the fact that her sister's appearance has changed a little in the two years since they last saw each other.

Though Rebecca's mane of thick blonde hair remains, it is cut to a shoulder length now instead of hanging to her lower back, which gives her more of a professional look, as opposed to the aura of a free spirit she has always conveyed.

Kate also observes that Rebecca, whose build has always been a blend of athletic and curvy—something Kate secretly envied—is now decidedly more slender, almost to the point of being slight.

It is, however, when Rebecca finally lifts her head and looks toward her sister standing at the foot of the back steps that Kate sees the most significant change.

Her older sister's face is as beautiful as ever—precise features, radiant skin, striking sky-blue eyes.

Everything that Kate's isn't.

What is different, however, is the fact that Rebecca is smiling—not just smiling politely, as the two sisters had been taught to do whenever greeting another, but smiling in a display of genuine happiness, which is something Kate has never before associated with the often-troubled woman she'd grown up with, only to grow apart from.

Kate cannot recall anyone—with the exception, at times, of Max—ever being so pleased to see her.

Startled and puzzled, Kate stares silently at her sister.

Still smiling, Kate's children still clutching at her, Rebecca says, "Hey, Katie."

Eventually, Kate replies, "Hello, Becca."

The driver places the two suitcases on the edge of the driveway, then returns to the rear of his vehicle to close the trunk. Rebecca thanks him before ushering Max and Callie onto the grass so that the driver has enough room at the end of the driveway to turn his vehicle around.

As he opens the driver's door, the young man pauses and nods to Rebecca. "Good luck."

Rebecca thanks him again, and she and the children remain still on the grass until the man drives off.

Then Rebecca says to the twins, "Do you guys think you can carry your auntie Becca's suitcases?"

The two are more than happy to do so. Kate briefly takes note of her excited daughter's eagerness to help before resuming eye contact with her sister.

"How was the trip?"

"It was good. The past few days have been long ones, though. Rushing to put some of my things into storage, giving away the stuff I'll never use, that kind of thing. I'm glad to finally be here."

Rebecca and the twins start toward the steps.

"I'm about to make dinner," Kate says. "Chicken and rice with tomatoes. Hope that's okay with you."

"That casserole Grandma used to make?"

"Yes."

"Oh, that sounds perfect."

As Rebecca moves closer, Kate observes yet one more thing that is different about her sister.

Her breasts—which have been another cause of envy for Kate from when she was ten—are notably smaller.

Though surprised by what she sees—alarmed, almost—Kate keeps her glance brief.

Turning, she climbs to the top of the steps and holds open the back door as the twins, each lugging a suitcase, lumber in a single file up the stairs, followed by their aunt.

Rebecca pauses to look at the backyard. Scanning it, she smiles fondly until the swing set, with its eight hanging chains, comes into her line of sight, and then a look of concern crosses her face, canceling any hint of joy.

She looks at Kate, who observed the sudden shift in her sister's mood and understood its cause.

Recognizing that there could only be one question on Rebecca's mind now—*Did the vandals do that?*—Kate nods.

Visibly disturbed, Rebecca takes one more look at the row of empty chains, and then reclaims her smile, obviously for the sake of the children, and resumes her climb upward.

After dinner, Kate cleans the kitchen table, and then sits Callie and Max down at it to do their homework. She tells them that she is going to help Auntie Becca get settled, and heads upstairs.

Through Callie's open bedroom door, Kate can see that Rebecca is unpacking, her two suitcases laid flat on the single bed and several summer blouses draped over her left forearm.

Kate knocks gently on the doorframe, drawing her sister's attention.

"Hey," Rebecca says. "Come in."

Kate enters and walks to the foot of the bed. "Can I help you unpack?"

Rebecca answers, "I've got it, thanks." She takes a quick look around. "It's weird to be back in this room," she says.

When they were children, first spending their summers here before becoming year-round residents, this room had been Rebecca's, while Max's room had been Kate's—a detail that Kate hadn't recalled until now.

Rebecca adds, "It's crazy how much smaller it seems."

No longer needing to play the role of beloved and carefree aunt, as she did during dinner, Rebecca is once again displaying the unusual behaviors Kate initially observed. She seems quieter, less frantic, and as she moves from the bed to the closet, there is a steadiness in the way she carries herself that only deepens Kate's confusion.

Putting the blouses on hangers, Rebecca says, "I want to ask you about what's been going on, if you don't mind."

Though Kate isn't eager to talk about that, she says, "Okay, what do you want to know?"

"When did it start?"

"Last week," Kate says. It takes her a moment to pinpoint the exact day. "A week ago last Sunday, actually."

"You said they broke into the cottage and stuck a knife into the wall."

"The bedroom wall, yeah."

The blouses hung, Rebecca returns to the bed. She considers what Kate has told her, and then asks, "And they cut all the seats off the swings?"

"Yeah."

Rebecca thinks about that, too, before asking, "What else?"

"Someone threw a rock at the living room window."

"Did it shatter?"

"It left a crack. A big one. But Derek was able to replace it the next day."

Rebecca nods. "That's good. What else?"

"That's it as far as physical damage goes. I had a few hang-ups the other night, and then two weird texts the next day."

"Weird how?"

"Someone saying they're sorry they missed me last night, that they hope they'll see me soon, that kind of thing."

"Couldn't those texts have been meant for someone else?"

"Eddie traced them to one of those prepaid cell phones. Certain details about the whole thing led him to rule out the texts being a mistake."

Again, Rebecca nods thoughtfully. "Anything since then?"

"No, quiet." Kate pauses. "Something's on your mind, Becca. What is it?"

"Nothing. I'm just bothered by this whole thing, trying to understand it. Like you said, it's creepy. But I hope my being here makes you feel a little safer."

Kate can't find it in herself to give her sister the response she is seeking, so instead she shrugs and says, "The more, the merrier, right?"

Rebecca carries two pairs of jeans toward the closet, but this time she pauses at the window to look out at the cottage. "Speaking of, what's your tenant like?"

"He's nice."

Rebecca hangs the jeans, and then returns to the bed. Smiling slyly, she says, "Oh, yeah?"

"Yeah," Kate says. "Listen, now might be a good time for us to go over some rules."

Rebecca picks up several bras, all of which, Kate notes, are padded. "I figured you'd want to talk about this, Katie. But first, I need you to know that I'm not the person I used to be. I had a medical thing I went through, and when I came out the other end, things were very different for me."

"What kind of medical thing?"

Rebecca looks at Kate. "Breast cancer."

"Jesus, Becca. When?"

"It started about two years ago."

"Why didn't you say something?"

Rebecca tilts her head to one side, as if to say, *Are you seriously asking that?*

Kate's initial response is defensiveness, though she is able to recognize it as a clear example of the learned behavior she is hoping to unlearn.

Making sure her tone is soft, Kate asks, "What happened?"

"It started with a lump. I did chemo, and everything was fine for seven or eight months, but then suddenly it was two lumps, one in each breast, so my doctor recommended a double mastectomy. That was a year ago. After that I had some reconstructive surgery."

Kate's eyes again go to the padded bras.

Aware of her sister's line of sight, Rebecca says, "Yeah, basically I'm a teenage boy now. But not having them to carry around has relieved a lot of my back problems. And the plastic surgeon did a good job with the nipple realignment."

Kate struggles for what, exactly, she should say, then finally settles on, "I'm so sorry."

"Don't be. My reaction to every problem has been to run." Rebecca smiles. "You may have noticed that."

Kate acknowledges the joke with a polite chuckle.

Rebecca continues. "But here was something I couldn't run from. I had to stay put and face it. I'd never done that before. Anyway, while I was recovering, I spent a lot of time flat on my back, thinking about the things I've done and the things I should have done and the things I wish I hadn't done. It was my long-dark-night-of-the-soul kinda thing, you know? Lots to regret and lots to get depressed about. And then one day I woke up and saw all the changes I wanted to make, laid right out in front of me like a pathway. But the thing is, it wasn't a pathway forward. It was a path into the past. And I knew in my gut that I had to follow it. I had a lot of things to make right before I had any hope of moving forward."

"That's why you wanted to come back."

Rebecca nods. "I told myself I was going to ask, try to open things up between us, and if you said no, then that was your choice and I would move on, because there were plenty of other relationships that I'd fucked up over the years and wanted to at least try to repair. If I couldn't earn your forgiveness, then at least I would be able to tell myself that I tried and maybe one day make my own peace with all the shit I did. Of course, when I called and asked, our conversation didn't go as smoothly as I wanted it to. We each fell back into our old pattern—I triggered you, you triggered me; I said something, you said something. But if I've learned one thing in the past year, it's that patterns can be broken—if you want them to be, that is. So you don't have to worry about me pulling my usual shit. I'm not here to meet anyone. I'm not looking to fuck around. I'm here to help you take care of your children. And you, if you'll let me. I'm here to be your big sister again. And if I can, I'll help you figure out what the hell is going on."

"I'm not sure there's anything you can do that Eddie isn't already doing. Leo, too."

Rebecca shrugs. "You never know, right?"

Kate is uncertain what Rebecca means by that, though she doesn't bother to ask her sister to clarify.

Rebecca makes another trip to the closet, pausing as she makes her way back again to look out at the cottage. "So he's a nice guy? Your tenant."

"Yes. Very nice."

"What's his name?"

"Jack."

Rebecca nods and returns to her suitcases. "Any potential there?"

"Potential?"

"For you? Is he attractive?"

Kate's instinct is to deny. "Haven't really thought about it. Why?"

"Two years is long enough, don't you think? I'd imagine Leif would have expected you to move on by now."

Kate isn't accustomed to discussing such matters with her sister. After all, Rebecca's tendency toward openness when it came to her relationships with men played a role in directing Kate to her desire for privacy, if not outright secrecy, when it came to the opposite sex.

After a moment, Kate says, "Not enough hours in the day for everything. That's all it is, really."

"Well, maybe I can help with that, too."

Kate nods once. "Maybe." She pauses. "Listen, I'm taking tomorrow off, too, and I'll be making a grocery run. Are you on a special diet or anything? I can grab whatever you might need."

"I can get my own food. I'm not expecting you to support me while I'm here. I have money."

"I don't mind," Kate says.

"How about I go with you?"

"Yeah, sure. If you're feeling up to it."

"Please don't think of me as fragile, Katie. I'm healthy. I worked hard to get that way."

"Okay. I'm glad."

"I was thinking of maybe taking the kids out for ice cream after I'm unpacked, if that's okay."

"Sure. It's a special occasion, right? That's if they're done with their homework in time, of course."

"You're welcome to come with us, or you can stay here and have the house to yourself for a bit. It's up to you."

"Thanks. Like I said, let's see what time they're done with their homework."

Rebecca gathers up the final contents of her suitcases—several peasant skirts and a black cocktail dress—and hangs them up in the closet, after which she looks out the window again.

She asks, "Is that him?"

Kate steps to the window. Jack is setting up his hibachi grill on the pathway. By the fact that his hair is mussed, she assumes that he has just gotten out of bed.

She answers, "Yeah, that's him."

"He's a good-looking guy," Rebecca says. "In good shape, too."

"He coached wrestling where he used to teach."

"A wrestler *and* a teacher, too. I'd say he fits the bill nicely. Is he single?"

"Divorcing, I think."

Rebecca looks at Kate. "So what are you waiting for?"

Kate turns and steps away from the window. "I'm not so sure it's smart to get involved with my tenant."

"You said he's short term, right?"

"Yeah."

"So if it doesn't work out, you wouldn't have to deal with the awkwardness for too long. Anyway, as someone who has done more than her share of not-so-smart things, I don't think going on a date would be the worst thing you could do."

"I just don't think it's in the cards right now."

Rebecca shrugs, and then steps back to the bed, closing her empty suitcases.

Kate says, "You can put those under the bed for now. I'll bring them up to the attic tomorrow. And I'll check on Max and Callie now, see how they're doing with their homework. If they're done in time, maybe I'll come with you guys."

Rebecca smiles. "I'd like that, Katie."

"Then I guess I will."

———

Kate drives them to Saugatuck Sweets, where they each enjoy an ice-cream cone while sitting at a table in the flagstone courtyard.

They return home just before seven, which leaves enough time before the twins' bedtime for a movie on Amazon Prime. Of course, Max wants to watch *Mission: Impossible*, but Callie is quick to object. Kate suggests that they let their aunt choose, and though Callie rattles off several titles that she thinks they should watch, Rebecca chooses *Four Weddings and a Funeral*, a favorite of hers. Though disappointed at first, Max and Callie are eventually won over by the decidedly British humor.

Afterward, Rebecca joins the children as they get ready for bed—brushing her teeth while standing behind Max as he brushes his, and demonstrating to Callie, for the day when the twelve-year-old is old enough to wear makeup, how best to remove it.

Fifteen minutes later, when Kate comes upstairs to say good night, she finds Max under the covers on the cot and Callie and Rebecca in the last stages of changing the sheets on Max's bed.

Kate says to her son, "That's nice of you, Max."

Silent but smiling, he nods.

"There's a reason why he's my favorite man in the whole world," Rebecca says.

Kate notes her daughter's elevated mood before wishing them both a good night and heading downstairs.

A few minutes later, Kate is seated at the kitchen table, sorting through the mail, setting the bills in one pile, credit card offers to be shredded in another, and junk mail in a third pile.

Rebecca, barefoot and dressed in yoga pants and a baggy T-shirt, enters.

"I'm going to make some tea," she says. "That okay?"

"Of course. I reorganized my cupboards a while back. Tea's now in the one to the right of the stove."

Rebecca holds up an unwrapped tea bag. "Brought my own."

Standing at the sink, she fills the teakettle from the faucet, then steps to the stove and sets the kettle on a burner as she lights it.

Kate asks, "Everybody upstairs is all settled?"

"Yes."

Kate finishes sorting the mail and stands, tossing the junk mail into the trash can.

Then she takes the pile of credit card offers from the table, places it into her workbag for shredding when she goes back on Monday, and walks to a narrow utility closet, opens it, and slides the bag onto its shelf.

From there she crosses the kitchen to the security system keypad mounted on the wall by the back door.

Rebecca asks, "You going to bed?"

"Soon. You?"

"After I drink my tea, yeah. Actually, would you mind if I took a shower?"

"You don't have to ask, Becca. I want you to think of this as your home, okay?"

"Thanks."

Kate enters the code, activating the system. Stepping away from the keypad, she looks at her sister. "You can sleep in tomorrow morning, if you want. You must be tired from your trip. I can get the kids ready for school. I'll be up anyway."

"No, it's okay. I want to do my part. And anyway, I get up early now, too."

"Are you sure?"

Rebecca nods. "Yeah."

"Okay. I'll see you in the morning, then."

"Good night."

"Night."

Kate turns to leave but stops at the door when Rebecca speaks.

"I think this might be good for us, Katie. Maybe it's finally a chance for us to be a family again. You know, in this house, like we used to be."

Kate faces her sister. "Maybe it is, yeah." She pauses. "Listen, I've been meaning to tell you that I appreciate you dropping everything and coming here."

"There wasn't really anything to drop."

"Still, I needed help and you came, so I'm grateful."

"You're my kid sister, right?"

Kate nods.

"So maybe we can put the past behind us," Rebecca says. "We can't undo what's been done, I get that. But things don't have to keep being the way they've been. That only happens because that's what people choose to let happen. You've been pissed at me and I've been pissed at you for so long, it's hard to imagine a different way of being, but I'm willing to try if you are." Rebecca shrugs. "I mean, none of us knows how long we're going to be around, do we? I'm done wasting my life. It's time for me to be what I should have been all along."

"Which is?"

"More like you. Well," she jokes, "maybe without that New England stoicism of yours. You and Grandpa, cut from the same cloth."

Kate laughs. "Yeah."

"On the other hand, I was like Grandma—too much like her for either of us, I think. Because of that we were good at working each other into a frenzy." Rebecca pauses. "I'm ashamed of how I acted back then.

We found a safe life, with two people who loved us and cared for us, and I shattered it. And I kept on shattering it. I took away what meant the most to you, and I'm sorry for that."

Though Kate opens her mouth to speak, she finds herself struggling for words.

And then she laughs.

Smiling, Rebecca asks, "What?"

"The stoic strikes again."

Rebecca nods. "It's okay. We are who we are."

The water in the teakettle begins roiling. Rebecca turns the flame off and moves the kettle to another burner, then places the tea bag into her mug and fills it.

"You're sure you don't want any, Katie? It's Sleepytime."

"I'm sure, thanks." Kate waits until Rebecca has returned the kettle to the stovetop. "And I'm sorry, too, by the way."

Rebecca looks at her. "What for?"

"Shutting you out. Keeping you at an arm's length."

"I hurt you. I didn't mean to, but I did. Why wouldn't you do that?"

"Still," Kate says.

"Well, we're here now, right?"

"Yeah."

Rebecca takes a sip of her tea, then brings the warm mug to her chest, holding it with two hands.

"I'm looking forward to tomorrow," she says.

"Mornings are hectic here."

"I'm ready for it."

"Good," Kate says. "I'm off to bed."

Rebecca raises the mug. "Me too, after this."

"Night."

"Night, Katie."

TWENTY-SIX

The next morning Rebecca is up early enough to take over getting Max and Callie ready for school, giving Kate time to get started on the laundry, which she normally tackles on Saturday but wants out of the way today since Maria and Leif's party is tomorrow and she will no doubt be asked to help out with last-minute preparations.

A second load is in the final spin cycle by the time Rebecca returns from driving Max and Callie, along with Maria's two children, to school. Together, she and Kate finish folding and putting away the first load, after which Kate transfers the completed second load from the washer to the dryer, and then puts the third and final load into the washer.

Though Rebecca said the night before that she would go grocery shopping with Kate, she instead opts to stay behind to tend to the laundry, then go for a quick two-mile run, which is a habit she started as part of her recovery.

Rebecca suggests that Kate might want to start an exercise program of her own, stating that something as basic as a thirty-minute walk three times a week can have a positive effect on both physical and mental health. Kate thanks Rebecca for the advice but dodges the subject with her standard deflection, which is that she simply doesn't know where she'd find the time.

Ten minutes later, Kate is dressed and about to leave when Rebecca stops her at the back door. Offering a one-hundred-dollar bill, she insists on paying for the extra food Kate will need to buy.

"I'm working; you're not," Kate says. "Hang on to your money."

Rebecca replies, "I'm doing okay, moneywise. Please, I want to pay my own way. It's important to me."

Though Kate is curious how it is exactly that Rebecca comes into her money, she doesn't ask, simply takes the offered bill, folding it and stuffing it into the pocket of her jeans.

Kate asks, "Can I get you anything?"

"A mix of frozen fruit? Whatever they have is fine. I like to make a giant smoothie in the morning and then pretty much nurse it all day."

"Anything else? I mean, you need a protein, don't you?"

"I get my protein powder from Amazon. I have a delivery coming tomorrow. Really, all I need is the fruit. Oh, and maybe some carrots."

"Yeah, no problem. You can always text me if you think of anything else."

As Kate heads up the driveway in the Subaru, she decides to stop at the cottage to see if she can get anything for Jack. Parking on the edge, she exits and crosses the pathway to the front door. Jack is visible through the window, seated at the long table and hunched over his phone. Kate knocks, and he sits up abruptly, clearly startled from some deep thought. Seeing Kate, he walks to the door and opens it.

"Morning, Kate."

Even before Jack speaks, Kate has gleaned from his expression and the way he is carrying himself that something is wrong.

"Morning, Jack," Kate says. "Everything okay?"

Jack answers, "Yeah," but his tone is flat. He raises his phone, briefly showing it to Kate. Visible on the screen is a text exchange, and Kate infers that it has something to do with his low mood. But that is the only explanation that Jack offers, and lowering his hand again, he asks, "What's up?"

"I'm running to the store. If there's anything you need, I'm happy to get it for you."

"No, I'm good. Thanks."

"Are you sure? It's not a problem."

"Yeah."

Whatever it is that Jack has on his mind is preventing him from making eye contact with Kate, which is something he's never had a problem doing before.

Kate asks, "Are you sure you're okay?"

"It's just . . . New Hampshire stuff, that's all."

"Ah. Do you want to talk about it?"

"No. But thanks."

Kate suddenly feels compelled to offer him something—anything—that might lighten his mood.

"Hey, so I haven't forgotten that I owe you a dinner for all the yard work. Today's going to be a little hectic, but how about tonight?"

"I don't want you to trouble yourself."

"It's no trouble. I mean, we have to eat something for dinner. It probably won't be anything fancy, not that what I made the last time was fancy."

"Another night." Jack nods to his phone again. "I might have to make another run back up to New Hampshire."

"Jesus, that sucks. But listen, my neighbors are having a big family-dinner-slash-potluck party tomorrow night. A lot of local business-people are going to be there, and I figured since you're looking for work, it might be a good opportunity for you to network."

"I'm not sure I'm up for being around a lot of people. Plus, I wouldn't want to intrude."

Kate smiles. "Enough with the don't-want-to-intrude shit, okay? Anyway, Maria told me to invite whomever I wanted. And to be honest, I'm not one for crowds, either. You and I can sit in a corner and talk all night, if you want. We'll set up a buddy system and save each other."

Jack smiles at that, though only briefly. "Thanks. I'll think about it."

"I'd really like you to come, Jack. If you can. Okay?"

"I appreciate your saying that," he says.

Kate turns to leave, then stops a few steps down the pathway. Facing Jack again, she says, "Oh, and my sister is here, in case you see someone walking around."

"Good to know," Jack says. "How's it going, by the way?"

"Not bad, actually."

"'Not bad' is good. And your other problem?"

"Nothing in the past few days."

"Maybe they got it out of their system."

"Maybe," Kate says. "And hey, we'll probably be eating around six, so if you're here and change your mind, just wander on over, okay?"

"Thanks, Kate."

———

Kate drives to the Fresh Market as if on automatic pilot, at times so lost in thought that when she becomes aware of her surroundings again, she has no memory of making certain turns and stopping at various traffic lights.

At the market, without her children in tow, she completes her shopping in fifteen minutes, including checkout—a record that leaves her feeling a sense of accomplishment.

Exiting the store and steering her cart across the parking lot, Kate spots something on the windshield of her Subaru that slows her steady pace.

Pinned beneath the driver's-side wiper blade is a piece of white paper.

As she gets nearer, she can see that the paper has been folded horizontally, and when she is ten or so steps away, she determines that there is nothing printed on the part of the paper that is visible to her.

Reaching her vehicle, she rests the nose of her cart against the rear bumper and walks to the front fender.

At first she is hesitant to even touch the paper. Of course, it could easily be a flyer for one business or another—a restaurant or car wash or window-cleaning service—but glancing at the vehicles nearest to hers, she sees that none have anything at all pinned beneath their wipers.

Finally, Kate pulls the paper free, taking one more look around as she unfolds it.

Expecting some colorful advertisement that fills the page, Kate instead finds that the letter-size paper contains only one thing—a phone number.

The number is missing an area code, and the prefix is not any of those belonging to the Westport area, though Kate realizes that it's possible a new prefix could have been assigned at some point without her having heard about it.

And while a telephone number with no name is strange enough, the number is not handwritten, so this isn't a case of someone recognizing Kate's car and leaving an impromptu note.

Whoever placed this under her windshield wiper typed it up via a word-processing program on a computer and printed it out beforehand. And wouldn't that mean this unknown person would have to know that she'd be in this parking lot at this time? At the very least, they would have needed to have this page with them in case they happened to run into her.

And then one more possibility comes to her.

Could someone have followed her here?

Kate scans the parking lot once more, this time ignoring the cars and focusing instead on the people, hoping that she might spot someone walking away—someone who stands out, perhaps, by the fact that they are trying *not* to stand out.

But everywhere she looks all she sees are shoppers like her, some arriving and others either approaching their parked vehicles or already at them and loading grocery bags inside.

Groceries in the back seat, Kate gets behind the wheel and takes a picture of the note with her phone, then texts the photo to Sabrowsky, along with the message:

Came out of the grocery store and found this on my car.

When a reply doesn't come through after a half minute, Kate tosses her phone onto the passenger seat alongside the paper and starts for home.

———

Kate returns to an empty house.

Placing two of her cloth shopping bags on the kitchen counter, she calls for Rebecca but gets no response.

Two more trips out to the car are required before she has carried everything inside, and after putting the groceries away, Kate walks through the downstairs rooms, listening, and then pauses at the foot of the stairs leading up to the second floor before doing the same with the basement stairs, both times hearing nothing at all.

It isn't her sister, however, that she is listening for.

Unnerved by what she found on her windshield, Kate finds the stillness of her home disturbing, and yet she is determined to prevent heightened anxiety from spiraling into full-blown fear.

Toward that end she chooses her preferred means of distraction: motion.

Heading upstairs to Max's bedroom, she confirms that Rebecca has, in fact, finished the laundry, just as she'd promised she would. The boy's clothes are neatly folded and put away, as are his sister's.

Opening the hallway closet across from the upstairs bathroom, Kate finds that the sheets that Rebecca and Callie had taken off Max's bed last night have been put away as well.

Even the fitted sheet is folded perfectly—a skill that has always been beyond Kate.

Back downstairs in her bedroom, Kate discovers that her clothing—underwear and T-shirts, as well as the boxers she sleeps in—are all in their respective drawers, and her jeans and slacks and cotton blouses are all on hangers in the closet.

And in her bathroom, the silk blouse that she wore last week is hanging from the shower rod, indicating that Rebecca hand-washed it before placing it there to dry.

Returning to the living room, Kate is out of places to go. Uncertain what to do, she lingers in the eerie silence for several moments.

But in the absence of an immediate purpose, she is inviting the thoughts that she does best to avoid—thoughts of loss, despair, longing, and desperation.

It is the latter she is experiencing now, an overwhelming rush of it bordering on panic, but it is a desperation born of fear, not desire.

She feels a pressure building inside her head now, as well as a tightness clamping onto her skull, as though her scalp were constricting.

The precursors of a migraine.

Hurrying to the kitchen, she fills a glass from the faucet with tepid water, downs it, and then fills another, downing close to half of that.

After catching her breath, Kate finishes what remains and sets the empty glass down in the sink, but her hands are suddenly trembling and she knocks the glass over, cracking it. She places the broken glass into a paper bag and is dropping the bag into the kitchen trash when her cell phone rings.

Fearful, she looks at her phone and sees "Eddie Sabrowsky" on the display. Relieved, though only slightly, Kate quickly answers and says, "Hey, Eddie."

He asks, "Are you home right now?"

"Yeah."

"Good. Chief O'Neil and Leo are on their way. They should be there in a few minutes."

"What's going on?"

"Just sit tight, okay? Are the kids in school?"

"Yeah. Why?"

"Is there any chance Maria can pick them up?"

"What for?"

"I don't have a lot of time to explain, Katie. Can you call and ask her to do it?"

"Are my children in danger, Eddie?"

"No, they're not. I promise. This is Leo's idea. You know how he is."

"Then if they're not in danger, what's going on?"

"We've found something, Katie. They'll explain when they get there. I'm pulling up to my destination now, so I need to go. Just call Maria and have her get the kids."

"Eddie, wait—"

Before Kate can complete her sentence, the call is ended.

Kate quickly navigates to Maria's number and is about to place the call when she spots Rebecca returning from her run.

Moments later, still in her running clothes and sneakers, and with instructions to text Kate the moment she is on her way back with the twins, Rebecca pulls out of the driveway in Kate's Subaru as Kate calls the school's main office, informing the woman who answers that there is a family emergency and that Max and Callie's aunt will be picking them up in fifteen minutes. Kate manages to keep any hint of urgency from her voice, and as she and the woman speak, a ding comes through her phone's earpiece, indicating that a text has arrived.

Once she ends the call, Kate opens the messaging app, and though she is expecting nothing more than a text from Maria or maybe Leo or even Sabrowsky, she instead finds herself looking at a familiar series of numbers—the very numbers, in fact, that were printed on the paper she found on her windshield, only now they are preceded by an area code.

The text preview contains no words, only a small thumbnail of an attached photograph.

Kate's heart is pounding as she touches the preview with her thumb, opening the message.

What appears on her display shocks and terrifies her.

It is a photograph, taken at nighttime, of a lit window, which Kate immediately recognizes as her bedroom window, its blinds lowered just below the halfway point.

But clearly visible in that small, nearly square frame is Kate, facing the window and wearing only the loose-fitting boxer shorts she sleeps in.

Though the photo's quality isn't the best, it is good enough for her to see that she is holding her tank top with two hands.

More than that, her face is clearly recognizable, as are her bare breasts.

The first thing her panicked mind scrambles to understand is what she was doing when this photo was taken, and by her position in the room and what she is wearing and the fact that she is holding a shirt, she concludes that she was standing beside her nightstand and getting ready for bed—her nightly ritual.

Still staring at the photo, Kate next wonders when this photo was taken, though that frantic thought is interrupted by the arrival of another text.

Originating from that same number, this message contains only four words.

I finally caught you.

TWENTY-SEVEN

Kate is seated at the kitchen table, Chief O'Neil directly across from her. Leaning against the counter a few feet away, Leo Burke stands with his arms folded across his chest.

On the table, midway between Kate and O'Neil, is Kate's cell phone.

Both the chief and her father-in-law have taken a look at the photo Kate received, adding humiliation to her horror.

And though the text Rebecca promised to send as she and the twins were heading back home came through as Leo was placing the phone on the tabletop, the relief that news brought simply meant that Kate's feelings of violation and fear were free to come into clearer focus.

O'Neil says, "Obviously, that photo was taken from the woods behind your house. And by the quality, I'd say it was taken with a camera equipped with a telescopic lens, which means whoever took it wasn't standing on the edge of your yard. He was well into the woods."

"So much for the patrolmen parked on the street," Burke says.

O'Neil ignores the comment and asks Kate, "Any idea when that may have been taken?"

Kate shakes her head. "No."

O'Neil pauses before continuing. "The texts you received the other night—'Missed you last night' and 'Maybe I'll see you soon'—I can't help but wonder if that's what 'I finally caught you' is referring to. Or at least, that's what we're supposed to think, that your stalker has been out there for several nights, trying to get a photo of you in your bedroom."

Leo Burke says, "Of course that's what we're supposed to think."

Kate remembers that she closed the blinds not this morning but the morning before, prior to acting on the arousal she awakened with, which means that the previous night she had left the blinds partially open.

"Now that I think about it," she says, "I'm guessing that could have been two nights ago."

O'Neil asks, "What makes you think that?"

Kate shrugs, then says, "I remember closing the blinds yesterday morning."

"Do you generally close them every night?"

"Not if I'm sleeping with the window open, no."

"The window looked shut in the photo."

"I must have forgotten that night. Which I know is dumb of me, considering what's been going on."

O'Neil says, "How could you have known someone would trudge through those woods and take a picture like that?"

"It was still dumb of me," Kate says flatly. She pauses. "Anyway, won't the photo have metadata or something that will tell you when it was taken?"

"It should, unless the file was scrubbed prior to it being sent. Of course, to make that determination, we'll need a copy of it."

"So I need to forward it to you."

"Unfortunately, yes."

The idea of sending that photo to anyone causes Kate even more anxiety. She closes her eyes briefly and lets out a breath.

"I'm sorry," O'Neil says.

Leo Burke, his arms still folded across his chest, shifts his weight, and then asks Kate, "You normally go shopping on Saturday morning, don't you?"

"Yes."

"Why did you go today instead? Why are you home on a Friday?"

"I took a personal day yesterday and today. Yesterday Rebecca arrived, and I wanted to be here. And today I was going to help Maria get her house ready for tomorrow."

"What's tomorrow?"

"Another one of their big potluck-dinner things. I figured I'd get my shopping out of the way today."

O'Neil says, "The fact that the note you found on your windshield was printed out before means that whoever left it must have had it in his possession prior to arriving at the parking lot."

"I thought of that, too."

"And the fact that Friday isn't when you typically do your grocery shopping means that you were either followed or that somehow the person who left the note knew you were going to be there."

Burke adds, "Or he could have printed it out days ago and has been driving around with it, waiting for his chance."

O'Neil keeps his focus on Kate. "Did you notice anyone following you?"

"No."

"Is there something that maybe seemed like nothing at the time but stands out in your mind now? Someone in the store, maybe, anything?"

Kate shakes her head. "No. I'm sorry."

"It's okay, Katie. You're doing great."

Kate nods, then looks at her father-in-law and says, "Eddie told me you wanted the kids pulled from school because you'd found something. What is it?"

Leo Burke defers to O'Neil. Kate looks back at the chief.

"Eddie is friendly with Frank Mills, the owner of the Fresh Market. He called Frank and asked if he would take a look at the surveillance video of the parking lot. Nothing official, just as a favor."

"And?"

"There's footage of someone placing the note on your windshield. It was done roughly a minute after you went inside. That could mean

Daniel Judson

he was following you and got there when you did, or that he was there, waiting for you to arrive." O'Neil removes his phone from his shirt pocket. "Frank took a short video of the tape playing on his monitor. I apologize for the quality, but Eddie is there now, getting a copy of the video from all the cameras, on disk."

O'Neil starts the video, and then hands his phone to Kate.

She watches as a male dressed in jeans and a sweatshirt, wearing a baseball cap, lifts her windshield wiper with one hand. In his other is the long-way-folded paper.

The male's face is obscured, both because of the position of the camera, located atop a light pole, and the bill of the cap. The only detail Kate can make out is a bearded chin.

The video clip is ten seconds long and ends after the man drops the wiper onto the note and quickly moves out of frame.

Kate hands the phone back to O'Neil.

"Unfortunately, Frank's cameras aren't high resolution, so enlarging any stills from the source video will only produce blurred images. But at least we'll be able to determine things like height and weight and probable age."

Leo Burke says, "What I see is a male in his twenties with a slight frame."

Kate looks at O'Neil. "Is that what you see?"

"I prefer to wait until I watch the actual camera footage as opposed to a cell phone recording of it. But, yes, that's what it looks like to me, too."

"Isn't there more footage from other cameras you can look at that might show him better, or catch him getting into his car or something like that?"

"We'll be looking at all that, as well as traffic cameras in the area and cameras from nearby businesses. I know this video is short and not the best quality, but is there anything about this guy that looks familiar to you? Body type, body language, that kind of thing."

Kate shakes her head.

There is a lull as O'Neil returns his phone to his shirt pocket.

Finally, he says, "I'll send someone out this afternoon to have a look through the woods, locate the spot where this guy was standing, see what we can find. Maybe we can determine where he entered the woods. Is that okay with you?"

"Yes."

"I doubt we'll find anything, but it's worth a try."

Kate asks, "Why do you doubt you'll find anything?"

"Those woods are mostly pine trees," Burke answers. "Which means the ground is covered with pine needles, so it's unlikely we'll find footprints."

O'Neil adds, "Someone this careful, he's not going to leave chewed-up gum or cigarette butts for us to find. And if he left footprints, it's likely he would have ditched his shoes the first chance he got."

"And you think he would know about all this?"

O'Neil nods. "This guy, yeah."

Kate is silent again. The small sense of ease that being in the presence of a current and former chief of police had fostered is gone.

A moment into this silence, Burke asks, "Who's picking up my grandchildren?"

"Rebecca."

"When you called, what reason did you give for pulling them out of school?"

"Family emergency. But Rebecca's going to tell them she got them early so they could have some fun with her."

"But she's bringing them back here, correct?"

"Yes."

"Good."

With Burke done, Chief O'Neil resumes his questioning. "I need to ask you something, Kate. Since today isn't your normal shopping day, did anyone know that you were going?"

"Yes. My sister and Jack."

"Anyone else?"

"No."

"And Frank's market is where you typically do your grocery shopping?"

"Yes. Why?"

"I'm just trying to gather as much information as I can."

Kate looks at her father-in-law, then back at the chief. "You're not thinking one of them has anything to do with this, are you?"

"Of course not," O'Neil says. "That's obviously not a woman in the video. Nor is it Jack. And anyway, all this started before he arrived. We'll find out as soon as we can where the two texts originated from. It's an out-of-state area code, which, of course, doesn't mean the text came from out of state. Unless it turns out those texts came from a nearby cell tower, there's no reason to start thinking the worst or second-guessing the people in your life."

Kate pauses to take that in, and then asks, "Why do you think the number on the note didn't include the area code? And for that matter, why leave the note at all? To bait me into calling? But how could I have without the area code?"

O'Neil answers, "My guess is this asshole wants you to do exactly what you're doing right now. Struggle to make sense of this."

Kate looks at her father-in-law. "Is that what you think, too, Dad?"

Burke nods. "Yes. Leaving the number could also be a way of tricking you into answering. After the late-night calls and strange texts, you might be more inclined to ignore any unknown callers, no matter what came up on your Caller ID. But if the number from that note suddenly showed up on your display, your curiosity might make you pick up. Or you might assume it had to belong to someone you knew and take the chance and answer it. In either case, he'd get through to you. And if you didn't pick up, he'd be in your head while you stood there looking at your phone and trying to decide whether or not to answer."

Kate looks at the chief, who nods in agreement, and then she asks both men, "Then why print it out? Why not write it by hand? I mean, if he wrote it on a slip of paper, I'd have no reason to think the note wasn't from someone I knew. I'd have no reason to be suspicious of it at all."

"The most likely answer is that he didn't want us to have a sample of his handwriting," O'Neil answers. "I doubt we'll find any fingerprints or DNA on the paper. I don't know if you noticed from the video, but he's wearing what looks to me like latex or nitrile gloves. But we'll run tests on the paper anyway, see what we find. At least we can identify the type of paper he used."

"What good would that do?"

"It's a long shot, but if we do catch this fucker and find a ream of the exact same paper in his house, it will help. It's often the little things like that that can make or break a case."

"So in the meantime, what do I do?"

Burke says, "I'll be installing some floodlights on the back of the house this afternoon. Bigger than the motion-activated one you already have. That should keep him from staking out your woods again. And Monday, I'll be helping Eddie with the security cameras and the front lights he ordered."

Leaning forward slightly, O'Neil says to Kate, "Believe it or not, this happens more than you think. And it usually turns out to be some jerk with a grudge, or a sicko who has singled you out because you're a woman living alone with her children. But there have been no threats of physical harm, and I'll be honest with you, I've never seen a stalking case turn violent without there first having been any number of warning signs. This guy, he's not out of control. Just the opposite, in fact. He's very much in control. I understand that's probably not much of a comfort to you, but it matters, trust me. Until Eddie and Leo get the security cameras up and running on Monday, I'll continue to post a patrol car here every night. And if you're okay with it, I'll have the officer park at a point in your driveway where his vehicle will still be seen from the street but also give him clear line of sight to the woods."

"Which will be lit up like the World's Fair," Burke adds.

"Great," Kate says.

"It's that or you and my grandchildren come stay with me."

"Your house is even smaller than mine, Dad. And anyway, Rebecca's staying with us."

"I know," Burke says. "If she weren't sleeping on your foldout, I would be."

Kate decides not to mention that Rebecca has taken Callie's room, leaving the couch free.

"Just close your blinds at night," O'Neil says. "And keep the doors locked. If you don't keep living your life, this asshole wins. Right?"

Kate nods. "Right."

O'Neil glances at his watch. "I've got a meeting, so I need to run. At some point, Eddie will show you all the videos he's collected, on the off chance you might see something significant that we miss. Okay?"

"Okay," Kate says. "Thanks, Chief."

O'Neil stands, then looks at Burke, nods once, and says, "Leo."

Burke responds, "Jim."

Neither Kate nor her father-in-law speaks until O'Neil has exited through the kitchen door and begun walking down the back stairs.

Kate asks, "Do you really think we needed to pull the kids out of school for this, Dad?"

"Better safe than sorry, Katie. Don't you agree?"

"They're safe in their classrooms. And Rebecca was going to pick them up after school and bring them back home, along with Maria's kids, so it's not like they were ever going to be unattended. It scared the shit out of me when Eddie said you wanted me to send someone to get them. I thought they were in imminent danger, like someone was on his way at that moment to take them away or harm them." She pauses. "And frankly, Dad, that wasn't your call to make."

"I had information that you didn't, Katie. I saw the video clip of the scumbag. If he knows where you shop, he knows where my grand-children go to school."

"O'Neil doesn't seem to think he's violent."

"I wouldn't put too much stock in anything he says."

"Why not?"

"First of all, telling someone in your situation not to worry is part of the job. Second, I don't trust him."

"Because you think he botched Leif's investigation."

"Because he isn't the man he used to be, Katie. He's not the cop I chose to be my successor."

"Dad, please. I need you to tell me the truth. In your professional opinion, do you think this guy is going to show up here?"

"Let's just say I don't want to look back and wish we did more."

"What more *could* we do? The cottage is occupied, my sister is here, and a cop car is going to be parked at the bottom of my driveway. Plus, now you're telling me you're going to set up floodlights in my back-yard—another decision you made, by the way, without bothering to consult with me first. Aside from me and the twins going into hiding in some undisclosed location, tell me, Dad, please, what could we possibly look back on and regret not having done?"

"I know this scares you, Katie. You lived through this once before, and it didn't end well."

"Of course I'm scared. But I can't let my children know that. And I can't let the asshole who's trying to scare me know that. I can't give up my life. I can't walk away from this house, not even for a day. And not just because of a promise I made to my grandfather fifteen years ago. This place is all we have left of Leif. Their father, my husband, your son—he was killed trying to keep us safe. He was killed protecting everyone and everything in this house. If I give up because some kid is being a dick, it'll be like Leif died in vain. So, yes, do whatever you have to this afternoon, okay? Put up barbed wire if you want, build a fucking wall for all I care. But we're not leaving. And we're keeping what's going on from my children. Do you understand?"

It is clear by his expression that Leo Burke is not used to being talked to in this manner, but Kate doesn't care. She holds the man's stare until he finally nods and says, "I understand." He pauses. "Maybe the children shouldn't be here this afternoon while I work on the lights. They'll ask questions."

"I'll take them to Maria's with me."

"Good," Burke says.

Kate hears a car in her driveway. Standing, she moves to the kitchen window as her Subaru comes to a stop.

"They're back," she says.

She is heading toward the back door but stops when Burke speaks.

"I lost, too, Katie. When Leif was killed, I lost, too. My grandchildren are all I have left of him. I'll do whatever it takes to keep all of you safe."

"But I have to be the one to make the decisions when it comes to them," Kate says. "That's the way it has to be. Okay?"

"Understood," Burke says.

Kate hears her son and daughter laughing as they approach the house, and she knows by this that Rebecca is doing her part to keep them at ease.

Relieved they are being spared the fear she is feeling, Kate lets out a cleansing sigh. But by the way her father-in-law lingers, looking at her, she knows there is something else on his mind.

Max and Callie reach the bottom of the back stairs.

"What is it?" Kate says.

Before Leo can answer, Max opens the back door and enters, running straight through the kitchen and into the living room. He is followed by his sister, who races past her mother and grandfather in pursuit of her brother.

Seconds later, Max is bolting up the stairs, Callie right behind him.

Despite the commotion, Kate's attention remains focused on her father-in-law.

He says, "We'll talk about it another time."

"Talk about what?"

In a lowered voice, Burke says, "The will that you and Leif had drawn up when you were first married names each of you as the beneficiary should one of you pass, correct?"

"Yes. Why?"

"That's obviously not the case anymore, so you'll need to get a new will drawn up, one that determines, if something were to happen to you, who the children's guardian would be and who the conservator of their inheritance would be."

Caught off guard, Kate says, "Jesus, Dad."

"I know, Katie. It's not a pleasant thing to think about. But the way estate laws are here, inheritances pass from parent to children, so even if you didn't have a will, everything would go to Max and Callie, as it rightfully should. But as your next of kin, your sister could argue that she is due a share of your estate, too. She could also petition the court to appoint her as guardian *and* conservator, which, frankly, I would have a problem with. I could try to fight it, but there's no guarantee I would win. And do you really want to leave all this up to some judge? Are you comfortable with your sister not only raising your children but also being the one who manages your estate until they're eighteen?"

Kate hears Rebecca climbing the back stairs and whispers, "Can we talk about this later?"

"Of course."

Rebecca enters through the kitchen door. Kate steps away from her father-in-law, then smiles at her sister.

"Sorry, just passing through," Rebecca says.

"Max and Callie just ran upstairs. Are you playing tag or something?"

"Hide-and-seek." Rebecca extends her hand to Burke. "It's good to see you again, Leo."

The two shake hands.

"Thanks for picking up the children," Burke says.

"Is everything okay?"

"Yeah," Kate answers. "False alarm. I'll fill you in later."

Rebecca sighs. "Oh, thank God." She gestures toward the living room. "Well, I've got a game to win, so . . ."

She turns and leaves. Burke waits until Rebecca is climbing the stairs before saying to Kate, "You can use the same lawyer you and Leif used, or you can meet with my attorney. Whatever you want is fine with me. But the sooner you take care of this, the better, don't you think?"

Kate nods. "I'll be making lunch in a little bit. Do you want to stay?"

"No, I'm going to run out and get the lights."

"Right," Kate says. "How many do you think we need?"

"Two will do the job. One on each back corner of the house."

"Okay."

"It'll take me at least an hour to pick up the equipment."

"I'll make sure we're next door by then. How long will it take you to install everything?"

"Two hours, tops."

"Okay, good."

"Maybe the four of you should stay together for the time being. Strength in numbers."

Kate nods. "Yeah, we can do that."

"If it's okay with you, I'm going to stop and talk to your tenant on my way out. I think it's a good idea for him to know what's going on. And I'd like him to have my contact information, just in case."

Kate's initial reaction is to ask her father-in-law not to do that, but she also isn't keen on the idea of filling Jack in herself. The photograph taken of her through her bedroom window is humiliating enough, and having to tell Jack about it would only deepen that humiliation.

"Do what you think is best, Dad. We obviously need all the help we can get. And Jack seems like a helpful guy."

———

While Rebecca is making lunch for Max and Callie, Kate retrieves her strongbox from the top shelf of her bedroom closet. Sitting on her bed, she places the metal box on her lap and opens it.

She spends the next few minutes sorting through its contents, among which are the deed to the house; the twins' birth certificates, as well as her own; her and Leif's social security cards; various insurance policies, life and home; the title to her Subaru; Leif's death certificate; their marriage certificate; and the now out-of-date will.

Removing the will from its envelope, Kate glances at the first few paragraphs, then sets the document aside.

The items that remain in the box are banking records relating to a savings account and a college fund, as well as Kate's teacher's pension.

The college fund currently holds $150,000—half of the payout from Leif's life insurance. The savings account holds $220,000—the other half of the life insurance payout plus another $70,000 that Kate and Leif, because they lived in a mortgage-free home and rented the cottage in the summers, had managed to save over the course of their marriage.

Kate has always been comforted by the fact that she has these assets to fall back on, but the discussion with her father-in-law has left her suddenly with a sense of unease about these funds.

Just one more thing to be uneasy about.

Yes, she needs to address this issue, should something happen, and appoint someone to take care of her children, as well as be a responsible steward for not only the high-value property but also the $370,000 in cash.

But whom to pick?

Of course, the candidates are few—her sister, her children's grandfather, her best friend and neighbor. And yet that pared-down list doesn't make the decision she faces any easier. Should she choose one of them to serve as both guardian and conservator? Or should she choose one for one role and one for the other? The likely candidate for conservator is their grandfather, but because of his age, should someone be named as backup? The same question would apply to Leo Burke being their guardian. And in either case, who would that backup be? Could she trust Rebecca—truly trust her? Until recently, Rebecca's life has been chaotic, and though she seems to have changed, old habits have a way of resuming. And then there is the matter of Rebecca's bout with cancer. What if it returned? What if she were sick for a prolonged period of time? What if she didn't survive?

And while Kate loves and trusts Maria, Derek isn't her favorite person in the world, so there's that to consider. And anyway, how exactly would Maria being their guardian work? Would Max and Callie live with her? If so, what would happen to this house? The house Kate had promised to never sell. A house that any developer would buy and more than likely tear down so that a McMansion could be erected.

Her mind reeling, Kate piles the papers back into the box, locks it, and returns it to the upper closet shelf.

She understands why she has allowed this matter to slip her mind for so long. Who wouldn't put off having to make such a difficult decision? Who, as lost as she has been in grief and fear and anger, could even hope to find what it takes to face this?

As a result, however, Kate has unwittingly left her children unprotected, and that is an exposure she cannot allow to continue.

TWENTY-EIGHT

Cleaning Maria's house is the distraction Kate needs, and working alone for most of the afternoon allows her to fall into a groove that prevents her from thinking too much. Losing track of time, she doesn't check her watch for what feels to her like two hours, tops, but when her cell buzzes in her pocket and she anxiously checks the display for who is calling, she sees that the time is four forty-five.

The incoming call is from Sabrowsky, and Kate answers right away.

"Hey, Eddie."

"You sound out of breath."

"Just cleaning. What's going on?"

"Chief O'Neil wanted me to fill you in on a couple of things. The first is that nothing was found in the woods. I actually went in there myself, just to double-check. There's been a significant amount of growth since we were kids. All the paths are covered over, and it's more like a jungle now than the place we used to be able to run through. I did manage to find the spot where our guy was standing when he took the picture, but with all the pine needles and peeled-off bark, there was no trace of him."

Kate realizes that Sabrowsky, too, has seen the photo. More than that, he likely has a copy of it with him, either printed out or on his phone. How else would he have been able to establish the photographer's line of sight?

She cringes at the idea of her friend seeing her half-dressed.

"You there, Katie?"

"Yeah. What else did the chief want you to tell me?"

"The two texts you received when you got back this morning were sent from Bridgeport."

"Bridgeport?"

"Yeah."

"What does that mean?"

"Well, it's a lot closer than New Jersey, so that's a concern. But it also means that the sender was about forty-five minutes from your place, figuring in traffic. We know the note was placed around ten, and you received the texts right after I called you a little before eleven."

"Jesus."

"Yeah. The good news is, knowing it came from Bridgeport will help us narrow down our search of traffic cameras. The bad news is that will take time."

"How much time?"

"I just finished looking through the recordings from all the surveillance cameras in the parking lot, and there is no video of our guy getting into a vehicle, so now we have to check surveillance cameras from nearby businesses, hoping one of those caught him. From there it's a matter of patching all those cameras together until we see him get into a vehicle—that is, if we're lucky. Once we know what vehicle we're looking for, then we can start looking at traffic cameras."

"How did the parking lot cameras miss him?"

"Often there are blind spots when you set up security cameras like that. Either our guy somehow knew where a blind spot was and slipped through it, or he lucked out. Maybe he's smart, but I've got a feeling he's just lucky. Anyway, at least this rules out everyone who knew you were going to the store. They were where they were supposed to be when the texts came through, right?"

Kate recalls seeing Jack's Jeep parked by the cottage, both when she left for the supermarket and when she returned from it. And right after she and Sabrowsky had ended their call was when Kate saw her sister returning from her run.

Kate answers, "Right."

"The other thing I need to tell you is that our guy never shows his face to the cameras. We have about twenty seconds of footage total, among all the cameras, and he has that cap on the entire time and never looks up. But it does look to me like he's on the young side. It's the way he carries himself, his build, everything. I just can't help but look at him and see someone in his twenties, possibly even early twenties. You know what I'm talking about. The two you saw outside the cottage the night all this started, you pegged them as being teens or a little older. It's the same here. Which brings us back to the possibility of this being a former student of yours, someone with a grudge. The chief wanted me to ask you again if you can think of anyone who might have a reason to think that you wronged them. A former student who didn't get into college and maybe blames you? Or who maybe had a thing for you but you shot down."

Kate says, "First of all, gross. Second, we've been through this already. I can't think of any student I've ever taught who'd want to make my life miserable."

"No one's implying that you had any kind of inappropriate relationship with a student, Katie. But teenagers have wild imaginations—especially teenage boys. You could simply look at one, and he'd get the wrong idea. Christ, for that matter, you could ignore one, and he'd convince himself that it meant something."

Kate shrugs. "If that's true, then that could be every boy I've ever taught."

"You're an attractive woman, and you stand up in front of teenagers all day. I'm sorry we keep coming back to this, but you can't think of anyone who looked at you too long, maybe checked out your body too much, made a point of it so you'd notice, anything like that?"

Kate closes her eyes and says, "No. And for God's sake, Eddie, please stop asking me shit like this."

The line goes quiet, and then finally Eddie says, "Sorry. I'm just following orders here." He pauses again, but this time Kate gets the sense that he is holding something back.

She gives him a moment more to speak, and when he doesn't, she says, "There's something you're not telling me, Eddie. What is it?"

"I just keep thinking that there has got to be a motive for this, right? Someone is going to great lengths to fuck with you without leaving any tracks. I know the chief wants to believe this is an idiot with a grudge or some pervert, and it may still be one of those, but for me that just doesn't add up. Like I said before, this looks almost professional. Even more so now. And then there's the photo of you. I mean, catching you at that moment, getting that shot, that was someone in your woods for more than just one night. That was either someone with enough patience to wait around for hours, night after night, or someone who figured out your routine and knew exactly when to slip into your woods. Either scenario requires effort and commitment, and to me that means terrorizing you like this is a means to an end, not the end itself. There has to be a goal here. This isn't just terror for terror's sake."

Kate says, "I don't even want to ask what you think that goal could be."

"It wouldn't matter if you did, because I don't have a clue. But if this is some organized psychological-warfare thing being waged against you—if this is more than just a bizarre stalking case—then maybe something similar to this has happened before, if not around here then somewhere else. And if it has happened before, maybe we can use that to reverse engineer this whole thing, you know? Maybe those investigations, if there were any, will show us something we haven't found yet."

Kate says nothing. Her eyes are closed, and for a moment, she has willingly shut down, not wanting to take in any more information.

After a moment, Sabrowsky asks, "You okay?"

Kate opens her eyes again. "Oh, yeah. I'm great."

"This is going to trigger shit for you, Katie. I mean, how could it not? I know you have to put on a brave face for the kids, but you've got to be ready to snap by now, no?"

"I'm ready to do . . . something," she says.

"I have some lorazepam. I can swing by with it after dinner."

"No, that shit just makes me stupid. It's tempting, trust me, but I can't."

"If you change your mind, you know how to reach me."

"I do, yeah. So hey, what do I do about the number the texts came from? Do I block it?"

"That phone is probably a burner, which is a phone someone uses once or twice, then destroys or throws away. I doubt he'll use it again, but maybe you should leave it unblocked for tonight, just in case. Who knows, contacting you from it again might be the mistake we're waiting for him to make."

"So I'm going to sit around all night, staring at my cell phone and hoping it doesn't ring."

"It'll feel creepy, I know. But Steve Schulze is watching your place tonight. You remember him, right?"

Kate does. Six six, powerlifter's build, all business. And as much of a hard-ass as Leif was, maybe even more so.

"I remember him, yeah."

Attempting a joke, Sabrowsky says, "Hell, even I'm scared of that guy." Then he returns to a serious tone. "You'll be good tonight is what I'm trying to say. Anything goes wrong—anything—just call Schulze's cell, and he'll be at your door in thirty seconds. Do you have it, by the way? His number?"

"No."

"I'll text it to you."

"Thanks," Kate says flatly.

"No problem. Hey, I'll see you tomorrow night, right? You're still going."

"I guess, yeah. So far, anyway. That is if I don't have a breakdown between now and then."

"Well, call me if you feel one coming on, okay? I could always come over. We could hang out, have a few beers or something."

"You're off tonight?"

"Yeah."

"Then shouldn't you be spending time with Sara?"

Sabrowsky pauses. "I guess you haven't heard."

"What?"

"We split up. A couple months ago."

"I'm sorry to hear that."

"Shit happens."

"Are you just separated?"

"No, she filed for divorce. Wants the house, the car, everything."

"Oh, God. I'm sorry, Eddie."

"You've got bigger problems. Anyway, yeah, I'm around if you need me."

"Good to know. But I'll be fine."

"And you should definitely go tomorrow night. It'll be good for you to be around people. Not just morale-wise. Remember, there's safety in numbers."

"That's what Leo said earlier."

"He's not wrong. Anyway, I'll text Schulze's cell to you after I hang up."

"Thanks, Eddie."

"Hang tough, Katie. This will end, I promise. I'm on this."

———

Kate prepares dinner while Rebecca and the children play a board game.

224

After putting the meal on the table and calling everyone in from the living room, Kate checks from the front window to see if Jack's Jeep is still there—it is—before joining her family in the kitchen.

She informed him that they would be sitting down to eat around six, so by six fifteen she stops listening for the sound of him at the door and gives her full attention to those seated at the table.[1]

She takes note of the fact that Max is far more outgoing now that his aunt is here.

Engaging in conversation, he is once again the happy boy he was prior to his father's death.

———

Rebecca keeps the twins up until ten, then spends the next half hour getting them to bed, after which she showers, says good night to Kate, and turns in.

The lights Leo Burke installed in the afternoon—powerful floodlights that would be overkill in a maximum-security prison—are equipped with sensors, so the pair automatically turned on at twilight and will automatically turn off again at dawn.

Even with the blinds closed, the harsh white light seeping in around the narrow gaps at the edges is enough to make Kate's bedroom overly bright. And it isn't just the seepage coming in from outside; the blinds themselves, backlit, glow like night-lights.

But even if her room were its usual cave-like darkness, Kate doubts she'd be able to sleep. The headache she's been fighting since this morning has taken root and is now beginning to grow, triggered by light as well as her utter state of exhaustion.

And it doesn't help that her cell phone, charging on her nightstand, is a means by which someone with ill intent can bypass the many measures put in place around her and, at least virtually, enter her bedroom.

Another provocation like any of the ones that have come before, she thinks, *and I will explode.*

Sitting on the edge of the bed, she tries taking a series of long, deep breaths, hoping that doing so might at least return her headache to the nearly tolerable base level it has held all day. But after a minute she feels no relief and gives up.

She remembers what Jack said during their first dinner together about headaches and knowing all the tricks to ease them, but looking at her alarm clock she sees that it is ten forty-five. Desperate, she grabs her cordless phone, exits her bedroom, and crosses the living room to the front window.

The cottage windows are lit, so Jack is awake, but realizing that she hasn't memorized his number, she makes a quick trip back into the bedroom to retrieve it from her cell. Calling it from her landline, she returns to the living room and paces back and forth as she waits for him to answer, only stopping when he finally does.

"Hey, Kate."

"I'm sorry to call so late, but I'm getting one of my headaches, and I was wondering if you could help me."

"Yeah, of course. You want to come over?"

Kate hasn't thought this through—leaving her house and walking to the cottage isn't something she thinks she can do, even with the back half of the property lit up like a carnival and a trusted police officer posted near the bottom of her driveway.

Knowing that someone waited in the dark to photograph her through her bedroom window, and possibly for several nights in a row, how could she ever leave her house again at night, never mind walk alone up her driveway?

The only alternative is that Jack comes to her, but is that something she wants Schulze to see? Walking down the driveway, Jack would be in clear view, and all it would take for him to be seen is for Schulze to glance in his rearview mirror. And if Schulze didn't witness Jack exiting the cottage and mistakes him for some intruder, what then? For that matter, even if he recognized that the figure walking down the driveway is the current occupant of the cottage, what would he think of Kate receiving a visitor so late at night?

Kate's rushing thoughts have caused her pain to only increase.

Jack asks, "You there?"

"Yeah. I was just thinking. Maybe you could come here. Except—and I know this will sound weird—could you cut across the front lawn instead of coming down the driveway?"

"You don't want your night watchman to see me."

"It's weird, I know. If he sees you he might misunderstand, and it'll turn into a whole thing."

"I get it," Jack says.

"You don't mind?"

"Not at all. Give me five minutes?"

———

Kate changes into a pair of dark yoga pants and a tank top, over which she wears an unbuttoned denim shirt.

Despite the bedroom blinds being closed, she undresses and redresses in the bathroom, then ties her hair back into a ponytail and brushes her teeth.

Crossing through her bedroom, she is stopped in her tracks by the sound of her cell phone vibrating on her nightstand, and for a moment she is uncertain whether to check it—or, for that matter, whether to even approach the thing.

But she pushes through the fear and forces herself to walk to her bed. Picking up the phone, she turns it over and looks at the display, on which is a preview of a text from Sabrowsky. Kate opens the message and reads it.

Just checking in. Everything okay?

Kate's heightened state of alertness begins to diminish, though slowly.

She responds: Yes. Getting into bed. Exhausted.

Then she waits for the reply, which takes only a few seconds to arrive.

Good night.

She sends back, You too, and then returns the phone to the table.

Leaving her bedroom, Kate closes the door to block the light, darkening the living room significantly in the process. The dimmest light available is a Tiffany lamp on a table beside the television, but she doubts her eyes could even handle that, so she takes three votive candles from a drawer in the TV stand and, lighting each one, sets them together on the coffee table.

At the front door, she deactivates the security system, then flips to the "Off" position the switch that controls the motion-activated light mounted at the front of the house so Jack doesn't trigger it as he crosses the front yard.

From the vertical row of narrow windowpanes to the right of the door, Kate watches the cottage. It isn't long before Jack exits it, crosses to the row of trees that separates Kate's and Maria's properties, then turns and heads toward the main house.

TWENTY-NINE

Resting on the couch in the candlelit living room, Kate listens to Jack in the kitchen.

First he fills the teakettle with water and sets it on the burner, after which he opens and closes several cupboards before finding the one containing the coffee mugs, all the while moving carefully and making as little noise as possible. After he sets the mug down on the counter, there is nothing for him to do but wait for the water to boil. During this time the house falls silent, and Kate closes her eyes and tries to breathe through the pain.

Finally, she hears the sound of water roiling, which ends abruptly as Jack lifts the kettle off the burner. He fills a mug, sets the kettle down, and then walks into the living room, offering the mug to Kate, who sits up and takes it.

In a hushed voice, she says, "I smell peppermint."

Jack sits on the coffee table. "Yeah, it's peppermint tea." His voice, too, is muted. "I picked some up when I went shopping."

Kate raises the mug to her lips, but then immediately lowers it. "It's too hot to drink just yet."

"The idea is to hold it up to your face while it's still steaming and breathe in slowly."

Gripping the mug with two hands, Kate places it under her chin and inhales deeply. After fully exhaling, she says, "God, that smells good."

"You feel the steam rising around your face?"

Kate inhales again. "Yeah. It's hot, obviously, but it's also cool because of the peppermint. I feel this kind of evaporating thing going on."

"Good. Just relax and keep breathing it in."

Kate closes her eyes, inhales and then exhales, and opens her eyes again. "So you're just going to sit there and watch me," she jokes.

"Yep," Jack says.

"Thank God it's almost dark in here."

"Stop it; you look great."

"You're too kind."

Kate closes her eyes, and neither speaks for a moment. After a few more breaths, she says, "It's like there's a bubble of peppermint surrounding my entire head."

"It's nice, right?"

She keeps her eyes shut. "Very soothing."

"Just keep breathing, and try to relax a little more with each breath."

"You're hypnotizing me, aren't you?"

"Hush. Keep breathing."

Kate does as she is told—eyes closed, deep breaths, steady exhalations. A minute passes before Jack speaks again.

"How's the pain?"

Kate smiles. "Less. Wow. You weren't lying about knowing tricks."

"I never lie," Jack says. "Describe the pain you're still feeling."

"It's at the back of my head. My scalp is clamping down on my skull, like my skin is shrinking or something."

"Okay, so do you want to try something for me?"

"What?"

"Try to imagine yourself floating on your back in water. Can you do that?"

Kate exhales, and then nods. "Okay. Now what?"

"Imagine that your face is above the surface, but the rest of your head is below it. You're floating effortlessly, no problem breathing, no sense of sinking, just relaxing and drifting. And imagine that the water you're in is much cooler than the air around your face."

Kate nods.

Jack gives her a moment before continuing. "Really feel the difference in temperature, how much cooler the water around your head is. Feel the difference between it and the air touching your face. Feel it all over the part of your body that's submerged."

Kate remains silent, breathing in the smell of peppermint and imagining herself floating in water.

Jack asks, "What kind of water is it? An ocean, a river?"

"It's a lake. A big lake."

"That's good. Is it day or night?"

"Night."

"Good. Think of as many details as you can."

Kate imagines her clothing, soaked with cool water, clinging to her body. And with her ears beneath the surface of the water, her hearing is muffled.

She imagines, too, a broad sky cluttered with stars.

Jack doesn't speak for several more moments.

Finally, he asks, "How are you feeling?"

"Like I could doze off."

"How's the pain?"

Kate opens her eyes. Jack is still seated on the coffee table, but he has leaned forward since she last saw him.

"I can feel the back of my head unclenching," Kate says.

"The tea should be cool enough to drink by now. Take a sip."

Kate does. The instant the warm peppermint touches her tongue, her face tingles. Swallowing it sends a current of warmth spreading through her core.

"Okay, that's witchcraft," Kate says.

"Only a little bit. Just keep drinking the tea and relaxing."

Kate takes several more sips. Jack leans back and looks around the room.

After a pause, he says, "Beautiful old house."

"Thanks."

"Do you know when it was built?"

"Nineteen ten."

Still studying the room, Jack says, "You can tell this was built by craftsmen. The moldings, the plank floors, the built-in bookshelves."

"We're lucky," Kate says.

Jack faces her again. "Did you eat enough today?"

"Yeah."

"Are you sure?"

"Yes."

"Do you want me to make you something?"

Kate shakes her head, then says, "Wow."

"What?"

"That's the first time I've been able to move my head today without searing pain."

"See?"

"That's crazy."

"I left the box of tea on your counter. You definitely should have that around."

"I can get my own."

"It's a box of tea, Kate. It's no big deal."

Kate pauses before speaking again. "Listen, I've been thinking, I should pay you for all the yard work you did."

"Not necessary," Jack says. "A dinner is more than enough."

"Yeah, about that. How come you didn't come over tonight?"

"I wouldn't have been good company."

"You didn't seem yourself this morning. What's going on?"

Jack shrugs. "New Hampshire stuff."

"I don't know what that means."

"Just . . . closing that chapter of my life. Lots of things to take care of."

"What kind of things?"

Jack hesitates.

Kate backs off. "You don't have to tell me if you don't want to."

"It's not that I don't want to," Jack says. He takes a breath, lets it out. "For starters, Elle's father wanted me to forfeit any claim on the house Elle and I bought."

"Is that really his place to demand that?"

"He bought it for us when we got married. Well, technically, Elle's mother did. Her side of the family is wealthy."

"But your name was on the deed?"

"Yeah."

"So they bought you out?"

"No."

"That doesn't seem fair."

"Fairness isn't one of her family's priorities." He pauses. "And they blame me for what happened to her."

"What happened?"

"A few months ago she had a breakdown."

"Jesus."

"She's struggled her whole life with bipolar depression. That was our marriage, really—months of her in a deep depression followed by months of her in a manic state. When she was manic, she did a lot of crazy things. A lot of things that were hard to deal with, aftermath-wise. But the worst was when her manic episodes pushed her into paranoia. She'd accuse me of things that weren't true—that I was having affairs with other faculty members, or that I was plotting to kill her. It got really scary when she started to accuse me of having affairs with students. Toward the end—for the last two years—every day with her was damage control."

"Where is she now?"

"A private hospital."

"How awful."

"She's getting the best care money can buy, though, so that's good."

"And her family blames you for her breakdown?"

Jack nods. "Yeah."

"Do you mind me asking what triggered her breakdown?"

"I wish I knew. She just grew more and more paranoid. She'd have these screaming fits, always around dinnertime for some reason. She'd accuse me of something terrible and tell me over and over again to just confess, just tell her the truth, get it over with. Usually I could calm her down, eventually. Or ride it out until she got tired. Then one day I couldn't calm her down. By midnight she was still going strong."

"God, Jack. I'm sorry. So the trips up there are to, what, sign papers?"

"Yeah. But I also visit her." He pauses. "She has been texting me from the hospital, asking me to come see her, pretty much since I got here. I think she smuggled her phone in. The meds she's on seem to be helping, but she still has her moments. She finally threatened to harm herself if I didn't come up."

Kate remembers Jack telling her this morning that he might need to make another trip up.

"That's a terrible way to live," she says.

"It's over and done with now."

"What do you mean?"

"Her family found out she'd been texting me and took her phone. Her father called me this afternoon to tell me I 'wasn't to lead her on anymore' and that 'any further attempts to communicate with her would result in legal action.'"

"He sounds like a fucking asshole."

"Oh, yeah. But in his mind he thinks he's protecting his daughter, so . . ." Jack doesn't finish his thought.

"Still, that's no excuse for being cruel," Kate says. She looks at Jack for a moment. "Do you mind if I ask you a question?"

"No. What's on your mind?"

"When I rented the cottage to you, you paid me out of an envelope of cash. It looked to me that you had maybe five hundred leftover. I don't mean to embarrass you or put you on the spot, but is that all the money you have?"

Jack smiles. "You've got enough to worry about, Kate. You don't have to worry about me, too."

"That's not an answer."

Though his smile remains, Jack says nothing.

"If it is—if that's all you have to your name—I could help. Like I said before, I can give you a break on the rent and return some of your money. And I will pay you for everything you do around here. At the very least, I'll stock your refrigerator. The last thing I need is you starving to death out there."

"I'm hardly starving, Kate." He shrugs. "But I guess maybe there was a part of me that needed to bottom out. Back to square one, as broke as I was the day I graduated college, no choice but to start over again. You know what I mean?"

Kate nods. "I do, yeah."

She gets the sense that there is something more Jack wants to say.

"What are you thinking?" she says.

"When I went up the other night, she didn't want me to leave, so I hid during bed check and lay down next to her on her bed. She kept saying that she hoped we would work things out, but I knew it wasn't real. She was just . . . grasping. She fell asleep, but I didn't. I waited all night for morning to come, and then I got out of there. I think that was when I finally realized there was nothing I could do for her. Sneaking out of the hospital and driving away, that's the moment I knew I was on my own. To be honest, in a way, her father cutting us off was a relief. I know that sounds horrible."

"It doesn't. I get it."

"Anyway, I think I've achieved my goal of rock bottom. It's time for me to get off my ass."

"Then you definitely should come to Maria's party tomorrow night. Like I said before, there'll be a lot of businesspeople there, which is the whole reason Derek is throwing it. If you're ready to start looking for work, it's the place to be. Plus, their parties are fun. Lots of games and lots of drinking."

"What time are you getting there?"

"I'll be there all day, helping set up. Usually people start arriving around five or six, though."

"It's a potluck, right?"

"Yeah."

From upstairs comes the sound of a door opening, followed by footsteps in the hallway and another door closing. Jack looks toward the sound.

"That's just one of my kids going to pee," Kate says. "Sounds like Max. Callie tends to stomp when she's just woken up."

"Will he come down?"

Kate shakes her head. "No, he'll go back to bed."

They wait silently, listening, and after a moment the toilet flushes, and then the bathroom door opens and Max returns to his bedroom, closing the door behind him.

Jack looks at Kate. "Listen, it's late. I should probably go, let you get some sleep. Hope I didn't bring your headache back with my tale of woe."

"Not at all. I actually feel like I could fall asleep."

Still watching Kate, Jack hesitates before whispering, "I got a visit from your father-in-law today. He filled me in on what's going on. You know if there's anything I can do to help, just call."

"Thanks."

"I guess you're about as safe as a person can be, though. Cop in the driveway, and those new lights out back."

Kate shrugs. "It's a fine line between safe and imprisoned."

"Is that how you feel? Imprisoned?"

"Maybe. All I can do is wait around for something to happen. It's frustrating."

"I'd be frustrated by that, too."

"And I'm not looking forward to Monday."

"What's Monday?"

"The surveillance cameras go up. Leo and Eddie will be installing them. Eddie is the one who put our security system in after Leif died." She pauses. "And here you were thinking you were renting a nice little cottage in Westport."

"The security doesn't bother me."

"It bothers me," Kate says. "It's not how I imagined my life."

"I suppose you could always move, right? I mean, if it came to that, if it looked like this asshole wasn't going to stop. Cash in, move on, start over. I have to be honest, it took me a while to get to the point where I could finally let go, but once I did, it was a relief."

"I can't sell."

Jack nods. "I get it. And this bullshit is bound to end sooner or later, right? Leo seems to think all the precautions will scare off whoever's doing this."

"Everyone seems to have a theory of how to put this to an end. But we went through this kind of thing before, and that time it lasted two years. Of course, back then we thought it was just kids getting revenge against a hard-ass town cop, so it was different. We rolled with it as being an unfortunate part of Leif's job. It was easier for me to do that then because I wasn't sleeping alone. It helped that Leif was next to me."

"Yeah, sleeping alone is a hard thing to get used to." He takes a breath in, then lets it out and says, "Speaking of sleep, I should get going. Are you done with your tea?"

"Almost." Kate takes a final sip, and then hands Jack the empty mug.

He asks, "Do you want more?"

"No, thanks."

"You should stay put, not get up too fast. I can let myself out."

"I'll need to deadbolt the door and set the alarm."

"Oh, yeah," Jack says. He holds up the mug. "I'll put this in the sink and meet you at the door."

"You can leave it here on the coffee table."

"Nonsense. You keep a tidy house. I don't want to start leaving messes for you to clean up."

Jack stands and walks into the kitchen, placing the mug into the sink. When he returns to the living room, Kate is waiting by the front door.

"Thanks for this," Kate says.

"It's nice to be able to deal with a problem I can actually fix."

"I'll see you tomorrow night?"

"I'll do my best, yeah."

"What does that mean?"

"I think for the time being it would be better for me if I could play things like that by ear. I'm not sure I'm ready to be around a lot of people. I hope you understand."

"I do. But if you do show up, we'll be happy to see you."

"Thanks."

They look at each other for a moment, and then Jack opens the door. "Good night."

"Good night, Jack."

He exits, and Kate closes the door, locking it and resetting the alarm. Then she watches through the narrow windows until Jack has made it to the cottage and goes inside.

Back in her glaringly lit bedroom, Kate pulls her comforter off her bed and grabs her pillow. Warily, she checks her cell phone, but no new messages or calls have come through.

Leaving the device on the nightstand, she brings the comforter and pillow with her as she exits the room, once again closing the door behind her.

Stretched out on the couch with the comforter over her, she removes her yoga pants and drops them to the floor, then sits up and takes off her overshirt, dropping that as well.

Even undressing in this manner—hidden under a comforter, making certain she is nowhere near any windows—causes Kate to feel the same rush of adrenaline she might feel just prior to taking some kind of risk.

She wonders if she'll ever again get naked anywhere other than her bathroom—a concern that matters now, considering the feelings she is starting to have for her tenant.

Her younger tenant with whom, unfortunately for him, she has certain things in common.

Sitting up, Kate leans toward the coffee table and blows out the votive candles. Then she lies back down and waits for sleep.

THIRTY

Kate wakes to a morning sky crowded with clouds the color of lead.

She hasn't thought to keep an eye on the weather, figuring that Maria and Derek would, but once she is up and the coffee maker is started, she checks her phone for today's forecast.

By noon the chance of rain will be 50 percent, with that number increasing every hour until it reaches 100 percent by five o'clock. It isn't until after midnight that the chance of rain lessens to 90 percent, and then holds at that number for three more hours. Kate immediately texts Maria, asking if the party is still on, then sets her phone down on the kitchen counter.

After pouring a mug of coffee and pocketing her cell phone, Kate deactivates the alarm, exits through the kitchen door, and sits on the top step of the back stairs. It is a chilly morning, but after sleeping with the house sealed up tight, Kate needs fresh air. Bracing herself against the cold, she looks to her right and confirms that Schulze's SUV is no longer in the driveway, then faces straight ahead and surveys the back woods.

She recalls being afraid of those woods as a child—that is, until Rebecca all but dragged her into them one winter afternoon to prove once and for all that no evil witches or deranged hobos or packs of vicious animals called them home. From then on there was no keeping Kate out, and she quickly came to learn every inch of the forest by heart—every winding path, every dip in the uneven ground, every tree, standing and fallen.

To a large degree, it was there that her imagination was born, and whenever a book she was reading contained a scene set in some magical forest, it was this expanse of woods that she saw in her mind's eye.

Here is where her most beloved characters fought or dwelled or loved.

Kate's interest in the woods waned once she entered high school, though she would still take walks through them on occasion, often in the autumn when the leaves were turning, but also whenever she needed to escape the tension that Rebecca's dramatics caused in their grandparents' home.

Kate recognizes, of course, that she has come full circle, now that the woods are once again a source of fear.

Never as a child or teenager did she imagine that one day someone would use these woods as a place from which to observe her unseen, waiting with a camera for the moment she passed a window in a state of undress.

By the time she is close to being done with her coffee, Kate has grown curious as to where her stalker stood as he waited—what spot, exactly, on that once-familiar terrain offered him the best view of her bedroom window.

But to find that out would require her to venture in those woods, which isn't something she is dressed for or, for that matter, up to doing.

And anyway, what good would it do her to stand where her violator stood?

Still, she needs to do something, is always at her best when she is in motion.

She recalls what Jack said last night regarding problems that can actually be fixed.

There is one thing that she can do—that she must do, and that no one else can do for her.

Taking her final sip, Kate stands to head back inside, stopping as she reaches for the doorknob when her cell phone buzzes in her pocket.

On the display is Maria's reply.

Yes, Derek says the party is still on. God help us.

Kate composes and sends her response.

God help us indeed.

———

Kate showers, dresses in jeans and a flannel work shirt, and then sits at the kitchen table with a notebook and pen.

She stares at the blank page for a moment before writing a list of three names:

Rebecca

Leo

Maria

Then she draws two columns, titling one Pros and the other Cons. And at the very top of the page she writes Guardian in bold letters.

Over the next few minutes she assigns to each person the reasons for, and the reasons against, them being selected as her children's legal guardian.

Rebecca's pros are the facts that she's the twins' aunt and that she is adored by them. Under Cons Kate writes: "Reliability? History? How does she make her money?"

Leo's pros are obvious—he is their grandfather, and being retired means he would be able to fill the role of guardian on a full-time basis.

His cons are just as obvious—his age, as well as his tendency to be overprotective, though Kate understands, given everything that is going on, how that particular quality could also go into the Pros column.

As for Maria, the fact that she has children in the same age group is a pro. After writing that, Kate also adds a single word: "Lovely." As for what might disqualify her friend, Kate can only think of two things, so she adds them to the Cons column. "Works full time; Derek."

Knowing that this is only a start—barely a start, really—Kate lets out a frustrated sigh. Certainly there are other factors that she will need to take into consideration, but the last thing she wants right now is to be made even more despondent than she already is by this overwhelmingly difficult decision.

Flipping to an empty page, she draws up an identical chart, labeling this one Conservator.

But after staring at those same three names for another moment, Kate closes the notebook without adding a word.

———

While Callie and Max are eating breakfast in the kitchen, Kate strips the linens from the bed and cot in Max's room, then crosses the hall to Callie's room and strips that bed as well.

With three sets of sheets and pillowcases bundled together in her arms, she passes the front-facing window, stopping when something outside catches her eye.

Visible through the line of still-bare trees that separate Kate's property from Maria's are Rebecca and Derek—Rebecca in her running clothes, her hands placed on her hips and her chest still heaving from the run, and Derek in jeans and a T-shirt and, strangely, a pair of slippers.

Kate can only guess that the reason he is wearing slippers outside is that he left his house in a hurry, though why, exactly, he would do that is uncertain to her.

Standing not far from Maria's driveway, Rebecca and Derek are engaged in what appears to be an intense conversation. At one point Derek raises his hand, as if to calm her, to which Rebecca responds by placing her hand on top of his and parrying it downward.

The discussion continues for a half minute, ending with Derek turning abruptly and walking away. Rebecca says something as he makes his retreat down the driveway, but whatever it is she has told him does not cause him to stop or even look back.

Finally, too, Rebecca turns and retreats, walking with her arms folded across her stomach.

Kate does not know what, exactly, she has witnessed, though something she is certain of is that this was not a discussion between two people who barely knew each other.

As far as Kate knows, not once during the many winters Rebecca spent in the cottage did she and Derek interact with each other in any significant way. Though Kate and Leif, along with the twins, were often at Maria's house for dinner with Maria's family—and vice versa—Rebecca seldom took part, preferring to pursue her own social life, albeit a secret one.

Of course, it was no secret to Kate or Leif that Rebecca in those days preferred the company of married men—married men with means, specifically, with whom she would frequently engage in months-long affairs.

To her credit, Rebecca became involved with only one married man at a time, though Kate could never tell if that was a strange kind of virtue or an indication of obsession.

But how difficult would it have been for Rebecca to carry on an affair, brief or prolonged, with the married man living next door?

The well-worn pathway running through the narrow woods and connecting the two properties would have given him easy and discreet access to the cottage, day or night.

And whether or not Derek was actually a man of means back then, he certainly portrayed himself as one, and continued to do so even as his business was failing.

Only briefly does Kate wonder whether to mention this to Maria. Her friend is the type of woman who would want to know, but is it Kate's place to inform her? Hasn't Maria enough to deal with now?

And anyway, Kate's assumptions could be all wrong. Derek being Derek, he is more than capable of saying the kind of thing that would set anyone off. So maybe what Kate saw was nothing more than an innocent conversation gone bad.

THIRTY-ONE

Kate is placing the sheets on the cot in Max's room when Rebecca, finished with her shower and dressed in jeans and a T-shirt, enters.

"Let me give you a hand, Katie," she says.

The fitted sheet is already down, so Kate tosses one end of the top sheet to her sister. Rebecca catches a corner, and the two lay the sheet flat and begin to tuck in the sides.

Kate is silent as she works.

Rebecca looks at her several times before asking, "Everything okay?"

Kate nods but still says nothing.

Rebecca watches her closely for a moment more. "You sure?"

"Yeah. Had a bad headache last night, that's all. Didn't really sleep well."

"I'm sorry. How are you now?"

"It's mostly gone."

"Mostly?"

"I'll be fine. I can live with it if it stays the way it is."

"You shouldn't have to 'live with it,' Katie."

"I'm used to it."

Rebecca decides not to push the matter. "You know, we just changed the beds and washed the sheets yesterday. Remember?"

Kate stops midtask. Shaking her head, she says, "Jesus. Force of habit, I guess." She resumes making the cot.

"You've got a lot on your mind. What time are you going next door?"

"Probably around ten."

Rebecca glances at her watch.

Kate asks, "What time is it now?"

"Quarter to nine."

Again, Kate nods. With the top sheet set, she picks up the bundled-up comforter and tosses it across the cot. Together, she and Rebecca spread it out until it is lying evenly, and then sweep it with their palms to smooth out its surface.

Moving from the cot to the bed, Kate unfolds a second fitted sheet, which she now remembers Rebecca folded and put away yesterday. Walking to the other side of the bed, Rebecca waits as Kate struggles to find a corner. Rebecca is about to offer help, but before she can Kate suddenly loses her temper and throws the still-folded sheet onto the bare mattress.

"Fuck!" she yells. Then she freezes, and the anger passes as quickly as it came. She looks at her sister. "Sorry."

Rebecca picks up the sheet and begins unfolding it. "It's okay," she says. "You know, we haven't had a chance to talk about what happened yesterday. Why Leo wanted Max and Callie pulled out of school."

Kate lets out a breath, further composing herself. With the sheet ready, Rebecca hands a corner to Kate.

As they make the bed, Kate tells Rebecca about the phone number left on her windshield while she was shopping, and the photograph that was texted to her from that number not long after she got home.

Now it's Rebecca who freezes. "Jesus," she says. "Were you nude?"

"Yeah. Partially, anyway. And I had to forward the photo to Chief O'Neil."

"Which probably means every cop in the department has seen it."

Kate shrugs. "Maybe. I don't know. I don't want to think about that. Eddie has; I know that much."

Rebecca continues placing her side of the fitted sheet onto the mattress. "Yeah, well, that probably made his day," she says.

"What does that mean?"

"Let's just say you don't know him like I do."

"I know you two have your history, Becca, but he's been nothing but helpful to us. And not just since all this started. Since Leif has been gone, he's been there for us in every way possible."

"I'm sure he has," Rebecca says. "I'm sure he feels a tremendous loyalty for Leif. But he doesn't have the problem with men that he has with women."

"What problem with women?"

"I'm just saying he tends to do one of two things—idealize a woman and obsess over her, or objectify a woman and demean her. I wouldn't be surprised if he has idealized you, and that's why he's always there for you."

"I don't think so, Becca. I mean, of the two of us, you were the one he pursued all through high school."

"That's the thing, though, Katie. It didn't end after high school. For years he wouldn't leave me alone. Even after he and Sara got married, I'd still hear from him. He'd text me nonstop for days, really intense stuff about how he felt about me and what I mean to him, and then he'd disappear for a few months, only to pop up again. The only way I could finally get him to stop was to tell him about my cancer, that my breasts were gone and I'd lost my sex drive. I didn't hear from him after that. But I know him. He can't live without his obsession. It's what he thinks is love. He told me a hundred times that he never 'loved' Sara the way he loved me. It was always me, and always would be. Maybe when I was no longer his ideal woman, he started looking for someone else to obsess over. And there you were, a widow living alone. Someone who'd need him the way he needs to be needed."

Kate shakes her head. "No, I don't believe that, Becca. I don't think that's the case. He's never given me any reason to think . . ." Kate trails off.

Rebecca asks, "What?"

"I mean, last night he told me he'd come over if I needed him to, but it wasn't anything."

"Are he and Sara still married?"

Kate pauses. "He said they're divorcing."

"I'm not surprised. Actually, I'm surprised it didn't happen sooner. I'm not trying to freak you out any more than you already are, Katie. I've been wanting to warn you about him for a while. If Eddie thinks he's in love with you—if he has idealized you—then he can be trouble. Take his help, yes, but keep your distance." Rebecca pauses. "Of course, the good news is, if he is secretly 'in love with you,' then the person who is doing this shit to you is fucked."

Kate has stopped making the bed. Standing straight, she looks at her sister. "I really didn't need this, Becca."

"I couldn't not tell you."

Kate nods, but tensely, her anger visible. Then she says, "Is there anything else you should tell me?"

"What do you mean?"

Before Kate can respond, her cell phone vibrates in her pocket, triggering a wave of terror. Her breathing stalled, she takes the device from her pocket and looks at the display. Her hands tremble as she reads.

Rebecca asks, "What is it?"

"It's from Maria. She says she was finally able to talk sense into Derek. They canceled the party."

Exhaling, Kate returns the phone to her pocket.

"Are you okay, Katie?"

"Yeah. Why?"

"Because you went white as a sheet. Does that happen every time you get a message on your phone?"

Kate nods—stiffly, not tensely.

Rebecca says, "Jesus, Katie. Your eyes went blank for a second. I could see the fight-or-flight reflex kinda shut off your brain. Your adrenals must be shot."

Suddenly Kate is struggling to keep back tears. "I feel like I'm going to have a heart attack."

Rebecca walks around the bed and places her hands on her sister's shoulders, looks at her squarely, then pulls her close, embracing her.

Kate does not fully surrender to the hug.

Leaning back, Rebecca says, "Listen, I've got an idea. Get one of those prepaid phones and put only the essential numbers in it. Shut your phone down for a while and leave it in a drawer and forget about it. You can't live like this. Adrenal burnout is a very real condition. And your Saturday is suddenly open, so you could run out and do it this morning. I'll stay here with the kids."

Kate steps away and returns to her chore. The tears she fought—stubbornly—linger in her eyes.

"I don't want to leave you without a car," she says. "In case there's an emergency."

"Then ask Jack if he'll drive you. That way, too, you won't have to go alone."

As is always the case after a burst of numbing fear, Kate's thinking is slow. "I don't know," she says. "I'd hate to bother him."

"I doubt he'd be bothered, Katie. Anyway, what have you got to lose by asking? And maybe you can invite him to dinner tonight, now that we're all free, so I can actually meet the guy. Max says he's nice, and Callie seems to think he's cute."

Still gathering her faculties, Kate doesn't respond. She breathes in and out, several times, then dries her eyes with the back of her hand.

Finally, she looks at Rebecca and says, "I need you to tell me something first."

"What?"

"Did you and Derek have an affair?"

Rebecca forces an uneasy smile. "Why do you ask that?"

"I saw you two talking after your run."

Rebecca nods. "Oh." She, too, takes a breath, lets it out. "I wouldn't call it an affair. But yes, we slept together a few times."

"How long ago?"

"Three years, maybe four. I don't know. I'm sorry. I know Maria means a lot to you. Are you going to tell her?"

"There's no point. Unless there's any chance it will happen again."

"It won't. That's what we argued about. He wanted to, but I said no."

Kate understands now why he was outside the house in his slippers. He saw Rebecca and rushed out to talk to her.

"God, I hate that man," Kate says.

Rebecca laughs. "Yeah, there's a lot to hate there." She pauses. "I'm not that person anymore, Katie. I need you to believe that. And if that's something I have to prove to you every day for the rest of my life, so be it. I used to hate myself and want to hurt myself, and I hurt a lot of other people in the process. I've done things I'm ashamed of. Terrible things. Unforgivable things. But those days are over. I promise you that. I will never be who I used to be. I couldn't if I wanted to, and I don't want to."

"It's as simple as that?"

"Yes. I'd rather die than cause anyone pain ever again, especially you."

Kate takes that in, nodding. "And I'm sorry for any pain I caused you," she says finally. "I don't want to be the person I used to be, either—when it comes to us, I mean. It wasn't easy, shutting you out."

"I didn't give you much of a choice."

"Still, I could have been less judgmental. I should have realized there was a reason you were acting the way you were."

"So maybe we can start over. Pick up where we left off."

"We can try," Kate says. "I don't think we can try to pretend the last twenty-five years never happened. But I guess we shouldn't let those years cancel out everything that came before. When we were all we had. Right?"

"Right."

Kate's cell phone vibrates again, the buzzing muffled but still clearly audible in the small room. Rebecca watches as Kate first freezes, then pushes through her initial reaction and removes the device from her pocket.

Looking at the display, Kate is puzzled.

Rebecca asks, "What is it?"

"It's from Chief O'Neil. He wants to meet with me."

"I wonder what he wants."

Kate shakes her head. "He didn't say." She keys in a response and sends it.

"What did you say?"

"I asked when."

Almost immediately, Kate's phone buzzes again. She reads the text. "As soon as possible. At Compo Beach."

"That's weird," Rebecca says. "Why doesn't he just come here?"

Again, Kate's response is to shake her head. She sends another text.

"What did you say?"

"That I could be there in a half hour."

Neither speaks as they wait for O'Neil's reply.

Finally, that text arrives.

Kate reads, "'I'll meet you there.'"

Speechless, she looks at her sister.

"Go," Rebecca says. "I'll finish this."

"I'll be leaving you without a car."

"We're not going anywhere. And if there's a problem, Jack's in the cottage, and Maria is right next door. We'll be fine. Go, Katie."

Hesitant, Kate doesn't move.

Then, without another word, she turns and heads for the bedroom door.

The Cottage

Driving, Kate struggles against a rising panic.

Though she tries to tell herself that Chief O'Neil asked to meet in person to deliver good news, the idea rings false, and with every mile farther from home she gets, the opposite scenario seems only more likely.

When Compo Beach is finally in view, the certainty that she is moments from something terrible causes Kate's heart to pound.

Parked at the far end of the otherwise empty parking lot is Chief O'Neil's marked sedan.

Kate steers toward it, moving alongside the wide beach leading down to the Long Island Sound.

The sky that was gray when Kate first awoke has darkened significantly, and its reflection on the water's flat surface appears almost black.

As she turns into a spot several spaces down from the chief's vehicle, the man, dressed in his uniform and a department-issue raincoat, emerges from behind the wheel.

He waits while Kate parks and shuts off the engine. Releasing her seat belt, she exits her vehicle as well, closing the door and then walking to the front fender.

Chief O'Neil gestures toward the beach, indicating that he wants Kate to meet him there. Then he crosses onto the sand and heads straight down the beach.

Kate follows a diagonal path until she catches up with him at the water's edge.

THIRTY-TWO

Kate's first impression of Chief O'Neil is that he's noticeably uncomfortable.

Though she is facing him, he looks out over the water pensively. And despite the twilight-like gloom created by the canopy of low-hanging clouds overhead, he is squinting.

Even if she didn't know the man as well as she does, there would be no mistaking his unease.

Kate asks, "What's going on, Chief?"

O'Neil shakes his head once. "Nothing good, I'm afraid."

Kate's heart sinks as her gut tightens. Still, she does her best to maintain an outward calm. After scanning the water briefly, she looks back at O'Neil. "Okay, so what does 'nothing good' mean?"

"The photo that was sent to you yesterday, of you in your bedroom, a printout of that was received today by Doug Banks, the superintendent of the Fairfield school system, your superintendent."

Closing her eyes, Kate cringes and says, "Jesus."

She reopens her eyes when O'Neil speaks.

"It came in this morning's mail," he says. "At his home. No letter, nothing, just the copy of the photo. Doug is a friend of mine, and he knows of our connection, so instead of calling the Fairfield police, which he should have done, technically, because that's where he lives, he called me. We met, and he gave me the photo and the envelope it came in. And he assured me that no one else has seen it or even knows about it."

Kate nods absently. "My heart is racing, but the rest of me is numb," she says. She, too, looks out over the dark sound, then asks, "Why is this happening?"

"I might have the answer to that," O'Neil says. "I explained to Doug what has been going on, and asked if he would keep this between us, which he agreed to do. But he suggested that you might consider taking a leave of absence while this plays out. Obviously, the photo was sent to him to embarrass you. And if Doug would have called the Fairfield police, it wouldn't be long before every cop in that department saw it as well, because unfortunately that's the way cops are, even my own. That, of course, would only add to your embarrassment. But now the concern is whether or not copies will be sent to anyone else. People you know, colleagues, or any of your students, for that matter. That makes me think that this is a threat to your livelihood. Would you be able to keep your job if a photo of you was spread around town? Could you survive a scandal like that? Would you even want to? Or would this end up driving you out of town? And is that what this is all about? Does someone hate you enough to want that?"

Struck with a sudden feeling of defeat, Kate is too overwhelmed to respond.

O'Neil looks at her for a moment, then faces the water and says, "Sending the photo to your employer was a targeted attack. This guy, your tormentor, he's a sniper. He could have spread copies all over town as his first move, but he didn't, he went instead for the one person who could dramatically alter your life. He sent a message. Of course, that doesn't mean he won't escalate at some point, but for now I think you have a little time. Time to think, time to act. I haven't told anyone about this. Not even Leo or Eddie. And Doug has agreed to keep this between us. So for now, I'm willing to sweep this under the rug. If Leo knew he would likely overreact, and Eddie, well, I don't think he has slept in days."

"What do you mean?"

"All he cares about is this case. Right now he's going through security camera footage that we collected from every stop within two blocks of the Fresh Market. Yesterday Eddie was searching for any reports of cases similar to this one. I'm considering asking him to take a leave of absence as well because I can't justify the man-hours he's putting in. Which brings me to my next point."

Kate looks at him. "Which is?"

"There isn't much that law enforcement can do in these types of situations. I could send the envelope and copy of the photo out for testing, but the envelope has been handled by God knows how many people during the mailing process, and it's doubtful anything would be found on the photo. Our guy isn't sloppy. I'm going to get shit from the selectmen, because it looks like favoritism, because that's what it is, but I'll post an officer in your driveway tonight and tomorrow night. Monday the security cameras go up, correct?"

Kate nods.

O'Neil continues. "Good. I hate that my hands are tied like this, because I know this feels world ending to you. The only things I can suggest are the same ones I'd tell anyone in your situation—change your numbers, lock your doors, don't go places alone, don't answer calls that are blocked or from numbers you don't recognize. And remember, Kate, you have options that others in your situation don't. You can sell and relocate—if it comes to that, I mean. We're not there yet; there's still the possibility he'll screw up in some way. And everything he does just adds to the list of charges we can throw at him. Half the homes in Westport have mortgages that are underwater. If a place sold for a million ten years ago, it's maybe worth six hundred thousand now. Not a lot of people could sell if they wanted to. But your place has special value because your lot can be subdivided. The only properties that are selling are new constructions. A developer would easily pay a million plus just for the land."

"I'm not selling," Kate says.

"Like I said, we're not there yet. But I need you to know that, officially, there's very little that we can do. Unofficially is a different story, but even then, there are limits." O'Neil pauses. "So it's up to you what we do next. We can keep this to ourselves for now, or we could bring everyone up to speed. It's totally your call."

"I don't know; maybe not telling anyone yet will make it seem less real. And you're right; Leo would go nuts."

"How much do the twins know?"

"They know about the smashed living room window. And they see the police car in our driveway at night."

"Did they ask why it's there?"

"I told them it was friends of their father keeping vandals away. They don't need to know about the other stuff. It helps that their aunt is here. She keeps them distracted."

"That's a difficult way to live," O'Neil says. "Keeping a secret to protect others. I sympathize. How old are they now?"

"Twelve."

"I'd imagine it would be hardest on Max. If the photo of his mom was spread around town, I mean."

Kate once again closes her eyes and cringes. She sees the face of her son, and then remembers their conversation about bullies as they sat side by side on the swings.

Opening her eyes again, Kate says, "You said you think I have time, right?"

"That's what I believe, yes. If his goal is to make you want to leave town, it's likely he'll want the threat to your livelihood to hang over you."

Kate nods decisively. "You should probably fill Eddie in, but otherwise I want to keep this quiet. For now at least."

"You got it, Kate. Try to enjoy the weekend with your family, if you can. Think about whether or not you'll take a leave of absence."

"I'm not going to be doing that."

"Do you think that's wise?"

"What this asshole doesn't know is I don't give a shit if anyone sees that picture. Not anymore, not after what you've told me. And if it does get out and parents complain and I get forced out of my job, another thing he doesn't know is I've got enough money saved to cover my expenses for an extended period of time. I don't have mortgage payments to make, and I could rent the cottage year-round at fifteen hundred a month, which would easily cover my property taxes. I'm not going to live in fear of what he may or may not do. And I'm not going to be chased from my home."

"But what about your children?"

"They lost their father, Chief. They heard the gunshots that killed him. I mean this in the best possible way, but they'll survive this. We all will. Max might need some help, true, but Callie doesn't take shit from anyone. And anyway, what kind of life lesson would I be teaching them if I ran away from everything we know because of some bully?" She pauses, then looks at O'Neil. "So fuck him, okay? Let him do his worst, because you know what? The worst has already happened. The man I loved bled to death in front of me. And nothing has been the same since. I'll do whatever needs to be done. I'll change all my numbers; I'll cut him off in every way possible. And if he ruins my life, then I'll just live in my fortress with my family. That's pretty much all I do anyway. I'll spend the next six years preparing my children for college. I'll drive them to school every morning, and pick them up every afternoon. And once they're off at college, then I'll figure out what to do. By then no one will remember some stupid scandal involving a public school teacher and photographs. No one will care anymore."

Chief O'Neil asks, "And if he keeps this up? Keeps applying pressure? Will you be able to handle that?"

"I'll have to. It's as simple as that."

"And if, God forbid, he escalates?" O'Neil says. "What then?"

Kate shrugs. "I'll make sure I'm ready for him."

"And how are you going to do that?"

THIRTY-THREE

The rain arrives at noon.

Though little more than a light drizzle at first, the downpour that was forecast begins less than a half hour later.

Kate is standing in the checkout line in the Stratford Walmart when the heavy rain comes, the drops pounding on the flat roof, sending a steady crashing sound echoing throughout the store.

Though she rushes across the already flooded parking lot to her car, Kate's hair and clothing are soaked, but she doesn't care about that.

With the motor running so the heater and defogger work, Kate removes the prepaid cell phone from its packaging and proceeds to activate and then charge the phone.

Once the device is up and running, the first text that Kate sends is to Rebecca, so her sister can contact her, should she need to.

Kate considers sending texts to Maria and Jack as well, informing them that she has a new number, but she decides to hold off until later because the drive from Stratford to Orange will take longer than anticipated, given the rain, and the last thing she wants is to keep Leo Burke waiting.

Greyson Guns, a firearms dealer and shooting range, is tucked in the back corner of a small plaza on the north side of Route 1.

As Kate parks in the crowded lot, she spots Leo Burke waiting under the awning at the shop's front door, a duffel bag in hand.

Within minutes, he and Kate have made their way into the busy indoor range.

Even with ear protection on, Kate is initially unnerved by the sound of steady gunfire to her left and right, but by the time she is facing a silhouette target with Leif's off-duty pistol presented in the high-ready position, she is focused to the point of tuning out any and all noise.

Kate's first two shots are dead center, but as she continues to fire, her accuracy suffers significantly, with several shots, to her dismay, landing well outside the human-shaped silhouette.

Leo waits until she has emptied the first magazine before pausing to explain that what is happening to her is common. The first two attempts were instinctive point-and-shoot shots, meaning that she simply presented the firearm and pressed the trigger without any preconceived notions of what to do and what not to do. But as she proceeded, Kate began overthinking the process—gripping the weapon with too much force in an effort to manage the felt recoil, snatching the trigger instead of pressing it, and focusing on the target to monitor where her shots were landing as opposed to keeping track of the front sight and confirming that it was, in fact, aligned with the dark circle at the center of the silhouette before resetting the trigger and firing again.

It takes another seventeen-round magazine of nine millimeter, but with Leo's coaching, Kate soon enough resumes hitting the paper target with shots that Leo, nodding in satisfaction, deems combat effective.

Using the third and final magazine, as well as a clean target, Kate is instructed by Leo to hold the weapon at the low-ready position, then press out to the high-ready on his command and fire two shots in rapid succession into the torso, making certain that she pauses after the first shot to realign the front sight before sending off the second.

When Kate has done that seven times, Leo instructs her to use the remaining three rounds to attempt what he calls a "Mozambique Drill." This involves landing two shots in rapid succession into the torso before placing a third into the silhouette's head.

The new challenge immediately invites overthinking, but Kate pushes through that reflex and relaxes. At the low-ready, she waits for Leo's command, and when it comes, she extends her arms forward, aligns the front sight with the target, fires, finds and aligns the front sight again, and fires a second time.

Then she shifts her focus to the head and raises the pistol until the sight is between her right eye and where she wants the shot to go.

Quickly focusing on the front sight once more, she fires. Returning the now-empty pistol to the low-ready, she looks downrange at the target and finds that the round has struck the head at dead center.

———

Driving back to Westport on a rain-swept I-95, Kate remembers Leif.

Briefly she recalls the first time he took her to the range, back when they had gotten engaged and he'd moved into the house.

So young, then, their whole lives ahead of them. How could either have known that it was there, on her property, that he would die?

Had they not reunited after college, he would still be alive. Of course, that would mean there'd be no Max and Callie, so she can't wish, not even for a second, that the chance meeting that brought them back together—running into each other in a grocery store late one winter night—hadn't occurred.

It would have been so easy for them to have missed each other, then and possibly forever. He could have left for the store five minutes earlier or five minutes later. And she could have satisfied her craving for ice cream by stopping at the convenience store a half mile from her house instead of opting for the supermarket and its better-stocked frozen section, three miles away.

But the ache that his absence causes still is equal to the ache that overtakes her whenever she imagines her life without him—a life without their children, yes, but also without the home they made together, the meals they shared in the kitchen, the outdoor chores and indoor renovations, as well as the sanctuary that was their bedroom.

After long workdays, on weekends, during cherished vacations and holidays, that is where they slept late every morning they could, and where they shared intimacy whenever one or the other brought the urgent need to bed at night.

She remembers priding herself on never once having refused him. Even during difficult times, when one conflict or another would arise between them, she and Leif always managed to find their way back to reason—a journey that usually began in the safe haven of their bedroom at night.

Very little of that life remains, and every project taken in and every chore completed is simply a means of keeping the momentum she relies on to carry her through from one day to the next.

Busy-ness, as a distraction from all that is gone.

The fact that her bedroom will no longer offer the comfort of darkness is too much for Kate.

And with the traffic on I-95 being slowed by the weather, she has only made it to Stratford when she realizes what she must do next.

———

Parked again in the Walmart lot, Kate uses her new phone to text Rebecca, asking her sister if she would measure the window in Kate's bedroom and send the dimensions back in a reply text.

Kate is in the crowded store and heading for the window treatment aisle when the text from Rebecca comes through.

It takes Kate less than a minute to find a light-blocking shade with the correct measurements. Picking out a pair of heavy curtains two aisles over takes a few minutes more. But ten minutes after having entered the store, Kate is back in her Subaru and heading home.

It crosses her mind that since Jack worked construction, she could use the new blinds and curtains needing to be installed as an excuse to invite him over.

But the idea of doing it herself will bring a sense of pride that she very much needs, so she sets that urge aside for now.

———

Kate showers and changes clothes—a post-range precaution that Leif had always followed and insisted that Kate also take part in whenever they returned from shooting practice.

As Rebecca and the twins work on a jigsaw puzzle in the kitchen, Kate clears out the top drawer of her nightstand to make room for the lockbox Leo Burke gave her. Once it is in place, she tests the device by entering the three-digit code. The instant the final key is depressed, the box unlocks and the spring-and-piston-activated lid begins to rise, quickly but smoothly.

Inside the box is the nine-millimeter pistol, a loaded magazine inserted in its grip, along with two spares.

After confirming that the lockbox is functioning properly, Kate presses the lid down, locking it in place, and closes the drawer.

Retrieving Leif's toolbox from his workbench in the basement, she sets about removing the existing set of blinds and brackets, after which she installs their replacements. Though her bedroom is already gloomy because of the dark clouds and sheets of rain, the light-blocking shade transforms afternoon into twilight.

Once Kate has installed the thick curtains and drawn them closed, she has re-created the solemn darkness she became accustomed to a long time ago.

And just as important, she has sealed herself inside a space that no one can peer into from outside.

———

At four o'clock, the rumble of thunder can be heard in the distance.

Maria calls to invite Kate and her family over for dinner, but Kate passes, stating that all anyone seems up for is a quiet and lazy night in. And while that is mostly true, Rebecca's brief affair with Derek four years ago plays a part in Kate's decision.

Bringing her sister into her friend's home would feel to Kate like an overt act of disrespect, not to mention guaranteeing for those in the know an awkward evening. For the first time since Maria informed Kate that she was going back to work full time, Kate is actually grateful that their interactions will now be limited. Chief O'Neil is right about keeping secrets to protect others being a difficult way to live.

The list of people Kate needs to protect—from any and all kinds of harm—is growing.

With this in mind, Kate gets her notebook from her workbag in the kitchen utility closet and returns to the page where she wrote down the names of those she is considering assigning as guardian.

After studying the three names for a moment, she draws a line through Maria's, leaving behind Rebecca's and her father-in-law's. Flipping to the next page, she does the same with the list of possible conservators.

A moment more passes before Kate strikes Rebecca's name as well, leaving Leo Burke as the only option.

And just like that, the decision has been made.

Turning back to the previous page, Kate reads through the column marked CONS, her eye landing on the final of the three that she listed alongside Rebecca's name.

"How does she make her money?"

She circles it, then closes the notebook.

———

Despite the rain droning outside—snaps and pops as drops drill into the already saturated yard, combined with a steady thudding on the roof above—the house seems quieter to Kate now that she can't be reached by anyone other than those she's given the new number to.

Rebecca and Maria have it, of course, as well as Leo Burke and Eddie Sabrowsky. Kate considered not including Chief O'Neil—she liked the idea, for some reason, of limiting herself to four people—but decided that she'd better send the new number to him, too.

Only being accessible to five people, all of whom she trusts, gives her a feeling of optimism.

All that remains is changing her landline number, which she will take care of tomorrow. For the time being, the ringers on all extensions have been silenced, and the volume on the answering machine is turned down to zero.

As she makes dinner, Kate enjoys the newfound feeling of peace. Whatever is coming her way in the next few days or weeks is coming her way, and there isn't anything she can do about it. For now—for however long this will last—she and her children are safe. Rebecca is safe. Leo Burke, though out of the loop for now, is safe.

She wants to lock herself into this moment—into the present—just as she has locked herself inside her home.

Because of the clouds, night comes earlier than usual, as does the patrol car. At five thirty it turns into Kate's driveway, rolling past the cottage and parking in the same spot that the vehicle the night before did—alongside the house, and facing the woods.

The sensor-activated floodlights, tricked by the early dark, come on just moments later.

It isn't until Kate has formed lean ground chicken into four patties that she realizes she hasn't informed Jack that the party has been canceled. Nor has she passed on her new number to him. After washing and drying her hands, she takes out her phone and keys in his number, then presses "Talk" and starts counting the rings.

Jack answers on the second ring.

"Hello."

"I'm glad you answered," Kate says. "Thought you might not because of the strange number."

"I figured it was you. Your sister told me you were getting a new phone today."

Kate pauses. "Oh, yeah? When did she tell you that?"

"She stopped by, around noon, I guess. She wanted to let me know that your neighbor's party was canceled."

"Oh, that was nice of her. I meant to tell you sooner; it's been a hectic day."

"I'm thinking that the lack of cars in their driveway and along the street would have tipped me off that plans had changed."

"You're still just sitting around and looking out windows," Kate teases.

"Actually, I'm officially no longer a bum. I got a job."

"You're kidding?"

"Nope."

"Doing what?"

"Working for a landscaper. Fifteen an hour off the books, which isn't bad. I start Monday. That is, if we all haven't drowned by then. Anyway, it gets me outside again, which is one of the things I liked when I worked home construction during the summers."

"That's great news, Jack. Hey, how about to celebrate you come over for dinner? And you wouldn't have to cut across the front yard this time."

Jack hesitates, and Kate's gut tightens at the sudden silence.

"What?" she says.

"Your sister already invited me. Well, actually, Callie did."

"She had the kids with her?"

"Yes. And Max asked me if I'd show him some wrestling moves."

"Really," Kate says. "I had no idea."

"They said they wanted it to be a surprise." Jack pauses. "To be honest, I think they're trying to fix us up."

Kate smiles—for the first time today, she realizes.

"Are they now?" she says.

"You can give them some excuse, if you'd rather not have company tonight. Tell them I have plans that I forgot all about."

"No need. I think it's sweet of them. But I don't want you to feel obligated to come."

"I was looking forward to it."

"Okay, then. It's a date. I guess."

"They told me to be there at six."

"That works."

"And Callie told me to ditch the tie this time."

Kate laughs. "Yeah, she's not shy when it comes to expressing her opinion, is she?"

"I'll wear it anyway," Jack says. "I think I look good in a tie."

"I think you look great in a tie."

"Tie it is, then. I'll see you in a little while."

"We'll be here."

Kate ends the call and turns to head into the living room, but Rebecca and the twins are standing in the door, causing Kate to stop short in the middle of the kitchen.

The three are smiling, and Rebecca says, "Sorry, Katie. They swore me to secrecy."

"I was going to set the table for five," Callie says, "and wait for you to figure it out."

Kate asks, "Is that so?"

"And Max told him that he had to bring ice cream."

Kate looks at Max. "You did?"

Max nods. "And tomorrow he's going to show me how to wrestle."

"Yeah, Jack just told me that. Wrestle, though, not fight, right?"

Adopting one of his sister's habits, Max rolls his eyes and says, *"Yes."*

Then, drawn by the sound of an action scene coming from the living room, he exclaims, "This is my favorite part." Slipping past his aunt, he hurries back to the TV.

Callie follows him, saying, "You've seen this a hundred times already. You know it's not going to end differently, right?"

Rebecca remains in the doorway.

"I like him," she says. "Jack. And not just because he said nice things about my paintings."

"Oh, that's right. He's an admirer."

"Nice to have at least one." Rebecca pauses, her tone turning serious. "Can you tell me what the chief wanted?"

Kate lowers her voice. "Later. After the kids are in bed. I wanted to talk to you about something anyway."

Rebecca smiles nervously. "Am I in trouble?"

Kate shakes her head, then whispers, "It's about Max and Callie. And the house and everything. And what happens if something were to happen to me."

"I hope this doesn't mean Chief O'Neil gave you bad news."

"It's not that. Leo and I had a discussion yesterday. I need to update my will, that's all. But we'll talk about it later, okay?"

"Yeah, sure."

"Right now I have to turn four chicken patties into five."

"Yeah, again, sorry about that. I tried to explain to them that you needed to know Jack was coming, but they wanted it to be a surprise. Do you want help?"

"No, I'm fine. Just tell the kids in fifteen minutes that it's time to set the table."

Rebecca's focus shifts to the top of Kate's head.

Alarmed, Kate says, "What?"

Rebecca points to Kate's hair and draws circles in the air. "You might want to do something about that."

Kate realizes that after her shower she merely combed her wet hair back and tied it into a ponytail.

"Oh shit. Maybe I do need your help."

"Go get ready," Rebecca says. "I'll take over in here."

THIRTY-FOUR

Callie holds center stage at dinner, performing as much for Jack as for her aunt, telling stories about her friends at school and the teachers she likes and the teachers she doesn't.

And Max is more animated, interjecting his opinion about certain friends or teachers on occasion, and maintaining his presence in the conversation even when he wasn't speaking by looking often at those seated at the table as opposed to down at his plate.

It doesn't take long before the adults realize that Callie has no intention of surrendering the spotlight, so they resign themselves to simply eating their meals and enjoying the entertainment, though every now and then Jack is asked a question, which he does his best to answer in the brief window of time he is allotted.

After dessert, they gather in the living room to stream a movie, Kate and Jack on the couch, Callie and Rebecca on the love seat, and Max stretched out on the floor and facing the television, his head propped up on several pillows.

There are moments when Kate forgets the outside world, only to remember her situation again and experience a sudden rush of fear.

She does her best to remind herself to remain in the moment and enjoy this time with her family and guest.

After the movie, Max suggests a game of Scrabble, so they move the coffee table to the other side of the room to clear space, and then set up the board on the floor.

Three games later—all of which Rebecca wins—it is ten o'clock. Jack announces that it's time for him to get back and turn in. Kate walks him to the front door as Rebecca leads the twins upstairs to get ready for bed.

Though the rain is lighter now than it was four hours before, it is steady, and as Kate opens the door, a burst of cool, damp air rushes past her.

"It's like I opened the door to a cave," she says.

The umbrella Jack arrived with is leaning in a nearby corner. Kate hands it to him.

"Don't forget this."

Jack takes it and says, "Thank you. This was great."

"A deal's a deal, right?"

"That's what they tell me. Speaking of, what's a good time for me to teach Max some moves?"

"Anytime. We're here all day. But if something comes up, you guys can do it another time."

Jack shrugs. "What's going to come up? I'm just waiting now for Monday morning to come."

"Why don't you come over for breakfast, then? Get some calories in you for your first day."

"Yeah?"

"Yeah. You guys can do your thing after."

"Okay." Jack pauses before extending his right hand. "Well, thanks again. For dinner. For everything."

Kate takes his hand, and they shake.

Turning away, Jack raises the umbrella and points it through the door, ready to open it. But before he can, Kate places her hand on his shoulder.

"Hold on," she says.

Directing Jack to take a few steps back, Kate quickly swings the door until it is almost closed. Leaving it ajar, she turns Jack so he is facing her, then closes the distance between them quickly, placing her left hand on the back of his head as she moves to pull him even closer.

Kissing him flush on the lips, she closes her eyes.

Finally leaning back, she opens them again and exhales.

They linger face-to-face for a moment, and then Kate smiles and says, "Okay, you can go now."

"Are you sure this time?"

She laughs. "Yes."

Opening the door, Kate steps aside, and Jack once again faces out and prepares to open the umbrella. "See you in the morning?"

Kate nods. "Yes. Definitely."

—

By ten thirty, Max and Callie are in bed.

Seated at the table in the dimly lit kitchen, Kate sips peppermint tea as she waits for Rebecca.

She is halfway through when she finally hears her sister coming down the stairs.

Entering, Rebecca says, "Hey." She is dressed in a silk robe.

Kate says, "There's water in the kettle if you want some tea. I don't know if it's still warm enough."

Rebecca steps to the oven and touches the kettle. "Yeah, that should work." She retrieves a mug from the cupboard and sets it on the countertop, places a tea bag inside, then fills it from the kettle.

After walking back to the table, she sits across from her sister. "How'd the good night go?"

"It went fine," Kate says.

"Max and Callie seem to really like him."

"Yeah."

Rebecca takes a sip, waits for Kate to say more, but when Kate doesn't, she asks, "Anything wrong?"

Kate nods. "I've been trying to put it out of my mind all night, but someone might be trying to get me to lose my job."

"That's what Chief O'Neil wanted to see you about."

"Yeah. I don't want to talk about that now, though. I'm trying to stay calm. But I need to ask you a few questions. Personal questions."

"Okay."

"I'd like to know how you make your money."

"Oh, that," Rebecca says.

"I've decided I'm going to name Leo as conservator, to take care of my estate until Max and Callie are twenty-one. There's the house, college accounts, and savings, and he would be in charge of renting the cottage. But I want to ask if you'll agree to be their guardian. It's obvious to me that you've changed. Max and Callie adore you. And Max is happy for the first time in a long time. The thing is, you always seem to have money, and you've never talked about a job, and all those winters that you lived in the cottage, you didn't ever work." Kate pauses. "So I guess I need to know that you're not, I don't know, selling drugs or running scams or cons or something like that."

Rebecca laughs lightly. "Nothing that colorful, I can assure you."

"And all that you've been through with your cancer and the surgeries, that costs money. I'm concerned you might be majorly in debt."

"I'm not," Rebecca says. She pauses. "The whole thing is pretty simple. A long time ago, someone died and left me a substantial inheritance."

"Who?"

"Someone I was in love with. We met years and years ago, not long after college. To the dismay of his family, he left me five million dollars, which of course I immediately began to burn through, and continued to burn through for years. Out of that five million, about fifty thousand is left. Obviously, that wouldn't last long, and my fine arts degree is pretty worthless, so I was planning on using that money to go to grad school. I have a friend in California who's a marriage counselor. She's the most fucked-up person I know—more fucked up than I ever was—but she earned her master's online, and in a few years built herself a good practice. If she can do it, I don't see why I wouldn't be able to as well. I was also thinking of occupational therapy, which would let me put my art degree to work. There are actually government assistance programs that would help pay for school. And the starting salary for an OT is seventy-five thousand, so that's not bad. I mean, for around here that's probably the bare minimum, but I did tend bar for one summer during college, so I could always pick up shifts somewhere if I needed to."

Kate needs a moment to take all that in. Then finally she asks, "So who was this man you loved? You never talked about him."

Rebecca shrugs. "You and I weren't really talking back then, were we? But he was great. He was older and he was married, but he was great." She pauses. "Maybe I didn't say anything because I didn't want you judging me. I didn't want your disapproval."

Kate nods but says nothing.

Rebecca asks, "Have you ever read John Updike?"

"Yeah. Well, a long time ago."

"In one of his books he describes a love affair between two people by saying something like the woman in her put the man in him at rest, and vice versa. Charles put the woman in me at rest. Being in love with him was grounding. I was almost *not* crazy when I was around him. I was almost normal. When he died, I slipped right back into my old behavior, but worse than before. I was me again, with a vengeance."

"How did he die?"

"He was murdered by his wife."

"Jesus."

Rebecca shrugs again. "Who knows, maybe that's why I'm considering becoming a marriage counselor." She laughs. "I never really made that connection until now. But then again, I haven't told any of this to anyone until now."

"Saying things aloud can do that," Kate says. "Make them more real."

Another pause, and then Rebecca says, "I was so mad when I was cut out of Granddad's will. Mad at him, mad at you, mad at everything. It felt like retaliation at the time—retaliation and rejection—but I realized finally that I didn't give him any choice. He was right to leave everything to you."

"If it's any consolation, there was less than twenty thousand dollars left. He didn't want to leave the house, so he hired round-the-clock nurses. That drained his savings pretty quickly."

"I wish I had been there. Toward the end, I mean. I wish I'd been better to him. And Grandma. And you."

Kate nods, and then says, "How long were you and Charles together?"

Rebecca smiles at the memory. "Three years."

"You were his . . . what?"

"Mistress, yeah. Kept woman, the whole thing. But it was more than that to me. It was everything. He was everything. Like Leif was for you. That's why I wanted to stay and help you after the funeral. I knew what you were going through. I knew what you'd lost. I knew what had been taken from you."

"I'm sorry," Kate says. "I'm sorry I was so cold to you."

"I didn't give you any choice, either. Anyway, I think I was meant to face the ordeal that followed alone. I was diagnosed a few months after."

Neither speaks for a moment.

"So," Rebecca says finally, "if you want me to be Max and Callie's guardian, I would be honored, yes."

"The house would go to them," Kate says. "My savings, too. Like I said, Leo would be in charge of all that until they're twenty-one. I'd want you to live here with them, though. I'd want them to finish growing up here. But I'm not going to pass on the same burden Grandpa gave me. When they're adults and they're ready to start their lives, they can do whatever they want with the property. They can sell it, or they can tear the place down and put up two brand-new homes to raise their families in." Kate pauses. "So are you okay with all that?"

"Yes, very. But nothing's going to happen to you, Katie, so we don't have to worry about any of this. Right? The cameras are being set up Monday. I'm here. Leo isn't far away. And, of course, Jack is right up the driveway."

"For the next three months, at least."

"Who knows, maybe longer."

"Yeah, let's not jump to any conclusions here, okay?"

"Maybe jumping in is exactly what you need to do now—as in, jumping in with both feet. Has there been anyone in the past two years?"

Kate shakes her head.

"Yeah, me neither," Rebecca says.

They fall silent again for a moment.

Finally, Rebecca asks, "When will you be making the changes to your will?"

"I'll call our lawyer Monday, tell him what I want. Then it's just a matter of him drawing it up and me getting there to sign."

"Every lawyer I've ever dealt with has always taken his sweet time. I hope your guy is different. I'm sure you'd like to get it all settled so you don't have to think about it anymore."

"I seem to remember back when Leif and I did our will that he didn't get back to us for over a week. Maybe he'll be quicker this time."

"Just try to focus on the relief you'll feel when it's finally done."

"Yeah. And after that, it'll just be this other shit I'll have to worry about."

"You're surrounded by people who care about you very much. That's got to help."

Kate nods. She is tempted to tell her sister about today's development—the photo sent to the superintendent of Fairfield schools—but decides against it.

It's late, she's tired, and all she wants is to sleep.

Rebecca lets out a long sigh. "Well, I'm going up," she says. "Are you going to be okay?"

"Yes. I'll be turning in soon, too."

Reaching across the table, Rebecca lays her hand palm up. Kate accepts the invitation and joins hands with her sister. Rebecca squeezes once, then releases and stands.

Offering a smile of support to Kate, she picks up her mug, says good night, and leaves.

Kate remains seated. She listens to Rebecca climbing the stairs, then finishes her tea.

———

Kate changes in the bathroom, then crosses her solemnly dark bedroom and sits on the edge of the mattress.

Opening her nightstand drawer, she first looks at the lockbox containing Leif's pistol, and then her eye moves to the cell phone lying beside it. The device—her old phone—is shut down, and for a brief moment Kate is tempted to restart it to check for any calls or texts that she may have missed.

But she knows it's not worth the risk. Nor is there any point in undoing all the work she did today to protect herself from a man who is, for all intents and purposes, an intruder.

At one point she will need to start the device again so she can manually transfer all her remaining contacts to the prepaid phone.

That can wait, though, for another time.

She slides the drawer shut and gets under the covers.

THIRTY-FIVE

In the cottage, while Kate observes, Jack teaches Max several basic takedowns.

Kate recognizes the techniques from her days attending Leif's high school matches—the double leg takedown, the single leg takedown, and a hip throw. She is pleased that her son is an attentive student and a quick learner, but Max has always excelled at the subjects that hold his attention, unlike his sister, who excels at everything regardless of whether she is interested or not.

Since they have no mat to break their falls, when Jack demonstrates a move on Max, he is careful to stop at the moment when Max's balance is compromised, after which he has Max attempt the takedown on him. Only during Max's attempts at the double leg takedown—dropping low, he wraps his arms around Jack's knees, drawing them backward as he drives his shoulder into Jack's hip—does Max actually manage to bring Jack down. But despite his size, Jack is agile enough to maneuver during the fall and land on the wood floor without injury.

As they continue to work on that technique—Jack offering pointers, Max listening carefully and then applying them—Kate hears a vehicle in her driveway. Moving to the front door, she arrives as a Ford F-150 passes the cottage. Recognizing it as belonging to Sabrowsky, Kate excuses herself and steps out onto the pathway.

The Ford parks at the bottom of the driveway, and Kate starts walking toward it. Getting out from behind the wheel, Sabrowsky looks first at the house, scanning the windows as though he is expecting to see someone looking out at him. Then he catches Kate out of the corner of his eye and heads up the driveway to meet her.

Sabrowsky is dressed in jeans, a black denim shirt, and cowboy boots. Kate can't remember the last time she's seen her friend out of uniform.

As they approach each other, Kate smiles and asks, "What's going on, Eddie?"

Sabrowsky nods toward the cottage. "Anything wrong?" There is a look of concern on his face—or at least a look that Kate reads as concern.

"No, not at all. Jack is just showing Max some wrestling stuff."

Again, Sabrowsky nods, but his expression doesn't abate. "Oh," he says.

Kate realizes that she may have been mistaken in her interpretation of her friend's expression. As they meet midway between his truck and the cottage, she gets the sense that something other than why she'd be at the cottage on a Sunday midmorning is on his mind.

Standing face-to-face and just a few feet apart, Kate does her best to maintain her calm and asks, "What's wrong, Eddie?"

Sabrowsky forces a smile. "Just very tired."

"Chief O'Neil said you were working too much."

"But it looks like it may have paid off, because I actually have some good news for a change."

"What?"

"I went through the videos that were pulled from the shops surrounding the Fresh Market, and I may have identified the vehicle our guy was driving off in after he left the note on your windshield. It passes by quickly, is only visible for two seconds, but the driver has the same cap on that our guy was wearing, and we can see a little bit more of his face—just enough to confirm that he has a beard."

"That's what I thought when I saw the clip the chief showed me."

"Unfortunately, the license plates aren't visible, but the car appears to be a green Chevy Malibu, '05 or earlier."

"I don't imagine there are a lot of those still on the road."

"Surprisingly, there are quite a few. But one was reported stolen recently, and where it was stolen is interesting."

"Why?"

"Because it was stolen in Bridgeport."

"Where the text was sent from."

"Exactly."

"Jesus," Kate says. "This guy knows all the tricks, doesn't he?"

"Yeah, well, so do I," Sabrowsky says. "That's not the good news, though. The good news is the Bridgeport PD has already pulled video from the area where the Malibu was parked when it was stolen. They haven't gone through them yet, but they agreed to make copies for me. I'm picking them up later today. So we may still find this asshole, Katie, and soon."

Kate sighs. "That would be awesome."

The expression that Sabrowsky erased a moment ago with a smile returns.

Kate says, "But there's something else, isn't there?"

"I have a question, but it's not an easy one to ask."

"What?"

Sabrowsky glances at the house again, and then looks back at Kate and says in a lowered voice, "Is there anyone who would benefit from you selling your house?"

"I don't understand."

"Are you obligated to, say, split whatever you'd earn from cashing out with your sister?"

"No. Why?"

Sabrowsky hesitates before answering, and Kate gets the sense that he doesn't want to say what's on his mind.

"Why, Eddie?" she says.

"I found a couple of cases similar to this one. Homeowners being harassed—vandalism, letters in the mail, that kind of thing. In one case in California, a married couple was dealing with harassment directed specifically at the wife. Weird anonymous letters started arriving, accusing her of being a prostitute, and then the same kind of letters were sent to her employer and church. And her close friends started getting letters, too, allegedly from her, confessing to affairs with their husbands—affairs that never happened. This went on for over a year, and it affected her health pretty badly. Her hair started falling out because of the stress; she couldn't eat; she became depressed. Their lives were turned upside down. They decided to sell and move away, start a new life, but before they put the house on the market, there was a break in the case. The person sending the letters got in a car crash, with a letter ready to go in the car with her. Long story short, the husband was behind the whole thing. The house was in the wife's name, and he wanted her to sell it so he could steal the money and run off with his girlfriend—the one sending the letters. I read that and started wondering if something like that is what is happening here."

He looks back at the house once more, almost nervously, then faces Kate again and says, "Not that I want it to be her, but the first person I thought of was Rebecca. I mean, it's something she's capable of. It's something I could imagine her doing."

"She's not the person she used to be," Kate says. "And she's come here to start over. If I sold the place, she'd have nowhere to live."

"And she definitely would get nothing."

"Yes."

Eddie nods, thinking about that, and then says, "Again, I'm just asking to rule it out, but Leo doesn't have any kind of financial claim, right? Not that I can imagine him doing something like this, but he hasn't really been the same since Leif was killed, has he?"

"He doesn't have a claim," Kate says flatly. "And why would he want to make me leave town and take his grandchildren with me?"

"Right," Sabrowsky says quickly. "Yeah, of course. Loss can screw a person up, but Leo would never do anything to hurt his grandchildren, would he?"

"Never."

"Has anyone shown interest in the property recently? A Realtor or developer? Someone calling or leaving their card, asking if you were interested in selling, that kind of thing."

"No. Why?"

"There were some other cases like this one—a cluster of them, in fact, on Long Island. Unrelated people in different towns, in both Nassau and Suffolk Counties, some married couples, some single or divorced women. It started with random vandalism, and then escalated to letters containing photos of the women as they were running errands or coming out of work. Really creepy stuff, and like the case in California, always directed at a woman—the wife, a single mother, a divorcée. Eventually, there were threats of violence. And because all the incidents were in different locations, law enforcement didn't connect them. To each town's department, these were isolated activities."

"So what happened?"

"Some of them cashed out and ran. Others held off. The thing is, this was during the recession, and Long Island was hit particularly hard back then, because home prices were already inflated to begin with, and right before the market came crashing down, prices were rising higher and higher. You buy a home for four hundred thousand, and six months later, its value has gone up another fifty or hundred grand. So when the housing market finally crashed, thousands of homes were suddenly worth less than what they had bought for, in some cases by half, which means the mortgages were underwater. Those owners couldn't have sold if they wanted to. But the houses that were targeted, they either were owned outright or their value was greater than what was still owed to the bank. Those owners could sell. And the people out on Long Island who cashed out, their homes were torn down, and new constructions were put up. Not by a bunch of different developers, though. Each of those homes in all those different towns was bought by one company, the Castello Construction Company, which, it turned out, was owned by a New York developer whose real business was laundering money for the Russian mob."

"I'm trying to follow, Eddie."

"What if that's what's going on here? You own your home, no mortgage. The lot is subdividable, so two new constructions could be built—or worse, two of those awful two-family homes that are popping up everywhere around here. If you sold for a million five, and the developer put in another five hundred grand in construction costs, that's a two-million-dollar investment for two properties that would probably sell for two-point-five million each. That's a profit of three million, and the only thing standing in the way of that is you."

"So wait, you think that this Castello Construction Company is behind this?"

"They're in federal prison, so no. But what one man can do, another can, right? Maybe someone heard about what was done on Long Island and decided to copy it. Or maybe they came up with it on their own. And real estate values still aren't back to what they were before the recession, even here. So to someone looking for a big payday, your property checks all the boxes. All they'd need to do is motivate you to sell. And if they did learn from what was done on Long Island, they'll have a Realtor in their pocket ready to tip them off when your place is about to go on the market. Then they swoop in with a cash offer, promising a quick sale, and look to a scared widow like angels sent from heaven."

"But you said on Long Island there were threats of violence. I haven't gotten anything like that."

Sabrowsky appears reluctant to respond, but finally he says, "Not yet."

Kate feels the blood leaving her face. Realizing what he has done, Sabrowsky immediately backtracks.

"I'm sorry, Katie." He shakes his head. "You're right; your guy hasn't made any threats. If anything, it seems like he's bending over backward not to cross that line. So far, he hasn't committed any felonies, because, unfortunately, in this state voyeurism is just a misdemeanor. So is revenge porn, which is essentially the crime he committed when he sent the photo of you to your boss. This is probably exactly what Chief O'Neil thinks it is—some loser with a grudge or with nothing better to do."

Kate looks away for a moment.

"You know, you do this, Eddie. You say scary things, and then you try to take them back."

"I know. Like I said, I'm tired." He pauses before continuing. "So no one has approached you about selling, but has anyone maybe encouraged you to sell? Even casually? Maybe made a comment that didn't seem like anything at the time?"

The last few days are a blur, and at first Kate is shaking her head in denial, but suddenly she can recall two recent conversations in which someone did exactly that.

Jack, on the night he sat in her living room and helped her with her migraine.

And Chief O'Neil, yesterday morning at Compo Beach.

Her next thought is that she does not want to share this information with Sabrowsky, but she can see by the way he is looking at her that he knows her too well and has witnessed the journey from denial to realization to reluctance she has quickly taken.

"What?" he says.

Kate shakes her head. "Nothing."

"Tell me, Katie."

The reluctance leaves her, and she answers, "Jack mentioned it once, that's all. And Chief O'Neil did, too. Yesterday morning."

"The chief said that?" Eddie's tone is mildly incredulous.

"Yeah."

"Well, that's kind of weird, don't you think? I mean, that they both would say that. And the chief recommended Jack when you were looking for a tenant."

Kate raises her voice. "What are you saying, Eddie? That for some reason Chief O'Neil wants me to sell my house, and he planted Jack here to talk me into it?"

"No, of course not. All I said was that it was kinda weird. I guess I should learn to think before I talk."

Lowering her voice but still riled, Kate says, "Yeah, you should."

"I'll get right on that, I promise. I'm sorry I upset you."

"No, I'm sorry," Kate says. "I'm tired, too. We're all tired."

"My gut says we'll get a break soon," Sabrowsky says. "I think our guy's luck is about to run out."

"God, I hope so."

"Just hang in there, Katie."

"Thanks, Eddie."

"Anything for you, you know that."

Sabrowsky turns and starts back down the driveway toward his truck. Kate looks at the cottage just as Max and Jack exit. The boy steps off the pathway and calls excitedly to his mother, then cuts across the grass and heads toward her while Jack remains in the open doorway.

When Max reaches Kate, they turn toward the house, and Kate sees that Sabrowsky has stopped just feet from his truck. At first Kate thinks he is looking at her and Max, but then she realizes his attention is focused behind her.

Kate follows his line of sight and sees that Jack has stepped out of the cottage and is standing on the pathway.

He has locked eyes with Sabrowsky as well.

Continuing to the house, Kate gives all her attention to Max, who can barely contain himself.

Pausing inside the front door, Kate watches as Sabrowsky steers his F-150 up the driveway.

Jack is still standing on the pathway. He observes the pickup as it approaches, and then nods once at the driver as the vehicle passes.

———

Doubts creep into Kate's mind as the day progresses, though she keeps busy, which allows her to dismiss them.

The last thing she needs is to question everyone in her life.

Still, she comes to wonder if she has perhaps allowed things to move too quickly with Jack.

Not that she suspects him of anything—of course not, the whole idea is ridiculous; she refuses to give in to that level of paranoia—but Eddie was right when he asked what she knows about the guy.

And though Jack and she have spent time together and enjoyed several long talks, all too often what people tell you is not who they really are.

She is reminded at lunch, with Max and Callie seated at the kitchen table, that her priority is her children, the house they live in, her work, and their education.

Is there room for anything more, even with Rebecca's help?

And anyway, is it just too soon?

By midafternoon Kate realizes, however, that a natural break is coming—on Monday she will return to work, the kids to school, and her tenant will begin his new job.

Life will get in the way then, no? She could easily let it get in the way, and in doing so ensure that this whole romance thing slows down and, possibly, loses its momentum.

That wouldn't be terrible, she tells herself. And if Sabrowsky is wrong about her living nightmare ending soon but right about matters taking a turn into threats of violence, what kind of relationship could she hope to begin under those circumstances? Would new love and the resumption of a sex life matter then?

And would she really want to drag Jack, with his own problems to deal with, into all that?

After dinner Kate receives a text from Jack, asking how everyone is doing, but she doesn't reply right away, and when she finally does, an hour later, it is with a single word—*fine*.

Her curtness, combined with the atypical delay, must have been perceived by Jack exactly as Kate intended it to be, because he doesn't respond.

And later, when everyone is in bed and Kate is checking the doors and security system, she looks out at a dark cottage, which tells her that Jack has gone to sleep without texting her.

Was he waiting as he passed his evening for a message from her? Was he bothered by the fact that she appeared to have, as her children would say, "ghosted" him?

Though she is, of course, concerned that she has caused him confusion, at the very least, she can't allow herself to dwell on that.

Nor can she deny that, as much as she suppresses her doubts, they always find a way to reemerge.

You can always sell and move, Jack said.

And what has Leo Burke said repeatedly about Chief O'Neil?

He isn't the man he used to be.

Finally in her darkened bedroom, Kate fears that a sleepless night is ahead when her new cell phone, on the nightstand, vibrates.

Dreading what she might see, Kate looks at the display and sees that she is receiving an incoming call from her father-in-law.

Her heart pounding, Kate answers quickly.

"Hey, Dad. What's going on?"

THIRTY-SIX

Three hours earlier, Leo Burke leaves his home in Westport and drives to I-95, then follows the highway south to the city of Bridgeport.

Waiting at the bottom of the exit ramp is Chief O'Neil's marked sedan, which the former Westport chief commences to follow through narrow streets until they arrive at a small used-car dealership and repair shop surrounded by an eight-foot chain-link fence topped with razor wire.

Taking up a quarter of a city block, the lot is crowded with a dozen vehicles placed impossibly close together, though the scene outside the fence isn't much different—five Bridgeport PD–marked SUVs, as well as an ambulance, are parked at a variety of angles on the blocked-off street.

A half block away, Chief O'Neil pulls to the curb and stops, Leo Burke doing the same. The two men exit their vehicles and meet on the narrow residential street.

Burke asks, "Any update on Eddie?"

"He's fine. The knife passed through his arm without hitting bone. Luckily, the hospital is four blocks away." O'Neil gestures toward the crime scene. "C'mon, I'll take you in."

Burke follows him to the perimeter, which is guarded by a uniformed Bridgeport officer. Recognizing O'Neil, the officer glances at Burke before stepping aside to allow both men past.

They pass two more officers as they walk through the open gate. Crossing the small lot, they reach the auto shop. Its two bay doors are closed, but its office door is open. As O'Neil leads the way inside, Burke looks down and sees a line of blood droplets leading across the wood floor to a set of stairs.

Another uniformed officer is posted inside the office, and O'Neil asks her where Detective Boylan is. The cop replies, "Upstairs, sir. He said to send you up."

O'Neil continues through to the stairs, Burke behind him. As they climb, O'Neil looks back and says, "The Bridgeport PD provided Eddie with security camera footage. He used it to track our suspect here. He was off duty, told Boylan that he just wanted to drive by and take a look at the place for himself, but when he got here, he saw a bearded male with the same build and height as our guy through the office window. Eddie wanted a good look at the male's face, so he decided to approach him under the pretense of looking to buy a used car. Almost immediately, Eddie sees sitting on the desk the same cap that our guy was wearing in the footage from the market. We're talking identical. The next thing Eddie knows, the suspect pulls a knife and attacks him. They struggle, and the suspect runs upstairs, with Eddie right behind him."

O'Neil and Burke reach the top of the stairs. Turning and walking down a corridor, they enter an apartment.

Roughly ten feet from the door, a lifeless body is facedown on the floor, a wide puddle of dried blood pooled around its head. Inches from its right hand is a chrome-plated subcompact pistol.

"He was going for the weapon when Eddie fired," O'Neil explains. "A single discharge, one round to the head."

Burke shakes his head. "Shit."

"Yeah, exactly," O'Neil says.

Burke takes a few steps closer to the body, positioning himself so he can better see the face. Then he kneels down for a closer look.

"He's a kid," Burke says.

"His name is Mark Hillman. He's nineteen."

Burke looks up at his former protégé. "One of Kate's ex-students?"

"It doesn't look that way. He grew up here in Bridgeport." O'Neil pauses, then adds, "Boylan has already spoken to his mother."

Burke stands. "When did you get here?"

"Boylan called me right away. I was here for an hour, then called you."

Looking down at the body once more, Burke sighs and says, "Eddie fucked up."

"Yes and no."

Burke looks at O'Neil. "What do you mean?"

O'Neil gestures to the corridor behind Burke. "We're through there."

Burke follows him back into the hallway. They pass the stairs and continue to another part of the upper-floor apartment.

This room is part storage, part office—cardboard boxes are stacked in the corners, and a makeshift desk fashioned out of an old door and milk crates occupies the center.

A plainclothes detective and a uniformed officer are behind the desk, on which are several notebook computers and a printer, as well as a camera with a telephoto lens attached. Burke's eye is on the camera as the detective steps away and approaches the two visitors.

O'Neil introduces Boylan and Burke.

"I know Leo," Boylan says. "Good to see you again."

Burke is still studying the desk and its contents.

Next to the printer is a half-used ream of printing paper.

———

Kate is leaning against her kitchen counter, her arms folded across her stomach.

Standing a few feet away, Leo Burke gives her a moment to process what he's just told her—both of them for the past ten minutes speaking in whispers so as not to awaken those asleep upstairs.

Finally, her voice still hushed, Kate says, "So how many photos of me were on the camera?"

"At least a hundred. I didn't see them, but Boylan said they were shots of you around town, leaving your school, that kind of thing. And there were dozens of shots of your bedroom window taken from the woods, but none like the one that was texted to you. Apparently, he's been trying to get that shot for a while. Possibly for months."

"How do you know it was months?"

"The seasonal change in the foliage of the branches visible in the photos taken from the woods. It's the same with the photos of you doing your shopping and walking to your car in the school parking lot. Some were taken in winter, some in the fall."

Kate shakes her head, says softly, "What the fuck."

Burke waits another moment before speaking. "The printing paper found in his apartment is similar to the paper that was left on your windshield. It'll be a few days before they'll know whether that page is an exact match, but I don't think it really matters. This guy—this kid—had everything right there. Prepaid cell phones, stolen cell phones, camera, printer, photo paper, everything. And since the garage he worked at and lived above was also a chop shop, he likely had the skills necessary to steal cars off the street." Burke pauses. "But the name Mark Hillman means nothing to you."

"Nothing. Never had a student with that name. Never met anyone with that name. Why was he doing this? Any clue?"

"Bridgeport PD found files and files on his computer, all of them full of the same kind of secretly taken photos of other women, as well as drafts of letters to them—harassing letters with details about their day, comments on the outfits they were wearing, creepy stuff like that."

"But only my photos were on the camera."

"Right." Burke shrugs. "I know, I wondered about that myself. Maybe you were his most recent target. Boylan will scour every device found in the apartment for any communication this kid may have had with someone else, in case he had an accomplice. And, of course, Boylan will examine the kid's online presence—chat rooms where he may have interacted with other weirdos."

"Are there such things?"

"Apparently there is an entire subculture on the internet devoted to idiots who do this kind of thing. Guys who swap photos they've taken of unsuspecting women and make derogatory comments about them to each other. In some cases it all stays online, but in others it spills over into the real world, like with our guy. I guess what's the point of violating someone's privacy if that person doesn't know about it, right?"

"So O'Neil was right. It was just some creep."

"A creep who wanted you living in fear. Fear that he created and fed. And not just you but other women as well."

"How does someone so young build such an elaborate . . . hobby? And he knew all kinds of tricks to remain anonymous. Where did he learn that?"

"He's probably been at this for a while, Katie. And I'm sure he learned everything he needed to know on the internet."

"Okay, but why me?"

"Boylan wondered if Hillman maybe had a run-in with Leif at some point. The photos of you go back at least nine months, but it's possible that he could have been at it longer than that. Since Leif was killed, even."

"So we're back to that," Kate says. "Back to some kid getting revenge against a town cop."

"For all we know, it could have been Hillman who was behind all that vandalism you went through before Leif was killed."

"Is that what you think?"

"I'm not sure what to think. But that would explain a lot of things."

"Why would a Bridgeport teenager have a problem with a Westport cop, though?"

"Towns like ours attract criminals from all over. Bridgeport, New Haven, even places up north, like Waterbury. The vast majority of those caught breaking and entering here are from out of town."

Kate is quiet for a moment. "How is Eddie?" she says finally.

"Twelve stitches, but he's fine."

"How much trouble is he in?"

"O'Neil put him on administrative leave, obviously; that's procedure whenever there's an officer-involved shooting. But he shouldn't have gone there. He should have passed the information on to Boylan and let him investigate."

"He was trying to help. And by the way you described it, he was attacked."

"I know. But there's going to be an investigation, and with every investigation there's always the risk of politics playing a role. The city prosecutor might charge Eddie just to make points. But O'Neil is behind him, and so is Boylan. And the union will cover any legal costs he might face."

"Poor Eddie."

"He cares about you, Katie. I still have connections in Bridgeport City Hall. I'll make some calls Monday. He'll be fine, I'm sure."

Kate shakes her head. "Hard to believe that idiot just leaves his hat lying around. But you always said he'd screw up somehow."

"They always do."

"Is Eddie staying at the hospital overnight?"

"No, they sent him home. Obviously, he won't be in any condition to set up the cameras tomorrow."

"Maybe we don't need them anymore," Kate says.

"It might be too soon to let our guard down."

"At the least, this is a chance to rethink the whole thing. I told you, Dad, I don't want to live like that if I don't have to. Cameras, floodlights. Maybe Boylan will find something in the next few days that confirms it was this Hillman guy and no one else, and this'll be over, once and for all."

"I think you should still keep the lights," Burke says.

"Maybe set them to manual? So they're not on from dusk to dawn."

"Motion activated would be better."

"Then they'll come on every time a deer walks through the back-yard. And we already have the motion-activated light back there. It's just not as . . . alarming when it comes on."

"We'll talk about it."

"Dad, I love you and I'm grateful for you and everything you do, but I have to be the one to make the calls, remember?"

"I can't be expected to be shy with my advice, Katie."

"Advice is fine. Advice is welcome. As long as you know the final decision is mine."

Burke nods. "Fair enough."

"By the way, I'm calling my lawyer tomorrow about getting a new will drawn up. I'm assigning Rebecca as guardian and you as executor of the will and conservator of my estate."

"I think that's the best solution, all things considered."

"I'm glad you agree, Dad."

Burke glances at the wall-mounted clock. Kate does as well. It is 1:51 a.m.

"You've got school in a few hours," he says. "Will you be okay?"

"Yeah. I've worked on less sleep."

"O'Neil told me about the photo that was sent to Doug Banks."

Kate nods, then asks, "When did he do that?"

"Tonight. He said he'll call Banks in the morning, fill him in."

Though her father-in-law doesn't say so, it is clear to Kate that he is unhappy about having been once again kept out of the loop.

"I'm sorry, Dad," she says. "I didn't say anything because I didn't want you to worry. There wasn't anything you could do anyway. I wanted to bear that burden on my own. I wasn't going to let him turn my life upside down, or the lives of those around me. Not anymore. I wanted off the roller coaster. I was ready to stand my ground and fight."

Burke smiles. "That's the Katie I remember."

Kate smiles as well. "Yeah, I remember her, too."

"You know, I think that's what Leif loved most about you. You weren't a pushover. I raised him with a lot of old-fashioned notions, especially about what marriage was and wasn't, but he forgot all that when you two got together. He saw you as his equal, which you were, of course. But I was proud of him for being a smarter man than I. I was proud of the choice he made when he married you."

"Thanks, Dad."

"You should get some sleep."

"Okay. You too."

Kate walks her father-in-law to the back door. They say good night, and he exits.

Setting the alarm, Kate pauses to watch through the kitchen window as Burke walks to his SUV, gets in, and heads up the driveway.

Kate is at her bedroom door when she hears someone coming down the stairs. She stops, uncertain if it is one of her children, but then Rebecca appears on the bottom step.

"Hey," Kate whispers.

Rebecca asks quietly, "Was that Leo driving off?"

"Yes."

"What's going on?"

"Eddie found him," Kate says. "He found the guy."

"Really? Wow. Good for Eddie."

"The guy's dead. Eddie killed him."

"Shit. Is Eddie okay?"

"He got injured, but he's fine."

"Oh, good." Rebecca pauses. "So who was the guy?"

"Never heard of him before in my life."

"How did Eddie find him?"

"Can I tell you tomorrow? I'm beat."

"Of course." Rebecca pauses again. "So it's over."

"Maybe. I hope. But it's a relief, knowing he at least won't be doing what he was doing anymore. I'll take that for now."

"I bet, yeah," Rebecca says. "This is great news, Katie. I'm happy for you."

"Thanks."

Rebecca returns upstairs as Kate enters her bedroom and closes the door.

She wishes she had asked her father-in-law to set the two floodlights to manual now so she could part the curtains and open the only window in the room for some fresh air.

But she can bear one more night sleeping in a space sealed as tight as a tomb.

THIRTY-SEVEN

Kate's Wednesday morning is hurried, even with Rebecca's help, and she makes it to school with minutes to spare.

It isn't until her lunch break that she has a moment to phone her lawyer to set up an appointment to discuss the new will. Because of his schedule and hers, the earliest he can get her in is Friday at five o'clock.

With that done, Kate decides to text Jack to apologize for her curt communication the night before. Since he is working, she doesn't expect to receive a prompt reply, but he responds within a half minute, stating that it is good to hear from her and that she did have him a little worried.

She replies with an offer to explain over dinner soon, which he accepts. Then she asks how work is going, and he responds with a thumbs-up emoji.

The remaining minutes of her break are spent texting Eddie, asking if he is okay, thanking him, and telling him to let her know if he needs anything. But he doesn't reply by the time Kate's next class begins, and she places her cell phone into her desk drawer.

Leaving at four, Kate still hasn't received a response from Sabrowsky. Driving home, she lowers all four windows of her Subaru to let in the cool spring air. The weather has lifted her mood, but her concern for Sabrowsky keeps her from fully enjoying the lightness she is feeling for the first time in too long.

———

After a chaotic dinner—Max, Callie, Rebecca, Jack, and Kate at the table, each more often than not talking over the other—Kate walks Jack back to the cottage, at which point she tells him that the person who has been harassing her won't be any longer.

"That's great," Jack says. "How did it come to an end?"

"It's a long story, but I'll tell you sometime when we're alone."

"I'll look forward to that. Maybe I can make dinner for you again."

"I'd like that."

"When might be good for you?"

"I have an appointment Friday night at five. I figured I'll have Rebecca take Max and Callie out for dinner. How about then?"

"That'd be perfect. And I'll make something more than chicken this time."

"It doesn't matter to me what I eat. I'm there for the company—and, of course, the entertainment."

"I'll be sure to put an act together by then."

Kate smiles. "Awesome."

———

It isn't until nearly eight, while Max and Callie are watching a movie in the living room with their mother and aunt, that Kate finally gets a call from Sabrowsky. Excusing herself, she answers as she walks into the kitchen.

"Eddie, I was getting worried. How are you?"

"Sorry, the painkillers made me sleep all day," he says. "I'm fine. A little dazed by the whole thing, you know."

"I feel terrible."

"Don't, Katie. I was doing my job. I'm glad he won't be bothering you anymore."

"I just don't want you to get into trouble."

"What's going to happen is going to happen. Listen, would you mind if I swung by in a little bit? I want to talk to you about something. In person would be better for me."

"Yeah, sure. We're watching a movie."

"How long till it's over?"

"I didn't mean that. Come over now." Kate pauses. "The thing is, Rebecca's here. It might be . . . awkward."

"I get it," Sabrowsky says. "I can meet you outside. It's actually a beautiful night. And it won't take long."

"Yeah, sure. I'll meet you at the bottom of the driveway."

"I'll be there in five."

"Wait, are you okay to drive? You're on pain meds."

"I'm fine. I don't take my next one till nine."

———

Five minutes later Kate is outside.

Leo Burke came by during the day and set the floodlights to manual, so the only source of light is the small, motion-activated light in the upper eaves at the back of the house, as well as the light spilling out of the ground-floor and upstairs windows.

Wearing a cardigan sweater against the evening chill, Kate watches the top of the driveway until Sabrowsky's F-150 appears on the road. Turning in to her property, the pickup rolls down the steep decline, passing the cottage and then stopping alongside the house, in the same spot where the officer assigned to watch duty has parked since Friday night.

Sabrowsky, his left arm in a black sling, meets Kate at the bottom of the driveway.

"Hey," he says, forcing a smile.

Despite his assurances on the phone and the smile now, Kate can tell that her friend is in pain. His eyes are glassy and bloodshot, his face pale.

"Look at you, Eddie," she says. "You should have stayed home."

"Probably, yeah. But there's some news, and I wanted to be the one to tell you."

"What?"

"Our tech guy went through Hillman's computer and cell phones, and he found no indication that Hillman shared the photo of you with anyone or posted it anywhere else online. There were a couple of print-outs, though, and a draft of a letter addressed to Chief O'Neil, accusing you of being a prostitute and instructing the chief to stop protecting you or Hillman would go to the newspapers. So it seems he had more planned for you."

"Jesus."

"But it's over, so you don't have to worry about that. O'Neil is holding the printouts himself, so they won't make the rounds through the station. And he wanted me to tell you that as soon as the investigation is over, he'll destroy them. Same with the digital copy you forwarded to him."

"Tell him I appreciate that."

"This kid was a piece of work, Katie. On his computers were letters to the other women he stalked and terrorized—threatening letters, sexual fantasy letters, even a blackmail letter to one he caught having an affair. Instead of money, though, he wanted nude pictures."

"How many other women were there?"

"Four."

"Is there anything that connects them? Or that connects me to them?"

"Not that anyone has found yet. But you were the first; we know that much."

"How do you know that?"

"The metadata from all the digital photos tells us when they were taken. Yours predate the other ones. And the earliest one was taken a week after Leif was killed."

"But why were mine still on his camera?"

Sabrowsky shrugs. "I don't know. Maybe you were his favorite and he couldn't bear deleting them."

Kate considers that for a moment, and then says, "O'Neil told me that Detective Boylan suggested this kid might have had a grudge against Leif. That maybe he was behind the original vandalism, before Leif was killed."

"That would explain how he came to choose you. If he knew about Leif, if they'd had run-ins and Leif pissed him off, which is what Leif was famous for doing, then he would have known what happened to Leif and that you were alone. It's possible you caught his eye, and he started stalking you. He got a taste for it, and that's why he eventually branched out to other women."

Kate glances at the empty swing-set chains, and then focuses on the woods beyond them.

Looking at Sabrowsky again, she asks, "If he's been taking photos of me for two years, why did the vandalism only start up again two weeks ago?"

"You're asking me to explain the thinking of someone who was deeply screwed up. I can't. Maybe as we dig deeper into his stuff, we'll know more. For now, just try to forget about him and what he did. He was an aberration, a freak show."

Kate nods but says nothing. There's a part of her that doesn't want to know any more than this, and yet there is one question she needs to ask.

"You don't think he had anything to do with Leif's death, do you?"

Sabrowsky shakes his head. "No, Katie. O'Neil investigated that, and so did Leo and I. The men who attacked your home were from New York. They likely targeted your place because a cop lived there, which meant there would be firearms they could steal. Hillman was a punk from Bridgeport who chopped up stolen cars. No one has found anything that suggests he had any connection with anyone in New York. In fact, it looks like the guy was a loser whose only friends were online losers like him." Sabrowsky pauses. "I know Leo thinks that O'Neil's investigation was flawed, and that by the time he and I looked into it, the trail had gone cold. But I'm certain that's all it was, Katie—two career criminals who thought a small-town cop wouldn't give them any trouble. If Hillman had been behind the original vandalism, then Leif being killed might explain why he stopped for as long as he did. Maybe he was afraid something he did would lead the cops to him. Two years go by, and secretly stalking you isn't enough anymore, so he starts up again, only this time he pushes the creep factor. He escalates from throwing eggs and annoying shit like that to things like terror tactics. But that's *if* he was behind the early vandalism. There's no record of Leif ever arresting Hillman. And there's no report of Leif's that mentions Hillman's name. Trust me, I looked. Like I said, you should just try to forget about him. He's dead and won't be bothering you or anyone anymore. Get your life back to normal, Katie. It's been a shitty two years. You deserve to live in peace. And if I've played even a small part in giving you that, then whatever happens to me will be worth it."

Kate feels a near-euphoric rush of goodwill for her friend. She reaches out and touches his shoulder, careful to avoid his injury. "Thank you, Eddie. For everything. I can't even start to tell you how grateful I am."

"Leif was the brother I never had. And you and I, well, we've known each other forever, right?"

"Right."

Eddie pauses, then says, "Leo told me that we're going to hold off on setting up the security cameras."

"Yeah. If we don't need them, I'd rather not have them here. It's not how I want to live. I know you already paid for the equipment, but if you can't return it and get your money back, I'll reimburse you."

"No, I should be able to return it. But I'll wait until you're sure."

"I'm pretty sure, Eddie."

"Well, I probably won't get around to it until after I get my stitches out next week, so I'll have them for a bit, in case you change your mind."

"Okay." Kate pauses. "If there's anything you need from me or need me to do—anything—just let me know."

Sabrowsky looks at the house. "Maybe you can give Rebecca a message for me."

"Sure."

"Tell her I'm sorry. She'll know what it means."

"Okay. I will."

Then Sabrowsky glances toward the cottage, and though he seems about to say something, he doesn't.

Looking back at Kate, he offers another forced smile. "It's getting time for my next pill," he says. "I'll see you, Katie."

"Call me tomorrow and let me know how you're doing."

"I will."

Sabrowsky turns and heads back toward his truck.

Kate says, "Hey, maybe you should come over for dinner some night. Rebecca's going to be living here for a while, and I don't want you to feel like you can't come by. Who knows, maybe you guys can be friends."

Stopping, Sabrowsky half turns toward Kate and says, "That might not be a good idea."

"Why not?"

"I'd want to be more than friends."

"Still, Eddie? After all these years?"

He nods. "Still, yes. After all these years."

Uncertain how to respond, Kate falls silent.

Turning again, Sabrowsky continues toward his pickup. "I'll talk to you soon, Katie."

As he gets behind the wheel, Kate moves onto the grass so he'll have room to turn his truck around, but instead Sabrowsky backs up the driveway and onto Old Town Road, then drives off.

———

Later, in her bedroom, Kate opens her only window by a few inches, and then lowers the blinds all the way to the bottom sill.

It's a start, she thinks.

She is standing by her nightstand, powering up her old cell phone, when Rebecca appears in the doorway.

Kate asks, "What's up?"

"Max and Callie are in bed. I'm about to turn in, too."

"So you'll take them out for dinner on Friday while I meet with my lawyer?"

"Yes, of course."

Kate nods. "I'll give you some money."

"I can pay for it, Katie."

"No, Becca. Save your money."

"We can fight about it tomorrow," Rebecca jokes.

"I'm going to win," Kate says.

Rebecca smiles. "We'll see." After a moment her smile fades. "So I guess I was wrong about Eddie."

"What do you mean?"

"That he was in love with you now."

"Oh, yeah. It's none of my business, so you don't have to answer if you don't want to, but what is it he's sorry about?"

"Back when he was still texting me, when he would pop up like he used to . . ." Rebecca doesn't complete her thought.

"What?" Kate says.

Rebecca hesitates, and then says, "He knew about the money Charles left me. A part of me used to suspect that's what he was really after. The last time he and I had any contact, when I told him that I had cancer, I also told him that treatments were going to eat away at what I had left. He offered to help me, but I told him that if he really wanted to help me, he would leave me alone. I told him I never loved him and never could. And he said that he hoped the cancer kills me." She pauses. "Basically, I did to Eddie what you did to me. You turned down my help and sent me away after Leif died, and a few months later I did the same thing to him. And if it crushed him half as much as it crushed me . . ." Once again, Rebecca trails off.

"And that's why you never heard from him again."

"Yeah. I'm assuming his apology is for what he said to me."

"He was angry and hurt from the rejection."

"I know," Rebecca says. She looks at her sister for a moment. "You know, I wonder about that day a lot."

"The day I sent you away?"

"No. The day you tried to stop me from going into the cottage with Eddie. That's when the trouble started—between you and me, me and Grandma and Grandpa, me and everyone. That's when I broke our second chance at a family. It took me a long time to see that—to see what it did to you. The fucked-up thing is, I didn't even really like Eddie. I knew he liked me, and I wanted to get it over with, you know. Having sex for the first time. I thought it would be best to do it with a boy I didn't care about, who couldn't end up hurting me by rejecting me after. And then I spent the rest of my life having to reject him."

"I remember when we were kids how Eddie used to want to hang out with us, whether we wanted him to or not. And Grandma was always sending him home when she called us in for dinner, but the next day he'd be back. I guess he has always been the type of person who wants most what he can't have."

Rebecca smiles slightly, then teases, "Yeah, well, that, plus I'm a goddess."

"Of course. That goes without saying."

"He used to tell me that all the time. I was his goddess, and he'd give anything to worship me. It was hard not to be flattered by that. But it was scary, too."

"I can imagine," Kate says. She recalls keeping Sabrowsky at an arm's length, even when they were children. By the time they reached high school, they each had different sets of friends. Sabrowsky made his return to Kate's life only during her senior year, when she started dating Leif. He and Eddie were essentially a package deal.

But even years later, when she and Leif married and he and Sabrowsky were young police officers in Leo Burke's department, Kate maintained her distance, though she was careful to never seem unfriendly.

Her sister's revelations only confirm for Kate what she had known instinctively from the day Sabrowsky showed up in their grandparents' backyard.

That strange and lonely boy who one summer morning walked out of the woods, asking if he could play.

Rebecca says, "There is a part of me, though, that wonders why I didn't just give in to him, at least early on. I guess back then I was the type of person who was suspicious of anyone who showed any hint of interest. You know what I mean? Like there had to be something wrong with anyone who liked me."

"We all have our self-esteem issues."

"You didn't."

"Sure I did. You were the better-looking sister with the better body. And you were smarter, too. You got straight As, and you didn't even try. But maybe seeing you hurting yourself triggered an opposite reaction in me. Maybe developing self-esteem the way I did was my coping mechanism for your lack of it."

Rebecca smiles again. "Well, then, you're welcome."

Kate laughs quietly. "Who knows what's going to happen, right? I never would have predicted that you and I would be here, talking like this. Maybe there's hope for you and Eddie. If that's something you'd want, I mean."

Rebecca shrugs but says nothing.

Then Kate laughs again and says, "No one has ever called me a goddess; that's all I'm saying."

"Leif must have had a name for you."

"Lots of them, sure. But none like that."

"Yeah, he was the strong, silent type. Jack, on the other hand; he's a different kind of man altogether."

"That he is."

"You know, if you ever . . . if the date goes well and you want to spend the night, just show me how to set the alarm and whatever else I might need to know."

"Oh, I'm not there yet."

"Yeah, we tell ourselves that, don't we? 'I'm not going to sleep with him until whatever date.' But then you smell him or he looks at you a certain way and the blood starts to flow."

"I can handle my blood."

"I'm just saying, Katie. If and when it happens, I'm here with the kids. Or if you don't want your first time with him to be in that crappy cottage, Max and Callie and I will camp out there some night, and you and Jack can have the house."

"I'll keep that in mind. Thanks." Kate sighs. "I got shit sleep last night, so I'm calling it a day. I'll see you at breakfast?"

"Yeah. Good night, Katie."

"Night."

As her sister climbs the stairs, Kate checks her powered-up cell phone for missed calls and texts.

There have been no recent calls, but the text icon on her display shows a small "3" above its right top corner, indicating that she has received three texts.

Her heart freezes slightly as she opens the app, but two of the messages waiting for her are notifications of recent credit card purchases, and the third is an offer from Greyson Guns for a yearly range membership.

As Kate connects the phone to its charger, her heart eases back to its normal pace and rhythm.

Within minutes of laying her head on the cool pillow, she is asleep.

THIRTY-EIGHT

Thursday morning Maria phones Kate to ask if D. J. and Alice can come over after school because Derek has a meeting.

"Basically, I'm wondering if I can borrow Rebecca for a little bit. I mean, since she's watching Max and Callie; what's two more, right?"

Kate finds it odd to hear Maria speak the name of the woman who had an affair with her husband, but she pushes past that and says, "I'm sure it will be fine, but I'll check with her. If it's a problem, I'll let you know."

"Thank you so much."

"Of course. So how is work going?"

"Exhausting, and I miss the kids, but it's good to be back. And it's good to have money coming in."

"Is Derek's meeting about new jobs?"

"I'm not sure, to be honest. We're not really talking all that much. He's in a foul mood, so I stay away from him. Apparently, he's been selling things, some of which were mine."

"Like what?"

"Like that nice Nikon digital camera. I went looking for it the other day, and he played dumb at first, but then he confessed."

"What the fuck," Kate says.

"Right?"

"What else has he sold?"

"Some of his mother's jewelry, which is fine with me, because the fewer reminders of her around here the better. Not telling me about it is one thing; I'm used to him keeping secrets. But apparently the money he got from everything he sold is gone already, and that I do have a problem with."

"I don't blame you."

"Enough about my problems. How are you?"

"I've got some good news, actually. It's over."

"What is?"

Aware that her children might overhear, Kate lowers her voice. "My problem."

"Seriously?"

"Yeah."

"You must be so relieved."

"Pretty much, yeah. I woke up this morning dreading taking a look at my phone, but then I realized there wasn't any reason to."

"After everything you've been through, it might take a while to fully sink in. But it must feel good when you realize there's nothing to worry about."

"Oh, God, yeah. And the last few days, it got pretty bad, things you don't even know about yet."

"I'll pick up D. J. and Alice around six. You can tell me what happened then."

Kate still isn't ready to be in the same room with her sister and her friend. "How about you text me when you're home, and I'll bring them over?"

"Are you sure?"

"Yeah, that way you can get dinner started while we talk."

"Sounds like a plan."

"Cool."

"I'm really happy for you, Kate. This is a big win, for all of us."

———

At seven that night Kate returns from Maria's.

Pausing her Subaru outside the cottage, she beeps the horn once. Through the front door window she sees Jack stand and look toward the door, then head for it.

Exiting, he crosses the pathway and approaches Kate's vehicle. He is wearing jeans and a hooded sweatshirt, and his unshaved face is reddened slightly from hours spent in the spring sun.

Kate asks, "How was your day?"

"Rough," Jack jokes. "But that's my own fault for being inactive for so long."

"But you like it?"

He nods. "Yeah. I can see myself doing this for a while."

"That's good. Did you eat yet?"

"Yeah. I was starving. Now I'm going to take a shower and read a bit, then get into bed. Six a.m. comes a lot earlier than I remember it coming."

Kate smiles. "Five a.m. does that, too. We're still on for tomorrow night?"

"Yes, if that still works for you."

"It does. See you then."

"Have a good night."

"You too."

Jack steps back as Kate shifts into gear and continues down the driveway. Returning to the cottage, he waits at the front door until Kate enters the house.

———

For the first time in too long, Kate is facing an evening that has the potential to be free of fear.

She experienced the same as she drove to work in the morning, checked her phone between classes and at lunch, and then walked to her car at four thirty—no dread, no distraction, no overwhelming worry.

Driving D. J. and Alice next door, no emotion passed through her that needed to be masked, nor did she feel any concern about leaving Rebecca, Max, and Callie alone at the house for the hour she spent bringing Maria up to speed.

And as she spoke with Jack outside the cottage, firming up their plans for tomorrow night, she felt something that was more than mere fearlessness.

A genuine sense of optimism caused her heart to swell and open, and every nerve in her body vibrated excitedly.

What was it she said to Rebecca about being able to handle her blood?

Blushing as she enters the house, Kate passes through the kitchen, cleaned after dinner while she was at Maria's, and finds her sister and children in the living room, watching an episode of *Arrested Development* on Netflix.

"You're back," Rebecca says.

Kate nods, watches the program for a moment, and then says, "I'm assuming everyone is done with their homework."

Seated on the floor, Max replies, "I finished mine before dinner."

Kate looks at Callie, who is beside her aunt on the couch. "How about you?"

Her eyes on the television screen, Callie answers, "All done except my algebra."

Kate raises her eyebrows and is about to ask the inevitable question—*What are you doing watching TV?*—when Rebecca speaks.

"She's having trouble, so I'm going to help her before bed."

"What is she having trouble with?"

"Substituting values for variables."

Kate nods. "Yeah, okay, you can help her with that. Thanks."

"How can you not remember seventh-grade algebra?" Rebecca teases. "Mr. Swift's class? Mr. 'Not-So-Swift,' who also coached track and wore those short shorts?"

"Jeez, I haven't thought of him in years. And yes, I have forgotten my seventh-grade algebra."

Kate immediately realizes her mistake and winces in anticipation of what her daughter will say to that.

Right on cue, Callie asks, "If I'm not going to remember it, then why do I have to bother learning it?"

Max shushes his sister as Kate half turns in the doorway, readying to make a fast retreat.

She says to Rebecca, "I'll let you handle this."

"Gee, thanks. I think."

———

By nine Max has brushed his teeth and is under the covers on the cot in his room.

In the room across the hall, Callie is sitting with her aunt on the bed, the two holding a workbook open between them.

Standing in the doorway, Kate says, "Not too late."

"Half hour," Rebecca answers.

"Okay."

"Good night, Katie."

"Good night."

Callie looks up from the workbook and says, "Night, Mom."

"Good night, Callie."

Crossing the hall, Kate steps into the doorway to her son's room. Lying on his right side, Max is reading a paperback. Kate enters the room, though she remains not too far from the door.

"What are you reading?"

Max holds up a tattered copy of *To Kill a Mockingbird*.

Kate asks, "Is that assigned reading? You're kind of young for that book."

"It's Auntie Becca's. She said she was my age when she read it."

Kate recalls the hours they spent in the cottage as children—sometimes playing house, sometimes reading quietly together.

Then she suddenly remembers Rebecca's first drawing, how she showed it to Kate as though it were nothing, despite the fact that, to Kate's surprise, it was a detailed depiction in pencil of the space they occupied.

Kate asks her son, "Are you enjoying it?"

"I just started it, but yeah."

"You won't let it interfere with your schoolwork, right?"

"I won't."

"Promise?"

"Promise."

Kate waits a moment, then says, "You like having your aunt here, don't you?"

Max nods. "She's great."

"I'm glad."

"And she keeps Callie in line."

"That's good, right?"

"Yeah. Maybe you two will get along better."

"Me and Auntie Becca?"

"You and Callie."

Kate's first instinct is to deny that there are any problems at all between herself and Max's sister, but then she realizes there would be no point in doing that. "It was getting that bad?"

"Yeah."

"You think I'm too hard on her."

"No. She asks for it."

"But we've been better the past few days, haven't we?"

"I guess."

"You're not sure?"

"No, you have."

Kate can tell that her son has something else to say.

She asks, "But?"

Max shrugs. "I don't know."

"Yes, you do. Please tell me."

He shrugs again. "You haven't really been yourself lately. Not all the time, just sometimes."

"I know. I'm sorry. I've just had a lot on my mind."

"Because of what's been going on? The swings and the picture window?"

"Yes, but we don't have to worry about that. It's been taken care of."

"By who?"

"Eddie, and others in the police department. Your grandfather, too. We're lucky; we have a lot of people on our side."

"Was it the brothers? The Dolans?"

"No, it was someone else."

"Who?"

"Just some guy with mental problems. But it's taken care of, I promise. He won't bother us anymore."

Max nods. "Good."

"I wasn't ever going to let anything happen to you. You know that, right?"

"Yeah." Max looks back at his book. "Auntie Becca says this is a story about a brother and a sister."

"It is. And their father, and the small town they live in."

The corners of his mouth turn upward as he gives in to his mischievous smile.

"Maybe I'll write a book about Callie someday. And you and Dad and Auntie Becca and Grandpa."

"Oh, yeah? Is that something you might want to do? Write a book?"

"Maybe."

"It's a lot of work."

"Did you ever try to write one?"

"Your aunt's the creative one, not me," Kate says. "But I bet if that's what you decide to do, you'll be great."

"I might want to be a cop, like Dad and Grandpa were."

"I'm sure you'd be a great one."

Max thinks about that, then nods and says, "I'm going to read a little more."

"Your sister's coming to bed in a half hour. Just don't stay up past that, okay?"

"Okay."

"I'll see you in the morning."

"Night, Mom."

"Good night, Max."

———

It is cold tonight—from four in the afternoon to sundown, the temperature drops rapidly from seventy degrees to thirty-five—so Kate opens her bedroom window by only an inch, though, of course, she lowers the blinds all the way to the sill.

Moving through the darkened house, Kate checks that the doors are locked, and then sets the alarm, bypassing the partially open bedroom window. She remembers the kiss that she and Jack shared at the front door, though she can't for the life of her remember how many nights ago that has been.

Pausing at the living room window, she takes note that the cottage windows are dark, and that Jack's Jeep is parked in its spot. In her elevated mood, she fantasizes about deactivating the alarm she just set and slipping out of the house and across the front yard, sneaking into the cottage and waking him as she climbs into bed beside him.

Fortunately, he made clear his physical exhaustion, as well as a plan to turn in early, so she doesn't have to struggle even for a second with whether or not to actually act on her fantasy.

Still, she allows herself a moment to envision taking that leap—laying her naked body upon his in the dark back room of the cottage— before turning and stepping away from the glass.

Back in the bedroom, washed up and changed into her tank top and boxer shorts, Kate hurries through the chilled air and gets under the covers.

She is stretched out on her back and contemplating her state of arousal when the living room becomes suddenly alive with flickering blue and red lights.

Kate kicks off the cover and rushes to the bedroom door, and there she determines that the lights—police lights, by the color and rapid flashing—are coming from the direction of Maria's property. Passing through the living room, she steps to the east-facing window to the left of the TV and sees through the bare border trees two marked Westport PD SUVs, moving nose-to-bumper down her neighbors' driveway.

Kate runs back to the bedroom, careful not to make too much noise as she moves, and grabs clothes from her hamper—jeans, socks, and a sweatshirt. She is scrambling to get dressed when her cell phone, on its charger on the nightstand, vibrates.

Her jeans on but unfastened, Kate retrieves the phone. On the display is Leo Burke's number.

She answers quickly, making no effort to hide her urgent concern. "Dad, what's going on?"

"I wanted you to know that O'Neil is on his way to your neighbors' house."

"Yeah, I know. I just saw them pull in." Wedging her phone between her cheek and shoulder, Kate zips up her jeans. "What's going on, Dad?"

"It has nothing to do with you, not directly, anyway."

"What does that mean?"

"I'm sorry, there's no other way to say this, Katie. Derek Hogue is dead."

Her sweatshirt in hand, Kate suddenly stops. "What?"

"They found him in his truck an hour ago, parked at Compo Beach."

Kate is frozen, both physically and mentally. She asks the only question she can think to ask. "What was . . . how did he . . . ?"

"Suicide," Leo Burke answers.

Kate continues to struggle with both finding her words and getting them out. Finally, she pushes through the confusion and asks, "How?"

"He shot himself. O'Neil is next door to break the news to his wife. And he's going to want her to go with him to identify the body, so she's going to need someone to watch the kids."

"I'm almost dressed. I'll be out the door in thirty seconds."

"Rebecca will stay with Callie and Max?"

"Of course. I'll bring Maria's kids back here, put them on the fold-out couch."

"I hate to ask you this right now, but do you know if he owned a firearm?"

"I don't. Why?"

"It's not important. We'll talk more tomorrow."

Kate is torn between wanting to follow up on that question and needing to get out the door, but in the end she doesn't have to decide either way.

"Go help your friend, Katie. I'll call you tomorrow."

Though her curiosity lingers, Kate says, "Yeah, okay. I'll talk to you then, Dad."

Ending the call, Kate drops the phone onto the bed and finishes dressing—sweatshirt, socks, then mud boots from the utility closet in the kitchen.

Deactivating the alarm, she exits through the back door, locking it behind her.

The shortest distance to Maria's property is the well-worn path off the front yard that cuts through the line of border trees. Kate hurries to it, following it until she clears the narrow woods and can see Maria's house clearly.

A uniformed officer—Schulze—is standing by the open back door and looking inside. O'Neil has already entered.

Kate crosses the yard swiftly, reaching the driveway in time to hear her friend cry out in shocked anguish.

THIRTY-NINE

The next morning, Rebecca looks after the children—her niece and nephew, and D. J. and Alice, all at the house—while Kate keeps an eye on Maria.

Sitting with her friend at her kitchen table, Kate consoles her when she breaks down in tears, and calms her when her grief gives way to bouts of frantic anger, during which she repeats the same question: *Why would he do this to us?*

Kate has no answer, of course, so all she can do is hold her friend's hands and say in a soft voice, "I don't know, Maria. I don't know."

And when Maria shifts back to grief again, she then asks the only question that matters: *What do I tell my children?*

It is more a plea than an inquiry.

Kate recalls asking her friend the very same question about her own children in the hours following their father's death.

She remembers Maria offering care the way a nurse would—taking charge, remaining calm, speaking clearly in a steady, almost emotionless tone.

In the minutes following Leif's death, and the hours that followed that, there wasn't a breath Kate took that Maria wasn't there for—right there, either beside Kate, holding her close, or facing Kate, her hands on Kate's shoulders, assuring her that Max and Callie were safe, that Derek had them, and that they didn't know yet their father's fate.

That night there was much to occupy Kate—Leif's officer brethren, quick to arrive and doing so in force, including, of course, Sabrowsky and Chief O'Neil, both men with urgent questions that needed answering. And Leo Burke was there, too, his grief already manifesting as the slow-burning rage that would linger inside him for months and months.

Kate lost track of time that night, couldn't say now when the ambulance arrived or when it left, couldn't put in order who spoke to her—or even what they asked or said. In shock, her thoughts were quickly reduced to the struggle of balancing her desperate need to have her children near—to hold them, feel their heartbeats, never let them go—with the instinctive desire to protect them for as long as possible from the news that their lives were forever changed—as hers and Rebecca's had once been.

But for Maria the experience is different. She had been brought back home at 5:00 a.m. by Schulze, who found Kate waiting, which allowed him to leave Maria in her care and depart.

All Maria has during these early-morning hours is Kate—no distractions, no questions, just the static of confusion and grief and anger as they sit together in a suddenly empty home.

At six thirty, Kate calls the office at Fairfield Warde High School and tells the secretary that she is taking a personal day due to a death in the family.

By seven, Maria is as composed as she is going to be. She tells Kate that her children need to know, and that she wants them with her.

"Of course," Kate says.

"My mother is driving down from Litchfield. She'll be with me when I tell Alice and D. J., so you don't have to sit through that."

"I'm here for the duration."

Maria nods. "Thank you. And I'm going to need your help, Katie, which is why I want you to go home, eat, shower, spend some time with your kids. You know how my mother is, so I'm hoping you'll come with me when I go to the funeral home later today."

"Of course. Whatever you need. Rebecca can take care of Max and Callie, so I can be here twenty-four seven."

Maria thanks her again, then says, "This all feels familiar, doesn't it? Except it's you taking care of me this time."

"I've got big shoes to fill."

Maria offers a strained smile, but then her eyes close tight and her lips purse. Seconds later, tears are falling from her eyes.

"Jesus, what is going to happen to us?"

"One step at a time, Maria. We'll figure it out together. You can count on me; you know that."

Opening her eyes, Maria takes in a deep, cleansing breath, then lets it out and says, "God, I am so scared."

"I know."

"It's not just the future that I'm afraid of, though. I'm afraid of what I'll find when I start going through his credit cards and bank accounts. And I have no idea of the size of debt he has left me to deal with." She pauses. "Plus, he had close to a dozen different cell phones over the years, and there's really only one reason for a man to have so many phones. I know he hasn't been faithful, but I don't know who with or how many secret girlfriends there have been. I turned a blind eye for the sake of the status quo, but there was also a part of me that just didn't want to know. You can't be hurt by what you don't know, right? I guess I'm going to find out all of that now, though."

"What do you mean?"

"Chief O'Neil is sending someone by later to collect all of Derek's phones."

"I don't understand."

"He needs them for the investigation."

"I didn't think in the case of a . . ." Kate trails off. Then she regroups and tries again. "Why would he need to go through Derek's devices?"

Maria shrugs. "I don't know. I didn't ask."

Kate can think of only one reason for O'Neil to seek such materials—he suspects foul play. But she keeps that to herself and instead says, "You don't have to turn anything over to him if you don't want to. Technically, he should get a warrant, listing everything he wants to look at."

Maria shakes her head decisively. "No. It's time for the truth to come out. The ugly truth, all of it. I've lived in denial for too long."

Another thought crosses Kate's mind that she knows not to express: it is likely that among Derek's devices is the phone that he used to communicate with Rebecca during the course of their affair.

Phone calls, texts, possibly even photographs.

Kate asks, "Where are his phones now?"

"He kept them in a fire safe in his office. I was cleaning one day, and he left it unlocked. When I opened it up, I knew exactly what I was looking at. I remember thinking for a moment that this was my way out. I could turn any one of those on and find the evidence I needed to make him move out and not have it be my fault. And for another moment I thought of just throwing them out to spite him. He'd go look for them one day and they'd be gone, and he'd know I knew." Maria pauses. "Instead I just closed the lid and said nothing."

Kate considers pointing out to her friend that she could ask O'Neil not to reveal any information he may find that casts an ill light on her deceased husband.

She even considers offering to speak to the chief herself, if that is what Maria would prefer.

But Kate knows that her motive isn't to make things easier for the grieving woman sitting across from her—or at least that isn't the entirety of her motive.

While her instinct now is to protect her sister, which is a desire she has not felt for a very long time, another motive is the fact that she herself had knowledge of the affair.

Would it matter that she found out only recently? Would Maria's passive acceptance of her husband's infidelities remain, should one of those faceless women turn out to be someone so nearby? Someone

Maria, mainly out of loyalty to Kate, has always disliked? Someone who, even at this moment, is watching over Maria's children?

The best thing would be to come out and tell Maria the truth. Kate knows this, of course. She even draws a breath and opens her mouth slightly, ready to do just that. But she stops herself and stays silent.

Now isn't the time.

And anyway, maybe that particular phone is elsewhere. Or was tossed out two years ago. Maybe, with luck, and for the sake of all involved, that whole matter will remain in the past.

———

Kate waits for Leo Burke's call.

It still hasn't arrived when she leaves at one o'clock to drive Maria to Collins Funeral Home.

Because of the complications of burying a victim of suicide, there is some uncertainty as to when Derek's remains will be released by the coroner, so out of an abundance of caution Maria chooses a Monday-morning burial with no calling hours the night before and a private graveside memorial service prior to the interment.

Upon Kate's return home at two thirty, she is tempted to at least send a text to her father-in-law and ask if he has heard any news, but she decides against it.

There are more pressing concerns that require her attention.

Rebecca kept Max and Callie home from school—their presence helped keep Alice and D. J. calm as the two waited to be reunited with their mother—so Kate spends the rest of the afternoon playing board games with her family, all four of them seated on the living room floor.

It is obvious to her that Derek's death has reminded the children of their own father's passing, and spending the hours before dinner in this manner seems to her the best course of action.

Scrabble, Pictionary, the Monopoly board that has been in the house since Kate and Rebecca were children—multiple rounds of each game played quietly, no real attention paid to who won and who lost.

And although her sister's onetime involvement with Derek was a long-ago mistake, it is clear to Kate that Rebecca has been affected by his death as well, and that she likely regrets that the last interaction she had with him was an argument.

Kate recognizes that her role now is that of healer, and it is one that she commits to fully.

At four she remembers to call her lawyer to cancel the appointment, though she takes that opportunity to tell him what it is she needs so he can begin drafting the new document, which she should have done to begin with.

It isn't long after that she looks out the living room window and sees that Jack's Jeep is parked outside the cottage. Eager to catch him before he begins preparations for their date, she retreats into her bedroom and calls him from her cell phone to tell him the news.

"Oh my God, that's terrible," he replies.

"Obviously, we'll need to do dinner another time."

"Of course. If there's anything I can do, please just let me know."

"Thank you. I'd invite you to have dinner here, but I don't think any of us are up for company. First their father, then their friends' father."

"I understand. It must be difficult for you, too."

"It helps that so many people are counting on me now. It keeps my mind busy."

"How is your sister handling it?"

Kate can't recall saying anything to Jack about Rebecca and Derek's history. "Did I tell you about them?"

"No," Jack answers. "But I heard them arguing the other morning."

"Oh," Kate says. She pauses, then asks, "You were able to hear what they said?"

"Yeah. They woke me up, so I was still in bed. Your father-in-law asked me to keep an eye out, so when I heard voices, I went to my window to see what was going on. I'll be honest; it was kind of strange what they said."

"What do you mean?"

"Your sister kept asking him if he was involved with someone, and he kept insisting he wasn't."

"Involved with whom?"

"Either they didn't say or I missed that part."

"What else did you hear?"

"He said he wanted to get back together, and she said no. That's what struck me as odd, you know. At first she was asking if he was involved, demanding that he tell her the truth, and then when he said he wanted to get together, she flat-out refused, like it was out of the question. Then he tried to touch her, like he was trying to reason with her, and she turned and walked away."

"Apparently, Derek had girlfriends. And Maria knew."

"Jesus," Jack says. "Poor woman. I can't imagine what she's going through right now."

"I should probably give her a call and check in."

"Obviously, if there's anything she needs that I can take care of, I'm here."

"Thanks, Jack. I'll definitely let you know. Maybe a take-out dinner for them some night this week would be a good idea. That's something you and I could do together, actually."

"Yeah, sure. It'd be good to see you, even for a little bit."

Kate smiles, only to realize that it's possibly the first time she has done so all day. "Same here. If I don't talk to you again, have a good night."

"You too."

Kate ends the call.

———

Rebecca and Kate are in the kitchen making dinner when Leo Burke finally calls.

Answering her cell phone, Kate steps away from the counter and says, "Hey, Dad."

"Katie, we need to meet."

The man's tone, dead serious, sends a wave of unease through Kate. "What's going on?"

"How soon could you get to my house?"

"I could leave right now. Why?"

"Is Rebecca there?"

Kate's unease heightens, but she does her best to hold steady.

"Yes, of course," she says. "We were making dinner."

Rebecca turns from the counter and gives her sister an inquisitive look.

Kate replies with a confused expression paired with an exaggerated shrug before directing her attention back to the phone call.

Her tone a little firmer this time, she asks again, "What's going on, Dad?"

Kate hears at first only silence, and then Leo Burke finally speaks. "It's about your friend's husband. I'll explain when you get here."

Kate remembers what Maria said this morning about Chief O'Neil's request for her husband's devices.

"Yeah, okay," she says. "I'm on my way."

———

The sun has set when Kate arrives at her father-in-law's house.

A small saltbox colonial, the house is dark, though the front porch light is on, and the narrow driveway that runs the length of the half-acre property is empty.

Kate wonders if her father-in-law parked his Ford Explorer behind the house, though of course that wouldn't explain the dark windows. Still, she pulls into the driveway and rolls to its end, only to find that the back parking space is empty as well.

Picking up her cell phone from the passenger seat, Kate begins navigating to the most recent incoming call—Leo's number—but stops when a vehicle pulls into the driveway behind her, its headlights flooding her car's interior with a glaring light.

She is blinded until the headlights go out, and even then it takes a moment for her eyes to adjust enough for her to identify the vehicle behind her as Sabrowsky's Ford F-150.

Eddie has already exited his pickup and is walking toward Kate's Subaru. He is dressed in jeans and a dark leather jacket, his left arm held close to his chest by a black sling.

Kate lowers her window as her friend reaches the driver's door.

"Hey, Katie."

"What's going on, Eddie? Leo called and told me to meet him here."

"Change of plan," Sabrowsky says. "He's meeting with Chief O'Neil. I'm supposed to bring you to them."

Kate raises the window and shuts off the engine, pockets her keys and phone, and exits her vehicle.

Inside the cab of the pickup, Kate pulls the passenger door closed as Sabrowsky starts the engine.

Leaning back in his seat, he winces, drawing in air through clenched teeth.

Kate asks, "Still hurts?"

Sabrowsky nods. "Sometimes it will throb like a motherfucker. I don't even have to be doing anything. I could just be sitting there and, boom, there it goes again."

Kate notices that his speech pattern is slower than usual, not yet a slur but close.

She asks, "When was your last pill?"

"I don't know. A few hours ago."

Taking a close look at Sabrowsky's face, Kate sees that his eyes are glassy.

"Maybe I should drive, Eddie."

"I'm fine. I promise."

Kate fastens her seat belt, and Sabrowsky shifts into gear, reversing out of the driveway and onto the street. Despite being limited to one arm, he controls the large vehicle effectively.

Shifting into drive, he eases down on the accelerator, bringing his pickup up to speed gradually.

Kate asks, "So where are we going?"

"Compo Beach."

"Where Derek was found."

Sabrowsky nods. "Yeah. Apparently, Chief O'Neil called Leo and asked him to meet him out there. Then Leo called me and told me to pick you up at his house and bring you to them."

"Any idea why?"

Sabrowsky shakes his head. "Something's going on, though. I mean, why would the chief be at a crime scene that's eighteen hours old? And why ask Leo to meet him there?"

Kate considers sharing her suspicion regarding the nature of the investigation into Derek's death, but she decides it isn't her place to do so. Knowing Sabrowsky's obsessive tendencies, O'Neil might be intentionally keeping his officer out of the loop.

And there is also the matter of Sabrowsky currently being on administrative leave to keep in mind.

Shrugging once, Kate answers, "I don't know."

"So it looks like we're both in the dark," Sabrowsky says.

Kate doesn't respond.

They ride in silence for a moment, but then Sabrowsky winces again. Taking his right hand off the wheel, he reaches around and briefly cups his left shoulder. Then he returns his hand to the wheel.

Kate takes another close look at her friend.

"You look tired, Eddie."

"I'm not really sleeping."

"The painkillers don't help with that?"

He shakes his head. "No. If anything, they seem to agitate me."

"What are you taking?"

"Percocet."

"No wonder. That drives everyone crazy."

"Really?"

"Yes. Leif was on that once, and it completely changed his personality. He was snapping at everyone, couldn't sleep except for a few hours, and then he'd have insane nightmares. I finally called his doctor and got his prescription switched."

"Maybe I should ask my doctor to prescribe something else."

"I would at least mention it to him."

"Thanks, Katie. I will."

Sabrowsky makes the turn onto Hillspoint Road. Compo Beach is a little over a mile away, down a more or less straight road with a speed limit of twenty-five.

If that weren't the case, and if Sabrowsky didn't keep his eyes ahead and stay just under the speed limit, Kate would have insisted that he stop so she could drive the rest of the way.

———

The far end of the Compo Beach parking lot is cordoned off with yellow police tape strung between a half dozen orange traffic cones.

A pair of bright fluorescent lights mounted atop a tow-behind unit, complete with its own generator, illuminates the area.

Kate is reminded by it of the way her backyard looked after Leo installed the two floodlights.

Sabrowsky stops just inside the parking lot's entrance and studies the scene three hundred feet ahead.

Kate does as well. Two uniformed officers are talking with a man and a woman, both wearing khaki pants and dark polo shirts. Standing off on their own, fifty feet away, are Chief O'Neil and Leo Burke.

Derek's pickup is at the heart of the cordoned-off area, and among the Westport PD vehicles parked on this side of the yellow tape is a van marked STATE POLICE MAJOR CRIMES UNIT.

"Huh," Sabrowsky says.

Kate asks, "What?"

"Major Crimes isn't usually brought in for a suicide."

Again, Kate holds back what she knows.

They continue to monitor the scene, which doesn't change—the two uniformed officers are still talking to the pair of state police investigators inside the yellow tape, and beyond it, Chief O'Neil and Leo Burke, standing face-to-face, continue their conversation.

Kate asks, "Should we get closer?"

"I'm sure they see us. We should wait until they wave us in."

Another moment passes, and then O'Neil and Burke are nodding together, as if in agreement. O'Neil removes his cell phone from his pocket and begins working the keys with his thumbs.

He finishes and is returning the phone to his pocket when Sabrowsky's cell phone chimes. Picking it up from the center console, he looks at the display.

Then he lays the device back down, shifts into gear, and says, "Here we go."

FORTY

Chief O'Neil and Leo Burke put another fifty feet between themselves and the yellow tape in the time it takes Sabrowsky to roll his F-150 across the empty parking lot.

He kills the engine and the lights, and then Kate and he exit the pickup and join the two men standing shoulder to shoulder and waiting for them.

"Sorry to bring you out here, Katie," Leo says. "But you needed to hear right away what we have to tell you."

The understanding that this meeting was to be about Derek is suddenly gone, and in its abrupt absence, Kate's unease returns, though she does her best to keep it from showing.

"Okay," she says tentatively. "What is it I need to know?"

"Before we start," O'Neil says, "I want you to know that your family is safe. I sent Schulze to your house. He's parked on your street, and after everyone goes to bed, he'll take a position in your driveway and remain there until morning."

Kate feels that all-too-familiar escalation from a nagging dread to utter fear. "Why? What's happened?"

O'Neil answers, "We have reason to suspect that Derek Hogue didn't kill himself."

Sabrowsky asks, "Why do you think that?"

"He had a number of cell phones at his home, one of which contained a text exchange with an unknown person that took place minutes before he drove here last night. According to that exchange, he was coming here to meet someone."

"I don't understand," Kate says.

Leo answers, "No cell phone was found on Derek's person or anywhere in his vehicle. It's unlikely he came here to meet someone without bringing a phone with him."

"He could have forgotten," Sabrowsky suggests.

Chief O'Neil shakes his head. "The text exchange was an unfriendly one. The unknown sender was demanding that Derek do something, and Derek was refusing to do it. I don't think under those circumstances he would leave his home without at least one of his devices."

Kate asks, "The sender was demanding Derek do what?"

"It's never stated explicitly. In fact, the two went out of their way to remain vague. They avoided using a name, or even gender-specific pronouns. But there were references to someone they called 'the target.'"

Leo says, "Derek Hogue didn't drive out here to commit suicide. He came here to meet someone, and that someone killed him in a way that would make it look like a suicide."

"How can you be so sure, Dad?"

Sabrowsky answers, "If he did have a phone on him, then someone took it."

O'Neil adds, "And whoever took it likely believed it was the phone that contained the text messages about the meeting."

"So Derek left that phone at home on purpose," Kate says.

"Yes," O'Neil says.

"Could the one he had on him have been stolen? I mean, someone could have found him . . . after, and decided to take it, right?"

"He still had his wallet and watch."

"There's more, Katie," Leo says. "There were two sets of fingerprints on the pistol that was found on the seat beside the deceased. Derek's and Mark Hillman's. And Hillman's fingerprints were on the magazine and the rounds it contained, but not Derek's."

"So you think the pistol belonged to Hillman."

"Yes. And whoever staged the suicide knew what he was doing, which means he was a professional. It's doubtful that a professional would stage a suicide so effectively, and yet not properly wipe down the weapon or the magazine and the rounds it contained."

O'Neil says, "The killer wanted to make certain we connected Derek Hogue with Mark Hillman."

"Why?"

Again, Sabrowsky offers the answer. "Derek and Hillman were partners."

Kate looks at her friend, then back at her father-in-law and the chief, both men nodding. Then the chief speaks.

"Two sets of fingerprints were found on the camera at Hillman's apartment, the one that contained all the photos of you. The first set belonged to Hillman, but the second set was unknown until it was compared with Derek's. They're a match."

Kate remembers something Maria recently said.

"Maria told me that her digital camera was missing. She asked Derek what happened to it, and he claimed he sold it."

"He didn't, Katie," Leo says. "He was the one who took the photos of you. He had access to the woods behind your property. And since he was your neighbor and the husband of your closest friend, he knew your schedule—when you left for work, came home, did your shopping, everything. That includes when you went to bed. Which explains why your photos were still on the camera, even though they predated the ones found on Hillman's computer. Derek has been taking them for two years, and when they were needed by Hillman, he provided them."

Kate's mind is slowed by shock, and it takes her a moment to speak. "Why?"

O'Neil says, "He was a contractor, Katie. And he was severely in debt. On one of his other phones was a text exchange with an unknown party that we suspect is the same unknown party he came here last night to meet. They were discussing ways to terrorize their 'target' into selling. In another conversation they discuss ways to run their target out of town. You were the target, Katie. And whichever way they got you to give up on your house, it was going to be Derek's responsibility to get you to sell to him."

"But he's broke. How could he afford it?"

"The unknown party had a developer that would provide the funds. Derek would get the contract to build the new constructions—that was his cut. And the unknown party would share the profit with his developer."

"Derek was being coerced, that much was clear," Leo says. "He resisted throughout, offered several times to find another target, but whoever was pulling his strings was fixated on your property."

"Why?"

"We don't know."

"But there was an escalation over the past few days," O'Neil says. "Derek's resistance turned to defiance. And it got him killed."

Struggling to understand, Kate looks at her father-in-law, then turns to her friend beside her, whose expression is grave.

Kate looks back at O'Neil and Leo. "Why was there an escalation? What happened in the past few days?"

Leo and O'Neil look at each other. Finally, Leo answers, "A few days ago, you decided to change your will."

"But what does that have to do with me selling my property to Derek?"

"It doesn't."

Exasperated, Kate laughs tensely. "I'm sorry, I just don't understand."

"I'm assuming you told Maria about updating your will."

"I must have, yeah."

"She told Derek, and Derek told his partner."

Kate shakes her head impatiently. "I still don't understand. How would me changing my will affect their plan to get me to sell?"

"That's the million-dollar question, isn't it?" O'Neil says. "Whatever their reason, Katie, it was important enough for them to consider killing you."

"We think that's what Derek refused to do," Leo says.

Kate has no words, not that she could have uttered them if she did—her lungs are empty, echoing her pounding heart.

Sabrowsky steps in and says, "But this doesn't make sense. What would they gain by preventing Kate from changing her will?"

Instead of answering, Leo asks Kate, "The changes you told me you were going to make—your sister as Max and Callie's guardian, and me as conservator—who else knew about that?"

"I told my lawyer, but that was a few hours ago."

"Did you share it with Maria?"

"Not that I remember, no."

"And Rebecca?"

"I told her, yeah. But you're not suggesting that she has anything to do with this."

Burke looks at O'Neil and nods, and O'Neil says to Sabrowsky, "Let's you and me take a walk."

Kate can sense that Sabrowsky is looking at her, but her eyes are fixed on her father-in-law.

The chief turns and walks away, and after a pause, Sabrowsky follows.

Leo waits until the two men are out of earshot before speaking.

"Derek and the person controlling him—blackmailing him, essentially—knew about the conversation you and I had regarding your will. It was the day after you and I had our discussion that our unknown person texted Derek and informed him that a change in plans might be necessary. Their exchange indicates they met that night in person, and it was the next morning that things turned unfriendly, so it's our belief that it was during that face-to-face meeting that they discussed killing you. What we can't account for, however, is how our unknown suspect knew what he knew. It came from him; he's the one who brought up the possible will change, not Derek. So what I'm about to ask you is important, Katie. Do you remember exactly when you spoke to your sister about it?"

"Not off the top of my head, no."

"Was it hours after you and I first discussed it? The next day?"

"It was either the next day or the day after that. Or maybe it was a few days later. I honestly can't remember."

Leo pauses before continuing. "You're aware that Rebecca and Derek had an affair a few years ago."

"Yes. I take it their texts are on one of Derek's phones."

"They are. Is it possible that they are still involved?"

"No, it's not."

"How can you be so sure?"

"I can account for Rebecca's whereabouts since she's been here, every minute of every day."

"Affairs can be conducted via texts and phone calls. And she stands to benefit, should you die with an invalid will."

"But the original plan was to get me to sell. She wouldn't benefit from that."

"Unless Derek and his partner offered her a cut."

"I'm sorry, Dad, but I just don't believe she is capable of that. She really has changed. And anyway, Jack overheard her and Derek arguing last week about getting back together. Derek wanted to; she didn't."

"How did he overhear that?"

"You asked him to keep an eye out. He heard raised voices out his window and took a look. Rebecca and Derek were standing at the end of Maria's driveway. Rebecca had gone for a quick run, and Derek rushed out to catch her alone."

Leo Burke nods thoughtfully as he takes all that in.

Kate glances past him at Sabrowsky and O'Neil standing fifty feet away. O'Neil is talking, Sabrowsky listening carefully.

Then Leo speaks, and Kate shifts her attention back to him.

"Katie, I can think of only one other way for Derek's associate to know what he knew, and when he knew it."

There is a part of Kate that doesn't want to ask, but eventually she breaks down and she asks, "How?"

"He has you under complete surveillance."

"What does that mean?"

"Not just visual but audio, too. It's possible that your house is bugged. For an unknown period of time, someone has been listening to everything said and done by you and everyone in that house, including my grandchildren."

"Jesus, Dad."

"Does Maria know the code to your alarm system? Does she have a spare key?"

Kate nods. "Yes. I have a key to her house, and she has a key to mine."

"If Derek knew the code as well, he could have gained entrance and installed devices while you were teaching and Max and Callie were at school. Unless it was physically wired into your electrical system, any listening device would be battery operated, so depending on how long this has been going on, someone would have to get in and out of your house regularly to change the batteries. Of course, being a contractor, Derek would have the skill necessary to hardwire a system, in which case he wouldn't have to deal with the battery issue at all."

"Where would a listening device be?"

"They could be anywhere."

"'They'?"

"He would have likely planted several, in multiple rooms. You and I were in the kitchen when we discussed your will. I'd imagine another device would be in the living room, maybe even your bedroom."

Kate's reaction to the idea of suffering such an utterly thorough violation is to close her eyes and shake her head. There is nothing that she can do except to surrender to the understanding that she and her children, for an undetermined period of time, have had no privacy. For a moment, her breathing stalls, and only when her lungs start to ache does her autonomic nervous system signal her diaphragm to move.

Finally, she says, "I want you to find each device and tear them out, Dad. Every last one of them."

"I will, first thing tomorrow."

"Why tomorrow?"

"I think it would be best if we kept this from the children. Once they leave for school, I'll get to work. And I'm sorry, Katie, but I would strongly encourage you to reconsider your decision regarding the security cameras. Eddie still has the equipment, and I think, with what we know now and, more importantly, what we don't know, that it should be installed as soon as possible." Leo pauses. "I know it's not how you want to live, but it's the way it has to be, at least for the time being, don't you agree?"

Kate takes a breath, pushes down the fear and the anger and the feeling of utter defeat, then exhales and nods. "Yeah," she says.

"Good."

"Is there any hope of tracking down Derek's partner?"

"We're working on that. He hid his trail well—very well—but there's the data from all of Derek's cell phones to go through, and cell-tower records that will have to be pulled. I'm hoping that will give us something."

"Be honest, Dad. How good are the chances you'll find him?"

"If he got careless and made a mistake, like Hillman did and Derek did, the chances are good."

"And if he didn't, then I'm back to locking my doors and drawing my shades, only now I can add looking over my shoulder every time we leave the house to the routine."

"O'Neil is going to process a carry permit for you. Firearms aren't permitted on school grounds in this state, but he has already talked to

Doug Banks, and he's given you permission to have your pistol with you, provided that it's kept safe and concealed at all times."

"How am I going to do that? Keep it nearby but concealed while I teach?"

"Leif's mother owned a purse designed for everyday carry. It has a hidden but easily accessible compartment. I still have it. I'll bring it tomorrow morning."

Her thoughts scrambled, Kate nods absently.

"Will you be okay tonight?" Leo asks. "Going home, knowing now what you know."

"That someone is listening to everything any of us says or does?"

"Most likely, the surveillance isn't active."

"What does that mean?"

"I doubt anyone is monitoring you every minute of every day. It's more likely that the hidden microphones are transmitting to a digital system, one that only records when voices or certain sounds are picked up. Then those recordings are reviewed at a later time."

"That's a small comfort, Dad."

"If you don't think you can handle that tonight, then bring everyone to my house."

Kate shakes her head. "No, you're right. It's better that the kids don't know. They need to sleep in their own beds. And then I'll have all day tomorrow to figure out a way to explain the security cameras."

"You can always blame it on their overprotective grandfather."

"Yeah, I was leaning that way," Kate says. She glances once again at Sabrowsky and Chief O'Neil, and then looks back at her father-in-law. "I really thought this was over."

"I know. Me too. But you and the children are safe. You need to remember that. And you have a lot of people who are going to make sure you remain safe."

"Speaking of, Dad, would you mind driving me back to my car? Eddie really shouldn't be operating heavy machinery in his condition."

Leo nods. "Yeah, I'll take you."

"And maybe someone should drive Eddie home, or at least follow him."

"I'll pass that on to O'Neil."

Kate looks out over the water, its smooth surface reflecting the darkening sky, a blackness interrupted only by the faint flicker of Venus. She cycles through a few breaths, steadying herself.

Leo gives her a moment, and then he asks, "How are you feeling, Katie?"

"I'm not sure. Numb, like I took one of Eddie's painkillers, but a little manic, too."

"That's the shock and adrenaline. Perfectly understandable, all things considered."

"I think I'll email my lawyer now, ask him to draw up the new will right away so I can sign it."

"That's probably a good idea. I'd be happy to drive you to his office when it's ready."

"Yeah, I might want that, Dad. Thanks."

"I'll go let O'Neil know we're leaving."

Leo turns and steps away.

Kate says, "Don't forget to tell him about Eddie, please."

"I won't."

Katie watches as Leo approaches Sabrowsky and the chief. He says something, after which, Sabrowsky turns his head and looks directly at Kate.

She can't tell by his expression if he is bemused or hurt, though the safest bet, knowing him, is to assume both.

Though she is grateful for all that he has done, unintentionally insulting him, even in a minor way, isn't something she can care too much about.

The three men talk for a moment more, and then Leo returns to Kate. "Eddie will meet me at your house in the morning," he says.

"Did you two set a time?"

"He said he can be there by eight. I might get there a little before."

Kate nods. "Okay."

"Chief O'Neil will issue the carry permit first thing in the morning. Do you think you'll need another session at the range?"

"No, Dad. I feel ready."

"Good," Leo says. "Then let's get you back home."

FORTY-ONE

Once more, Kate is riding in silence, this time with Leo in his SUV. At his house, she gets into her Subaru, then backs down the driveway to the street and begins the second leg of her trip home, with Leo following close behind.

As she turns into her driveway, she sees that he has parked alongside Schulze's patrol vehicle, no doubt chatting with the officer through their open windows as he waits for Kate to make it safely inside.

Instead of walking from the end of the driveway to the back door, which is closer, Kate opts for the front door, if only to give her a few seconds of extra time once she's inside the house to put on the mask of calm and ease that she must wear for the sake of her children, who are eating dinner at the kitchen table with their aunt.

This time closing and locking the door behind her doesn't bring the same sense of security she has come to count on.

Steel-reinforced doors and solid walls have shielded her from prying eyes, and windows were easy enough to avoid.

But now there are listening ears to be aware of, which means there are conversations she cannot have, no matter how badly she needs to have them.

Kate musters a smile just as she reaches the kitchen, and as she enters, both her children and sister look at her and smile, each expressing happiness in one way or another that she is back home.

They are mid-meal, and though she has no appetite and likely won't for a while, she joins them at the table.

Rebecca asks, "Do you want me to make you a plate?"

Kate shakes her head. "No, thanks."

Rebecca watches her sister for a moment. "Everything okay?"

Kate answers, "Yeah. Long day. For all of us."

Though Rebecca nods in agreement and doesn't ask a follow-up question, it is clear to Kate that her sister isn't buying that answer.

Nor is she fooled by Kate's smile and upbeat mood.

Averting her eyes, Kate makes small talk with Max and Callie, but it isn't long before she gives her sister a glance meant to indicate that they will talk later.

———

By ten o'clock, Max and Callie have been in their room with the door closed for a half hour, and Rebecca is taking her bedtime shower.

In her bedroom, Kate is grateful for the sound of running water coming from upstairs. Knowing what she knows, white noise, as such, is better than silence, and as she sits alone, still in her jeans and sweatshirt, she runs through the many conversations she has had in her home recently—or at least as many of them as she can remember.

She thinks, too, of conversations she has had outside her home, beyond the reach of however many listening devices may have been planted. Sifting through what her tormentor does and does not know strikes her as an important thing to do, though there is really only one specific detail that she cares about.

As best as she can recall, Kate's discussions with her father-in-law about taking possession of Leif's pistol occurred elsewhere. And if her recollection is correct, then her tormentor is ignorant of what sits in a locked box in her nightstand drawer, which gives her at least one advantage.

Despite the rush of courage and resolve this instills, Kate still finds it difficult to accept that she and her family have been so utterly violated, and the feeling of vulnerability that stirs is even greater than the vulnerability Kate experienced when she first received the photograph of herself, topless as she undressed for bed in this very room.

It is also difficult to cope with the awareness that someone—some unknown person with evil intent—was more than likely listening in on last week's morning indulgence, and that the sounds Kate made as she struggled for orgasm, not to mention her vocalization when release finally came, exist somewhere as a recording.

Adding to that feeling of violation is Kate's memory of her husband's devotion to her pleasure, and the delight he found in her process—the building, the getting close, the reaching, and the final letting go.

The idea that someone has stolen that from her—taken what for so many years only she and Leif shared—is almost too much to bear.

As the shower continues to produce its white noise, Kate realizes that there is another reason that it brings her a degree of comfort.

Not only does it provide a brief semblance of privacy by covering the sound of Kate's breathing and movements, but it also reminds her that there is another being in her home, one who has vowed to never let harm befall the children she is here to care for.

As Leo is fond of saying, there is strength in numbers, and as Kate and her sister protected each other when, for a period of time, they were all they had, there is no doubt in Kate's mind that they would do the same now.

How else is Kate to live with the terrible knowledge that someone wanted her dead, and that that someone pressed the husband of her closest friend to commit the act?

Though she tries not to, Kate can't help but envision a number of ways that Derek could have done what he was asked to do.

The times, the places, the methods he could have used.

The access he had, and how Kate wouldn't, possibly until the very last moment, understand his actual intent.

Kate can only imagine the horror that would tear through her like a storm when she realized that someone so close to her, someone she trusted, had come to kill her.

The upstairs shower ceases abruptly, and Kate is once again sitting in an unnerving silence, keenly aware of every breath she takes.

When enough time has passed for Rebecca to dry off and dress, Kate picks up her cell phone and texts her sister, asking her to come downstairs and to bring her own phone with her.

———

Dressed in her robe, her hair still wet, Rebecca stands in the doorway to Kate's bedroom.

Before her sister can speak, Kate raises her hand and holds her index finger vertically to her lips. Then she lowers her hand and composes a text.

Leo says the house is bugged.

She sends the text, and Rebecca reads what appears on her phone's display, then looks at her sister, dumbfounded.

Kate sends another text. He and Eddie will be here in the morning to search for devices.

Rebecca reads that, and then replies: Do they know who?

Kate shakes her head as she thumbs the keyboard.

Derek wanted to get the house. He and Hillman were partners, along with someone else.

Rebecca's face goes white. She almost speaks but catches herself and texts: Partners with who?!

Again, Kate shakes her head.

Rebecca types frantically: How do they know?

Derek had cell phones. O'Neil got them from Maria. He and Leo think Derek was murdered.

Rebecca's shock deepens. Visibly shaken, she stares at her sister for a moment before responding. What else do they know?

Kate replies: Too much to text, will tell you in the morning when it's safe to talk. But I need to ask you something.

Rebecca nods once and waits as Kate works the keys. She looks at the display when the text comes through.

Do you know how to use a gun?

Looking up, Rebecca nods again, quickly, and responds: Charles had guns. He taught me. Then she sends a quick follow-up: Why?

Kate replies: Derek was supposed to kill me. His partner killed him because he refused.

Horrified, Rebecca breaks the silence. "My God," she whispers.

Kate steps to her nightstand, then waves for Rebecca to join her there. Opening the drawer, Kate reveals the lockbox inside.

With Rebecca standing at her side and watching, Kate enters the passcode slowly, one digit at a time. The spring-loaded lid opens, revealing the pistol and spare magazines.

Rebecca mouths, "Loaded?"

Kate nods. Closing the lid, she steps back so her sister can confirm that she correctly read the digits Kate pressed.

Rebecca repeats the procedure, and once she has depressed the last key, the lid rises.

Pressing it down until it locks again, Rebecca then steps away, allowing Kate to slide the drawer closed.

They stand face-to-face, and Rebecca draws a breath and opens her mouth, readying to speak again, but Kate raises her index finger to her lips once more.

Still, it is a moment before Rebecca exhales the breath held in her lungs and closes her mouth.

Kate texts: Schulze is parked in the driveway again, so we're safe for tonight. The alarm is set.

Despite Kate's assurances, Rebecca's expression of shocked horror remains.

Kate writes and sends one last text: We'll talk in the morning, okay?

Rebecca nods, then responds: I won't silence my phone tonight in case you need me.

Kate mouths, "Thank you."

Rebecca lingers, unwilling to step away from her sister.

Then she lurches forward suddenly, pulling Kate close and embracing her tightly.

"I'm sorry," she whispers.

Caught off guard by the gesture, as well as her sister's surprising strength, Kate asks in a hushed voice, "For what?"

"For everything," Rebecca says. "For all of this. You don't deserve it."

For a few seconds Kate is hesitant to match the fullness of Rebecca's embrace, but finally any and all resistance melts away and she closes her arms around her sister, holding her as close as possible and with as much strength as she can muster.

———

Kate can't sleep, though she isn't surprised by this.

Her bedroom, its door and only window closed, grows stuffier as the hours pass.

And, of course, there is much on her mind, but it's really the raw emotions she has yet to process that keep her far from rest.

A steady current of anxiety has looped through her body since her conversation with Leo Burke, and while her concern for the safety of her family is what occupies her most, she also feels compassion for Maria, who will soon learn the truth about her husband's death, including the fact that Kate is the reason for it.

A man Kate didn't particularly care for, and whom she at times even casually derided, refused the order to kill her.

And yet, at the same time, he was part of a plan to drive her from her home through a campaign of harassment and humiliation.

How can this not elicit a sweeping storm of reactions, psychological as well as physiological?

How could she ever hope to find the peace necessary to sleep, knowing that two men debated whether or not to murder her?

And that one of those men is still out there, maybe far away, maybe somewhere very nearby, as sleepless at this moment as she is?

———

The least Kate can do is lie still and rest her exhausted body.

She imagines that she is sinking into the mattress, and that with every minute that passes, the stresses on her nervous system and immune system and adrenals are washing away, bit by bit.

Each moment of motionlessness is time that her muscles are not rigidly flexed, her stomach not clenched, her joints and bones not required to fight against gravity.

At one point her body suddenly flinches, and she realizes that she has managed to slip into a twilight state of consciousness, but when she looks at the clock on her nightstand, she sees that barely fifteen minutes have passed since she last checked the time.

Still, thinking that perhaps some level of unconsciousness is possible after all, Kate switches off her alarm clock, just in case.

———

Kate sits up, suddenly alert.

Beyond her heavily shaded window is the sound of an engine running.

Her clock reads 5:55 a.m., and even in her groggy state she knows that means sunrise is underway.

Getting out of bed, she hurries to her window, moves the heavy curtain aside, and peers through the blinds just in time to see the Westport PD vehicle parked at the bottom of the driveway complete the process of turning around and then drive from her line of sight.

Putting her robe on over her boxers and tank top and stepping into her slippers, Kate opens her bedroom door and steps into the living room. Pausing at the bottom of the stairs, she listens for an indication that the occupants of the two bedrooms are up, but she hears only silence.

Entering the kitchen, she doesn't bother switching on the light; the glow from the microwave display and hood exhaust light, combined with the blue light of dawn, are enough to see by.

Her long night of poor sleep has left her with the early-warning signs of a headache, so she decides to hold off on her morning coffee and have peppermint tea instead. Taking the kettle from the stove top, she brings it to the sink and holds it under the faucet as she opens the tap. As the kettle fills, she looks out the window overlooking the backyard and sees something odd.

Emerging from the border trees separating her yard from the back woods, dressed as he was last night, is Eddie Sabrowsky.

With his left arm in its sling, he has difficulty maintaining his balance as he trudges through the overgrown shrubs, but finally he clears that barrier and steps onto the open grass.

As he walks toward the house, he glances up and sees Kate in the window. Grimacing from the pain his journey through the woods no doubt caused, he raises his right arm and waves.

Shutting off the water and leaving the half-filled kettle in the sink, Kate steps to the back door and deactivates the alarm system.

She unlocks the dead bolt and opens the door just as Sabrowsky reaches the bottom of the stairs.

He pauses and looks up at her, his eyes still glassy and his expression grim.

Kate asks, "What's going on? Everything okay?"

"Everything's fine, Katie. Just checking things out."

"You're kind of early. Leo isn't going to get here until around eight."

Sabrowsky nods and starts up the stairs. "There are some things I need to take care of first," he says.

Kate glances at the end of the driveway, sees only her Subaru parked there.

She asks, "Where's your truck?"

Reaching the top step, Sabrowsky stands face-to-face with Kate but doesn't answer.

Something about his face—pale and pained, his eyes wild and unfocused—causes Kate's heart to fall into her stomach.

It is when she sees that he is wearing leather gloves that fear springs through her body.

Her tone of voice flat, she asks, "What are you doing here, Eddie?"

He nods, relieved. "Good," he says. "You haven't figured it out."

Kate's gut clenches. "Figured out what?"

Sabrowsky quickly scans the kitchen behind Kate, then looks at her again.

"Let's just get this over with, Katie, okay? There isn't a lot of time."

FORTY-TWO

A burst of strength overtakes Kate—arms, legs, and core, all suddenly, savagely powerful—and she grasps the edge of the door with two hands, but before she can swing it more than a few inches, Sabrowsky takes a lunging step forward, blocking the door with his body.

It is a sacrifice move, because his left shoulder is what makes contact with the door, but Sabrowsky ignores the blow to his injury and shoves the door open with enough force to send Kate stumbling backward into the kitchen.

As he breaches the threshold, Kate turns to run, but he is quickly behind her, grabbing a fistful of hair with his right hand and pulling it like a leash until the distance is closed between them and she is pressed against him.

His mouth close to her ear, he whispers, "For the sake of your children, stay quiet. Understand?"

There is impatience in his voice, and menace, and the feeling of his body so close to hers causes Kate to stiffen and freeze. Still holding her hair, Sabrowsky eases the door shut with his foot, then guides Kate to the kitchen table and sits her down.

Standing over her, he releases her and cups his left shoulder, bending forward slightly at the waist and whispering, *"Fuck, fuck, fuck."*

He takes two steps back, twists and bends a few times more, but then the pain passes and his movement ceases. He takes a deep breath, and then returns to the door and flips the dead bolt.

For a second Kate thinks of running, but she is too stunned by fear and confusion to move, and anyway, what would she accomplish by doing so, except risk waking the entire house?

The strength she'd felt just seconds ago has drained away, leaving behind weakened legs and arms that are trembling.

Sabrowsky takes a position again in front of Kate. He glances quickly at the microwave's digital clock and then says to her, "You normally wake the children at six forty-five, correct?"

Kate nods once, stiffly.

"And on weekends, when you don't wake them, they sleep in until at least eight, right?"

Kate pauses, and then says, "Yes."

Sabrowsky's voice takes on a tone of reason and calm. "Good. So we're going to move like little mice, okay, Katie? You do everything I tell you, when I tell you to do it, got it? With luck, by the time the kids get up, this will be all over."

Kate is hesitant to speak, but fear mixed with curiosity gets the better of her. "What will be over?"

"Please, Katie," Sabrowsky says. "Everything you say and do from now on determines whether or not the children live. I can get what I need either way, but Leif was a brother to me, and I'd rather not harm his children. In fact, I'm doing everything I can to avoid that. Understand?"

Again, Kate nods once. "Yes."

"I'm going to need you to get dressed, so we're going to head into your bedroom. Quiet as mice, okay?"

Sabrowsky steps back and offers his right hand to Kate. It takes a moment for her to accept it. He pulls her up from her seat, steadily but gently.

"Lead the way," he says.

Kate walks into the living room, Sabrowsky close behind her, his hand firmly on her shoulder. As they pass the stairs, they each look up,

Kate first, and then Sabrowsky, both making sure that no one has exited the bedrooms above.

Entering the bedroom, Kate heads straight for her nightstand, but Sabrowsky whispers, "Not there."

Kate stops, and he directs her to stand at the foot of the bed, after which he retrieves her cell phone from its charger and pockets it.

From where he stands, Sabrowsky can see through the bedroom door to the bottom of the stairs, which he pauses to check.

Kate glances at the top drawer of the nightstand, and then quickly looks back at Sabrowsky.

"You seem to know our morning schedule down to the minute," she says. "You're the one who's been listening to us, aren't you?"

Despite his manic state, Sabrowsky is slow to react. He nods for a moment, and then says, "Leo knows about that, then. That's what you two talked about last night when you were alone."

Though fear continues to race through her, Kate does her best to appear calm.

But Sabrowsky knows her, has for most of their lives, and he sees through her mask.

"You're surprised right now, Katie. That's good. That tells me Leo doesn't know who has you under surveillance; otherwise he would have warned you. I need to know, though: How did he figure it out?"

"Does it matter?"

"Very much, yes."

"The conversation Leo and I had about me updating my will was at noon, and that night Derek got a text about it on one of his phones. Leo and I knew we were the only ones who knew about that conversation at that point."

Sabrowsky takes that in, as if gauging its importance. Then he says, "He knows about Rebecca's affair with Derek, correct? Those texts were on one of his phones?"

"Yes."

"What else does he know about them?"

"I don't know what you mean."

"Did he tell you anything else about the two of them, what they were up to, the crap they pulled?"

Kate can't hide her confusion. "What are you talking about, Eddie?"

Sabrowsky shakes his head, dismissing the question. "Did you know about their affair, too? Did you know that Derek and Rebecca were fucking? In that cottage? Night after night?"

Kate wonders now if she has mistaken mania for anger.

"Yes," she answers.

"How did you know?"

"Rebecca told me."

"Back then or recently?"

"Recently."

Again, Sabrowsky pauses to take that in. Watching him, Kate gets the sense that he is bothered as much by the fact that the affair is common knowledge as he is by the affair itself.

She considers addressing that, but before she can, Sabrowsky asks, "Does he suspect her?"

"I don't understand."

Though he keeps his voice hushed, Eddie is suddenly impatient. "Does Leo think Rebecca and Derek were working together? Does he think she was part of what was happening to you?"

Aware now of his volatility, Kate keeps her tone even. "He asked me if I thought that was possible."

"And what did you tell him?"

"That I didn't think it was."

Sabrowsky takes in a breath, and then lets it out. "This is important, Katie. Did you give him reasons why you didn't think that?"

"I told him I knew where she was every minute since she got here."

"Anything else?"

"That Jack overheard Rebecca and Derek arguing one morning."

"What about?"

"Getting back together. Derek wanted to but Rebecca refused."

"And did Leo seem convinced?"

"Yes."

Another inhalation and exhalation, and then Sabrowsky says, "Okay, good."

"Why is that important, Eddie?"

Sabrowsky dismisses that question as well. "Did Leo say anything about how your house ended up being bugged?"

"What do you mean?"

"Does he have a theory about how someone could gain access?"

"He assumes it was Derek. Maria knows the code to the alarm system and has a spare key." Kate stops short. "It wasn't Derek, though, was it? You installed the alarm system. After Leif was killed, you set it all up for us. So you know the code as well."

Sabrowsky says nothing.

Kate asks, "You don't think Leo will figure that out sooner or later?"

"He won't."

"How can you be so sure?"

"You don't have to worry about that, Katie."

She scoffs, shaking her head in disbelief. "You did all this. You terrorized me while pretending to be looking out for me. Everything you said and everything you did, that was part of it. Get me scared, then come over and calm me down, only to get me scared all over again. That's what you said was happening. And you did that for what, Eddie? For money?"

Sabrowsky doesn't respond. For a moment, he teeters, his eyelids fluttering.

Kate decides to press him.

"I don't understand," she says. "What does changing my will have to do with me selling my house?"

His episode of instability passes, and Sabrowsky shakes his head. "We're not doing this, Katie."

"Doing what?"

"Discussing the whys and hows."

Kate continues to press him nonetheless. "Leo says you wanted Derek to kill me. Because I was going to change my will, you told Derek that the plan had to change. Fucking with me so I'd give up and sell wasn't enough anymore. But how does killing me get you the house? Your plan doesn't make any sense."

Sabrowsky seems to have stopped listening, allowing his attention to wander. Kate watches him silently, waiting for some kind of reply.

Then Sabrowsky's faraway look fades, and he focuses once again on Kate.

"C'mon," he says. "Time for you to get dressed."

FORTY-THREE

"Pick out some clothes," Sabrowsky says. He pauses before adding, "And some nice underwear, too."

Confused, Kate remains still.

"I need you to look like you were planning to spend the night."

"Spend the night where?"

Sabrowsky shakes his head. "That wasn't the deal, Kate. What I say, when I say it, remember?"

Kate hesitates, creating a brief standoff between herself and Sabrowsky that ends with him, suddenly angry, stepping to her dresser.

"We don't have time to screw around," he snaps.

He opens the top drawer and looks at the contents—Kate's underwear, consisting of a dozen light-colored bras and panties. He begins sorting through them in a rush, stopping only when a black bra and matching thong are revealed at the bottom of the drawer.

Removing them, he holds them up before tossing them onto the bed. "These," he says.

Her confusion deepens, and Kate asks, "What the fuck are you thinking, Eddie?"

Sabrowsky walks to the closet, opening it and putting his back to Kate as he searches through her clothes.

Again, Kate glances at her nightstand drawer.

Sabrowsky selects a pair of jeans and a red silk blouse, turns and throws both items, still on the hangers, next to the black lace underwear.

"Get dressed. Now."

"What for?"

He shakes his head dismissively. "Don't push it, Katie."

"Can I at least change in the bathroom?"

"No."

"Then turn around."

"It's not like I haven't seen you naked before, Katie."

She refuses to move. Still agitated, Sabrowsky reaches around to the small of his back. Removing a pistol, he stands with his arm lowered and his hand hanging alongside his leg.

Kate's heart flails wildly at the sight of the firearm, beating against her sternum like a caged animal. Her face flushes, but her body turns rigid and cold.

It takes all she has to maintain the appearance of calm. "Won't that wake the whole house, Eddie?"

Sabrowsky raises and extends his arm, pointing the weapon at Kate's chest.

"Here's what's going to happen if you don't stop fucking around. You're going to come with me to your son's room. That's where the children are, right? Then you're going to choose which one dies first. Then you're going to watch me put a bullet into their heads, one at a time. Like I said, I get what I want whether they live or die."

Kate nods. "Okay," she says. She raises her hand in a calming gesture. "Can you just not point that at me?"

Sabrowsky returns his hand to his side. "No more shit," he says.

"Yeah, okay, no more shit."

"So get going."

Kate unties and opens her robe, sliding it off her shoulders and dropping it to the floor, then steps out of her slippers. Pulling her tank top up and over her head, she drops that, too. Finally, she hooks her thumbs into the waistband of her boxers and bends forward as she pulls them down to her ankles before stepping out of them as well.

Stepping to the bed, she reaches for the underwear, putting on the thong first and then the bra. Next is the silk blouse, followed by the jeans.

Satisfied, Sabrowsky returns the pistol to the small of his back. Walking back to the closet, he selects a pair of black heels and brings them to Kate.

"Put these on."

Using the foot of the bed to balance herself, Kate puts on the shoes.

Sabrowsky studies her. "Good," he says. "Now was that so bad?"

Kate doesn't respond.

Sabrowsky nods toward the farthest corner of the room. "I'm going to need you to stand there."

Kate walks to the corner, her heels clicking on the wood floor.

Sabrowsky reaches for his back pocket, removing a six-inch-long, narrow-handled screwdriver. Walking to the back wall, he crouches down at the electrical outlet and uses the tool to back out the single screw holding the cover in place.

Setting the plate, screw, and screwdriver down, he reaches behind the exposed outlet with his finger, grabbing hold of something and pulling hard.

In his hand is a black cylinder roughly the size of a triple-A battery. Attached to it is a pair of exposed electrical wires.

Sabrowsky stuffs the listening device into his pocket, and then puts the cover back into place and resets the screw.

He tells Kate to lead him to the kitchen, and as she exits the bedroom and crosses the living room, she makes no effort to step softly.

Sabrowsky repeats the procedure at the outlet closest to the kitchen table, after which he tells Kate to lead him into the living room and sit on the couch while he uncovers an outlet below the bookshelf and removes the device hidden there.

Then he stands to one side of the picture window that overlooks the front yard, leaning his right shoulder against the wall.

Kate glances at the clock. It is six fifteen.

In a quiet voice, she asks, "Now what?"

Sabrowsky looks out the window, but instead of scanning the property, he fixes his attention in one direction.

Kate knows he can be looking at only one thing.

The cottage.

"Now we wait for your boyfriend to leave for work," Sabrowsky says.

———

Kate listens for sounds from upstairs, indications that her children or sister have awoken.

But so far the house remains silent.

Sabrowsky looks out the window frequently, checking on the status of the cottage, and when he isn't doing that, he is either looking at Kate or staring down at the floor.

For the first five minutes, whenever her captor's attention is elsewhere, Kate glances toward her bedroom, wondering if she could make it to her nightstand and retrieve Leif's pistol from the lockbox before Sabrowsky could overtake her—or worse, make good on his threat and rush up the stairs to Max's bedroom.

Those moments when Sabrowsky stares at the floor, his eyes unfocused, are when Kate is most tempted to quietly slip off her heels, jump up from the couch, and bolt.

As strong as that compulsion is, however, Kate's caution is stronger, and eventually she surrenders to the understanding that this fantasy is not her way out of what is to come.

A few more minutes of waiting in silence passes before Kate speaks.

"If you're so desperate for money, Eddie, you could have asked for help. You didn't have to do this."

Sabrowsky maintains his silent vigil for a moment, and then finally says, "No, I did."

"Why?"

"They're the reason Leif is dead."

"Who is?"

"Hillman and Derek."

"What are you talking about?"

Keeping his eyes on the cottage, Sabrowsky shrugs indifferently.

Kate asks, "Why are Hillman and Derek the reason Leif is dead?"

"They tried this once before. Years ago. The vandalism. But they didn't know what they were doing. They didn't know how to escalate things. Derek had made a promise to some very dangerous people. Eventually, those people lost their patience and took matters into their own hands, sent those two animals here to do terrible things."

"How do you know this?"

"My investigation for Leo revealed more than I let on at the time."

"Why didn't you tell anyone that?"

He shrugs again, this time half-heartedly. "My marriage was ending and I needed money. I figured why send Derek to prison for what he did when I could bleed him for all he's worth? Hillman didn't have any money, but he was helpful in tracking down Derek's associates." Sabrowsky pauses. "I killed them for what they did to Leif."

"Jesus, Eddie."

"You have no idea what I'm capable of, Katie. I had no idea until my best friend was taken from me."

Kate needs a moment to process that.

"You didn't kill Hillman in self-defense, did you?" she says finally. "You murdered him."

"That freak didn't deserve to live. The things he did to women." Sabrowsky takes a breath, lets it out. "The men that were sent here the night Leif was killed, they were supposed to make it look like a home invasion. Beat Leif and leave him for dead, rape you and your daughter,

363

torture your son. Of course you'd sell after that, right? Hillman's job was to take photographs of the aftermath, and if you didn't sell, start sending them to you, one at a time, until you finally gave in. And since no one would want to buy a house where such terrible things had happened, Derek was supposed to swoop in like a hero and make you a cash offer. The house would be torn down, a pair of two-family constructions would go up, and the developers would walk away with three million in profit. But you already know that."

"You're the reason Derek went broke."

Sabrowsky nods. "Yeah, I bled the fucker dry. I saw it coming, though, and I knew once that money stopped, I'd have no choice but to make my own deal. So I had Derek start taking the pictures of you at home, and Hillman followed you around town. When the time came, they're the ones who broke into the cottage and left you the first message."

"But I saw teenagers that night."

"That's what you thought you saw, Katie. It was dark, you were startled, and everyone has their bias. So we ran with it. Derek even flattened his own tires to keep you thinking that. He and Hillman didn't know how to escalate, but I do. It was important to give you hope at first that this wasn't what had happened before and that it could be easily explained away. I didn't want you or Leo or O'Neil pressing the panic button and putting you in lockdown too soon. There were things that needed to be done still, but I also needed you to gradually lose hope, a bit at a time. I needed you to come face-to-face with all the things I knew you fear." Sabrowsky's mood suddenly darkens. "But instead of selling, you dug in. Leo mentioned the will, and I knew when I heard that conversation that if you didn't break, well, we'd only have one direction left to take. And that wouldn't work with Leo as conservator."

"And what makes you think Rebecca is just going to sell you the house?"

"She won't have a choice now."

"What do you mean 'she won't have a choice'?"

"You don't have to worry about that," he says.

Still looking out the window, Sabrowsky suddenly stands straight. "Finally," he says.

Kate hears the sound of a car door closing, followed by an engine starting.

She listens as Jack's Jeep drives off. Then Sabrowsky steps away from the window and faces her.

"C'mon," he says. "Let's go."

FORTY-FOUR

Sabrowsky and Kate leave through the front door.

As they walk across the path toward the driveway, Kate's heels make a sharp clacking sound on the slate. It takes only a few steps for Sabrowsky to instruct her to take off her shoes and carry them.

Moving up the driveway alongside her, Sabrowsky glances to the right, peering through the border trees that separate Kate's property from her neighbors'.

There is no activity in any of the points in Maria's yard from which anyone standing outside would have a clear view of the two people making their way toward the cottage.

The only other possible exposure is Old Town Road. Someone out for an early-morning walk, or even just driving by, might happen to spot Sabrowsky with Kate, so when he isn't checking to his right, he is looking straight ahead.

His concern about being seen—and the only explanation for it—causes Kate's focus to narrow significantly.

In this surreal tunnel vision, she no longer feels the pavement beneath her bare feet or the chilled morning air cutting through her blouse.

All she is aware of is the man beside her, the empty cottage ahead, and those in the house behind her.

She is utterly detached from any and all other aspects of her life.

It takes less than a minute for them to reach the cottage. Sabrowsky instructs Kate to try the doorknob, scanning the road again quickly as she does.

"It's locked," she says.

Sabrowsky removes a key from his pocket with his gloved hand, and then holds it up for Kate to see.

She asks, "How did you get this?"

Sabrowsky shakes his head, refusing to answer. "Get inside."

Taking the key and inserting it into the lock, Kate says, "You knew the lock had been changed. You got a copy from Tony, didn't you."

He again declines to respond. "Just get inside, Katie."

Once Kate has unlocked the door, Sabrowsky pushes it open far enough to shove Kate through. Taking one last look at the road, he follows her inside, withdrawing the key from the lock and pocketing it before closing the door.

Kate backs into the kitchen as Sabrowsky, facing her and matching her pace, pursues her.

"You're not thinking straight," she says. "You're in a corner, I get it, and you're trying to find your way out, but this isn't going to work."

Kate continues moving backward while Sabrowsky presses forward, the distance between them—maybe two yards—remaining constant.

He glances down at her left hand. "Drop the shoes."

Kate hangs on to them. Though she is clearing the kitchen area, Sabrowsky is only midway through it. Taking two steps to his right, he puts himself within reaching distance of the counter.

In the dish drainer by the sink is a large kitchen knife. Grabbing it, he resumes his course.

Kate glances at the six-inch-long blade in his hand.

"So that's it, Eddie? You're going to kill me?"

"I won't have to, Katie."

Her eyes remain on the knife. "Oh yeah? Why not?"

"Because you're going to do it yourself."

She meets his stare. "Fuck you, I am."

He extends his arm, pointing the knife at her chest. "You're the reason Rebecca moved away," he says. "You stole this house from her. You stole the life she could have had, here, with me."

"I didn't steal anything, Eddie."

"You could have ignored your grandfather's will. You could have shared the house with her, or at least let her stay in the cottage year-round. But no, you had to be the judgmental bitch and punish her. 'Cause that's you, holier-than-thou, better than everyone. And what the fuck did she do that was so wrong? Break some stupid rules? Piss off your dick grandfather and bitch grandmother?"

"It was more than just that, Eddie, and you know it."

"She broke up your family; is that it?"

"Yes."

"You guys were my family, Katie. You broke up my family when you sided with them."

"Jesus, Eddie, that was twenty years ago."

"No, it started twenty years ago. You've been driving her away ever since. You made that choice, over and over again. Even Leif thought you were being harsh. He wouldn't tell you that, but he told me. But Kate has to be Kate. That's what he'd say: 'Kate has to be Kate.' You wouldn't even let Rebecca stay after he was killed. You wouldn't let her help you. It was more important to you to keep hurting her. It was more important to keep getting your revenge."

"You knew how destructive she was, Eddie. You know the shit she pulled. I was protecting myself. Anyway, things are changed now. She's here. To stay."

"Yeah, now that you need her. Now that you can use her."

Kate shakes her head. "This isn't you. It's those painkillers fucking you up. You don't have to do this. We can both just walk away and never talk about this again. You can go home and call your doctor, get your medication switched, and that'll be the end of it, I promise."

"You're a terrible liar, Katie."

"I'm not lying. Just walk away, Eddie."

"It's too late for that. Anyway, you know too much now. You're too smart for your own good. I couldn't let you live if I wanted to." He pauses. "Which I don't."

Kate has backed into the living room. The bathroom and bedroom doors, both open, are twenty feet behind her. She continues her slow retreat, each step keeping him at a distance while also bringing her nearer to the only place she can go.

"Drop the shoes, Katie. And it would be better if you took off the blouse and jeans."

Her back straightens in defiance. "No. I'm not going to cut my fucking wrists, if that's your plan."

"It can go either way. I stopped by to check on you and found you here, dead from a suicide. Or I found you here after having been stabbed to death by the man you spent last night with. Is that what you want? To drag your boyfriend into this?"

"No one is going to believe either story."

"After everything you went through two years ago, and what you've gone through this past few weeks, who can say what was going on inside your head? Distraught, depressed, guilt ridden, broken—people have killed themselves for less."

"But I didn't spend the night here. Rebecca knows that, and Jack knows that."

"Rebecca will say what I tell her to say. And I'll make sure it looks bad for Jack.

"The thing is, Katie, all I need is to create confusion. The bigger the mess, the better. Either case, O'Neil will want to believe the easy answer, because that's what he does, and Leo won't accept it, because that's what he does. The two of them will turn on each other; Leo will want to do his own investigation, and who will he ask to help him? Me. And just like last time, I won't find anything that contradicts O'Neil's conclusion. You came out here last night to fuck a guy you barely know, and in the morning, something happened; he either brutally murdered you or you took your own life." He pauses. "You were the one who sneaked into the cottage this time, Katie. And just like Rebecca had to, you paid for it. Except you won't have to live with it like she did. You won't have to spiral into self-hate. I'm showing you the mercy you never showed her."

Kate is just steps from the bedroom, and the distance between her and Sabrowsky remains unchanged. In her mind she plays out her desperate move—turning and bolting through the open door, slamming it shut and locking it before Sabrowsky can get to it.

But then what? Wait, helpless, as he attempts to break it down? Open the window and scream for help while he hurries to the house and makes good on his threat to kill her children?

"This is justice," Sabrowsky says. "It's important to me that you know that. I'm righting a wrong here. Rebecca gets what should have been hers. And I get Rebecca."

"How? How are you so sure Rebecca will go along with any of this?"

"Like I said, you don't have to worry about that."

As Kate takes one more step backward, something over Sabrowsky's shoulder catches her eye—motion at the far end of the cottage that for a brief moment stops her reeling mind and draws her focus.

The door is open, and Rebecca is standing in it.

In her hand is Leif's pistol.

"C'mon," Sabrowsky says. "Get into the bedroom, get out of your clothes, and sit on the bed."

Though she is focusing on Sabrowsky, Kate can see that Rebecca is now moving through the kitchen, quickly but carefully.

Her right arm comes up, the pistol aimed directly ahead.

Backing into the bedroom doorway, Kate knows that she needs to distract Sabrowsky, so she asks the only question she can think to ask. "Do I have to get undressed?"

"I'm afraid so."

"Why?"

"Because that's how I want people to remember you. The 'good' sister in black lace underwear, dead on a stranger's bed."

Kate moves farther into the room, and then stops when she is all but up against the wall.

Sabrowsky is two steps away from entering the doorway when Rebecca, midway through the living room, halts and raises her left arm, adding that hand to her grip on the pistol.

In a calm and steady voice, she says, "Turn around, Eddie."

Though Sabrowsky pauses, he doesn't face Rebecca, merely turns his head and glances over his shoulder at her.

Then he looks at Kate and says, "You don't know her, Katie. You have no idea what she's done."

"Step away and drop the knife," Rebecca orders. Her voice, however, is less steady than it was just seconds before.

Sabrowsky doesn't comply. "Are you going to shoot me, Becca? Do you even know how to shoot?"

"Yes. And yes." Still, the uncertainty remains in her voice.

"You know why I'm doing this, Becca. You know why I have to."

"Just step away, Eddie. Now."

Losing his patience, Sabrowsky looks over his shoulder and snaps, "I'm doing this for you!"

"I know why you're doing this. I don't care."

"You don't care?"

"Step the fuck back, now."

"You don't care?!"

"I'm going to count to three."

"You know I know."

371

"One."

Sabrowsky faces Kate. "She hated you; you know that. Just like you hated her."

Force suddenly returns to Rebecca's voice. "Two."

"She wanted you to hurt as much as she did."

"Three."

"That's all that mattered to her. That you hurt, too."

Rebecca shouts, "Eddie!"

Sabrowsky turns suddenly, stepping out of the doorway and into the living room, the kitchen knife still in his hand.

"I thought a count of three was all you were going to give me, Becca? You didn't shoot, though. Why not?"

He takes a few steps toward her, and then stops. Rebecca holds her ground, but her hands are shaking.

"Don't make me do this, Eddie."

"You know I'm right," he says. "You know this is the only way. I do this, and we get everything. You, me, the kids—we're set for life. We can go wherever we want, do whatever we want. And we take our secrets to the grave. No one will ever know. *Ever.* Do you understand what that means?"

"Stop."

Sabrowsky takes another few steps, stops again, and drops the knife. It lands tip-first into the wood floor.

"You can't kill me, Becca. I know you can't. You're broke. You're old. And the way you are now, what you've been through, what they cut from you, no one will want you. No one but me, that is."

Kate steps into the doorway, and Rebecca glances at her, saying nothing.

"He has a gun," Kate says.

Rebecca focuses on Sabrowsky again. "You can't kill me, either, Eddie. Without me, you get nothing. Without me, you go to prison. And you know what happens to cops in prison."

Motionless, Sabrowsky stares at Rebecca.

"It's over, Eddie."

"You're really going to reject me again." He pauses, then scoffs. "Everything I've done, you don't fucking care."

"You were weird as a kid, but now you're just delusional."

Sabrowsky takes another step, but this time Rebecca counters by taking two steps back.

"You don't want to hurt me, Becca," he warns. Then he laughs once, but there is hostility in the smile that accompanies it. "Not again, you don't."

"Please just raise your hands, Eddie."

"No," he says flatly. "You want this; I know you do. It's all you've ever wanted. I'm giving it to you, right now. All you have to do is take it. Just tell me, 'Kill Katie.' That's all you have to say. 'Kill Katie for me.' Then nothing that happened before matters." He takes two steps toward her. "You understand that, right? You understand what that means."

Rebecca holds her position. "Enough, Eddie."

He shakes his head decisively. "No," he says. "I decide from now on what is and isn't enough."

Then he steps forward again.

Rebecca adjusts her hands, securing her grip on the pistol.

"You're going to have to do it, Becca. You're going to have to kill me."

Sabrowsky takes another step, and Rebecca reacts by covering the trigger with her index finger.

"Please," she says softly.

He takes yet another step, putting roughly six feet between himself and the knife sticking out of the floor.

Kate's eyes go to that knife, and she quietly steps out of the bedroom doorway, then moves to her right, positioning herself out of the line of fire, but also creating for herself a straight and clear path to the knife.

Sabrowsky says to Rebecca, "You can't do it. You know I'm right. You know we deserve this life."

"Last warning, Eddie," Rebecca says.

He continues forward, taking one step, and then one more. Again, Rebecca counters by taking an equal amount of steps back.

She is halfway through the kitchen now, Sabrowsky on the threshold between it and the living room.

"It's over, Eddie," she says.

"Then you're going to have to kill me, Becca. I'm not going to prison for you."

"I didn't ask for this, Eddie."

"Didn't you?"

"Eddie."

"Didn't you?"

Kate makes a break for the knife, taking quick, light steps, but Sabrowsky is too focused on Rebecca to notice.

Reaching the knife and grasping the handle, Kate frees it from the wood, and then pauses cautiously.

Sabrowsky is still a good eight feet away.

Though Rebecca doesn't dare look at Kate, she is aware of her sister's position—Kate gets that sense by the way Rebecca's eyes are fixed straight ahead. Kate also believes her sister understands the problem that the remaining distance creates.

Kate has managed to make it this far unnoticed, but can she make it the rest of the way?

Softening her tone, Rebecca says to Sabrowsky, "You need help. We'll make sure you get it. I promise."

It is clear to Kate that Rebecca is attempting to distract Sabrowsky. Kate takes two steps forward, and then pauses, as a test of his attention.

His focus remains on Rebecca.

"Don't patronize me," he says.

"I'm not; I swear."

"It's too late for that anyway."

"It's not."

Rebecca has moved even farther into the kitchen, the cottage door now just feet behind her.

Kate takes two more steps, but more than that and she would place herself directly behind Sabrowsky—and in the line of fire.

"You know that I know," Sabrowsky says. "Right? You have to. Why else would I do all this? What other choice would you have?"

"Last warning, Eddie."

"You said that already."

"Enough."

"Yeah, you said that, too."

Less than a foot between her and the door, Rebecca stops.

"Nowhere left to go," Sabrowsky says. "It's now or never, Becca. It's the sister who stole from you, or it's me."

He presses forward, but finally it's a step too far for Rebecca, and she fires.

The sound of the gunshot tearing through the confined space of the cottage is deafening, and reflexively, Kate flinches and drops into a crouch, but she doesn't take her eyes off Sabrowsky.

Though the nine-millimeter hollow-point round has struck him dead center in the chest, his only visible reaction is to take two unsteady steps backward, as if lightly shoved off his balance. Stunned, his body freezes, but he remains standing, and after staring at Rebecca for a moment, he finally looks down at the blood flowing from his wound.

Raising his head, he faces Rebecca again and says in a hushed voice, "Fuck."

Though horrified, Rebecca holds her ground, continuing to aim the pistol at him with two shaking hands.

Then her expression shifts from fear to anguish, and she whispers, "Jesus, Eddie. *Jesus.*"

His body still stiff, Sabrowsky reclaims one of his two lost steps, but it is more of a clumsy stagger than controlled forward motion.

Kate, too, has been rendered motionless by shock. The knife still in her hand and her ears ringing, she remains crouched.

Sabrowsky continues to stare at Rebecca for a moment, and then he bends forward slightly and begins to reach around to the small of his back, his movement slow but deliberate.

Rebecca speaks his name one more time, pleading for him to stop, but he doesn't.

Kate has a clear view of his back, and she can see him grab his pistol and remove it from his waistband—not with any kind of speed, but smoothly, steadily.

She calls out to Rebecca as Sabrowsky swings his arm back around, warning her of his weapon, but before his hand even passes his hip, Rebecca fires again.

This time Sabrowsky's body is jolted by the round puncturing his sternum, and almost immediately he drops to one knee, his head slumped forward.

Still, the pistol remains in his hand, pointed at the floor.

The concussive wave generated by that second gunshot pierces Kate's ears, deepening the already severe ringing, but through it she can hear Sabrowsky's suddenly raspy breathing.

In a full panic now, Rebecca rocks back and forth nervously, uncertain whether or not to lower her firearm, and confused as to why Sabrowsky has not yet been incapacitated.

The expression of dread on her sister's face tells Kate that she is struggling with the idea of possibly having to fire again.

The terrible noise, the smell of cordite, and the sight of what she has done to another being—these are all assaults on her senses that leave her mortified and conflicted.

Rebecca takes a step toward Sabrowsky, and then retreats two steps, her outstretched arms wavering, her horror increasing with every second that she must wait.

"Eddie, please," she says.

As though Rebecca's voice has pulled him from a light sleep, Sabrowsky raises his head abruptly. He looks at the floor for a moment, dazed, before finally focusing on the woman in front of him.

Rebecca says again, "Eddie, please. Drop the gun."

Looking down at his hand curiously, Sabrowsky appears almost surprised by the weapon in his grip.

He laughs once—scoffing more than amused—and meets Rebecca's stare yet again. Seconds later, he turns his head and glances over his shoulder, searching for Kate.

Finding her, he raises his arm suddenly, moving with a speed that catches Kate off guard.

He brings the pistol to bear on her, his anger evident in his focused and determined eyes.

Again Kate freezes, but before Sabrowsky can find his aim, Rebecca fires one more time.

Instantly, Sabrowsky collapses, landing on his side on the floor.

It takes a few seconds before Kate can think of what to do. Dropping the knife, she hurries into the kitchen, crouching down in front of Sabrowsky and taking the pistol from his hand, then quickly standing again and moving back several steps.

Holding the pistol in two hands, she points it at the fallen man before looking at Rebecca.

Slowly lowering down to the floor, holding the pistol loosely in one hand, Rebecca sits and stares at Sabrowsky.

It is clear to Kate that her sister is on the verge of going into shock—and in no condition to be handling a firearm. Stepping to her without taking her eyes off Sabrowsky, Kate kneels down beside Rebecca and, holding Sabrowsky's pistol in her left hand, eases Leif's out of Rebecca's hand with her right.

She places Sabrowsky's weapon on the floor beyond Rebecca's reach.

"Hey," she says softly. "You're okay, Becca. We're okay."

Rebecca is unresponsive at first, fixated on the man dying just feet away, but finally she can turn from that and look at her sister.

But whatever calm Kate hopes to instill is contradicted by the sound of Sabrowsky's breathing.

Raspy, ragged, and shallower, and more infrequent following each tortured exhalation.

These are sounds Kate never wanted to hear again—sounds more terrorizing than gunshots.

Leif had struggled in the same horrible way during the final minutes of his life, as Maria and Kate attempted to stem the waves of blood leaving his body.

It is when Kate hears the sound of sirens approaching that she is unable to sit by and listen.

Stepping to the kitchen counter, she lays Leif's pistol down, then opens the drawer to the left of the sink and removes the small stack of dish towels it contains.

Kneeling, she rolls Sabrowsky from his side and onto his back, quickly folding one towel into a makeshift compress and leaning over him as she applies it to his chest.

Within seconds the cotton is soaked through. Kate tosses that towel aside, her hands already slick with blood, and folds the next. Before setting it in place she can see that the three shots Rebecca fired are grouped within inches of each other.

Leaning over Sabrowsky again, Kate applies the fresh compress to his chest, covering all three holes and pressing down with one hand while preparing the third and last towel with her other.

She is placing it on top of the second towel—it, too, sodden with blood—but even with all her weight pressing down, she is unable to slow the rate of blood loss, never mind stop it.

Kate persists, however, even as her hands are painted dark brown to her wrists.

Even as Sabrowsky is racked by violent seizures, his breathing an erratic, desperate wheeze, Kate doesn't give up.

She remains over him even as his breathing stops and his face pales and his body goes lifeless beneath her.

Even then she remains, holding back the still-flowing blood and listening to the sirens growing nearer.

FORTY-FIVE

For the first twenty-four hours, during those few moments when she is alone, Kate relives the chaotic aftermath.

The first to arrive on the scene was Officer Schulze, who had been driving home at the end of his shift when he'd heard over his radio the call of shots fired at Kate's address.

She hadn't heard the man enter the cottage because of the ringing in her ears and realized he was there only when he placed his large hands on her shoulders and gently moved her away from Sabrowsky.

Sitting her on the floor beside her sister, he paused to meet her eyes and establish a moment of cognition before returning to the fallen officer and checking for a pulse.

Finding none, he looked at Kate with an expression of confusion and concern.

Within minutes, several other patrol officers arrived, all of whom Kate recognized, and who, of course, recognized her. Schulze was kneeling in front of Rebecca then, his hand on her shoulder as she stared at him blankly.

Shock was setting in, Rebecca was trembling, and Kate put her arm around her sister's shoulder, drawing her close.

They sat together like that for a while, Rebecca leaning against Kate as Kate watched the officers talk among themselves and make calls on their cell phones, though she could not hear a word that was spoken.

At one point a young female officer Kate had never seen before arrived, looked at Kate and her sister seated on the floor, and then spoke to Schulze for a moment before exiting the cottage.

She returned with a sweatshirt bearing the Westport PD logo on its front, and crouched down, offering it to Kate. The officer communicated with hand gestures that Kate could get out of her bloodied silk blouse if she wanted and put on the sweatshirt. Kate nodded, and the officer positioned herself in front of Kate and held up the sweatshirt like a curtain. Kate removed her blouse, and as she put on the sweatshirt, the officer remained in front of her in an effort to give her some semblance of privacy.

Moments later, Kate and the officer—her name tag read BARNES—helped escort Rebecca outside, Kate on one side, Barnes on the other. The driveway was already lined with vehicles, one of which was an ambulance. A pair of waiting EMTs draped first Rebecca and then Kate with emergency blankets, directing them to the back of their vehicle.

Kate and Barnes carefully sat Rebecca on the rear bumper, and one of the EMTs began tending to her. Barnes and the second EMT urged Kate to sit as well, but instead she stepped away and looked down the driveway toward the house.

Parked next to her Subaru at the bottom of the driveway was Leo Burke's Ford Explorer, and standing beside it with him were Max and Callie.

Though their grandfather was talking to them, no doubt consoling them and telling them that everyone was okay, their eyes were fixed on their mother, expressions of horror and fear on their faces.

And as Kate continues to relive those events, it is what she saw in her children's eyes that causes her continued pain.

———

On Sunday, Kate makes the decision early that, for a day or so at least, she will keep Max and Callie home from school, because she can't imagine not having them near.

It is a feeling she knows that Rebecca shares.

So as though on vacation again, they leave after breakfast that morning for a day trip—Kate behind the wheel with Max in the passenger seat, and Rebecca and Callie seated in the back.

Passing the cottage on the way up the driveway is both surreal and difficult for Kate.

Surrounded by yellow police tape, its door closed and sealed by a red sticker marked "Do Not Enter," the place is once again an unoccupied space standing one hundred feet from their home.

For Kate it is impossible to even just glance at the cottage and not be back inside it—face-to-face again with Eddie Sabrowsky and his long-concealed hatred for her, trapped along with him in his delusion, and the target of his frustration and rage.

There have been moments since yesterday morning when Kate is confronted by the understanding that someone she came to trust was intent on doing her harm, and had been for a long time. Just the thought of that—suddenly flashing to the instant of that terrible realization—is enough to cause Kate to suddenly flinch, as if struck by an unexpected blow.

She does her best to hide this reaction from her children, of course, but there is no keeping it from Rebecca. Though Kate and she have yet to speak to each other about the violence that they endured together, they have for the last twenty-four hours barely spent a waking moment apart, devoting their focus and energy to taking care of—or simply being with—the children.

It is an unspoken understanding between Kate and her sister that making Max and Callie a priority is the only way back for all of them.

As the Subaru reaches the top of the driveway, Callie has a sudden thought. "Hey. Where is Jack staying?"

Kate looks at her daughter in the rearview mirror. "Your grandfather said he could stay with him until the police are finished with the cottage."

Kate decides not to address the fact that she will also have to hire a professional crew to thoroughly clean the cottage before it is habitable again.

Callie nods. "Oh. That was nice of Grandpa."

"It was."

Satisfied, Callie looks out her window, but then Max has his own thought. "Would he even want to live in it again?"

Kate says to him, "I don't know." Then she offers a consoling smile. "We'll see, I guess."

Max thinks about that, and then says, "I hope he comes back."

Kate makes a right turn onto Old Town Road. Passing Maria's house, she notes that, as was the case yesterday morning, there are no vehicles in the driveway.

The house, too, appears unoccupied.

Glancing in the rearview mirror again, Kate sees that Rebecca is also studying the house. Then she faces forward and meets her sister's eyes in the mirror.

It is obvious to Kate that Rebecca and she are thinking the same thoughts.

No doubt by now, Maria has been informed that her husband didn't kill himself but was instead murdered.

No doubt, too, she knows by whom and why.

And it is likely that included in all that information is the fact that Rebecca and Maria's murdered husband once had an affair.

———

They travel north, taking a ride through Litchfield County, and then stop for lunch at the White Horse in Cornwall.

Rebecca and Kate carry the conversation, both during the drive and as they eat, mostly asking Callie about the music she is currently listening to and what movies Max is looking forward to seeing.

Kate gets the sense by the way in which Callie participates in the conversation that her daughter understands the need for the distraction, but Max maintains his usual reticence, giving only brief or at times even just one-word answers.

———

That night, they play board games, everyone seated on the living room floor, while episodes of *The Office* stream on the TV for background noise.

Though Kate has already arranged to take a personal day, and Max and Callie won't be going to school, the usual bedtime for the twins of nine thirty is kept.

Kate believes that in this regard life as usual is the right action to take.

———

Dressed for bed and listening to the shower running upstairs, Kate stands in her bedroom, paralyzed by memories.

Chief among them is the memory of undressing in front of Sabrowsky at his command.

But there are other memories, too—the nights of fearing the ringing of the landline or the buzzing of her cell phone as it sat on its charger on her nightstand; the bright lights that her father-in-law installed outside her window; the listening when the house was quiet for sounds that would indicate danger.

She remembers, too, being awakened in the dark hours of the morning by a deer moving through her backyard and then, moments later, observing from her living room window those two figures running from the cottage—figures that, due to her personal bias as a high school teacher, she mistook for teenage boys.

It is this very memory—the cottage that night, and then what she discovered in it the next day—that adds credence to a thought that came to her as she drove back to Westport in the late afternoon, all topics of conversation having been exhausted and the occupants of her Subaru silent and lost in thoughts of their own.

Kate waits for the shower to stop, and then waits until she hears her sister in Callie's bedroom before she takes her cell phone from its charger and sends a text to Rebecca, asking if she will be coming down for tea tonight.

Rebecca replies: Yes. Down in a minute.

Kate responds: Meet you there.

Five minutes later, the teakettle is on the stove, and Kate and Rebecca are seated at the kitchen table.

Kate asks, "How are you doing?"

Rebecca shrugs, then lets out a long sigh and says, "Not looking forward to going to bed. Couldn't sleep last night, and then when I did, I had nightmares. But I guess that's to be expected, right?"

"Would it help for you to talk about what you dreamed?"

"I don't know. Probably not. All of us getting away today helped, though on the drive back I started getting that sick feeling in my stomach. And then when we turned onto our road, I felt like I was going to throw up."

"Yeah, me too. I'm better when Max and Callie are around, because I have to be. But the minute I'm alone, my mind starts flashing to things."

Rebecca nods. "Same here. To be honest, I'm having a hard time imagining being able to come back from this, you know? I mean, how do you? How do you get from here, back to something that even resembles normalcy?"

"I was thinking about that today," Kate says. "I had a couple of ideas I wanted to run by you."

"Like what?"

"I'm going to ask Leo to disassemble the swing set tomorrow. No one really uses it, and we don't need the reminder sitting there every time we go outside. Plus, I know he'll feel better if he has something to do."

"I haven't even thought to ask. How is he?"

"Eddie became like a son to him these past two years." Kate pauses. "And I think him being around so much was a way for Leo to keep a connection to Leif."

"So all that is heaped on top of the fact that Leo almost lost his grandchildren and his son's wife," Rebecca says.

"Yeah, exactly."

"Then maybe Jack being at his house will help. I mean, Jack is another connection to Leif, right? And Leo's house is only a two-bedroom, so I'm guessing Jack is in Leif's old room."

"I didn't think of that," Kate says. Then she laughs. "There's kind of a weird symmetry there, no? Leif and Jack having each slept in the same bedroom."

"Maybe that's the universe telling you that Jack's the one."

Kate laughs again. "I'm not so sure about that."

"Have you heard from him?"

"Jack?"

"Yeah."

"He sent me a text last night, told me to let him know if there's anything he can do."

"You should have him over for dinner some night soon. Max and Callie have definitely taken to him, and it might be another step toward things being normal."

"Maybe," Kate says.

"Why just maybe?"

It takes Kate a moment to find the words. "I can't imagine I'll be . . . I don't know . . . good company anytime soon. You said it yourself, how to come back from what happened. How do you go from someone you've trusted wanting to kill you, and then trying to, to trusting someone enough to let him get close?"

"I get that, Katie. But Jack likes you; that's obvious. And he doesn't seem to be the kind of guy who'd want to rush things. Just the opposite, in fact."

Kate nods but says nothing. To explain her concerns—that Jack only recently extricated himself from a complicated and difficult situation and might not be eager to jump into another one—would mean betraying his trust.

Rebecca watches her sister closely, and then says, "I get that, too. They call a double mastectomy surgery, but it's really . . . amputation. Or, at least, for me it was. I'm nowhere near ready to be sexual with a man again."

"I'm so sorry you had to go through that alone."

"Don't be. I mean, it sucked, yeah, but it had to happen that way."

The water in the kettle begins roiling. Rebecca stands and hurries to the stove, taking the kettle off the flame before its shrill whistle can start.

"Do you want tea tonight?"

"Sure," Kate says. "Thanks."

Rebecca opens the cupboard, removes two mugs and sets them on the counter, then says, "You said there were a couple of things you wanted to run by me. What's the other?"

"It's pretty big. You would have a say whether or not it happens, of course."

"A say in what?"

"I've been thinking since this afternoon about just having the cottage torn down and all the pieces hauled away."

Rebecca stops and looks at her sister. "Really?"

"Yeah."

"You don't need my approval for that, Katie. This is your place."

"I've been thinking about that, too. I want to add your name to the deed. That way, in case something were to happen to me, it would be one less thing for you to have to deal with. End-of-life shit is a pain in the ass, trust me. And anyway, it should have been that way from the start. I shouldn't have gotten caught up in Grandpa's need to punish you."

Now Rebecca needs a moment to find the right words. "I appreciate you saying that, Katie. I don't know what else to say."

"You said you wanted to be more like me," Kate jokes. "Congrats, you're officially a stoic now."

Rebecca laughs.

Kate waits a moment before saying, "I'm not making excuses, but back then I was just too afraid to break any of his rules, even after he was dead. I thought I was respecting him by following his wishes to the letter, but that wasn't the case. That was just me being too much like him for my own good. I loved him, and I know you did, too, but he wasn't the most forgiving man. I think he thought being that way was a strength or an indication of character. And obviously so did I. But we were both wrong."

Again, Rebecca needs a moment. "I was wrong, too. About a lot of things."

She turns back to the counter and places a tea bag into each mug, then fills them with steaming water before placing the kettle back on the stovetop.

"Hey, but what about Jack?" she says. "If you have the cottage torn down, I mean."

"I'll refund his money. And I'll help him find a new place, if he wants. Like Max said: Would anyone really want to live in it after what happened? Would you?"

Rebecca shakes her head. "No." She carries the mugs to the table, setting Kate's down. "There's the matter of the income it generates, though. Would you want to give that up?"

"I don't care about that. Plus, renting it out is a hassle I don't really need anymore. Of course, you co-owning the house with me means that you live here, too."

Rebecca sits across from her sister. "But Max and Callie can't keep sharing his bedroom."

"I would have an addition put on. Probably off the living room. Another ground-floor bedroom and bathroom for you. I can pay for it. And it would be nice to open the house a little."

"That's generous of you, Katie. I have my money, though. I could use that."

"No, you need that for school. And something we haven't talked about is you needing a car."

"I was going to have mine either shipped or driven here."

"You're still driving that same old BMW?"

"Yeah. I think I've crossed the country over ten times with it."

"So how many miles are on it?"

"It's closing in on two hundred thousand."

"Maybe you should leave it there and sell it."

"But then we'd only have one car."

"I was thinking of giving you the Subaru and getting a new one for myself. Yours probably isn't going to last much longer. Subarus last twenty years, and mine's only ten years old, so you'd be set for a while. Plus, it's safer."

"Okay, now I really don't know what to say."

"We could all go car shopping this week. It'll be another reason to get out of the house. As for the cottage, we have time to think about what to do. We couldn't do anything anyway until it's no longer a crime scene."

"How long will that take?"

"Chief O'Neil said to expect a week, just to be safe. And that would give us time to move all your paintings up to the attic."

Rebecca shakes her head. "No, we wouldn't have to bother with that. It's probably for the best if they're destroyed and hauled away, too."

"Are you sure?"

"Yeah."

"Why?"

"They're just reminders of a time I'd like to forget," Rebecca says. "A time when I hated myself." She pauses. "So you really want to do all this?"

"Yes. I have to reschedule signing the updated will with my lawyer. When I'm there, I'll ask him about adding you to the deed." Kate cocks her head suddenly. "I can't remember; what day is it?"

"Sunday."

"Derek's funeral is supposed to be tomorrow."

"Have you heard from Maria?"

"No. I looked a little while ago, and there are still no cars in her driveway."

"Could she have taken the kids and gone to her mother's?"

"Yeah, maybe."

"You should text her. She probably doesn't even know about what happened yesterday."

"That's not really something I can put in a text. Plus, it's kind of late."

"That's true." Rebecca pauses. "She probably knows by now, right? About Derek and me?"

"That would explain her going silent like this."

"I'm sorry, Katie."

"She suspected he had girlfriends. I guess there's a difference, though, between imagining some anonymous stranger and finding out it was actually someone you know."

"But she can't blame you for her husband's affair, even if it was with your sister. And anyway, you didn't know, so it's not like you kept it from her."

"I did know at one point, though, and I didn't tell her."

"Should you have? Under the circumstances?"

"She might think so." Kate shrugs. "Or maybe I just didn't like keeping a secret from someone I care about."

"It was something stupid that happened years ago. Sometimes it's better to keep things like that in the past, don't you think? Sometimes we have to bury things for the sake of others. And then learn to live with that secret as best we can."

———

By nine the next morning, Leo Burke is in the backyard taking down the swing set.

Some bolts loosen easily, despite the rust that has built up over decades of rain and snow. Other bolts he needs to spray first with WD-40 and then let sit for several minutes before they will give.

Three bolts, however, won't budge, so to get those joints apart, he hacksaws through each connecting metal tube.

In just over two hours the disassembly is complete, and the pieces are in the back of his SUV, ready to be taken to public works and disposed of.

To thank him for his efforts, Kate invites him to lunch, but he offers to take everyone to the diner instead. Kate gets the sense that he recognizes the importance of getting away from the property as often as possible, at least for the time being.

While Max, Callie, and Rebecca are upstairs getting ready to leave, Kate decides that now is a good time to have a private conversation with her father-in-law. Stepping outside through the back door, she joins him by the rear of his vehicle.

"So how are you doing, Dad?"

"I'm fine," he answers. "How is everyone here?"

Kate remembers him saying last week that they were probably too much alike for her own good, and his response is a perfect example of one of those ways in which they are similar.

She answers, "Shocked and confused, but we're hanging in there."

"It's good that you kept Max and Callie home from school today. This can't be easy for them, considering."

"Yeah."

He looks toward the house. "I'm proud of what they did—Max calling the police from the landline when they heard the first shot, and Callie calling me from her cell. I kept her on the phone as I was driving here, and she held herself together very well. She was scared—for you, because you weren't in the house and that meant you had to be in the cottage—but she remained calm and answered all my questions." Pausing, he faces Kate again. "She reminded me of her father then. Very much."

"I knew they made the calls, but I didn't know the rest," Kate says. "Thanks for telling me, Dad."

"Of course. I'd like to tell them how proud I am, but I know that would just embarrass them. They're at that age now. But maybe somehow you could tell them for me. Or Rebecca could, since they're so close."

"I don't think it matters if you embarrass them. They should hear that from their grandfather."

Leo nods, considering that, and then looks toward the house again. When he looks back at Kate a moment later, tears have welled in his eyes.

"I don't know what to do with what happened," he says. "Or with what could have happened if your sister hadn't been here. Chief O'Neil let me read your statement. I feel foolish for having trusted Eddie as much as I did."

Kate is caught off guard by the admission of fault, as well as the uncharacteristic vulnerability her father-in-law is displaying, but she knows better than to call attention to it in any way.

The ability to be embarrassed isn't exclusive to his twelve-year-old grandchildren.

"He fooled us all, Dad," she says. "It wasn't just you."

Leo shakes his head. "I don't mean just that. I was so . . . desperate to replace Leif, as if he even could be replaced, that I forgot one simple fact."

"What?"

"That Leif is here. In you. In your children." He pauses again, and then says, "If I promise to work on my control issues, would you be okay with me being more involved here? I'm not thinking of anything drastic. Maybe a Sunday dinner every week—or a few times a month, at least, if every week is too much. Or a movie now and then, all of us together."

Kate smiles. "I think that's a great idea. And a Sunday dinner every week wouldn't be too much. It sounds just right, actually."

"There are a lot of decisions that will need to be made in the future. Applying to colleges, taking tours of campuses, picking which one to go to, since I'm expecting Max and Callie will be accepted by many. They are, of course, your decisions to make. But if you feel the need to run any of those kinds of things by me, I would be more than happy to listen."

"I was counting on that, actually."

Leo nods. "Good," he says.

"And I'm sorry if you've felt resistance from me. I didn't realize until recently that I tend to do that, to keep certain people at an arm's length."

"Well, Leif's mother was like that, too, so it's safe to say I bring that out in people. But like I said, I promise to work on that."

"You're welcome here anytime, Dad. For any reason, for no reason, whatever, just come by. I want things to be different. They need to be different. Okay?"

Leo nods again. "Okay."

He looks away once more, but this time his focus is on the cottage.

"I know of a cleaning crew," he says. "When you're ready, of course. They do good work, won't leave a trace behind."

"Yeah, that might not be necessary."

Leo turns to her. "What do you mean?"

"I have a decision to make, and I'd like to hear your thoughts before I make it."

———

The next day, Tuesday, Kate goes car shopping, taking along her children and sister.

And at Kate's request, Leo meets them at the Subaru dealership on the Post Road in Milford to offer his advice.

Two hours later—after a test drive and filling out the loan paperwork—Kate drives off the lot in a new Forester, Max riding with her, as Rebecca, with Callie in the passenger seat, follows in the Outback.

Later that day, Kate, Rebecca, Max, and Callie go for a long joyride in the new vehicle, and then stop at Tutti's on their way back for pizza.

When they left at two o'clock, Maria's driveway was still empty. And upon their return at five thirty, it remains so.

Before joining everyone in the living room for a movie, Kate slips into her bedroom and sends Maria a text, asking how she is doing. After waiting a few minutes and receiving no reply, Kate pockets her phone and leaves the room.

Despite the fact that the device is set on vibrate and she will feel it buzzing in her pocket should a text come through, Kate checks it twice during the movie and then again after it ends.

Hours later, after getting into bed and connecting the phone to its charger, Kate checks one last time, but there is still nothing.

———

By Wednesday, the moments of calm and normalcy begin to outnumber those when Kate struggles, secretly, with the aftereffects of Sabrowsky's assault and subsequent death.

Max and Callie seem more at ease, as does Rebecca, who, if secretly struggling at times like Kate, hides it well.

It is over dinner that night that she asks her children if they feel ready to go back to school.

"We don't want you to fall too far behind," Kate points out.

The decision is made by all that tomorrow will be the resumption of their daily lives.

———

On her lunch break, Kate receives a text from Rebecca.

Call if you have a chance. Not an emergency.

Kate makes the call. "Hey, Becca, what's up?"

"There are moving trucks next door."

"What do you mean?"

"I went for my run and came back, and there still weren't any cars in the driveway, but when I got out of the shower, these two big moving trucks were there."

"Any sign of Maria?"

"I don't see her car, but there's a big old Mercedes parked behind one of the trucks."

"That's her mother's car. Anything going on?"

"I'm looking out the window now. Nothing, just the two trucks and the car. They must be inside."

"Do you have plans today?"

"Just looking around online at graduate programs."

"If you can keep an eye out every once in a while and let me know what you see, I'd appreciate it."

"Of course," Rebecca says. "I'll text you."

"Thanks."

"Oh, wait, hang on, someone's coming outside. It's one of the movers and an older woman. Maria's mother, I'm guessing."

"But no sign of Maria."

"Hang on, someone else is coming out. Nope, it's just another mover. And now they're all going back inside again."

"I'm meeting with my lawyer at four, so I should be home by five."

"Okay, I'll keep you posted."

"Thanks."

———

Throughout the afternoon, Kate checks her cell phone between classes for updates.

Rebecca reports after one o'clock that the movers have begun to remove items from the house, loading large pieces of furniture into one truck and cardboard boxes of varying sizes into the other.

At no time does Rebecca report seeing Maria. A text sent after two o'clock states that the Mercedes is gone, and then forty-five minutes later another comes through, reporting that the car has returned.

According to the text Kate reads as she is walking to her Forester at four, the movers are still at work. But as she is leaving her lawyer's office at four thirty, Kate receives one final communication from Rebecca.

Trucks and car have just left. And now there's a for sale sign out
front.

———

After dinner, Kate follows the path through the border trees, crossing Maria's driveway and knocking on the back door. When no one
answers, she uses the spare key Maria gave her to enter.

The kitchen has been gutted—the table and chairs removed; the
cupboards, some of which have been left open, are empty; and the
window above the kitchen sink is without a curtain.

All that remains are the major appliances.

Moving through the dining room and into the living room, her
footsteps echoing, Kate finds similar scenes in each room—furniture
gone, shelves empty, windows bare.

She continues on to the family room, and then to Derek's office,
only pausing once she has entered the ground-floor main bedroom.

The emptiness is palpable, the silence complete.

Her tour finished, Kate returns to the kitchen and removes the key
from her key chain, then places it on the counter by the sink.

Then she makes sure the doorknob is locked before exiting and
closing the door behind her.

FORTY-SIX

Callie asks, "When is Jack getting here to pick up his stuff?"

It is Saturday morning, and Kate and her daughter are stripping the sheets from the bed and cot in Max's bedroom while Max and Rebecca are grocery shopping.

Chief O'Neil came by yesterday afternoon, removing the seal from the cottage door and taking down the yellow police tape that has been up for six days. Kate immediately texted Jack to let him know that he could finally have access to his belongings.

He responded promptly, and their brief exchange was friendly and polite. In fact, Kate made a point of keeping it that way, and Jack made no effort to make it otherwise.

"He said he'd be here between nine and ten," Kate answers.

Bundling all the bedding together, Kate tosses them into the laundry basket. Callie is holding the stack of folded clean sheets, which she places on the cot before removing the fitted bottom sheet from the bed and handing it to her mother.

Kate unfurls it, and Callie takes hold of one end as they step to opposite sides of the bed and lay the sheet down.

Callie asks, "Is he staying for lunch?"

"No."

"Why?"

"I didn't invite him."

"Why not?"

"Because I didn't want him to feel obligated to stick around until then."

"I don't think he'd think that."

"We have too many things to do today anyway."

"But isn't lunch one of them?"

"Yes, but I'm not sure yet what we're doing or when we're doing it."

With the bottom sheet in place, Callie takes the top sheet from the pile and returns bedside. This time she unfurls it so that Kate can grab her end. Together they lay it down.

"He likes you, Mom. And you like him. You should at least ask."

"Let's just get the beds made, okay?"

Once the sheet is flattened and smoothed out, they begin to tuck its edges under the mattress.

As they work, Callie asks, "Are you afraid?"

"Of what?"

"That he might turn out to be a psycho like Eddie."

Caught off guard, Kate pauses before answering, "No, I'm not worried about that. And I told you, Eddie was on medication that affected his thinking."

"Mom, I'm not a kid."

"What does that mean?"

"I looked it up online. There's no 'may cause murderous intent' warning for painkillers. I know you're trying to protect us by telling us that, but it wasn't just the medication that made him do what he did. Was it?"

Her task complete, Kate straightens her back. Callie does the same, and for a moment they look at each other.

Finally, Kate answers, "No, it wasn't."

"So what was wrong with him?"

"It's a long story."

"I'd like to hear it, Mom. Please. I want to know."

"Why?"

"He was Dad's best friend, and you and Auntie Becca knew him since you were kids, right?"

"Yes."

"So what happened? I mean, how does someone go from being your friend one minute to doing what he did the next?"

Kate steps to the cot and picks up the folded comforter, and then returns to the side of the bed. After another pause, she lays the comforter on the mattress and starts unfolding it.

As Callie joins in, Kate says, "He had problems, Callie."

"Well, yeah, that's obvious."

"I don't think there's anything else I can say that will help you understand."

"Did he hate you? Like, for all this time? Since you were kids?"

"He resented me for something I did."

"What did you do?"

"I made a choice."

"What choice?"

"To not forgive Auntie Becca."

"Forgive her for what?"

Kate shrugs. "A lot of things. Mainly, though, it was the choices she started to make around the time she turned fourteen."

"What kind of choices?"

"Ones that she was too young to be making."

Callie nods. "Oh." She pauses, then adds, "Boys."

"Yes. Something people don't realize, especially when they're young, is that the choices we make can end up making us who we are. Auntie Becca made a choice that upset your great-grandfather and great-grandmother very much. It shocked them, actually. It upset me, too, but I still loved her. She was my big sister; I couldn't just turn my back on her. But then she just kept making the same kind of bad choices, and the more she did, the more upset our grandparents got. It especially bothered our grandmother. She was very prim and proper, and she and Auntie Becca would argue all the time. I tried to keep the peace for a while, but eventually it became just too much. Something clicked inside me, and, boom, that was it. I shut Becca out, which was how our grandfather handled things. I started to see what she was doing as being unforgivable. And the more damage she did to our family, the more unforgiving I became, not just toward her, but as a person. A choice I made became who I was."

"How old were you guys then?"

"When I shut her out?"

"Yeah."

"I was fifteen, and Auntie Becca was about to turn seventeen." Kate pauses. "We'd been close our entire lives, but I just didn't recognize her anymore. It was like she was a stranger."

"But how did your not forgiving Auntie Becca affect Eddie?"

"In his mind I was the reason they didn't end up together."

Callie nods again. "So he was one of the boys."

It takes a moment for Kate to answer. "Yes. But before that, when we were just kids, she was his favorite; that was obvious. He showed up at our house a lot, always wanting to play with her. In the summers, he was usually waiting for us when we got up, and then wouldn't go home until Becca told him he had to. Your great-grandmother didn't like that very much. She didn't like him to begin with, but more than that, family was very important to her, and he was intruding on that."

"How did you meet him?"

"When your auntie Becca and I came to live here year-round, we were playing in the backyard one morning and he just appeared, walked out of the woods and asked if he could play with us. He was kind of a sad case."

"What do you mean?"

"The way he was there most mornings during summer vacation and didn't want to leave when Becca and I were called in for dinner. It took me a while to figure it out, but I think Becca knew right away that he didn't want to go home." Kate pauses. "He'd often have bruises on his arms. I remember Becca got cut on a broken soda bottle once, and Eddie took off his T-shirt to stop her hand from bleeding. There were bruises on his chest and back. I think he and I were maybe eight or nine at the time."

"Oh my God," Callie says.

"Becca was always kind to him. And sometimes she stood up for him when our grandmother would complain about him always being around, which didn't go over very well. That was the first glimpse for all of us of the rebellious teenager Becca would become."

"Did they love each other, do you think?"

Though Kate is once again caught off guard by her daughter's question, she reacts by shaking her head dismissively. "They were children, Callie."

"Snape and Harry Potter's mother were children when he fell in love with her. And he loved her for the rest of his life."

Kate smiles. "That's true. But that's just a story. And anyway, in Eddie's case it was more like an obsession than love."

"Maybe it just looked that way to you. I mean, how can you know how he was feeling, right? That's kind of . . . judgy of you, don't you think?"

Kate shrugs. "Maybe, yeah," she says.

"It's interesting that Snape acted like an enemy but turned out to be a friend, and Eddie acted like a friend but turned out to be a bad guy."

Caught off guard a third time, Kate can only say, "Wow."

"What?"

"That's very astute of you, that's all."

"We learned about that in English."

"Learned about what?"

"Shape-shifters, archetypes, the hero's journey. I wonder if that's why he's named Snape, because it rhymes with 'shape' and he's a shape-shifter."

"Could be," Kate says.

"It's the same thing in the book Max is reading now."

"*To Kill a Mockingbird*?"

"Yeah."

"You read that?"

"Yeah. The last time Auntie Becca was living in the cottage. It's her favorite. In it Scout and Jem were afraid of the guy that lived on their street, and that everyone called 'Boo.' But he's the one who saves their lives on Halloween, and it turns out that he's just this shy and lonely guy."

Kate smiles again, this time proudly. "That's right. Good job."

"So we never really know what's going on inside someone, do we?"

"I guess we don't."

Callie pauses, and then says, "I think Jack's okay, though, Mom. He acts like a good guy, but I don't think that means he's going to turn out to be a bad guy. I don't think he's a shape-shifter."

"Have you been worried about that?"

"You can't help but wonder," Callie answers. "I mean, after what happened with Eddie. It has to be on your mind, right?"

"It's not."

"How come?"

"Jack's found a new place to live, so I don't think we'll be seeing him again."

"He doesn't want to stay?"

"It's not that. Your aunt and your grandfather and I, we've all decided that it would be for the best if we got rid of the cottage."

"Why?"

"There are a lot of reasons, but mainly none of us wants the reminder of what happened sitting in the front yard."

"But that doesn't mean Jack can't come back and visit," Callie says. "You like him, and he likes you. Isn't that what matters?"

"It's a bit more complicated than that."

"Complicated how?"

"It just is, sweetie. That's something you'll learn as you get older."

"What is?"

"You can like someone, or someone can like you, but that doesn't necessarily mean you're going to be good for each other. I think Jack would be better off with someone else."

"Why?"

"I need you to just trust me on this. Okay?"

Callie doesn't respond immediately. Then, finally, she says, "That stinks, Mom."

"It is what it is," Kate says.

"We don't want you to be alone, though."

"I'm not. I have you guys, and your aunt."

"That's not what I mean."

"This isn't something you have to worry about, okay? You've got a school year to finish. And then it'll be summer, and a lot of things are going to be happening around here that'll keep us all busy."

"I just think you're making a mistake, Mom."

"I appreciate you looking out for me like this, Callie. But sometimes when we face tough choices, the best thing to do is to choose what's best for others, not ourselves." Kate pauses. "And maybe if I had done that years ago, things would have turned out differently for a lot of people."

"What do you mean?"

"I could have forgiven Auntie Becca. I could have made the decision to keep on loving her instead of cutting her off. I realize now that there was a reason why she was acting the way she was back then. She wasn't very happy with herself, and sometimes when people aren't happy with themselves like that, they do things to hurt themselves, not realizing that in the process they are hurting the people around them, too." Kate pauses, then says, "And doing what I did, and for as long as I did, only made her want to hurt herself even more."

"But you said you didn't know that back then," Callie says. "Sounds like she didn't give you any other choice."

"There's always another choice, sweetie. And if you can't see one, then you need to look for it, no matter how impossible it seems. Especially when it's someone you love as much as I loved your aunt."

"You said 'loved.' Past tense. You love her now, right?"

"Of course I do," Kate says. "I never really stopped, I guess, which is why it hurt so much when I lost her."

"I don't think you have to worry about that happening again, Mom. Even I can see that she's changed. Max can, too."

"You and your brother have talked about that?"

"Yes. We're glad she's here, and that you two are friends again. It never really made sense to us that you guys weren't. We couldn't imagine ever hating each other like that."

"Well, that's good," Kate says. "It means you're both smarter than I."

"I don't know about smarter, Mom," Callie jokes. "Wiser, maybe."

Kate laughs. "That too." She looks at her daughter for a moment, and then says, "C'mon, let's finish making the bed, wise guy. We've got a lot to do today."

———

Kate is putting away canned goods in the pantry when she hears Max announce from the living room that Jack has arrived.

She is still dressed in her Saturday-morning work-around-the-house clothes—old jeans and a sweatshirt—when she leaves to meet him in the cottage.

Before leaving she stepped into her bedroom and removed the cash Jack gave her from the lockbox full of documents she keeps on the top shelf of her closet.

The wad of bills in her pocket, Kate enters the cottage to find Jack in the back bedroom, gathering his things.

Covering Eddie's bloodstains on the kitchen floor is a blue plastic tarp that Leo put down late yesterday afternoon to spare Kate from having to go inside and do so herself.

Even now, she pauses at the sight of the tarp before forcing herself to continue into the room.

She announces herself by saying, "Hey, Jack."

He appears in the bedroom doorway, a stack of folded clothes in his hands. On the foot of the bed behind him is his open duffel bag.

"Hi, Kate," he says. "Hang on one second, okay?"

He turns to the bed and places the stack into the duffel.

"No rush," Kate says.

Standing in the entrance to the living room, she looks around the cottage as Jack continues to collect his things in the bedroom.

Though there are no doubts in her mind regarding her decision to have this place taken down, being inside it again serves only to confirm her conviction to be rid of it.

It is impossible now not to remember Eddie Sabrowsky venting his hatred toward her in those terrifying moments when it was just the two of them, standing face-to-face.

Kate forces the memory from her mind and says, "Leo told me you found a new place."

Still in the bedroom, Jack answers, "I did, yeah."

"How soon will you move in?"

"Possibly on the fifteenth. I'm signing the lease after I leave here."

"Oh, good. That reminds me, I have your money to give back to you."

Carrying his duffel bag, Jack exits the bedroom and sets the bag down on the dining room table.

"I appreciate that. I didn't want to ask for it, but I'll need first- and last-month's rent."

"Of course," Kate says. "It's your money."

"Still, it's kind of awkward."

"Don't be silly." Reaching into her pocket, Kate approaches Jack. She removes the bills and hands them to him. "Here you go." Then she takes a few steps back.

Jack looks at the money, though Kate senses it is really a way of avoiding making eye contact. After a moment his brow furrows, and he finally looks at Kate.

"This is the whole amount," he says.

Kate nods. "Yeah. You were here for, what, two weeks? I'm not going to charge you for that, especially after this curveball."

"No, I insist," Jack says.

"Please, just take it. For the inconvenience. And as an apology."

"You've got nothing to apologize for, Kate."

"No, I do. You were a good tenant. I'm sorry you got dragged into this mess. I know more drama is the last thing you need."

"It was hardly your fault."

Kate shrugs, and then says, "Actually, it kind of was."

"How so?"

She shrugs again, though this time to dismiss the question. "So listen, I'll let you get going," she says. "I should get back to the house anyway."

She turns to leave but stops when Jack speaks.

"Hang on a minute, Kate."

She faces him.

Jack asks, "Is that all I was? A tenant?"

It takes a moment for Kate to respond. "No."

Jack takes a step toward her. "I'm sorry if by not being in touch much this week, I made you think I'd lost interest. I was really just giving you space so you could take care of yourself and the kids. I thought that was the best way to handle this." Jack pauses. "Of course, you didn't reach out to me, either, so I just assumed I was right for backing off.

But the first thing I did every time I came home from work was to ask Leo how you were." He pauses again. "I guess I was hoping he might mention that, which I realize now was probably the last thing on his mind when he talked to you."

"I just figured, you know, all things considered . . ."

Jack finishes her thought. "That I'd run for the hills."

"Yeah."

"I'm sorry you thought that. It's not the case, I promise."

"I appreciate you telling me that, Jack. I really do."

"Of course," Jack says. "So how is it going? How are you holding up?"

"I'm keeping my shit together okay when I'm around Max and Callie, but when I'm alone, it's a different story."

"That sounds pretty textbook to me."

"And frankly, being with someone—being alone with someone other than my children and my sister—isn't something I can even imagine right now."

Jack nods. "I can understand that."

"I really don't see the end to this yet, either. And I can't ask you to wait around for me to feel differently. That just wouldn't be fair to you."

"I'm not in any hurry, Kate, trust me. And my apartment's in town, so I'm only two miles away. You know how to find me when the time's right. And if I don't hear from you after a while, well, I know where you live, right?"

Kate laughs. "Right," she says. "You do."

———

Within a week, and with Leo's help, Kate finds a contractor that will both demolish the cottage and put on the addition off the living room.

Two days later, on the evening before the crew is to begin its work, Kate and Rebecca meet in Kate's lawyer's office while Leo watches his grandchildren.

There, the quick-claim deed is signed and notarized, making Rebecca a co-owner of the property.

Later, as Max and Callie are working on their homework and Rebecca is researching graduate programs online, Kate takes a moment to step outside.

It is the first summerlike night of the year—warm and mildly humid, the air still and the sky clear—and after a moment of standing on the pathway, Kate steps onto the front lawn, tripping the motion-activated lights and taking one final look at the cottage.

For the first time since the Saturday morning Rebecca saved her life, Kate is able to look at the structure without immediately experiencing a sudden jolt of fear.

Though she is grateful for the reprieve, and the deep calmness she is feeling instead, Kate is nonetheless eager for tomorrow to come. The contractor has assured her that the deconstruction and removal will be completed within a matter of hours, which means that by the time Max and Callie are home from school in the afternoon, the place will likely be gone.

How long, Kate wonders, until its absence is no longer conspicuous?

At what point—on what future day—will she look upon her front yard and see only a slope of uninterrupted grass running from the street down to the front door?

Of course, it is possible that the cottage will always be there, even when it no longer exists, and that the catalog of memories it evokes— good and bad, significant and minor—will continue to arise in Kate's thoughts with the same frequency with which they do now.

Maybe having it removed is a fool's errand. Maybe no matter what Kate does, no one will ever fully forget all that has transpired within its four walls.

But to let it stand would guarantee that those memories would always be at hand. At least with it gone, there is hope that all who live here will finally find peace.

Deciding that it is time to head back inside, Kate turns, but something catches her eyes and she stops.

In Maria's driveway, visible through the still-bare trees separating the two properties and lit by Kate's front light, is the Mercedes-Benz Rebecca reported seeing on moving day.

And parked directly behind the Mercedes is Chief O'Neil's marked sedan.

The vehicles appear to be empty, and the kitchen window is lit.

It isn't long before Kate observes two figures exiting the house— Chief O'Neil, with a small cardboard box in his hand, as well as, to Kate's surprise, Maria.

O'Neil waits in the driveway as Maria switches off the kitchen light, then closes and locks the back door. Maria joins O'Neil, and he walks her to the Mercedes, where they pause to speak for a moment before Maria gets in behind the wheel.

At no time between exiting the house and entering her vehicle did Maria once look in Kate's direction.

As O'Neil walks toward his sedan, the engine of the Mercedes starts, and its headlights come on.

Once O'Neil is inside his vehicle, Kate feels the urge to hurry across her front yard and follow the path through the border trees, catching her friend's attention before she can begin backing down the driveway.

Instead, Kate decides to remove her cell phone and send Maria a text, asking Maria if she would like to talk.

When Kate looks up again, she sees that O'Neil's vehicle has backed onto the street and is driving off. The Mercedes starts to reverse then, but stops abruptly after only a few feet. A patch of pale light appears in the dark interior, illuminating Maria's face as she looks at her phone's display.

But as quickly as that light appeared, it goes out as Maria places her phone down, after which the Mercedes resumes reversing.

On the street, the vehicle pauses briefly as its driver shifts gears, and then it, too, drives off.

———

Kate is washing her face when she hears her cell phone vibrating on her nightstand.

Taking a hand towel from the rack, she dries her face as she walks to her bed, then picks up the phone and sees on its display a preview of a text sent by Maria.

Her heart skipping, Kate quickly unlocks her phone and navigates to the full text.

As she reads, her heart drops.

You should have told me about your sister and Derek.

In Kate's mind a reply immediately begins to formulate—that she didn't know until recently, and then when she did find out, she wasn't sure if it was her place to say anything, and anyway she was so desperate to keep her life from blowing up even more than it already was, not to mention not wanting to hurt her friend, that she decided to keep the peace, like she had done as a teenager.

But the more she thinks about what to say and not say, the closer Kate gets to the realization that none of it would matter.

Cutting off Kate so suddenly and completely, and at such a tumultuous time in her life, can mean only that Maria is well beyond caring about the hows and the whens.

In the end, all Kate ends up sending is a two-word reply.

I'm sorry.

And then right away she sends a follow-up that she knows in her heart is futile.

Can you forgive me?

After a minute of looking at the display and waiting for a reply that does not arrive, Kate returns her phone to the nightstand and continues to get ready for bed.

Fifteen minutes later she is under the covers and once again looking at her phone.

Eventually, though, she understands that Maria's lack of response is the answer to the question she posed in her last text.

With the phone back on the tabletop, Kate switches off the light, but she doesn't fall asleep easily, and when she finally does, she dreams that she is in the empty cottage, standing face-to-face with Eddie Sabrowsky, her jeans and silk blouse soaked with his blood.

His clothing, too, is bloodied, and his face is pale, his eyes glassy but focused on her.

They stare at each other in silence before Eddie finally speaks.

His voice is ragged because of the blood filling his lungs, and all Kate can do is look at him and listen to the words he says.

What other choice would she have?

FIVE WEEKS LATER

FORTY-SEVEN

On a Saturday in June, Kate drives to the Walmart on the Post Road in Milford to shop for a pair of blinds and set of curtains for Rebecca's room, which is nearly finished.

Max is along for the ride, while Callie and her aunt take care of the grocery shopping.

Once both tasks are complete, the four will meet Leo in Norwalk for an early lunch at the Blue Cactus Grill—his favorite—followed by a visit to the Maritime Aquarium.

Fifteen minutes after entering the store, Kate and Max are leaving it with the blinds but no curtains, Kate having been unable to find the exact kind that she and Rebecca agreed upon.

Kate is placing the bag into the back of the Forester, Max already in the passenger seat, when her cell phone rings.

Closing the hatch, she takes the phone from her pocket, and seeing that she is receiving a call from Chief O'Neil, says to Max, "Hang on a second, sweetie," then answers.

"Hi, Chief."

"Hello, Kate. I was wondering if you were free for a talk sometime today. It shouldn't take more than fifteen minutes."

"Is anything wrong?"

"I just came across some information that I should make you aware of."

Kate recalls the night she'd seen O'Neil outside Maria's house, the chief holding a small box as he walked Maria to the Mercedes.

"I'm leaving Milford now," Kate says. "Can you meet me at the house, or would you rather I met you somewhere?"

"I can meet you at your house, as long as we're able to talk privately."

The fact that O'Neil wants to speak with Kate at all is unnerving enough, but his wishing to do so privately adds an element of genuine concern.

Kate checks her watch, and then says, "It's nine thirty now. Would ten fifteen work for you? We have lunch plans with Leo at eleven thirty."

"Ten fifteen would be fine. I'll see you then."

Kate is about to say, "Goodbye, Chief," but then she realizes he has already ended the call.

———

When Kate and Max return home at ten, Chief O'Neil is already there, his marked sedan parked on Old Town Road.

Parking her Forester at the bottom of the driveway next to Rebecca's Outback, Kate asks Max to go inside and help his aunt and sister unpack the groceries.

As they exit the vehicle, Max looks up at the police car on the road. Hesitant to leave, he looks at his mother.

"It's okay," Kate says. "I'll be right in."

She opens the rear hatch and removes the bag, handing it to Max, and though he accepts it, he is still staring up at the street. O'Neil has exited his vehicle and is waiting beside its driver's door.

Kate says to her son, "Go on, sweetie."

Carrying the bag, Max heads toward the back door.

Kate waits till the boy is climbing the stairs, and then looks up at Chief O'Neil, who remains at his vehicle, as if waiting for Kate to give him the all-clear. She does so by nodding once, and as he starts down the driveway, she walks up it.

He is not far from where the cottage stood when he stops to wait for Kate to close the remaining distance and join him.

She says, "Hi, Chief."

"Hello, Kate." He surveys the empty patch of ground at the end of the short pathway. Recently planted grass has only started to grow, tall but still sparse.

Then O'Neil turns his attention to the house, focusing on the new addition off the living room.

"That's coming along quickly," he says.

"Yeah, sometimes being Leo Burke's daughter-in-law has its advantages. We got the permits fast, and the contractor is a friend of his."

"Who did you use?"

"Roy Clayton."

"I know Roy. He's a straight shooter."

"Of course, when he came to give us his estimate, the first thing he asked was if we would consider selling."

Still looking at the addition, O'Neil smiles and says, "Of course he did. How much more is left to be done?"

"They finished hanging the sheetrock yesterday, so really all that's left is cosmetic stuff."

"That shouldn't take too long."

"Roy says he'll be finished by the end of next week at the latest."

O'Neil nods thoughtfully but says nothing.

After a moment, Kate asks, "What's on your mind, Chief?"

He faces Kate. "There was a lot of material to go through. Cell phones that belonged to Eddie and Derek. And Hillman, too. And then there were the recordings from inside your house that Eddie made. His transmitters were short-range, so we suspected that his recording equipment was likely hidden somewhere in your neighbor's house. A while back we found a reference to a hiding place in one of the text exchanges between Eddie and Derek. Eddie needed to know where the device was, in case anything happened to Derek and Eddie needed to get in and get it. Your friend met me at the house one evening, and I was able to locate the equipment right where it was supposed to be—under a floorboard in Derek's office."

"I know," Kate says. "I saw you two that night."

"The recording device was digital with a one-terabyte hard drive, and there were hundreds of hours of recordings. Apparently, Derek would upload each day's recordings to an online storage site, and then Eddie would download them from the site to his computer and listen. The device was the type that was always listening but only recorded conversations, the same way home surveillance cameras nowadays are always watching but only record when motion is detected. Of course, the device also captured other types of sounds." O'Neil pauses. "Obviously, all those recordings are evidence and need to be preserved, but there was one recording in particular that I deleted. A private one of you, early one morning."

Kate closes her eyes briefly, waiting for the wave of embarrassment to pass. Then she opens them again and says, "Thank you, Chief."

He pauses again. "Full disclosure, Kate. A copy of that recording was on Eddie's personal computer as well. And Derek's, too. I had concerns that either of them may have shared it with Hillman, knowing what we know about that sicko, but there is no indication of that in any of the email accounts that belonged to Eddie or Derek. I did make a call to my counterpart in Bridgeport, asking him to keep an eye out for such a file on any of Hillman's devices, but so far none has turned up. He agrees with me that, should a file of that nature be found, there would be no point in preserving it. As you know, male police officers can sometimes be guilty of indulging in locker-room behavior, and the last thing I want is a copy of that recording making its way through either department."

Kate takes a breath, and then lets it out. "The violations just keep coming, don't they?" she says.

"I took the same precautions with the photos of you, so I can assure you that all digital copies have been permanently deleted."

"I'm grateful, Chief."

"We look out for our own, Kate. Fellow officers, their spouses, and families, they're supposed to be able to count on us. And that's what makes what happened here so distressing. We failed to keep our promise because of the actions of one of us. It's betrayal by a loved one; there's just no other way to look at it. And how can one not be shaken to the core by that?"

"If it's any consolation, I don't think Eddie was himself. I don't think he could have kept himself from doing what he was doing even if he wanted to. He lost sight of what was right and what was wrong a long time ago. And after that, all that was left was grievance and getting what he wanted, no matter what the cost. That's not the thinking of a healthy person."

"You're perhaps more forgiving than I am," O'Neil says.

Kate laughs. "No one has ever said that about me before."

O'Neil studies Kate, and after a moment she gets the sense that there is something on the man's mind, and he is deciding whether or not to express it.

Kate is about to ask him what he's thinking when he says, "Everything in your statement pans out. Eddie was extorting money from Derek, essentially bleeding the guy dry, after which he became desperate for a new source of income. He coerced Derek and Hillman into their campaign of harassment, because he found out during the investigation he did for Leo after Leif was killed that Derek and Hillman were involved in the previous harassment and what it was they were up to. So he decided to re-create that. Find a developer to finance Derek, who would make a cash offer on the house once you were ready to sell. Eddie would use his influence to help you make that decision in the first place, and then he'd use it again to convince you that a short sale to your struggling neighbor was the best option for everyone. Part of the deal with the developer was a finder's fee once the property was Derek's, as well as a percentage of the profit from the sale of the new construction. But what I didn't understand is why Eddie's plan had to change when you and Leo discussed updating your will. Why would that matter to him if what he wanted was to get you to sell? Why did your changing the will cause him to abandon his original plan and decide instead to kill you? There was absolutely no mention of that in any of the communications between Eddie and Derek until that day, so why the sudden escalation?"

"He was listening to my conversations," Kate says. "Right? So he would know there was the chance that I would decide to assign Leo as conservator. Obviously, he thought he'd have a better chance at influencing Rebecca into selling than he would Leo. In fact, when he brought me to the cottage, he kept telling me that she would do whatever he told her to. He seemed so convinced of that."

"And did that confidence of his—that Rebecca would just fall into line—make any sense to you?"

"Of course it didn't. But Eddie's mind was twisted. I think he thought Rebecca would see what he did as a correction of a wrong that had been done to her. She would essentially get the house she was denied by our grandfather, and because of that she'd finally love Eddie."

"I agree that Eddie believed that. But maybe there was another reason he was convinced she'd do what he told her to do."

"What do you mean?"

"As part of my investigation, I took a statement from Jack, and he mentioned a conversation he overheard one morning between your sister and Derek."

"What about it?"

"He said that Rebecca kept asking Derek if he was involved, which he denied."

"Yeah," Kate says. "They had an affair a few years ago. Jack said Derek asked her if they could resume it."

O'Neil nods. "Jack mentioned that as well, yes."

"I'm sorry, Chief. I'm not really following."

"Eddie had no way of knowing the status of your will, correct?"

"Correct."

"So for all he knew, if you died, Leo might be in charge of everything until Max and Callie reached adulthood. That's why killing you wasn't part of the original plan. But when he found out you essentially had no will, he realized there was a way of getting more than just a finder's fee and a percentage of the profits. He could potentially get it all. Your savings, Leif's life insurance, your life insurance, the income from renting the cottage—everything. And with all that money, there'd be no reason to sell the property. But the key was Rebecca. Everything depended on her rolling over and doing what he told her to do. And I'm sorry, Eddie had his problems, yes, that's clear now, but he wasn't stupid. Far from it, in fact. He had all of us fooled, and for a long time. That took cunning and patience. So he wasn't gambling everything on your sister's gratitude or sudden acceptance. He murdered his partners, and he would have murdered you, too, and I don't believe that he would have done all that without some guarantee that he would get everything he wanted."

"What are you saying, Chief?"

O'Neil reaches into his pocket and removes a cell phone.

"This was hidden in Derek's office along with the recording equipment," he says. "On it is a text exchange between Derek and an unnamed number that started about four years ago and ended one week after Leif was killed. This unnamed person and Derek were obviously engaged in an affair. The texts were intimate, and there was a somewhat steady exchange of photographs showing certain body parts, male and female. But there were other texts as well, a half dozen or so vague ones that reference something they called 'The Plan.' Though both Derek and this unnamed person are careful to never go into any specifics, one text sent by Derek to her states that she deserved a cut of the profits, to which the unnamed person replies, 'I don't care about the money.'"

O'Neil pauses to swipe the phone's display with his thumb, after which he holds up the device for Kate to see.

He asks, "Do you recognize this number?"

Kate reads the digits and then closes her eyes. A moment later, she opens them and answers, "Yeah."

"It's your sister's?"

Kate nods. "One of them, yes."

O'Neil lowers the phone. "When she was asking Derek if he was involved, she wasn't asking if he was involved with someone; she was asking if he was involved in the current harassment, because she knew about his role in the previous harassment. The text exchange about her deserving a cut occurred one month before Leif was killed, so she knew what Derek was up to for at least that long."

Kate shakes her head absently. Finally, she whispers, "Jesus."

"The morning after Leif was killed, Derek and Rebecca exchanged dozens of texts. He knew that the crew that had come to your home was sent by the people he promised your property to, but he swore that he had no idea they would go this far. The fact that he was being as careless as he was, saying what he was saying in texts, leads me to believe that he was telling her the truth. The man was in a panic."

Kate asks, "And Rebecca?"

"She was horrified. And outraged. She told him that he had to do the right thing and come forward, but he said he couldn't, that he had to think about his own family. He warned her not to say anything to anyone, because that could get both of them killed. She tried to convince him to at least send an anonymous tip to Eddie, or to even Leo, identifying the men, but he refused. They went back and forth like that for several days, and a few times they made arrangements to meet secretly to talk. Rebecca was pressing him—she wouldn't let up—and it got very heated toward the end. But then suddenly her tone changed. She told him he didn't owe anyone anything, and that he had to do what was right for him and his family, because no one else would. There was nothing in their exchange to explain why she made such a dramatic shift, though."

"Do you happen to know what day that was?"

"April twelfth, I believe."

"The day after Leif's funeral."

"Is that significant?"

"Yes. It's the day I sent Rebecca away."

O'Neil says, "I see." Then he looks toward the house. "Could you tell me a little bit about Rebecca and Eddie's history?"

"There was a sexual encounter when we were kids. Rebecca had just turned fourteen, and Eddie was twelve." Kate pauses. "She initiated it."

"And after that?"

"There were other encounters in high school, not a lot, maybe a handful, but they all followed the same pattern—Rebecca would pull away from him after, just like she did the first time, and that would set him off."

"Set him off how?"

Kate shrugs. "He would plead, cry, get angry, refuse to leave Rebecca alone, and then not show up at school for days at a time. Even when we were kids he was very erratic, but it got worse when we were teenagers."

"Did he ever threaten any kind of violence?"

"No. But I think every rejection genuinely broke his heart. It was obvious he was obsessed with her."

O'Neil considers that for a moment, and then asks, "Did you know that your sister was involved with a man named Charles Larson?"

"Yes."

"Did she tell you what he did for a living?"

"No."

"He started in real estate, and then bought several construction companies. Within a matter of years he became one of the biggest developers in California. When he died, he was being sued for fraud by a former business partner." O'Neil pauses. "It's probably just a coincidence that he happened to be a developer, and possibly a corrupt one. There's no indication in any of the texts that the scheme was Rebecca's idea. Derek was in that business, too, so he could have heard about it through any number of associates. If it was her idea, though, or even if she simply put the notion into Derek's head, then she's the reason Leif's dead. She would have been the one to put all that into motion. On top of that, Derek's telling her about his involvement in Leif's murder made her an accessory after the fact. Her silence allowed Derek and Leif's killers to evade justice. I can only assume that Eddie intended to use these facts to control her. 'Play my game, live with me in your sister's house for the rest of our lives, or be exposed and face charges.'"

Kate looks toward the house for a moment. Finally, she asks, "So what do we do now?"

"Unless you feel otherwise, I don't see any point in prosecuting your sister. Leif killed the crew that was sent here, and Eddie tracked down and killed the men who sent them. He murdered Hillman and Derek, too—the men who were terrorizing you. And then Rebecca killed Eddie." O'Neil shrugs. "I think that's about as much justice as we can hope to get out of this mess."

Still looking at the house, Kate nods but says nothing.

O'Neil holds up the cell phone, drawing her attention.

"I'm the only one who has seen what's on this," he says. "Maria was out of the room when I found it in Derek's hiding place, so I was able to remove it without her knowledge. It's difficult to understand why he hung on to this instead of destroying it, considering how incriminating these texts were. Maybe he thought it would prove he didn't have anything to do with Leif's murder, should he need to do that one day. Or maybe he couldn't part with the text chain with your sister. Either way, you and I wouldn't know what we know now without it. And without it, no one else but us will ever know."

Kate looks from the device to O'Neil. "What are you saying, Chief?"

"I'm going to leave what we do up to you, Kate. If you want your sister charged, I will do that. If not, then I need you to take this right now and make it disappear. Do you understand?"

Kate answers, "Yes." Still, she doesn't reach for the device.

O'Neil asks, "Are you aware that Rebecca received a substantial sum of money after Charles Larson died?"

Kate nods. "Yes."

"You have to ask yourself, if she had all that money and could afford to live anywhere in the world, why did she keep coming back here? Why spend most winters in that drafty old cottage? She had to have a reason, right? She's your sister, and I would think you know her better than anyone, so what do you think that reason could be? What was it that kept bringing her back here for all those years?"

·"Max and Callie," Kate says.

"Possibly. But they're twelve, aren't they? And she's been coming back here for over twenty years. What was her reason then?"

"I don't know. Maybe to claim the one thing she inherited from our grandparents."

"There's really only one way to know for sure," O'Neil says.

He takes Kate's hand and lays the phone onto her palm.

"I realize we don't know each other well, Kate, so feel free to tell me to go to hell. But the way I see it, you can send her away again, or you can pursue charges. It's your choice. But I think you should talk to her first, give her the chance to tell you what, exactly, she did and why. Otherwise, your family is broken all over again. Your children lose their aunt. You lose your sister. And your sister loses everything."

O'Neil gently closes Kate's hand around the phone.

"Like I said, it's your choice. Whatever you decide, I'm behind you. We take care of our own, and always will."

Feigning a migraine, Kate stays behind while Rebecca takes Max and Callie to meet their grandfather for lunch.

Prior to leaving, neither she nor her sister addresses the fact that Kate spent fifteen minutes talking with the chief of police in the front yard.

Still, there were moments as she waited for her niece and nephew to get ready that Rebecca looked at Kate expectantly, as if waiting for her sister to say something—anything—about the matter.

But Kate pretended not to notice Rebecca's obvious curiosity, and when Max and Callie were ready to go, she said goodbye to them and then retreated to her bedroom.

Sitting on the edge of her bed with the door closed, Kate listens as the Outback climbs the driveway and turns onto Old Town Road before driving away.

After lingering several minutes, Kate finally exits the bedroom and walks to the center of the living room.

Here, as she was that Friday morning she returned from grocery shopping to find the house empty, she is surrounded by an unsettling silence.

That was the morning she found the note on her windshield, and she makes the same decision now that she made then: to distract herself with movement.

She steps into the unfinished addition, walking carefully on the overlapping drop cloths covering the laminate floor, and observes the progress that has been made.

It isn't long before she takes stock of what remains to be done.

The walls and window trims are still unpainted; a pair of french doors, their glass panes taped to prevent breakage, stand in a corner, waiting to be hung; and the ceiling fan and light, still in its box, needs to be installed.

A few more days of work and the room will be done, ready to be furnished and occupied.

Unable to stay still for very long, Kate wanders the rest of the house—the kitchen, the pantry, the upstairs bedrooms, pausing always in each space for no more than a minute.

Then she is back down in the living room, standing in front of the picture window overlooking the front yard.

As she feared, the physical absence of the cottage has yet to free her of memories of it. Her mind is flooded with vivid recent scenes, as well as vague remembrances of long ago—a tangle of actions taken and things said and emotions that, in many cases, can still be felt.

But she tells herself not to be overwhelmed by this chaos.

She needs to be sharp and coolheaded for what lies ahead.

———

Seated at the kitchen table, Kate waits as Rebecca takes her bedtime shower.

Though the lights are off, the blue-white of the full moon low on the horizon, combined with the soft glow from the oven's digital clock, is more than enough to see by.

Five minutes after her shower, Rebecca enters the kitchen and approaches the counter to begin making her nightly Sleepytime tea.

It isn't until she has filled the kettle and placed it on the lit burner that she turns her head far enough to catch Kate in her peripheral vision.

Startled, she gasps, bringing her hand to her chest and laying it flat over her heart as she faces her sister.

"Jesus," she says. "You scared the crap out of me, Katie. Why didn't you tell me you were there?"

"Hasn't tea together before bed become our thing?"

"It has. I guess I was zoning out. Hey, how's your headache? Do you want some of that peppermint tea?"

"I didn't have a headache," Kate says. "I needed some alone time."

"You could have just said that."

"Lying seemed simpler."

Neither speaks for a moment. Rebecca watches her sister. Finally, she turns back to the counter and takes two mugs from the cupboard.

"So if you didn't have a headache, then why have you been so quiet? Something's wrong." Pausing, she places the mugs on the countertop and, keeping her back to her sister, asks, "Is it something Chief O'Neil told you?"

Kate answers, "Yes."

Rebecca nods, and then says, "You know, don't you?"

"Know what?"

"You want me to say it?"

"Yes."

Rebecca turns, and though she is facing her sister, her eyes are fixed on the floor at her feet.

She says, "You know, anytime I'd see you talking to O'Neil or Eddie or even Leo, I was certain that was it, you know, you were being told."

"Told what, Becca?"

"That I knew."

"Knew what?"

Rebecca looks at Kate. "That I knew about Derek, what he was up to two years ago."

"What was it you two called it?"

Rebecca shrugs dismissively. "I don't remember. 'The Plan,' maybe. Something like that."

"And you didn't care enough to tell us."

"It wasn't that I didn't care. I just didn't take it seriously."

"Why not?"

"Because I knew it was a stupid scheme that wasn't going to work. I knew you would never give up the house, no matter what. And Derek is—was—about as harmless as they come. I knew he didn't have it in him to do something more drastic."

"So you were just going to let him keep doing all the shit he was doing."

"Do you want the God's honest truth?"

"Yes."

"Maybe for me the idea of you being brought down a peg wasn't the worst thing."

"And what about you knowing that Leif wasn't killed in a robbery gone wrong?"

"I'm assuming the chief found our texts."

"Yes."

"If you read them, Katie, then you know that coming forward wasn't an option. It could have gotten all of us killed—you, the kids, me, Derek, and Maria. I had a choice to make, and I made the only one I could that would keep everyone safe."

"You had no way of knowing that Derek's men wouldn't send another crew to finish the job."

"A Westport police officer—the son of a former chief—was gunned down in his driveway. Chief O'Neil, every cop in the department, including Leif's best friend, not to mention Leo—they were all over it, Katie. You and the children were as protected as anyone could be. Trust me, I considered telling Eddie everything I knew, but then I'd have to admit my relationship with Derek to him, and that wouldn't do any of us any good. You needed Eddie focused, not off balance, because at that time you couldn't have asked for a better protector, or so we all thought."

"I need to know something, Becca. And I want the truth. Did you give the idea to Derek?"

"What do you mean?"

"The scheme to harass Leif and me into selling, did that come from you?"

"How would I even think of something like that?"

"Charles Larson. According to O'Neil, he was a developer, and possibly a corrupt one."

Rebecca scoffs. "Charles was the most honorable man I've ever known in my life."

"Despite the fact that he was cheating on his wife with you."

"You have no idea what you're talking about, Katie. But that's always been your thing, hasn't it? Judging people, never looking past the way their actions affect you to see that maybe there's something more going on, that they're struggling or hurting or maybe even crying out for help."

"You haven't answered the question."

"No, I didn't give him the idea. And I had no idea he was connected to such dangerous people until after Leif was killed." She pauses. "You really thought I could be capable of that? Of living with myself, knowing that I was the reason Leif got killed? Of coming back here to help you, pretending all the time that that never happened?"

"The way I see it, you're the reason our grandmother died. And you've had no problem living with that, or coming back here year after year, like that never happened."

Rebecca shakes her head. "Jesus, Katie."

"You could have gone anywhere else, Becca. Anywhere in the world. Instead, you chose to live out there, in the place where all this started, all your shit started. Why didn't you just stay away? Leif and I made it obvious we didn't want you here. Why didn't you just leave us alone?"

"I kept coming back for a lot of reasons, Katie. I love Max and Callie more than anything; that's one. But maybe the real reason— maybe why I kept returning even before they were born—is because I thought Grandpa was right. The cottage was all I deserved. Maybe coming back to it was my way of accepting his punishment. And yours. Maybe if you saw me doing that, then you'd see that I was sorry for everything, and then eventually you might even forgive me. Or at least forget enough that we could start over." Rebecca pauses. "For the record, Katie, I never would have let Eddie live here, or pretend to be a father to your children. I would have stopped him, one way or another, even if it meant going to prison."

Now it's Kate's eyes that are fixed on the floor. She is silent for a moment.

Finally, she says, "I'm trying not to be that way anymore. Judgmental, I mean."

"And I'm not the person I used to be. I've made a lot of mistakes, and maybe the biggest one was when I was fourteen. If I hadn't done what I did with Eddie, if I had listened to you and not gone through with it, our lives might have turned out differently. So maybe I did put this in motion. Maybe everything that came after was all my fault. If I could take it all back, I would, but I can't. You can keep on hating me, Katie, but I'm done hating myself. If you want me to leave, I'll leave. At least this time, I'd understand why. But if you want me to keep proving myself, I will. If that's what you need to let me be a part of your life—for us to finally be a family again—then so be it."

Rebecca pauses to give Kate the opportunity to speak, but when her sister doesn't take it, she turns to the stove and switches off the burner, then transfers the kettle to the one behind it.

She is returning the two mugs to the cupboard when Kate speaks.

"Chief O'Neil says you could be charged with a crime."

Rebecca nods. "I know." Then she faces Kate again. "You've got a lot to think about. The water in the kettle should be warm enough for tea, in case you want that. I'm tired, so I'm going to go to bed. You can let me know in the morning what you decide."

Rebecca crosses the kitchen to the door, pausing once more.

But Kate remains silent, her eyes still focused on the floor, so after a moment Rebecca continues through.

Kate listens as her sister climbs to the top of the stairs and closes the bedroom door.

The next morning, Kate is up before everyone else.

She dresses in a pair of jeans, a sweatshirt, and canvas sneakers.

Taking her lockbox down from the upper shelf in her closet, she opens the box and removes Derek's cell phone, then pockets the device and returns the lockbox to its place.

In the kitchen she starts the coffee maker, waiting patiently until a pot is brewed, and then pours a cup and carries it with her down the basement stairs.

At Leif's workbench in the far corner, she removes a hammer from his toolbox and sets it on the counter. Then she puts on a pair of yellow-tinted protective glasses.

A red-colored shop rag is next to a pistol-cleaning kit. After laying the rag flat on the bench, she places the phone on top of it before folding over its four edges until the device is covered.

Picking up the hammer, she pauses to take a breath, and then proceeds to smash the phone, striking it as hard as she can several times before putting the hammer down and unfolding the rag to confirm that the device has been broken into multiple pieces.

Closing the rag again, she carries it with her as she heads back upstairs.

Stepping out the back door, Kate walks down the stairs, and then crosses to the very edge of the backyard.

The morning is bright but chilly, the grass touched with spring dew.

With the bundled rag in her sweatshirt pocket, she holds her coffee with two hands and looks into the woods.

She recalls that morning decades ago when Eddie Sabrowsky first appeared in their lives, emerging from these woods to find two sisters playing with an antique dollhouse their grandfather had brought down from the attic in hopes of easing their overwhelming grief.

He asked the older girl who she was.

I'm Becca.

Becca what?

Becca Wallace. Who are you?
Eddie.

Then the boy looked at the other girl, the younger one, not blonde and outgoing like her older sister, but dark haired and cautious, watching him with uncertainty in her brown eyes.

He asked what her name was, and when she didn't answer, Rebecca did for her.

That's Katie. She's my sister.
Do you two live here now?

Rebecca nodded.

Are you playing?
Yes.

The boy stepped out of the woods and onto the open grass.

Would it be okay if I played with you?

Kate takes several sips of her coffee, and when the mug has been nearly emptied, she sets it down by her feet.

Taking the rag from her sweatshirt pocket, she unfolds it, then picks out the biggest piece from the pile of broken debris and casts it as far as she can into the woods.

Without urgency she repeats the process, piece by piece, each one flung in a different direction, until the rag is empty.

ABOUT THE AUTHOR

Photo © 2012 Tracy Deer-Mirek

Daniel Judson is the Shamus Award–winning (and four-time finalist) author of *The Temporary Agent*, *The Rogue Agent*, and *The Shadow Agent* in the Agent Series, as well as *Avenged*, *The Poisoned Rose*, *The Bone Orchard*, *The Gin Palace*, *The Darkest Place*, *The Betrayer*, *The Water's Edge*, *The Violet Hour*, and *Voyeur*. A Son of the American Revolution, former gravedigger, and self-described onetime drifter, Judson currently lives in Connecticut with his fiancée and their rescued cats. For more information, visit Daniel at www.danieljudsonbooks.com.